ALSO BY STERLING ANDERSON

GO TO SCRIPT

15 STEPS TOWARD BECOMING A SUCCESSFUL (ARTIST) SCREENWRITER

www.sterlingandersonwriter.com
www.sterlingwritersroom.com

FIVE
SECONDS
TO GO

BY

STERLING
ANDERSON

ISBN: 978-0-9861446-3-9

DEDICATION

To my beloved wife, Marcella Austin - Anderson. Who has shown me that it is undoubtedly true that when you have one person who shares your dream it becomes a journey.

I used to wonder why God never told me it was going to be my last five seconds to play or be a star. Now I wonder when it's going to be my last five seconds to talk to a friend or my last five seconds to see my parents or my last five seconds to live. I guess it all means every five seconds is a gift.

-- Rhee Joyce

Chapter 1

End Of The Phenomenon

That was the day that everything changed. Hot rays of sweltering sun beamed down. A looming dark cloud eclipsed the punishing humidity but did nothing to relieve the hoopsters beneath -- rife with sweaty compctition and altercations, punctuated by grunts and squeaks of rubber sneakers. Berkeley's legendary "Live Oak Park," the basketball asphalt jungle. Among the throng of wannabes, one stood out as the real deal. Shirtless, sweaty, at seventeen, Rhee Joyce was six foot three inches tall, his chiseled frame reminiscent of a da Vinci drawing. He leapt high in the air, past his defender, towards the rim, shifting the basketball from his left to his right hand. Admirers and foes alike watched in awe. All of them knew a future filled with opulent mansions, expensive cars, and beautiful women was inevitable as he sailed through the air. An opposing defender planted himself in front of Rhee, so Rhee changed his left hand layup to a right hand reverse -- one of his patented moves, which he had performed a thousand times.

Then something went wrong.

In midair, Rhee's left knee caught the left shoulder of his defender. A soaring bird whose wings got clipped, Rhee spun out of control and plummeted toward the blacktop with a crash.

Rhee rolled over and planned to walk it off. He ignored the searing pain as he tried to stand but went down. Hard. He tried to stand again, but his leg wasn't having it. Rhee rolled over, a grimace on his face. Spectators screamed from the sidelines. There were sounds of jangling metal as surprised palms slammed against the chain-link fence, other sounds of thuds on wood as more palms slapped against the worn benches, rattling the court with the yet-to-be-spoken bad news. Some of them covered their mouths with shaking hands. Others pointed at him, faces shocked, mouths agape. Some ran in small circles and jumped up and down in front of anyone with cell phones, feeling a pain that wasn't theirs.

"Call 911, call 911," someone hollered.

Players rushed over and circled Rhee to form a canopy of people above him. He registered concerned looks on their faces but swatted away the helping hands. He wasn't a punk. He was Rhee Joyce, the high school phenom, set to go one year to college and then straight on to the NBA.

When he stood, a pain like no other zipped through his bones and speared his brain. He went down for the last time. His butt hit the ground. He surrendered to the baked asphalt, the rough, hot ground on his back, looking straight up, through the downturned faces, everyone towering over him, so many heads floating in the blue sky; Rhee's first view of things gone wrong.

Aware his mouth was suddenly dry and fearful of further surrender he couldn't yet fathom, clutching his thigh, looking down his legs, he noticed for the first time the porcelain white bone sticking out of the skin around his ankle.

Chapter 2

Five Years Earlier

Sheets of rain poured onto the streets as a lone figure pedaled through them on a Sunday morning in front of Oliver Wendell Holmes Junior High School gymnasium. Six feet tall, gangly, thirteen-year-old Rhee Joyce came down from his bicycle and hurried inside to retreat from the rain.

He had already heard the sound of basketballs bouncing in the small gymnasium. It was Rhee's second favorite sound in the world. The sweet sound of the basketball falling through the rim was his favorite. Swish!

The hood of Rhee's sweatshirt was soaked. He had cut two armholes in a green, plastic garbage bag to keep the rain at bay. He pulled off the garbage bag and scanned the gymnasium for a place to put his bicycle. He kicked the kickstand, balanced his bike, and then stole glances all the way across the court at the man who showed two boys some fundamental basketball moves. Even though they were across the gymnasium, Rhee heard the man speak with enthusiasm about basketball. He sounded knowledgeable, so Rhee watched and listened.

He saw basketballs on a rack with wheels and carefully pulled one from it. Each methodical move he made was an attempt to be as silent and as invisible as possible. It seemed to work because the man paid no attention to Rhee. He continued to spew information to the two boys with blank looks on their faces. Rhee thought they looked bored.

He took a chance and bounced the basketball once, twice, three times. The two boys looked over as it echoed through the gym. He stopped his dribble and gave a small wave. The two boys small-waved back. He thought they looked his age. They dutifully turned their attention back to the spirited man who kept up his seamless lecture about the rocker step and the crossover dribble.

Rhee backed away from the basketball rack with a ball in his hand. He stood behind the three-point line of the other half court. A determined look formed on his face as he arced the basketball towards the rim. The swish of the net echoed off the walls.

The man and the two boys turned and looked. Swish was the universal language in most basketball gymnasiums. It was a pure sound, and it gave Rhee instant credibility.

He retrieved the basketball and used his peripheral vision to see that all three of them watched him. He dribbled the basketball between his legs and pounded the ball up and down the sidelines. He showed his handle while they continued to observe. The basketball was like an extension of his hands. He heard the man call out to him. "Hey." Rhee dribbled over to them and stopped. "Would you like to play a little two-on-two with my kids and me?" the man asked. He had kind eyes.

Rhee grinned widely and nodded. He nearly came out of his skin with anticipation. "Are you a coach?" Rhee asked.

The man smiled with his eyes as well as his mouth. His head went back as he laughed. He looked at his two sons. They also smiled with their eyes. Then all three of them laughed. "No, I'm not a coach. I'm a doctor."

"You're a doctor, really?" Rhee asked. "I sure thought you were a coach."

"I may be, one day if I'm lucky." The man pointed at his two sons. "Just promise me that you'll never ask that question anywhere near their mother." The two brothers giggled and nudged each other.

Rhee stood confused. This man with kind eyes knew more about basketball than most of the coaches Rhee had encountered. "Why do you know so much about basketball?" Rhee asked.

The man shifted a basketball to his hip and placed his hand on Rhee's shoulder. "I'm one of those guys who only knows just enough to make himself dangerous."

Rhee smiled. "My dad said, to know basketball, you have to know the history of the game. Do you know the history of the game?" Rhee asked.

"Like I said, just enough to make myself dangerous."

Rhee had a feeling the man with kind eyes knew a lot more than he led on. "Do you know anything about Dr. Naismith?" Rhee asked. The man squinted at him, impressed with Rhee's question.

"Not a whole lot -- just that there was a peach basket at a YMCA training facility in the late 1800s and a man of vision wanted the students to get a little exercise. Little did he know that ninety years later a man named Julius Erving would take off from the free-throw line and put that round ball through that peach basket." Rhee watched as Dr. Silva tossed the ball in the air a few times as he relayed the story of basketball's origins.

Rhee gave the man a suspicious look. "You know a lot."

"I know your dad is a very smart man to teach you the history of the game. "What's your name?" the man asked.

"Rhee."

The man smiled wide. "Great name, Rhee. I'm Bob Silva, and these are my two sons, Jordan and Taylor."

Rhee gave the two boys a cool nod. The two boys each gave cool nods back. "Nice to meet you," Rhee said. "Should I call you Mister Silva or Doctor Silva?"

"You can call me Bob, or sometimes I like being called LeBron James," Bob Silva said with a straight face. A slow, devilish smile spread across his lips, and Rhee knew he was the victim of a harmless joke. Bob Silva gave a wink. "Gotcha. Now I know you pay attention." Rhee smiled back. He was never going to call this man by his first name or LeBron James. Rhee's parents instructed him to never call an older man or woman by their first name. Rhee focused and registered on the name Doctor Silva. He repeated it several times in his head: *Doctor Silva, Doctor Silva, Doctor Silva.*

His eyes brushed over all three of them and then held on the two boys. Now that he was close enough, he realized he was wrong about their ages. Jordan looked younger than Rhee; Taylor looked older. Rhee turned his attention back to Dr. Silva and noticed he was nearly half a head taller. He tried not to say anything, but it came from his mouth sooner than he was able to retract it. "How tall are you?" Rhee asked.

Dr. Silva smiled wide with his eyes and his mouth. "I'm six foot five inches. Is that going to be a problem for you?"

"Nah," Rhee said.

Dr. Silva pointed at Taylor, "You and him against me and Jordan." Rhee kept from any protest. He figured he was paired with the elder instead of the younger son to give Rhee and the elder son a fighting chance.

Dr. Silva tossed the ball to Rhee. Dr. Silva crouched into a low, defensive position, and tapped the floor menacingly, even mockingly. Dr. Silva was determined to teach him a thing or two. Rhee passed the ball and urged Taylor to shoot the first shot. Dr. Silva rebounded the miss with authority then smacked the ball and grunted.

In the paint, Rhee placed his forearm on Dr. Silva's back and tried to force the older man away from the basket. But Dr. Silva shoved his way towards the basket and banked in a jump hook shot. Dr. Silva clapped his hands twice. "Winner's out. Toss me the ball." Rhee obeyed and tossed it to him. Dr. Silva threw the ball to Jordan and clapped for it to come right back. "Ball." Jordan threw his father the ball, and Dr. Silva squared on Rhee. Dr. Silva faked left and lowered his shoulder to drive right. Rhee plucked the ball away from him, clean. He dribbled it away. "You got lucky," Dr. Silva said.

Rhee smiled and unselfishly passed the ball to Taylor. Rhee continued to play a humble role and watched the competition heat up between the brothers as they squared up on each other. Rhee and Taylor soon found themselves behind by several baskets. Rhee decided it was time to measure his skills against the six-foot-five-inch Dr. Silva.

Neither Dr. Silva nor Jordan had any chance at stopping thirteen-year-old Rhee, whose arsenal of moves turned Dr. Silva and his younger son into ornaments. Swish, swish, swish echoed throughout the gym as Rhee made ten straight baskets. Before the last bucket was scored, Rhee handed the basketball to Taylor and whispered something in his ear. Taylor smiled wide as he looked at Rhee. Dr. Silva glued himself to Rhee and denied the inbound pass, which was exactly what Rhee and Taylor wanted. Rhee went back door, and Taylor lofted the ball up toward the basket. Rhee grabbed the basketball in mid flight, BAM, as he slammed it down with two hands to end the game.

Dr. Silva took the basketball and gave Rhee a suspicious look. "How old are you?" Dr. Silva asked. One of his eyebrows went up, letting Rhee know he had to tell the truth.

Rhee dipped his head, shyly. "Thirteen," Rhee said. He saw Dr. Silva give Rhee a pronounced, disbelieving, stare.

"You just went backdoor and dunked on me with two hands. There is no way you're only thirteen. You must be at least twenty-five," Dr. Silva said, while playfully messing Rhee's hair.

Rhee fought back a smile and went toward the drinking fountain as Dr. Silva studied him from behind. Rhee hoped they were going to play more games.

The second game lasted less than ten minutes. Rhee's teammate, Taylor, threw him the ball and cleared out. Rhee took it to mean he had permission to continue being dominant. The third game took even less time. The second Rhee touched the ball it was in the basket. It was odd that the more he took it to Dr. Silva, the harder the man played. Dr. Silva's chest heaved in and out. Drenched with sweat, he sucked in as much air as he was able to between breaths. Rhee stole a glance at Dr. Silva and seriously wondered if the man was having a heart attack.

Rhee pretended he needed a drink between games so his adult opponent would have a chance to back down. But it failed. The second he came back, Dr. Silva tossed him the basketball. It started all over again. Rhee wanted to ease up, but he felt it would be more disrespectful not to try. Play after play, Rhee squeezed past Dr. Silva's blocks, or wrestled the ball from Silva's possession, but Dr. Silva wanted to play more. Every time Rhee scored, Dr. Silva went lower, slapped the floor, and tried harder. Rhee never met anyone so determined to take a basketball beating.

Taylor and Jordan lost interest. The blank expressions returned to their faces as they lumbered around the court. Dr. Silva observed them as they passed the ball to their teammates with little to no enthusiasm and got out of the way. "Both of you, sit this out," their father said to his two less-than-enthusiastic sons. Rhee felt relief as he watched them jog away toward the bench with a fire they forgot to bring to the court. Dr. Silva wiped his brow, inhaled deeply, straightened his back, and slowly locked his eyes on Rhee. He tossed Rhee the ball with more force than before. "OK young man, let's see what you got."

Rhee held the ball on his hip. He looked over at Taylor and Jordan as the two brothers sat down on the bleachers. He could tell by their hand gestures that they were embroiled in a game of rock, paper, scissors. He turned back to Dr. Silva, who stutter stepped in place. "OK," Rhee said, innocently. An adult just gave him permission to show his stuff. Rhee eased into a triple-threat position and whizzed by Dr. Silva before he was able to react. The winning basket bounced off the glass backboard with a thud and plopped through the net.

Dr. Silva caught the basketball, slapped it and spun it in his hand. "Young man, you are a special player, even if you are only twenty years old."

Rhee covered his mouth to hide his wide grin. "I'm really thirteen," he said.

"Thirteen, my butt," Dr. Silva said. He extended his right hand toward Rhee. "What is your name, again?"

Rhee's hand enveloped Dr. Silva's. "Rhee Joyce," Rhee said. He leaned over and grabbed his basketball shorts. His legs burned with fatigue. He'd never played that many games in a row.

Dr. Silva stared down at him and then asked, "Well, Rhee Joyce, you ever heard the term, 'half man, half amazing?'"

Rhee let out an involuntary smile. "Yeah, Vince Carter," he answered.

"That's right. You know something about the older NBA players?" Dr. Silva asked.

Happiness grew inside Rhee. "Yes, sir. My dad told me I would never know the game of basketball unless I knew the players who played before me."

"Well, Rhee Joyce, like I told you before, your father is a smart man. I'd love to meet him sometime." Dr. Silva made a fist and tapped Rhee on the shoulder. "Well, you're half kid, half amazing, and I've just decided to take a personal interest in you." Dr. Silva offered his fist for young Rhee to dap. The two touched their fist. "Done," Dr. Silva said.

"Done?" Rhee asked. He tilted his head, unsure.

Dr. Silva gave a wide smile. "Done is what our family says when we see or believe something we have know doubt will happen." Rhee's eyes sparkled along with his grin.

For the next five years, Rhee witnessed Dr. Silva follow his career and help Rhee and his family promote the Rhee Joyce Phenomenon. He learned Dr. Silva had an unquenchable thirst for all things basketball, was a prominent doctor in the community, and had a lot of pull in the Sacramento area. He arranged for Rhee to meet and work out with the Sacramento Kings' players during basketball camps organized by the doctor. Good fortune came to Rhee when he turned sixteen. Dr. Silva's reputation grew to such heights that he became the Davis Senior High School varsity basketball coach. Dr. Silva's coaching notoriety soared as Rhee broke every scoring, rebounding, and assists record in the Delta League. The coaching doctor and young Rhee became attached at the hip. The two of them appeared in newspapers and prep magazines across the nation.

Rhee even drove with Dr. Silva to Berkeley to play at Live Oak Park, a legendary playground on the West Coast, similar to Rucker's in Harlem, complete with asphalt burns, paybacks, and ego busters.

His new mentor told him that Kevin Johnson, Gary Peyton, Jason Kidd, and many ex-college and pro players honed their skills at Live Oak Park, also called The Jungle.

Rhee's eyes were opened to a whole new world. He was amazed to discover the college and pro players sometimes took a back seat to the skills of the street players and hustlers. He saw a lot of the great players played in street clothes with old shoes. Some of Rhee's innocence was spoiled when he found out some of the best players he'd ever seen drank alcohol or smoked cigarettes and marijuana between games, including the best player Rhee ever faced. That player was named Rooster. Rhee soared over anyone who played against him, even Rooster, until he crashed landed against the asphalt on that blazing hot day.

Chapter 3

The News

Warm summer rain pelted the windows. A flood of get-well cards cluttered the room. The deluge of flowers emitted a sickly perfume that mingled with the usual hospital smells of antiseptic, disinfectant, blood, and vomit. "No!" eighteen-year old Rhee Joyce cried out. He sat up in his hospital bed, soaked in sweat. Salty tears ran down his cheeks. He closed his eyes and fell back on his pillow, staring at the speckled squares in the ceiling. Then a knock on the door jerked his head up. Rhee gathered himself and tried to suck the tears back into his eyes. "Come in," he said.

The door slowly opened. Dr. Silva entered. He wasn't wearing the blue jacket, white shirt, and blue tie he had worn while he coached Rhee's last varsity high school game. Dr. Silva wore a doctor's white frock over a white shirt and blue tie. He also wore a stethoscope around his neck. He looked older to Rhee than when they had first met at Oliver Wendell Junior High School. Rhee's mentor and coach now had graying temples and a receding hairline.

Rhee sat up, briefly hopeful. "Hey, Coach," Rhee said. He watched Dr. Silva part the blinds and let the light stream into the hospital room; he turned around, paused, and stared at his medical chart.

"You have a trimalleolar fracture."

"A tri what?" Rhee asked.

"You've broken the distal tibia, the distal fibula, and the posterior malleolus," Dr. Silva said. His voice and tone was not passionate like when he talked basketball. Dr. Silva's cadence was eerily monotone, professional, and drone. Rhee glared at his cast.

It made him feel like he was serving a prison sentence. "The operation necessitated pins, plates, and screws."

"When will I be able to play basketball again?" Rhee asked. He felt himself hold his breath as he waited for the answer. At first Dr. Silva said nothing. His silence gave Rhee a sinking feeling. Dr. Silva sat down next to him.

"As I told your parents, the operation couldn't have gone more beautifully. The surgeons you had were the best in the entire state."

Rhee felt tears fill his eyes so he closed them. "So when will I be able to play?" Rhee kept his eyes closed while he threw wishful prayers as far as humanly or spiritually possible.

"Rhee, the strength, stability, and range of motion to compete on a level that you're used to are not going to happen."

Life drained from Rhee. He felt like shattered glass. He opened his eyes when he felt he was sure to not cry. "I have to play basketball, Coach. It's my life," Rhee said.

Dr. Silva dropped his head. "I'm sorry, Rhee. I'm really sorry." Rhee's mentor dipped his eyes toward the floor. "I'm personally happy that you'll be able to walk without a limp, my friend."

Rhee's face felt hot. He felt nauseous. His throat felt tight. It was hard to breath. His skin itched and felt like it was crawling right off his body. He shook his head, vehemently. "I'm going to play again, Coach. You can believe that. No matter what you say, I'm going to play again. This is one hundred percent on the real." Rhee closed his eyes and prayed. He asked forgiveness for anything he'd done so wrong to deserve this nightmare. His coach, mentor, and doctor finally looked him in the eyes.

"Rhee hard times and adversity doesn't necessarily build character, but they certainly reveal it," Dr. Silva said.

A surge of anger went through Rhee's entire body. "What does that mean?" Rhee asked.

"Don't measure yourself by how many times you get knocked down. The only way we can truly measure ourselves is by how many times we get back up," Dr. Silva said and inched toward the door.

"Coach," Rhee called after him. Dr. Silva stopped. Rhee looked at the taut, silver cable that supported his leg. He felt the tears again. He knew he had to fight them back. He didn't want his mentor to feel he was soft or a punk. Rhee pulled a tissue from the box and blew his nose. "What about my scholarship to St. Aquinas? What's going to happen?"

"I don't know, Rhee. Coach La Bayne hasn't called me. Maybe he's talked to your parents."

Dr. Silva committed his hand to the door handle. "Coach." Dr. Silva let go of the door handle and dug his hand into the pocket of his medical frock. It took an eternity to look in Rhee's direction. "This is hell, right? I've died and gone to hell, haven't I?" Rhee asked.

Dr. Silva pulled his gaze off Rhee and gave the window a thousand-yard stare. His eyes slowly came back to Rhee. "Life is what you make of it, Rhee."

In all the years they'd known each other Rhee never said a disparaging word or talked back or used profanity in front of his coach. But Rhee felt he was being bombarded with coaching clichés by a doctor who was supposed to be his friend, protector, and mentor. Rhee felt a wave of panic that he was going to swear and talk back any second.

"What the hell am I supposed to do?" Rhee asked.

Dr. Silva said nothing. He only gave Rhee an unblemished look of disappointment. "I will give Coach La Bayne a call."

Rhee gave the slightest nod, more out of habit than genuine appreciation. He had no idea why he asked about St. Aquinas or his scholarship. He was only going to play college basketball the mandatory one year the NBA sanctioned. Every school that recruited him accepted he was going to be "one and done." Rhee was going to be a first-round draft pick. A representative from the NBA told him this when he was only a junior in high school. Rhee blinked back the tears. He turned his head and stared out the window. Tears rolled down his cheeks, but his face was devoid of any expression of sorrow. He was numb. He forgot that his mentor, coach, and doctor was still in the room.

"You were one of the best I've ever seen, if not the best. No one will be able to take that away from you," Dr. Silva said.

Rhee fought back the tears the best he could but they came freely. Then he heard the door click shut.

The hospital room door flew open. Rhee turned his head to see a jovial nurse enter the room. She wore a painted, happy smile she had obviously learned in training.

"Hooray! You're going home today. You excited?"

Rhee glanced at his cast. A sharp pain pierced his chest, as if someone had run a hot sword through his heart. No. He was not excited.

Chapter 4

The Tigress

Layers of steam rose up from the streets and sidewalks. The summer rain evaporated and made the roads smell newly paved. The air conditioner hummed an icy breeze in his face while Rhee hobbled on his crutches into the house. He glumly walked past a chair made comfortable for him by his mother with pillows and a blanket but instead went straight to his room. He flopped down on his bed and put his head in his hands. After a few minutes, he leaned his crutches against his desk, sat down in front of his computer, and waited for the humming and booting sounds to finish. As he usually did, he went immediately to his Facebook page.

The number of posts on his wall was insurmountable. Every one of his 1200-plus friends must have posted a message:

"Hey Rhee, hope you're doing OK."

"Get better soon. Rhee, you're the best!"

"You'll be back soon."

Rhee logged out of his page and went to his email. His inbox had blown up with 325 new messages. Rhee turned off his computer and glowered at his crutches before pushing them. They clanged to the floor. He plopped on his bed and stared at a spider crawling across the ceiling. Listening to his house, he heard the drone of the air conditioning along with low unidentifiable ticks and clicks, someone digging outside, neighborhood sounds, angry barks from a dog, a car that whizzed by, the roar of a distant lawnmower, murmured voices, all familiar but more painful and irritating than before. Rhee knew he was in for a lot of talk about "before."

He turned his head and took inventory of all the trophies, medals, ribbons, newspaper articles, and photographs that littered the bookshelves, desk, chest of drawers, and walls. When he managed to get his cast in a suitable position with his crutches out of the way, Rhee picked up a large scrapbook the size of a New York City telephone book. Another horrible pain like a hot needle plunged straight into his ankle. He rubbed his cast.

Rhee grabbed the book with both hands and forced himself to look. It felt thicker than ever. He flipped through articles and pictures, a few yellowed with age, neatly pasted within blue borders, some of it his work, most of it his mother's. All were testaments to his brilliant high school basketball career, including a letter written to him when he was in ninth grade, four years before his injury.

The letter from Coach Bobby Knight before he retired from coaching symbolized everything to Rhee. It represented the highest achievement for high school players: to be sought after by prestigious coaches and programs. It represented the opportunity for a good relationship with his father, who loved Coach Knight. It meant Rhee was more than just a high school star. It meant he was a prodigy. The letter meant Rhee was special and not meant to be a mere mortal.

He continued to flip through the pages. The remote on his bed haunted him for attention. He picked it up and pointed at the flat-screen television on the chest of drawers. The flat screen's tiny light turned from red to green. A small light on the DVD player also went green. Images of Rhee appeared on the screen. He floated through defenders like he skated on smooth ice.

It was the semifinals of the Northern California Tournament of Champions. Rhee rewound the action of him stealing the ball, racing down the court, and windmill dunking. Everyone in the gymnasium leaped up in the air and cheered wildly, tears stinging his eyes.

A gentle knock on the door made Rhee quickly turn off the TV. He grabbed a tissue, wiped his eyes, and then pretended to read *ESPN The Magazine*. "Can I come in?" Mrs. Joyce asked. Rhee's mother stood in the doorway with a tray of freshly baked cookies. The smell of melted chocolate usually smoothed away Rhee's troubles. Not this time. He said nothing; he had nothing to say. "Rhee Raymond Joyce, I'm talking to you."

Rhee recognized his mother's willful Southern black woman tone and knew better than to mess with a sleeping tigress. "Come in then."

"Thank you," Mrs. Joyce said, as she breezed into his bedroom.

He wanted to give her a growl, but respect and fear disallowed it. "No problem."

He loved his mother with all his heart. She was a graceful, methodical woman with light brown skin and medium-length black hair. Adult diabetes had chipped away some of her beauty, but not much. She still had a face similar to the fifties actress Dorothy Dandridge. Her Alabama roots had graced her with a dignified demeanor and resourcefulness, and she retained a good dose of a Southern accent.

Mrs. Joyce reached into her apron and removed a cell phone. She offered it to Rhee. "This has been ringing so much since you were in the hospital. I bet you have more than 200 text messages and voicemails, but you already know that because, every time I tried to call, it only said your voicemail inbox was full."

Rhee gently pushed his mother's hand away. He wanted to shove it with more authority, but he knew better. "I don't want it."

She gave him a look that told him she was running out of patience. "Rhee, if you're not going to use your cell phone, then your father and I will stop paying for it."

"Then stop paying for it. I don't want to talk to anyone, and I don't want to see anyone, ever!"

"Now you're just being plain foolish. It's one thing to feel sorry for yourself, but being foolish is altogether childish." She tossed the cell phone on Rhee's bed.

He gave his mother a glare. It didn't stir up her wrath, but he knew full well he was being foolish. He just wasn't in the mood to hear it from her. He was now hard as a rock. That's what he said to himself in his head. It was basketball or die. He wasn't going to deal drugs. He wasn't going to bang. He would just die. He made a show of picking up the cell phone and tossed it on his desk with a clunk. "Cancel it, mom. I'm not using it anymore." He didn't tell her why; she'd find his body soon enough.

She moved around his room, setting the tray down and putting away the plastic trash bag. He wanted to shout at her to leave but knew that wouldn't end well for him.

Mrs. Joyce sighed as she plucked leftover tissues off the floor and bed. She tossed them in the wastebasket by his desk. She glanced at the warm cookies and then at her son, glowering on his bed. His strained silence was meant to shove his mother out of his room, but it had backfired. It forced her to say something: "There is life without basketball."

His back stiffened. His mother's words were exactly the last piece of advice he wanted to hear. He snatched a tissue and blew hard. Of all the trivial things she could have said about the weather or the paint color of his room or the cookies, his mother had to go straight to her knife-like opinion.

"A life that wasn't supposed to be mine," he mumbled.

Mrs. Joyce stopped. "I know you're hurt, Rhee. I don't blame you."

Rhee looked up and sent her a look he hoped was laced with fire and rage. *If you don't blame me, then get the hell out, and close the damn door!* This was what he wanted to say, but he knew better than to voice it.

"You're a winner, Rhee. You can still make something out of your life." Mrs. Joyce gave him an all-too-familiar look -- one that told him he was teetering on the edge and would be pushed off if he weren't careful.

Rhee took a deep breath to calm the explosion that mounted inside him. "St. Aquinas had their first practice today. I was supposed to be there."

"I know, honey."

"Not one person from the team called me. It's like they haven't even noticed I'm not there."

"Did you check your messages?" She folded her arms and waited for his response. He shook his head, knowing full well she baited him. "Then how do you know who called and who didn't call?" Rhee was tired of her little word games; he wanted her to leave him alone. "You have a lifetime to get noticed."

"If I have to spend my lifetime without basketball, then it'll be a very short lifetime," he mumbled.

Mrs. Joyce whirled on him. Her head was reloading authority-tipped ammo. The heat from her gaze seared his face. "What'd you say?"

His bed was quicksand, swallowing him up. He was pushing his mom's anger. Her patience frayed along the edges. His fight-or-flight instincts kicked in. He chose flight. Whatever he was going to do, he'd do it some place his mother didn't buzz around like a bee with a giant stinger. He reached for his crutches. His mother wiped a tear from her eye. He pushed the crutches away, and they crashed to the floor.

Mrs. Joyce let out a gun-cocked sigh as she picked them up and balanced them on the wall nearby. Her chamber of bullets was full, and she had many clips to back up any furry.

"Why didn't anyone prepare me for this?" Rhee asked through welling tears.

She looked at him as though there was no perceivable reply. His question hovered between them, sucking the air out of the room. "We all wanted you to make it, Rhee -- especially your father." The mention of his father made his gut cramp.

"Where is he?"

She examined her hands and picked an imaginary piece of lint off her blouse, then went back to her hands, studying them, and said, "He's in the backyard."

Rhee reached for his crutches. He separated them and stood.

Mrs. Joyce moved back so he could make his way to the window to look out. "I don't think you should bother him right now."

He watched his father out the window, gardening below in the baking sun.

Rhee turned to her just as she patted her hair then pressed her hands to smooth a crease on her skirt. He waited for his mother to explain, but she only came to look out the window. "Why not?" Rhee asked.

He knew the answer but tried not to fall into any more of his mother's verbal traps. Rhee boldly met her gaze, but she looked away this time. Rhee knew his mother was lethal. He only had to push her to the point of no return.

"He's still very upset."

Rhee pushed the sleeping tigress that hid inside her grace and dignity. His mother stayed poised. The tigress would have ripped him to shreds and tore out his heart with her teeth. He summoned the tigress. She'd kill him. "Upset? He's upset about what, mom? I'm the one that went from hero to zero. What happened to him?"

His mother's eyes narrowed. It was suicidal to wake the tigress, but Rhee didn't care. He wanted his blood all over the walls. Slowly, her demeanor changed. Her unwavering Alabama resolve started to surface. It was a resolve that gave him his fair share of trouble. It was a vicious tigress that had wounded him but not taken him out. He wanted out.

She crossed her arms and took an oak tree stance. "Your father is as disappointed as you. He wanted you to go to college."

He heard the cocked and loaded warning in her voice, but he couldn't turn back and run out now. "He doesn't give a damn about college. He wanted me to play the minimum year and then go onto the NBA. He told me. He told you the same thing. He wanted me to be a first-round draft pick so he could buy that big house he's been promising you."

He swore he heard a distant roar. Her wrath was on its way, and he knew he'd stirred it up.

"That's enough, Rhee," Mrs. Joyce said, her lips curling.

This meant trouble. He knew it. But Rhee wanted trouble. He wanted the tigress to use her claws and tear his throat.

"It's true. He's not mad because of me. He's mad because he had his own plans. I was only a means to an end."

Mrs. Joyce turned to face him. Her eyes leered. Her hands smoothed out her apron again and again, as if sharpening her claws. He waited to see her fangs. "There's more to your father than that, and you know it. You just want everyone to be as miserable as you."

"He wanted me to be the best so he could be king shit dad with guaranteed money and more beer to drink."

"I said that's enough. Your anger is taking you to a place you do not want to go. Just because you are in pain, doesn't give you license to be one."

He stared at his mother while the back of his head screamed for him to stop. The front of him wanted the tigress. His brain was on the back; his mouth was on the front. The inevitable train wreck was not going to end well. Rhee was going to be the first casualty.

"Tell him I know he doesn't care about me. All he cares about is himself."

The slap across his face came like a bolt -- although he knew it was coming. The sting of it slowed time. He wanted the claws to take his face clean off. He lifted a hand to his face and felt the heat coming off the mark he was certain was there. Anger dried the tears in his eyes, and he gave her a defiant look.

He wanted his mother to hit him so his pain was unquestionably shared. She failed to give him what he wanted, which was death by a fatal blow from the tigress. Without basketball, he had to die. He rubbed his face. The tigress had failed to kill him. The lion wasn't going to fail. He wanted the lion.

Tears welled in his mother's eyes. She pointed her finger at him. It shook with anger and disappointment. "You ever speak that way again, you'll get my fist next time."

It was a threat he knew she would make good on; he understood it loud and clear. But he wanted her claws, not her fists. Her eyes burned back at him with a fire Rhee had no use for anymore. He leaned on the crutches and rocked. He looked down at the floor and then slowly gazed up at her.

"OK, mom. You had your turn. I guess now it's his."

Her eyes were filled with his life, her faltering hope, her love, and her anger. Her eyes, which had seen everything in his life, searched his face now for clues to make things better or right, and she found none. Rhee could see he'd beaten the tigress. He moved past her, slowly, deliberately. He reached the door and never looked back to see the tigress crawl back inside his crying mother, but he heard it.

Chapter 5

The Lion

Clusters of storm clouds hovered. They did not break the heat and humidity, only darkening the moods below. Rhee stood out of sight so he could measure the heat of the lava pit he was about to jump into. He watched as his father turned gardening into a violent contact sport. He was a proud lion, ruthless, and at the height of his rage. It was perfect timing.

The bottom half of his postal uniform was flecked with dirt. His white tank top T-shirt had soil and sweat stains stretched over his barrel chest; his handful of gut leaked over his belt. Even in his late forties, his father was an imposing man. He sported a pencil-thin Duke Ellington mustache that never seemed to twitch into a smile.

He attacked the soil with a shovel, then dropped it and picked up a metal rake. He scratched the soil to make uniform lines and then ruined them with the shovel.

Rhee stayed a safe distance, plotting a way to entice his father's wrath. He was in so much pain he wanted the lion to finish what the tigress failed to do. Without basketball, with his leg in a cast, and without a future, he was a wounded gazelle. He wanted to die. This was the fastest way to get what he wanted.

"You got something to say, young man, or you waiting for Christmas?"

He understood his father's question all too well. He was waiting. Rhee was waiting for his world to change or end, for the sun to go down nine hundred times or his father to kill him. A part of him wanted to turn and run, but the other part took a bold step forward.

Rhee looked down. He saw insects and earthworms running

and squirming for their lives. If only he was that smart. "Nah. I don't have anything to say." His tone was defiant. If he were lucky enough, his father would put Rhee right out of his misery with one of the garden tools or his bare hands. The lion's paws made any tool seem too paltry to kill with, so the lion's paws were the best way to go, wielded by the man he most disappointed.

"Everything that happened is your own damn fault," Mr. Joyce grumbled. He gave Rhee a long, unwavering, glacial look. There was no mistaking the rhythm of the anger flaring in and out of his nostrils. It was the kind of look meant to shrink everything inside Rhee, to send him scrambling like a bug running from the shadow of a shoe. The lion was able to pounce and kill within seconds. You'd only ever see the lion leap -- he'd blind you before he landed.

Rhee was not scrambling. He was on the offensive. "I didn't get hurt on purpose like you think."

Mr. Joyce dropped the shovel and picked up the rake. Rhee was sure his father planned on throwing it. He feared no tools. He feared and craved the lion's leap and crush. His lips curled so he could spit his words through clenched teeth. "Are you being unmannerly with me, son?"

Rhee dropped his head. "No, sir." He felt the heat of his father's mounting rage. The lion was about to burst from his father's skin and be done with the kill.

"I hope not -- for both our sakes. I don't want to kill you, and you don't want to die," Mr. Joyce said. He was wrong. Rhee wanted to die and die fast. "I didn't raise you to be unmannerly. Best not give me attitude after all I've done for you," Mr. Joyce said. "Who the hell do you think paid for all those basketball camps and exhibitions all across the country?"

Rhee lost some of his nerve and muttered, "You did."

"Damn right. And when you wanted to meet Sonny Vaccaro, who made sure you got to Chicago and played in that All-Star Game?" Rhee leaned on his crutches. He felt his father's question didn't require an answer. He was wrong. "I didn't hear you, young man."

The battle was heating up. Rhee felt a fire blazing in his gut.

The flames of it dried his throat and licked at the bottom of his brain. He couldn't let it loose. But keeping it in, he might explode. Something had to give -- his pain or his life. *Please dear God, let me die right here, make it all stop*, Rhee prayed to himself.

"You did." Rhee said.

"Damn right, I did. I taught you everything you know about the game. I taught you how to play, and I taught you the history of the sport. So, if I'm a little upset, if I'm a little disappointed, that's my business. I earned it." Mr. Joyce dropped the rake, picked up the shovel, and hurled it into the soil where it stuck like a javelin. "I told you not to go to Berkeley to play street ball with a bunch of hoodlums."

His nerve inched to the surface. He'd spit in the lion's face. "You told Dr. Silva I could go there. You said, if I could play with the street players, I could play with anyone."

His father softened at that. It shook Rhee. He saw the hurt and sadness in his father's eyes. He'd much rather deal with the lion's murderous rage rather than with his father's sadness. It was easier to summon the lion.

"You could play with anyone, Rhee. You knew it. I knew it. The doctor knew it. You didn't have to prove it. There was no more reason to risk your future playing against drug dealers and felons," Mr. Joyce said. The edge in his father's tone drifted away. That cut Rhee even deeper. The lion had paused. Where had the lion gone?

"That's the best place to play against the best players. It still is." There was a well of hope within his father that was running dry. Rhee looked away when he saw maybe the last drop of it in his father's eyes.

"James is the best; Durant is the best; and Howard, Westbrook, Rose, Wade, Kobe, Love, Curry, and Paul are the best. They play or played in the NBA. Like the players you yourself played against, Irving and the Wall kid, they are men who have contracts and guaranteed money. Drug dealers and felons are guys who have nothing, nothing but rap sheets, enemies, and people they owe money to."

Rhee thought about Live Oak Park. He thought about the

gangsters, pimps, alcoholics, and felons who all taught him how to ball. He needed to defend their honor. "They have the love of the game, and they taught me how to play."

He waited for his father to speak. The stretch of cold silence gave him goose bumps. This was not the ugly and swift battle he'd been expecting against the powerful lion. This was a loving, disappointed father. This lingered, painfully so.

Mr. Joyce pulled the shovel from the dirt and thrust it into the soil again. "Well, Rhee, love is not going to pay the bills around here."

"What do you mean?"

"I mean you better get a job or you better figure out how to get back out on that court 'cause I can't afford for you to do nothing."

Rhee stared down at the ground.

"You standing there looking like a deer in the lights doesn't make me feel you're listening to me, son."

Rhee had no idea how wounded his father was, until now. He was even too wounded to be a lion. This was his father, a man, the man he loved, the last man he wanted to let down.

"I'm listening." His voice pitched like he'd involuntarily swallowed the pit of a peach.

"Then you better read it back to me so you and I both know you were listening."

"I need to get a job because you can't afford to take care of me," Rhee answered.

"I've been taking care of you all your life. It's time that changed. Playing basketball is no longer an option. You best start thinking about a real job."

Rhee's sides ached as if his dad had slowly inched a knife through his rib cage. "You said that..."

"What?" Mr. Joyce asked.

Rhee watched his father stab at the soil. "You said that my job was playing basketball."

Mr. Joyce stopped. He picked up the shovel, took a few steps, and narrowed the distance between them. Had the lion come back? Mr. Joyce held the shovel and was within striking distance. Rhee pictured the shovel colliding into his head. He kept his eyes on his father, who looked him in the eyes and then let his eyes drop to Rhee's cast. Mr. Joyce tapped the cast with the shovel. "That was when you had two good legs to play on, son."

His father might as well have chucked the garden spade through his eighteen-year-old heart. Less than two weeks ago, Rhee had loved his parents every single second of his life. It never occurred to him that the day would arrive when he'd come close to wishing he didn't have parents. A deep hole opened inside him. If it couldn't be filled with basketball, then what was the point of continuing? Neither the tigress nor the lion did what he needed. His mother and father shared their grief and pain. He had his own grief and pain.

Rhee entered the house and made a half-hearted attempt to find his mother before he took her car keys off the big ugly wooden key holder he had made in fourth grade. He nearly collided with her in the hallway. She was a wall he hadn't seen while looking down. He stumbled on his crutches, leaning back on them to avoid her and then leaning forward so as to not fall. "Can I take your car?"

"Where are you going?"

"Out," Rhee said. He was drained from the slow, tortured battle with his parents.

"And will you be home for dinner?"

"I don't know," Rhee said.

Outside, standing in front of the car that took him to games and took him to camp, keys cold in his hand, he tried to think of where it could take him now. He got in the car, crutches in the back seat. He buckled up and started driving. He felt sick knowing he would have to come back here, but right now, his hands on the wheel, feeling powerless over his fate, he was going nowhere.

Chapter 6

Jungle Legends

The summer clouds politely avoided the sun, promising to return as Rhee negotiated the curb of the sidewalk with his crutches. He paused at the sound of profane shouts rustling through the trees around the park. He mustered the courage to continue on, ready for the barrage of pity-filled stares sure to come his way. A fight between several grown men greeted Rhee around the corner.

On the street, people walked or lingered, hands in their pockets or fondling their phones, eyes darting around or looking down. Through the rattling chain-link fence, hands were in the air, waving off conflicts, throwing up surrender, expressing dismay. A full-court, four-on-four game had stopped. The arguing was at full tilt. Two men -- one shirtless, the other wearing a Phoenix Suns jersey with the number thirteen -- were pried apart as they shouted at one another.

The shirtless man pointed his finger and spit angry saliva. "That was a foul! You damn near broke my arm."

The man in the Phoenix Suns jersey waved him off and just turned and walked away. "I didn't foul you, man. Just play the game."

Two players grabbed and held back the shirtless man, enraged at being ignored. "You did foul me, fool. Go home and watch Magic Johnson videos 'cause you don't belong out here."

The shirtless teammates pulled their guy away so the game could resume. The game was back on and so were the killer crossovers, no-look passes, and windmill dunks. Other men stood on the sidelines and laced their shoes.

One of the men not in the game jumped up and down, stretched, and yelled, "I got next."

Rhee leaned on his crutches as his outstretched hand pushed open the cold metal of the chain-link gate to Live Oak Park -- The Jungle. The men who waited on the sidelines were not warming up and stretching. Instead, Rhee was immediately hit with the familiar sounds of crumpled paper bags as they swigged from hidden beer bottles. Pungent alcohol smells intermingled with the wafting smoke of cigarettes and marijuana. All of this was fuel that ignited spectator trash talking like they were in the games themselves. These were playground legends, once guaranteed the golden chalice of the NBA. Most of them exchanged stories of each other's one-time greatness. Every great play brought up arguments about greater plays in the past.

Otis Green was an ageless, toothless man, aged somewhere between forty-five and seventy. He stood on the sidelines. Both his pants and T-shirt looked like they'd been plucked from a forgotten pile at the Salvation Army, but his high top sneakers were brand new, without a scratch or a mark. They were signed with a black Magic Marker.

Rhee tried to be stealthy in his approach, but it was hard for him to go unnoticed. His reputation once preceded him, now it was his cast and crutches that told stories of his tragic demise. He stood beside Otis, who yelled at the players from the top of his wet lungs.

In one hand, Otis held a twisted brown paper bag; in his other was a cigarette. Rhee stood beside him, his eyes burning from a whiff of the smoke that switched directions in the wind and blew his way. His eardrums strained against Otis's shouts. "I told you fools to use the backboard. Willis Reed, Bill Russell, Bill Walton, and Tim Duncan used the backboard. Why don't you young punks stop all that 'And One' bull crap and use the damn backboard? I'll tell you why, 'cause none of you have an ounce of bird shit sense. That's why you're out here and not playing for the Knicks, the Celtics, the Trailblazers, or the Spurs."

This was church to most of these men, and they knew Otis felt he had the right to harass the congregation. When Otis turned and noticed Rhee, he lit up like a Christmas tree. He raised both hands and spilled some of the liquid from the twisted brown paper bag he was holding.

"Well I'll be damned. Rhee Joyce, as I live and breathe."

The announcement turned several heads. A few men raised their own brown paper bags in salute to Rhee's presence. Some of the players on the court glanced over. The sweet sound of basketballs hitting pavement gave Rhee a sense of being home.

Rhee suppressed his smile. "Hey, Mister Green. How's it look?"

"Mean, just like you was raised on," Otis said, with his eyes glued on the game in progress.

"Where are Booker and T-Bone?" Rhee asked. He took a half step back to avoid the choking smoke drifting his way from Otis's cigarette. Rhee was used to the old man keeping his eyes on the game in progress while he jawed with the guy next to him.

"Booker decided he best keep it on the down low for the time being," Otis said. He flicked his cigarette, and the embers flashed on the grass and went out.

"What happened?"

"Grab the ball, fool," Otis yelled. "Get on the damn ground and get them knees dirty. If Dave Cowens could get on the ground, y'all should be able to get on the ground too." Otis was on one of his famous tirades, so Rhee waited. "'Course none of you fools know anything about the two-time NBA champion, seven-time All-Star, 'cause you don't know anything about the game." Finally, Otis turned to Rhee, not missing a beat. "Booker robbed a liquor store. He's doing five to fifteen years up at San Quentin."

Rhee shook his head in disbelief. "That's not good."

"Don't get bent out of shape, young fella. Life happens, and the shit storm with it," Otis said. "Black men have different sentences for their crimes than white men. You best get used to that, young buck."

"What about T-Bone?" Rhee asked.

Otis stomped and pointed at one of the players. "You call that defense? I call it bullfighting. You just wave your cape and let the bull waltz on through and dunk the ball. Where is your damn pride, son?" Otis asked. "Play some damn defense." One of the players spit in Otis's direction. "T-Bone is all right. He's on the DL too."

"What'd he do?"

"Some say he shot his ole lady. Others tell it like she packed her bags and took the first train away from that fool."

"Feels like all the best players are going away or getting into trouble," Rhee said. He looked down at his cast.

Otis nudged him. "Not all of them are gone." He pointed at a group of men, all drinking and smoking. "Look at ole Harris and Snake. There's Booker's younger brother, Joe Willy."

"Where? Rhee asked.

Otis pointed. Joe Willy puffed on a marijuana joint, a crown of smoke around his head. "Don't forget young buck. Willy was a McDonald's first-team All-American himself -- just like you."

The entire park was littered with playground legends. All of them were past their prime, without any future or any hope. Rhee had a cold chill; he feared he was looking at himself in five years.

Otis turned to a coffee-colored man who had reddish hair, a ruddy complexion, and nursed his own twisted brown paper bag, his hands of dirty chipped fingernails holding it tight. "Hey, Red. Look who just showed himself. It's Rhee Joyce. Or I'm a liar."

Red kept his eyes on the game while he tossed back a swallow from his hidden drink. "Is he on one leg or two?" Red asked. "Last time I saw the boy he was rolling around on the ground like a Tijuana hooker with her leg broke off."

Otis nearly blew a fuse. "He's got two legs, Red. What kind of sick fool question is that?"

"Fat Shorty busted his ankle stepping off the curb. They cut his whole leg off from the bottom of his knee to the top of his ankle. That's his foot running around out there on the court now," Red hollered.

Otis's face scrunched up like he had just bit into a lemon. "Whatever you drinking, you best pour it out 'cause it's rotting the rest of that pea brain you got." Then he reconsidered that thought. "Or you could give it to me to hold on to."

Red grabbed his crotch, and Rhee knew what came next. "You best get over here and hold these nuts 'cause they so big I get tired of carryin' 'em myself," Red said, cracking an affectionate smile. His eyes fell on Rhee. "And that is Rhee Joyce, Otis. And you are a liar. You best stop talking and pay me back my five dollars."

Rhee chuckled and turned back to watch the action. A large, jet-black African-American man named Rooster, after the faded tattoo of a rooster on his shoulder, went up and rammed a two-handed dunk that ricocheted off the back of the rim.

Otis stomped his foot on the blacktop, spilling some of his sudsy libation in the process. "Damn, Rooster! I told you to use the backboard. You don't get no points for King Kong dunks that don't go in the basket."

Rooster turned and ran back on defense. When he passed half court, he gave Otis a middle finger salute. "Kiss my black ass, old man." He took three long strides and flew through the air, pinned a layup against the backboard, brought it down, and tossed the basketball the length of the court to a teammate who rocked the cradle and slammed the ball through the rim.

Otis stomped his foot again. "That's it. That's called defense. That's what I've been telling you, but you too thickheaded to listen. Defense wins championships." Rooster sent another middle finger to Otis. "Yeah, that's right. You just mad 'cause my shoes are signed by Dwight Howard. You stole your shoes from off somebody's porch." Rooster turned away and hid his laugh from Otis, who turned his attention to Rhee's cast. "How's that ankle?"

Rhee rocked back on his crutches when Rooster pinned another layup against the backboard and brought the basketball back down to earth. "Coach told me I'm going to set off the alarms at the airport security from now on."

Otis shook his head, twisted the brown paper bag, and stole a quick swig. He wiped his mouth with the back of his hand. "Damn, son. Sorry to hear that. When you went down, we all knew it was bad."

Rooster drove the middle of the lane and cut between two defensive players with a tomahawk dunk. Booming thuds as the defense guys went down hard. Several spectators on the sidelines covered their mouths and pointed. Sounds of handclaps as a few gave each other high fives. "I see Rooster brought his A-game today."

Otis waved Rhee off. "Pay him no mind. He only plays good when his wife puts him out of the house or when he gets out of jail. It makes him meaner than a bear with its head in a beehive. Brings his anger to the court." Otis paused, wiped his mouth, then asked, "How is the doctor?"

"He's good. Next year's team is supposed to go to state."

Otis shook his head in disbelief. "Without you? Hell nah. Not an oyster's chance to climb into a parking meter. Without you, they be lucky to make it out of sections."

"They'll be all right," Rhee said, his eyes on the court.

"I know they'll be all right, son. But they damn sure ain't gonna make it to state."

Rhee let the silence linger between them. They were going to respectfully agree to disagree.

"How's the ole man these days?" Otis asked.

Rhee's neck stiffened. His shoulders sagged. His eyes fell to his cast. "I'm not his favorite person right now."

"Damn shame. Sorry to hear it. Don't worry. My father didn't speak to me near three years after I got out of jail," Otis said.

Rhee tried to appear nonplussed about that.

"Which time, Otis? You've been to jail more times than my woman's been on a diet," Red chortled.

Several people in the stands and on the sidelines chuckled at Red's comment. His wide smile showed gold caps with diamond studs. Rhee bit down to keep his mouth from twitching into a smile. This was one of the reasons he came down here. He wanted to stop thinking about death and find the humor in life again.

Otis turned to Red and set him on fire with a gaze. He hissed through his teeth and pointed at him. "Red, you best put a sock in that mouth, 'for I come over there and beat you like a fat snake."

Red stood up like he'd accepted the challenge, but these two men had been cackling at each other since Rhee was in his early teens. The two old men kept their peacock struts up even if their feathers were all withered and faded.

"Come on and bring it over here with your bad self. I guarantee no fat snake ever went upside your head like I can't wait to do."

"Only head that's going to take a beating --" Otis stopped in mid-sentence, so genuinely excited he forgot about his verbal jousting. He used his forearm to nudge Rhee's shoulder and pointed toward the game. "Watch this kid with the ball. Name is Christian. He's Buster Riley's son."

A rail thin, light-skinned African-American kid dribbled down the court. He was about the same size and dimensions as Rhee.

"Watch him, Rhee. This kid has so much talent, he don't know what to do with it."

Young Christian shaked and baked, went behind his back, and made a killer crossover that left his defensive opponent stumbling backwards. Christian spotted up and drained a twenty-foot baseline shot. Otis bounced on his toes with enthusiasm. "He's only fifteen and still growing like a weed. Everyone wants him. Reminds me of Tiny Archibald, 'cept taller."

"That boy got game, but he's a long ways from Nate Archibald," Red piped up. Red wasn't as done with Otis as Otis was done with him.

"Damn it, Red! When I want your opinion, I'll come over there and beat it out of you," Otis said.

"Why you talking when you could be over here with my fists up against your big, crooked head?" Red asked.

They continued their daily banter, while Christian jumped into a passing lane, stole the basketball, and raced down court. Instead of an easy layup or dunk, Christian bounced the basketball and it slammed against the backboard. Out of nowhere, Rooster flew through the air, grabbed the ball, and with two hands jammed it through the rim.

Rooster held his head back, beat his chest, and hollered like a madman. He and Christian slapped hands three times. "Next.

School is still in session for anyone dumb enough to want to learn," Rooster yelled.

Five new players with fresh dry shirts started shooting baskets. The shirtless, sweat-drenched players headed toward the drinking fountain. Some unwritten rule allowed the shirtless winners of the game to drink from the fountains before anyone else. Otis leaned into Rhee. "I told you. That boy's like you. He's going all the way."

Rhee and Christian gave one another respectful nods, and Christian went to the drinking fountain, lined up behind a couple of shirtless players, tall as redwood trees. Rhee shaded his eyes from the sun that highlighted the old and crusty orange-painted rim. The net was a drunken cobweb. One more dunk, and it would be a swept-away memory.

Four years before, when Rhee first played at The Jungle, his fourteen-year-old hands were sweaty and the bounce of the ball on pavement hypnotic as a shirtless muscular man twice his age dribbled the ball in his direction. A shout from the sideline diverted his attention.

"D up, Rhee. D up." Rhee looked over and saw Dr. Silva clap his hands and give Rhee two fists of encouragement. Rhee got low, slapped the concrete, gritted his teeth, and the shirtless muscular man blew by him and dunked the ball with two hands and a strong swish singing from the nylon net. "Take that home to yo mamma," a deep voice rang out.

He tried to shake it off, but his confidence waned. He dribbled the basketball up court, got his pocket picked by his opponent, who flew back down the court and gave himself an alley-oop, then two-handed jammed again. The rim continued to rattle and shake when he retrieved the ball. "Oh, Lord. I must be a God myself," a voice cried out.

Rhee stepped out of bounds and tossed the ball to a teammate. When he jogged up court, Dr. Silva whistled for him to race over for a quick word. He handed Rhee some orange Gatorade. "No fear, Rhee. No fear," Dr. Silva repeated. "Don't think of their size and age. Play the way you know how to play." Dr. Silva put his hand on Rhee's shoulder. "It's time for you to separate yourself from everyone out there. Anyone in any life has the chance to separate himself from the others; it's a gift from God that should never be refused. You understand?"

Rhee nodded, "Okay," he said, but it wasn't something he'd understand for years to come. He raced back out to the court, curled around a screen, and clutched onto the basketball passed to him. The shirtless muscular man was so close to Rhee his sweat dripped on him as he pivoted away to protect the ball.

"No fear, Rhee. No fear," Dr. Silva hollered.

Rhee lowered his shoulder and burst toward the rim with the man glued to his hip. He stopped, squared up to shoot with two hands jutting in his face. He lifted his shoulders, and his opponent went airborne. He stayed on the ground, ducked underneath and shot the ball. The shirtless muscular man plummeted back down, clobbered Rhee, and sent him somersaulting backwards. The basketball went off the backboard and through the rim. "Ow!" Rhee said. He dusted the gravel from the torn skin of his elbow.

He looked up and saw a large, dark hand offering to help him up. The man lifted Rhee to his feet and gave him an encouraging pat on his butt. "Not bad, young buck. My name is Rooster. Welcome to my house." Rhee took Rooster's hand and was lifted up to his feet.

Rhee's thoughts swam back to the surface, and he leaned on his crutches and heard Red give Otis a tongue-lashing. "Why would you say something like that to the kid after his accident, Otis? Ain't you got no common sense?"

The gate squeaked as he pushed it open with his crutch.

"What'd I do? What'd I say?" Otis asked.

"You told him a damn lie, Otis. Ain't no one going to be as good as Rhee Joyce for a long ass time."

Several of the old one-time legends waved at Rhee as he departed. The Jungle was a place to come and test your skills against other past and future star players. It was also the graveyard for former basketball stars to come and watch their own legends die. Voices faded as Rhee hobbled away, leaving behind him all the moves and plays that made others look toward his bright future -- the future that was not to be. Rhee felt like his visit to The Jungle was his wake. He couldn't feel more down low if he were buried.

Chapter 7

A Bad Wheel

Rhee wore khaki shorts and a St. Aquinas T-shirt while the technician's buzzing cast cutter ripped at the last of the top half of his cast. It looked like his mother's electric hand blender, without the safety guard around the whirling blade. Flecks and shards of plaster flew everywhere. The technician wore a mask to keep the white cast dust from going up his nose. There was a pile of dust and cast bits on the floor around the technician's chair. He rose and offered his seat to Dr. Silva.

Dr. Silva removed a cast spreader from his top pocket. He sat down on the stool, and using the spreader like the wrong end of a pair of pliers, he carefully removed the rest of the plaster. Relief washed over Rhee as he felt the sensation of cool air instead of the hot, itchy cast. Once it was off, however, his relief evaporated. Rhee was appalled at how much thinner his left leg was than his right. His skin was three or four shades lighter than the rest of his leg. On the outside, he had a zipper scar that went from the base of his toe to his calf. The zipper on the inside of his leg was half the size. There was no way this looked like progress.

"You're going to have to soak the leg in warm water twice a day. Use a very soft towel and don't scrub the skin," Dr. Silva said.

Rhee slid off the examination table and put his bare foot on the cold linoleum floor. A pain shot through his ankle and leg that made him grit his teeth. The pain was insufferable. He tried to hide it, but he knew it showed on his face. "It feels OK." He was almost unable to stand on his left leg. "Yeah, I think it's good."

Dr. Silva slapped his knees. "Good! Then lace up your sneaks and come give me twenty-nine points and twelve assists tonight.

We could use you." Rhee continued to look down at his emaciated leg. An uncomfortable silence lingered in the air.

Rhee tried to turn and walk, but he almost fell. He was only able to back up and sit back down on the examining table. Dr. Silva studied him carefully. "You're a worse liar than an ugly rug, Rhee."

"You think?" Rhee asked, with a grimace.

Dr. Silva grabbed a rubber mallet and tested Rhee's reflexes. He made a knocking sound as he gently tapped the top of Rhee's knee. "It's normal for joints and muscles to be weak and especially tender after eight weeks of being in the cast." He brought a walking cast boot out of a box.

Deflated, Rhee asked, "Another one?" He hadn't prepared himself for another artificial apparatus. Dr. Silva held up the walking cast boot, but Rhee looked away. He knew his disappointment showed all over his face.

Dr. Silva turned to the technician. "Can you give us a minute?"

"No problem." The technician nodded and shuffled from the room.

Dr. Silva patted the examination table for Rhee to sit down. He did, but he couldn't be forced to look at the walking boot. "Some people come out of this surgery and only need a cane to walk. I can see you're in pain." He patted Rhee on the shoulder. "Don't let it bother you too much. It doesn't mean a lot right now."

"How long is it going to hurt like this?"

"Not long. Maybe a couple of weeks."

That sounded like an eternity, so Rhee looked away. "Great."

"I know what you're thinking, Rhee. All these weeks you've been wanting to do a layup, right?" Rhee nodded. "You wanna get up there and do a 360 dunk, am I right?" Rhee nodded, emphatically. "Well listen, you can't do it because you had a trimalleolar fracture."

There were those words again, Rhee thought, the scientific reminder and announcement of the end of his fantastic basketball-playing career. The words came out like a eulogy at a funeral.

Dr. Silva looked at Rhee a long time. Rhee fidgeted under the long silence.

Tears welled up in Rhee's eyes. He folded his arms. "Right."

"Like I told you before, you've got a lot of screws holding that ankle together. They are titanium, but your ankle is not. It could still shatter with too much weight or pressure."

Rhee wanted to conjure some miraculous super powers and laser the walking cast off with his stare. "How long do I have to wear it?"

"That's entirely up to you. If you do too much, it will extend the recovery time. If you take it easy your ankle will heal better and faster." Rhee's doctor and coach examined the walking cast boot. A ripping sound followed as he parted the Velcro and gently tapped Rhee's leg. "Raise it up."

Rhee did as asked and Dr. Silva carefully placed the boot around his ankle. He said nothing while Dr. Silva wrapped the Velcro around the walking cast boot. When he was finished he patted it. "Is that too tight?

Rhee slid off the examining table and was disappointed at how weak his ankle still felt. He took a few full steps. It was easier to maneuver, but the pain increased from the normal cast. He sat back down. An awkward silence fell between them.

"Wiggins and Parker went in the first round. Just like you said they would," Rhee said. Dr. Silva didn't respond. "Tyler Ennis even went. I never saw that coming."

"Are you feeling any pain right now?" Dr. Silva asked.

Rhee felt immense pain, but he was more annoyed that Dr. Silva had not engaged in the conversation. "I held my own against those guys, even though most of them were older than me."

Dr. Silva bent to examine the walking cast boot. He poked and prodded with furrowed brows. "Marcus Smart is a man amongst boys. He should've been a first-round pick. Parker is a five-tool player. He may be rookie of the year. Coach Krzyzweski was lucky to have him, even for one year."

"He's better than me."

Dr. Silva lightly patted the walking cast boot. "I'd argue against it. He may be bigger and play a different position, but you held your own."

Rhee's heart jumped. Dr. Silva's approval was still an addiction. "Ennis and Smart are both better than me. Wiggins got me a lot of times."

"He's a great player," Dr. Silva said. "He's struggling a little now, but he'll find his way. He comes from great pedigree."

The reality set in that these players were moving on with great promise in their futures; Rhee was sitting talking about his past.

"On two good legs, there are very few high school and college players in the country as good as you, Rhee. You held your own at all the camps."

Rhee attempted a smile that wanted to come but lost its life. The trill of a cell phone broke the tension in the room. Dr. Silva reached down in his pocket and pulled out his phone, looked at the number, then put it back in his pocket. Rhee noticed a real change in his expression. When Dr. Silva stood, it was all business.

"Rhee, I want you to listen to me. I've known you for a long time. I also know how much you can push yourself."

Rhee had a bad feeling that any ounce of hope he was clinging to was about to be sucked from his soul. Dr. Silva was in the house -- not Coach Silva: his friend, mentor and advisor.

"Your ankle is never going to be the same. It may feel the same, and you may think it's 100 percent. But the wrong amount of pressure may make it explode like a balloon." Rhee met his gaze but said nothing. "Do you understand?"

"What if it does come back? What if you're wrong?" Rhee asked. Dr. Silva looked down at his clipboard.

"In this case, Rhee, I'd love to be 100 percent wrong, but it's about 10,000 to 1."

"I'll take that, Coach. There aren't 10,000 in America better than me. You can bet that."

Rhee waited while his mentor measured him then sighed. "I'm going to tell you this one time only."

"As my doctor or as my coach?"

"Your mind and body is an eighteen-year-old athlete that hasn't reached its prime. In four or five years you may be bigger and stronger than you are now."

Rhee's heart felt like it may fly right out of his chest. He never imagined being bigger or stronger. He was going to make it to the NBA. No doubt, now that he realized he was going to change. He was going to become a man.

"But your ankle, Rhee. Your ankle is the ankle of an eighty-year-old man. When it heals, at best, it will be the ankle of a fifty-year-old man."

Rhee's heart sank. "But the rest of my body can make up for a fifty-year-old ankle, right Coach? You told me most NBA players have bad ankles, remember?"

"Yes, Rhee. Most NBA players have really bad ankles. But not as bad as this. Not as bad as yours."

"What about Grant Hill? He was told he'd never play on his ankle, right?"

"Grant Hill had a million surgeries, Rhee."

"Then I'll have a million, I don't give a f--" Rhee caught himself.

"He had contract money to afford all those surgeries. No one is going to draft you with a bad wheel, Rhee. You're like a fine racecar. You have the engine; you have the gears and the fuel. But you can't race at Daytona 500 with a bad tire. The speed will expose the tire, and you'll hit the wall."

"It doesn't mean I can't try to race. It's up to me if I want to crash and burn, right?"

"The best advice I can give you now is take all the frustration you're feeling right now and use it for something positive."

"Like what?" Rhee asked. He was ready to explode.

"Like college. You're still going to college, right?"

All this time, Rhee never equated going to college with not playing basketball. College was only a stepping-stone to enter the NBA. He looked for a sign -- any sign -- that indicated Dr. Silva might be convinced. But nothing in Dr. Silva's eyes or demeanor indicated he might change his mind.

A woman's voice crackled, startling him as it came through a speaker on the wall. "Dr. Silva. Dr. Silva. You are wanted in the OR. Dr. Silva you are wanted in the OR."

Dr. Silva looked at his watch. He gave Rhee a touch on his shoulder. Rhee felt the surge of pity. Dr. Silva's words broke through his haze of mourning. "Don't forget what I told you."

Rhee's eyes dropped to the floor. He put his hands over his face as the room seemed to close in on him. Dr. Silva or Coach Silva, whoever, was gone. His life was definitely over. The life he had now was not remotely desirable to him. Rhee shuddered. Thoughts of wanting to end his pathetic existence filled him as he hobbled down the hall. He listened to the hospital activity: phones beeped, nurses shuffled about, toilets flushed, some voices murmured encouragement, other voices slightly louder gave cheerful greetings. It felt to Rhee as though each patient would return to their regular life, back to work, back to family, business as usual. But not him. Rhee envied them all. His time here had only confirmed that his bright future had burnt out.

Chapter 8

Job Wanted

"I'm sorry that the school has decided to revoke your scholarship. But the athletic department's position is strict when it comes to injuries off campus. They feel you didn't honor your letter of intent by participating in an unapproved game after the designated high school season."

Rhee cocked his head and leaned on his cane for support, his mind reeling after the dire message that had just been spouted at him. The slender African-American, who delivered it in a cold, matter-of-fact tone, sported a trimmed goatee and closely cropped hair speckled with gray. "But I've been accepted to the school, right? I mean, I was all set to play here on full scholarship," Rhee said, with a plea in his voice. The Assistant Dean of Students at St. Aquinas waved his monogrammed pen in the air like a conductor. The Assistant Dean slid a pair of glasses onto his nose and looked down at a file. Rhee glared at him and wondered how many dreams of other students who sat in this chair had been extinguished by this man.

The Assistant Dean flashed a smile, as he'd already done a hundred times that day. "Yeah, you've been accepted to our school, lock, stock, and barrel. You've even been assigned housing."

"What does that mean?" Rhee asked skeptically. He squeezed his cane to keep from knocking the unctuous smile off the Assistant Dean's face.

"It means you're one of the lucky ones. Coach La Bayne signed off on your student housing and your meal card and all of your books for the first semester."

Rhee's pulse quickened and sharp hostility churned inside him. Three months had passed, and he was finally receiving audience from someone at St. Aquinas College, who carried no influence to let him play basketball, even on his bad leg. He wanted to spew accusations about the college and the coaches and all the full-court lies. He looked up and noticed the Assistant Dean's eyebrows furrowed while he looked at his cell phone.

"Your biggest problem is today's date," the Assistant Dean said.

Rhee found it hard to appreciate the man's little joke. He was one of the top five high school basketball players in the country and sure to go all the way to the NBA. Now he had no future in the NBA. In fact, he had no future at all. Yet, according to this man, that wasn't his biggest problem. "Today's date," was somehow his biggest problem.

"What do you mean?" Rhee asked.

The Assistant Dean pushed a few folders to the side and uncovered a desk calendar. He scanned around a few dates, "School starts in less than a week, and you haven't registered for classes. According to my records, you haven't officially enrolled."

"I signed a letter of intent, though."

"I understand, Rhee. But you missed orientation, and now all the classes are closed," the Assistant Dean said accusingly. "Now that the semester has started, the soonest you can sign up for classes would be the spring semester."

Rhee now understood the problem. The school that hounded him for three straight years was now not going to let him into their classes, at least not right away. "When is that?"

The Assistant Dean's eyes raced around the desk calendar, as if he'd lost his spot. "We're on a trimester system, so you'd have to wait until the end of February."

Rhee tried not to look as puzzled as he felt. He had no idea what a trimester meant. He kept thinking about the free housing and free books for one semester.

"What about the rest of the time? If I enrolled in February and my books and stuff get paid, what happens after the semester has ended? What about next year? Who is on the hook for that?"

The Assistant Dean made a steeple with his fingertips. His chair squeaked for oil as he spun around to a filing cabinet. Rhee fixated on the picture of a graduating teen, probably the Assistant Dean's son, jealous that he would never hear the same revoked scholarship speech. A file cabinet drawer slammed shut, and the loud boom snapped Rhee out of his trance. The Assistant Dean spun back around with a brochure in his hand, coaxing another oil deprived squeak from his chair. He opened the brochure and grabbed a pen. Rhee watched him circle some numbers, slide the brochure across the desk, and tap the circled areas with his pen.

"These are the total costs with housing, books, and a meal plan for an entire year."

Rhee pushed on his cane, stood up, and looked down at the lopsided ink circles on the brochure. After he read the numbers, he felt lightheaded. He reached back to touch the chair so he didn't fall. What he read was so staggering, his mind swirled. No one had ever discussed the cost of college with him. The moment was an awakening, like icy cold water poured over his head.

"How are my parents going to afford all that money?"

"That is the total cost. You can save a lot by living at home," the Assistant Dean said.

$35,000 a year circled his brain and clouded Rhee's thoughts. Then $35,000 times three made everything black. If he finished school, he would have an undergraduate degree and probably a six-figure student loan to pay off. "That's crazy."

"The good news is you don't have to worry about meals, books, or housing for the school year."

"You mean half the school year, 'cause, like, I can't start now, right?" He wanted to make sure the Assistant Dean's double-talk didn't go entirely unnoticed. And another half year to pay for added another $17,000 he'd have to come up with.

"Yeah, you're right. Coach La Bayne thought you were going to be covered the whole year, but since you can't come until February, that means you're only covered for a semester," the Assistant Dean said in a tone that made it completely clear he wasn't used to being corrected. "The bad news is your father makes too much money for you to receive financial aid for the tuition."

Coach La Bayne had deserted Rhee and his family. After being on his doorstep for three years, he hadn't even called him to check to see how he was doing after his surgery. The news of the end of his career was the end of his relationship with more than 200 colleges that had begged him to come to their schools.

"My father is a postal carrier. He doesn't make enough money to sling that kind of cash around. We needed me to play on scholarship."

"I understand. Unfortunately, he does have a decent income. All our academic grants and subsidies are for much lower income students."

Rhee and the Assistant Dean sat in awkward quiet until the chair squeaked to life again as the Assistant Dean pushed it back. He stood and crossed the room to another file cabinet. Rhee watched him with curiosity as a file drawer grated open. The Assistant Dean removed a file, slammed the cabinet shut with his hip, and returned to his desk. He plopped down hard in his chair, as if accentuating his difficult job. "We do have just a few foundation grants that haven't been filled yet." He looked up at Rhee. "Have you thought about what you might declare as a major?"

Rhee tried to wrap his brain around the question, but three times $35,000 added up in his head to $105,000. It might as well have been a million. Why didn't anyone ever mention the cost of college? He had received more than twenty letters from this school, every year since he was fifteen. No one ever mentioned $35,000.

"Rhee?"

Rhee's thoughts swam to the surface, just above the $35,000, and he took a deep breath.

"Rhee?" Rhee looked up and saw the Assistant Dean pinch his eyes with his thumb and index finger. He then leaned back and pressed his fingertips together, again. "Did you think about what you'd major in once you got here?"

"Yes, I did. It was basketball. Didn't Coach La Bayne tell you?

He came to my house a hundred times and told me I'd never have to worry about a thing. He never said it all would be taken back if I got hurt."

The swirl in Rhee's brain was numbers and promises and withdrawals. His starting salary as a pro player would have been at least a million. And the school would have made money from Rhee's fame, and whatever team he signed up with would have had extra coverage and a star player. It was dawning on Rhee that, as long as the school or the NBA could make money from their involvement with him, the pipeline of financial and moral support was open and running. But one bad landing, a snapped bone and a cast later, he was lucky to have crutches for support.

"You must have had hundreds of schools that promised you the world. Why did you choose this school?"

"Excuse me?" Rhee asked.

"I'm looking at your file. You aren't just a great athlete with nothing to offer. You have decent grades. You come from a good family. I know you could have chosen just about any school in America. You are definitely Duke material."

Rhee looked at the Jesus on the crucifix above the doorway, blood oozing down his face, adorned with a crown of prickly thorns. More blood oozed from his hands and feet where rusty nails were impaled. Suffering. All the times he had seen Christ on the cross, he'd never understood the meaning of suffering. Now it trumpeted in his mind. "You think it was a bad choice?" Rhee asked.

"Not at all. I'm just curious. To be honest, even I thought you were going to one of the powerhouse, high-profile schools, like Kentucky, Duke, North Carolina, or Kansas," the Assistant Dean said. "I'm not sure our little school would have even been on my radar if I were Rhee Joyce."

The truth surfaced and came out of Rhee's mouth before he was able to stop it. "My mother liked it here," Rhee said, barely audible, his shoulders slumped in defeat.

"Did you say your mother?" the Assistant Dean asked. A smile crept into his goatee. He fell forward in his chair and placed both his hands on his desk and Rhee noticed the surprise in the Assistant Dean's face. "You're kidding me, right?"

"She said the campus was pretty."

The Assistant Dean's hands slid off his desk, and he clasped them behind his head. "Man, I didn't expect you to say that. Wow!" Something changed in the Assistant Dean's expression. He unclasped his hands and shook a finger at Rhee. There was a grin stuck on his face. "You know what?" He asked Rhee in a kinder tone, the previous air of derision evaporated.

"What?" Rhee asked, unsure what had thrown the Assistant Dean or what he'd say next.

"I swear, that's something my mother would have said too, God rest her soul."

Rhee didn't know how to respond. The thought of losing his own mother made Rhee's hands sweat. He balanced his cane on his backpack next to his chair, looked down at his walking cast boot. A scratching sound erupted as Rhee made an adjustment with the Velcro, a little more snug.

The Assistant Dean picked up his glasses and looked at Rhee's file again. Rhee watched him scan through with a more sympathetic eye this time. "Have you ever thought about what you wanted to do after college?"

Rhee scratched his forehead. "No one exactly encouraged me to think about anything other than playing in the NBA."

The Assistant Dean acted as though they had something in common. Maybe they did. His attitude had definitely changed since Rhee mentioned his mom. He picked up the gold pen with his monogrammed initials and tapped what sounded like Morse code on the desk. "It's unfortunate you haven't decided on a major, because we have this one grant for declared majors, but you'd have to have applied for a writing or science award the beginning of your senior year in high school." He flipped through the file like he wanted to make something out of nothing. Then his eyebrow lifted. "Unless you get a job."

"A job?" Rhee asked, dumbfounded and unable to hide his confusion.

"There is a literary fellowship award. It is a large grant for English majors who work and maintain a 3.2 grade point average," the Assistant Dean said.

Rhee picked up his cane and leaned forward. "I don't know anything about English. Sometimes I can barely speak it." Rhee waited for the Assistant Dean to stop looking so determined, but he didn't. Rhee's file was still open on the desk between them, his good grades on display in black and white, evidence of his future potential. The Assistant Dean was locked in like a player who needed to sink a free throw to win the game.

"They don't expect you to have a PhD in English coming out of high school." The Assistant Dean threw his head back with a hearty laugh. The guy enjoyed his joke so much it forced Rhee to push out an unconvincing laugh. "All that's required is you have to have had a B-plus average in high school, which you did, and be one of the five English students that qualify. We still have two available. We were going to hold them until next year, but I think I could work with you."

"Seriously?" Rhee asked. "You mean it would pay for my school?"

"Almost a full scholarship, except for meals. You'd have to start school next semester."

Rhee's father had a job, so did his mother at one time. He knew friends with jobs. "Work? Like what kind of work?"

"Work, work. You know, work. Here is the scholarship declaration." He slid his finger over the text to help make it sink in for Rhee. "It says: 'Those students working twenty hours a week or more and maintain a B-plus grade-point average can qualify for the Caldwell Foundation Award.' You just need to declare English as your major and find a job by the beginning of next year. It would be great if you had the job now so I could start processing the application. The sooner we start the application, the sooner I can sign off on it. I think you'll have a good chance."

"Where am I going to find a job?"

"Anywhere, Rhee. Ask your parents or friends. Go online or go to the placement office at the Student Affairs building. It's about two buildings away from the gym. You will find the new job postings on Mondays." The Assistant Dean looked down at his cell phone again, the date flashed on the small screen. "That's today.

With any luck, you might find something."

Rhee pushed on his cane and stood. He balanced his backpack on his shoulder. The pain in his ankle was less severe, but he still limped. "How much time do I have to get a job?"

"Technically, until next year. But if you get a job right away, it'd increase your chances. All I need is a pay stub, and we can start the paper work."

"Any job?" Rhee asked, making sure.

"Just has to be a minimum of twenty hours a week, but I'm sure we can work with you if it's a couple hours less."

Rhee's mind raced, trying to sort out all the information he'd just received.

"If you don't find anything today, talk to a little old lady named Miss Cartwright. She's as old as California, and her mind is about forty-five seconds behind her actions. But she's as sweet as sugar. She gets all the new job postings. Tell her I referred you."

Rhee hoisted his backpack on his shoulder where it had fallen a little and grasped his cane to steady himself as he turned and walked towards the door. He stood under the Jesus on the crucifix. Rhee Joyce, McDonald's first-team All-American opened the door. A sizzling sound crept into his brain as he thought for the first time in his life about flipping burgers. "Thanks a lot," Rhee said, on his way out. The bitter taste in his mouth came out a little in his words.

Rhee stood alone in front of the bulletin board filled with job posting cards in various degrees of erosion. Some were tattered from being up so long. More were coated with food and grime by hands rubbing across them like a magic lamp to help the jobseeker read better. Others were partially ripped off with orphaned staples left behind. Now Rhee was the new hopeful, gripping his pen tight in his right hand. Narrowing his eyes to read the mostly illegible scribbling, he mouthed silently what he read: "Driver Wanted."

He wrote on the back of a piece of paper. "Must speak French or Arabic," Rhee read to himself. He scribbled over the number he had written.

"Window Washer," he whispered. Rhee envisioned himself washing windows while people pointed. "That's Rhee Joyce up there, the ex-basketball player; look at him now. He's a window washer." Rhee wrote down the number. Then he read the small print out loud. "Must carry own life insurance and not be afraid of heights?" Again, Rhee crossed out the number. "Damn!"

An elderly woman approached. She sauntered towards the board, but her lavender perfume raced ahead into Rhee's nostrils. She wore an old, threadbare pink sweater draped across her shoulders. Her hair was white like snow; her knee-high stockings crinkled near her ankles, and her faded grey shoes appeared comfortable, if not well worn. Rhee stepped back from the bulletin board to give her a wide berth. The fragile old lady fumbled with cards from her sweater pocket and then slowly and shakily lifted one of her arms to post new listings. She held the stapler in her hand like a five-pound weight. Rhee leaned his cane against the wall and reached over to give her a hand.

The old lady raised her eyebrows and peered up at him. "Thank you," she said.

"Are you Miss Cartwright?"

Her shaky hands matched her voice. "Yes, I am."

She handed Rhee the stapler along with a jumble of the new job listing cards. They had nearly finished when Rhee saw one of the postings right under his staple. It was clear as day and made trumpets go off in Rhee's head.

"Wanted: Basketball Coach."

Chapter 9

White Chocolate

Stifling air hovered over baking asphalt in the parking lot of Joaquin Moraga Junior High. The elegance and wealth on display refused to wilt under the heat of another unseasonably warm October day in California. Freshly cropped rose bushes took the place of the graffiti, empty bottles, potato chip bags, candy wrappers, and broken glass that Rhee was accustomed to seeing in a junior high parking lot. Jaguars, Mercedes, Range Rovers, Mini Coopers, and unidentifiable foreign vehicles politely made a line to pick up kids all taking their time to hop into their rides. Rhee climbed out of his mother's car, leaned on his cane, and reread the job listing to be sure it was the right school.

He folded the paper, closed the car door, checked the straps of his walking boot cast, and then crab-walked toward the school. He stopped when a turbo Bentley screeched to a halt in front of him. Three of his McDonald's All-American teammates had pointed these cars out and swore up and down they'd all have a fleet of the $250,000 cars when they reached the NBA.

The Bentley stayed idle in front of Rhee. He started to raise his cane and wave them to go by when a slick, well-groomed fourteen-year-old in jeans and a red cardigan sweater, opened the passenger door and unleashed a command. "I don't give a shit what time your meeting is. Come get me at five o'clock. I'll call you on your cell, and you better pick up!" he shouted and slammed the door. Hip-hop music with excessively violent lyrics still thumped from inside.

Rhee had never heard someone speak that way to a parent. He had little doubt that, if that were his mother or father in the Bentley and he had just spoken that way, Rhee would have been run over and then backed over.

The kid ran towards the school, an expensive leather messenger bag swinging across his shoulder, and disappeared into the small crowd of other kids. The well-coiffed driver of the Bentley, with flawless skin, looked like an actress or a model. She was a smartly dressed woman in a simple but fashionable white blouse and stared ahead with her hands on the steering wheel. She wore little makeup and didn't look old enough to be the mother of a fourteen-year-old. The large platinum diamond-studded bracelet and two large diamond earrings matched the audacious rock on her ring finger. She switched to a soft rock station, turned the music down to an eardrum-saving level, and then sat and waited for her resolve long after the bad-mannered brat had gone.

The woman waved at him. Rhee realized he was caught staring at her. He sheepishly waved back. "Hey," Rhee said, barely audible.

She gave another small smile, laced with embarrassment, gripped the wheel of her quarter-million-dollar car, and drove off, crushing trace amounts of gravel underneath the tires. Rhee took a beat to pull himself together before he turned toward the school. A brief look over the lush green campus, and his eyes fell on the sparkling new gymnasium. The rays from the sun bounced off the freshly cleaned windows, which made it an even more majestic sight. Rhee looked down at his watch. He was a little early. He limped across the school campus and stood in front of the large metal double doors. He took a moment before reaching for the metal bar to enter. This would be the first time he had stepped into a gym since cementing the final win of his grade school career. Never in his wildest dreams did he think the next time would be to coach a middle school team. He took a deep breath and balanced his backpack and cane as his hand finally hit the cold metal bar of the double doors. The metal bar vibrated in his hand as he heard the throb of rap music.

Lil Wayne's music boomed over the speakers. Rhee entered and gawked at a pristine gymnasium: brand new scoreboards, breakaway rims perched on glass backboards, modular bleachers with neatly numbered seats, and a crystal-clear sound system that some Division One colleges would be happy to sport. The polished wooden floor displayed the emblem of a soaring eagle with the words, "Home of the Eagles," handwritten above it. Rhee made a slow 360-degree turn. A large golden eagle was on the home team wall with its wings spread as if it were landing on an unsuspecting prey.

Rhee heard the unmistakable action of a basketball game in progress as the ball dribbled against the wood floor. Shouts and sneaker squeaks emanated from the far center court, as six young players were embroiled in a heated three-on-three game.

Five of the boys were African-American, and one was white. Rhee's attention on the game was focused on the boys, all of whom had skills. Each of them put down some solid hoop. Like many of the pick-up games across the country, the young boys battled verbally while they played.

"You fouled me, man."

"No, foul. Play the game, girl scout."

"I'd play the game if you'd stop sexually assaulting me."

"I ain't being sexual with you. Who do I look like -- your grandmother?"

"Don't talk about my grandma, unless you're tired of living."

"If you throw down like you play, call your daddy so I can slap him for raising a sissy."

Rhee suppressed his laughter and inched closer. The trash talk continued as the boys took every opportunity to raise their testosterone flags and challenge one another's masculinity.

Rhee stood at half court quietly observing. The white kid was an exceptional player, shades of a younger Stephan Curry mixed with a younger Tony Parker and Derek Rose. His opponents were formidable, but the white kid was unstoppable. He scored at will.

His killer crossover dribble left his young defenders in a time warp; Tim Hardaway in his prime would have been proud. He also had a deadly step back jump shot. It was money. His form was picture-perfect, and his no-look passes commanded attention from his teammates, or they got hit in the face with the basketball.

Rhee stepped just inside the half-court circle, exhilarated by the energy pulsating from the game in progress. The squeak of the polished floor, the player's deep breaths as they bumped and pushed each other; this was home for Rhee. He inched toward the action, until the white kid caught a pass, stopped the game, tucked the ball under his armpit, and stared at Rhee.

"What up, Dog? You wanna play, you gotta call next," the white kid said. His street vernacular raised Rhee's curiosity. *The kid's Eminem with a ball*, Rhee thought.

"Nah, that's ah-ight, playa, injury," Rhee said. He tapped on his walking cast boot. "Don't get this off for another week."

The white kid scowled. "Dag, I thought you had that cane and wore that boot 'cause you was just old."

The five African-American boys laughed. Rhee waited through the embarrassment of being one-upped. Two of the African-American kids whispered and pointed at him. One of them stepped up and took a hard look at Rhee. The white kid turned into a "triple threat" position to resume play, but the African-American boys kept their eyes on Rhee. "What up?" Rhee asked.

The white kid threw up his hands, exasperated. "What is this some kinda jack? Why don't you tell us your name so we can formally tell you to press and get to steppin'?"

Rhee had met and played against a lot of wiggas -- white guys who acted black. This kid took it to another level. He had already morphed into an imperial wigga: wigga squared, to the tenth power. A wild gaze came to the white kid's eyes. Rhee knew full well the white kid was "mad dogging" him.

"I'm Rhee. Rhee Joyce."

The African-American kids noticeably changed their attitudes when they heard his name. They looked at each other and then looked at Rhee. The white kid stayed with his "who cares?" expression. One of the African-American kids approached. "Hold up. Are you really Rhee Joyce, like Rhee Joyce?"

Rhee nodded. "Word. I'm here to check out the coaching job," Rhee said.

"Coach of what?" the white kid asked. Rhee ignored him and kept his eyes on the African-American kids. "What? You deaf too?" the white kid asked. "Let me help you out." The smart-mouthed white kid stomped over to the scorer's table, reached behind and pressed a button. The music abruptly shut off in mid-song. "That was probably getting all up in your hearing aid, right?"

Rhee cut the white kid some slack because he was such a good player. But now the white kid was a legitimate pain in the ass. It was time to bring this boy down a notch. The fastest way would've been to grab the basketball and show all the kids what was what, but that took two good legs. This battle had to get verbal, and Rhee knew no one needed qualifications to talk trash. You only needed a mouth.

One African-American kid was dark-skinned with a reddish hue in his complexion and had closely cropped hair. He was around six feet tall. He had big hands and big feet. He probably had at least five or six more inches of growth. He placed his hand on his chest and stepped closer. "I'm Kenny Providence. They call me 'Prov' around here." He wheeled around and pointed at a light-skinned African-American kid, who was thick and muscular. "You owe me five dollars, homeboy. This really is Rhee Joyce."

All the African-American kids looked at Rhee in awe. Two of them slapped a high five. Two others shared a small fist dap.

Prov's movements were smooth, like a kid with exceptional coordination. He reached out and offered Rhee his hand.

Rhee looked at the kid's hand, and then moved his cane to his left so he was able to shake. "What up, Prov?" Rhee asked.

"You looking at it," Prov answered. After he bumped shoulders with Rhee, he moved back and looked at Rhee like he was an icon. Rhee's eyes fell on each of the African-American kids, and they all looked back at him with a cool and restrained excitement. Silence now washed over the large gymnasium, until Prov pointed at the other players and made the introductions. "That's David Smith or 'Cub.'"

Cub was strong and wide. He was around five foot ten inches with light-brown skin. But his hazel eyes and freckles gave away the fact he was probably mixed race. Cub had substantial facial hair and a short Afro, cut on the sides of his temples into a fade, which gave him a little flattop. His well-proportioned body signaled that he was done growing.

"What up?" Rhee asked.

Cub came over to Rhee and offered him a fist dap. Rhee closed his fist and gently touched knuckles with Cub. "Respect," Cub said.

"It's your world, my man," Rhee said. Cub's eyes filled with excitement.

Prov pointed at another one of the African-American kids. "The ugly dude is Lambert Davis, or 'Lam,'" Prov said. Rhee laughed.

Lam was anything but ugly. He had sleepy, greenish, eyes, and was around six feet tall, with a coffee-cream color and a model-like sharp-cut jaw. He raised his chin and signaled to Rhee. "Happenin'?" Lam said. He gave Rhee a small respectful wave.

Rhee liked that Prov was respectful enough to introduce the whole crew. His voice echoed off the bleachers and walls as he announced each one. Rhee felt a twinge of exhilaration. He examined them as potential future players for the team. If he got the coaching job, he really had something.

"The short gangsta is Felix Duncan. He's the leader of the crew."

Felix was dark-skinned, coffee -- no cream -- and chubby. He hadn't yet grown out of his baby fat. He reminded Rhee of those athletes that were not born with perfect physical features but somehow gave little away in the skills department.

"How's it going?" Rhee asked.

"No one listenin' if I'm complaining, right?"

"Right," Rhee said with a smile. He instantly liked Felix. "So if you're the leader, why is Prov doing all the talking?"

"Leaders delegate, right?" Felix asked. "Go ahead, Prov keep talking. I'll say something if you step all over it."

All the African-American boys laughed along with Rhee. He warmed up to these kids. They had a routine like kids who grew up together.

"And skinny boy is Rama Nance," Prov said, while he pointed at Rama, who glared back at Prov, not thinking it was funny. Rama gave no indication that he even noticed Rhee.

"Don't nobody be calling me 'skinny' or 'boy,' or I bust them in the mouth," Rama said.

"Yeah, yeah, OK," said Prov waving Rama off.

Rhee kept his smile down. Rama was just shorter than Rhee, six foot two or three, with dark complexion and tight cornrows, gangly, a scar on the side of his face, and mistrusting, scowling eyes. A hard life was displayed in those eyes.

Prov pointed at the white kid. "White boy with all the attitude and mad, crazy skills is 'L.A.'"

L.A. chewed on a fingernail, disinterested in social niceties. He was a good-looking kid, around six feet tall, well built, made to handle himself on and off the court. He had shaggy brown hair that hung in his eyes. His hands and feet were a good size, and the lack of any facial hair indicated more growth in the future. With a few more inches, this kid was going to be a force on the court, an NBA lottery pick.

"What's up L.A.?" Rhee asked. He kept his gaze on him, but he refused to look at Rhee for more than a millisecond. The question bounced around the hard surfaces of the gymnasium and then faded to an uncomfortable silence.

"Come on, small soldier. Play your position and recognize who you're talking to; the dude is Rhee Joyce, man," Felix said.

"All I recognize is that y'all stopped playing the game when this buster came into the gym," L.A. said.

Rhee turned his attention back to Felix and the rest of the African-American kids. "You guys all go to school here?"

Prov moved toward Rhee in a respectful manner. "Nah. We at Marshall over in Oak Town," Prov said.

Rhee's heart sank; he had already invested emotionally in the possibility of getting the coaching job and thought these kids were going to be part of his team. Rhee looked up at the clock. "Why y'all all the way over here? Why aren't you guys in school?" Rhee asked.

"We got some kinda teachers' free day," Prov said.

"Yeah, free from gettin' shot," L.A. said.

"Shut up, L.A.," Rama said.

L.A. spun the ball on his middle finger and intentionally pointed it at Rama, who narrowed his eyes at him and stepped forward. But Felix grabbed his arm.

"Yo, let's just chill and live nappy," Felix said. He finally displayed his position with all the boys.

Lam and Cub nudged each other and sat down on the court. L.A. kept spinning the basketball on his middle finger and slowly pointed it at Rhee. Rhee felt the urge to walk over to L.A., slap him, and break his middle finger. The kid had skills, but he had no manners and a shitty attitude.

Rhee redirected his mounting hostility and focused on Felix. "So, Felix, you and your crew on the team at Marshall?" Rhee asked.

"We are, but 'White Chocolate' goes to school here."

Rhee slowly turned his gaze back to the smart-mouthed punk. "What does L.A. stand for White Chocolate?" Rhee asked.

"Stands for 'leave it alone' or 'lick my ass.' Take your pick," L.A. said.

The African-American kids reared back in disbelief. "Ah, hell nah. No you didn't say that," Felix said.

"I said it," L.A. shot back with venom in his voice.

Rhee gave L.A. a hard look that he hoped screamed, "You're pushing it punk."

L.A. gave Rhee an unmistakable look back that screamed, "So what?"

Rhee shook his head and then took a deep breath. He wanted to pick up his cane and beat this mouthy kid with it. "What up with all the hate?" Rhee asked.

L.A. spun the basketball on his finger. "Not hating, we just wanna ball. You came in here, interrupted our game, and wanna run your mouth like you on Oprah."

"Sorry about that. Y'all just go on with your game. But first I need to understand: if L.A. stands for 'leave it alone' or 'lick my ass,' then why don't they call you L.I.A. or L.M.A.?" All the African-American kids chuckled. "So you got game, but you can't spell. That's cool. I understand if you need more schooling."

The African-American kids belly laughed. Rhee stared at L.A. and waited for a comeback, but the kid was obviously too stunned to respond.

Felix glanced up at the wall clock. "Oh, man, we gonna miss the bus."

The rest of the boys snapped to attention. Lam and Cub leaped to their feet, and they all spread out to collect their things. L.A. was not in a hurry to leave; instead, he bounced the basketball between his legs several times and launched three-pointers. Rhee counted four out of five from behind the arc.

Rhee leaned on his cane and limped toward L.A. "What about you?"

L.A. stopped to watch his friends pull on their sweats and gather their backpacks and travel bags. All five African-American kids rushed up to L.A. "We outtie," Felix said.

"Yeah, late," Cub said.

"Peace out," L.A. said.

All the African-American boys took turns shaking L.A.'s hand, and they all embraced him. Rama tapped L.A. on the head with genuine affection. He grabbed the basketball out of L.A.'s hand, spun it on his middle finger and held it in front of L.A.'s face. L.A. laughed. He grabbed the ball off Rama's finger, and the two kids, shook, dapped, and hugged.

"Late," Rama said. He placed his right thumb and right pinky near his face like a phone. "I'll holler at you tonight." Rama turned and caught up to the other boys as they all left.

"Late," L.A. said.

These kids were genuine friends with the smart-mouthed wannabe gangster they called L.A., who dropped the basketball, grabbed his shirt, turned, and started to walk toward the boys' locker room but glanced towards Rhee. "I've seen you at Live Oak; you can play, no doubt," L.A. said, with a small grin.

"Oh, I see. Now that your homies are gone, you know me?"

L.A. pulled his shirt over his head. "I knew you the whole time, homie. I was just messing with you."

"Is that right?" Rhee asked.

"Thirty-seven points, fourteen rebounds, twelve assists, and eight steals."

Rhee tried to stay cool, but this kid played him like a drum. "You read about my last game?"

L.A. smirked. "I was there. Nice back door alley-oop to win the game, with only five seconds left to play. It was dope." He turned to go into the locker room. "Too bad it was your last five seconds, right?"

Rhee took the kid's hammer-fisted verbal assault with all the dignity he could. Then L.A. surprised Rhee by play-acting as though he were announcing the game as it happened.

L.A. put one hand over his ear and pretended to hold a microphone in the other. His voice echoed throughout the gymnasium. "Ladies and gentlemen, the score is tied, and we have only five seconds to go in the game, five seconds to know if the Delta League title will belong to the Davis High School Blue Devils or the Woodland Wolves. The Woodland Wolves players set their defense. Three players triple-team Rhee Joyce. The Wolves' seven-footer Mark Vail is standing down in the low post. The other Wolves player is also back with the seven-footer. They want anyone but Rhee Joyce to take the last shot."

Rhee's mouth dropped open. So far the smart-mouthed kid recalled the last game he played exactly as it happened, beat for beat, word for word. He was spot on with every detail and selling his color commentary like an auctioneer.

"The Blue Devils' Coach, Dr. Robert Silva, yelled something to his son, the sure-handed sophomore, Jordan Silva, who inbounds the ball. Three players shadow Joyce. The seven-footer Vail is still down in the post. Joyce breaks for the ball. Wait. Joyce goes back door. Silva lobs the ball up into the air. The seven-foot defender is going to intercept the ball, but wait... I don't believe what just happened. Rhee Joyce did the improbable. He went over seven-footer Vail and with two hands took the ball away and kissed it off the glass!"

"Jeez," Rhee mumbled, as L.A. finished.

"Ladies and gentleman, as the late great Chick Hearn once said, 'Turn out the lights, the coffee is cold, the butter is hard, and the fat lady has sung.'

"The Blue Devils' McDonald's All-American Rhee Joyce has played the most monumental performance of his high school career. He has given the Blue Devils' fans this stellar moment in time to tell their children and grandchildren about. A moment we were witness to tonight. The Delta League MVP has nearly pulled off a quadruple double with thirty-five points, fourteen rebounds, twelve assists and eight steals. Ladies and gentlemen, as you are my eyes, it may be decades before we witness a player with the monumental talent of the Blue Devils' Rhee Joyce. With five seconds to go in the ball game, Rhee Joyce just finished his last championship high school game with another miracle. The Blue Devils win."

L.A. cocked his head and looked at Rhee with a mad dog gaze. He grabbed his crotch, turned, and trotted toward the locker room.

"Hey," Rhee yelled.

L.A. disappeared into the locker room. He popped his head around the corner, just enough so Rhee could see him. "What?"

"How'd you do that?"

L.A. sucked on his teeth and disappeared. He left Rhee awestruck. Who was that kid?

Chapter 10

Coach Of The Year

Rhee entered the main office where the latest flat screen computers sat atop architecturally designed, sleek, white desks. He slid up to the long counter that separated the students from the staff and faculty. Behind the counter, everyone hustled about, making sure they did their jobs without stepping on one another. He shifted his weight on his cane. A young African-American woman stood over a desk with her back to him.

"Excuse me," Rhee said.

She turned around, and Rhee almost forgot why he was there. Her hair was braided and scrunched tight in back; a sprinkling of freckles, large amber eyes, and full, shapely lips accentuated her tailored, navy-blue dress, which hugged her slender figure.

"Can I help you?" she asked.

Rhee derailed. He'd been away from his cell phone, text messages, emails, Facebook, Twitter, and the rest of his social media so long that this attractive girl knocked him for a loop. Not too long ago, attractive girls were something he took for granted. Rhee had female admirers, but he was so focused and dedicated to basketball, he never got caught up on dating or the tangled web of a relationship. He returned a few selected phone calls of girls he liked. He even went to his junior and senior prom. He was polite and attentive and snuck in his share of heavy petting. But when things headed in any direction toward exclusivity, Rhee carefully slipped the knot. Basketball was his true love. Girls liked his attention and his Spartan reputation. None of the girls believed he was stuck up. They all accepted his unavailability as a byproduct of his stature. All in all, he had managed a respectable mystique with girls his age -- until now.

Time stood still while Rhee waited for the young woman to recognize him. It never happened. It took so long for Rhee's brain to move into gear that she scowled at him with annoyance.

She spoke slowly, "Can I help you?" Her voice was laced with impatience.

Rhee cleared his throat and searched for composure. "Rhee Joyce." He flashed a polite smile. She stared at him like he was an ant or a piece of navel lint she might flick away.

"What can I do for you?" she asked, all business, no cooing.

Rhee's smile flipped upside down. He collected himself. He wasn't a predator. It just got beneath his skin, with mounting regularity. Less than six months since his accident and he was already such a nobody. "I'm here about the coaching position."

She reached under the counter and handed him a piece of paper. "Fill out this application."

Rhee was set back by her indifference. He might as well have been someone sent to wash her car. She frowned over the counter at his walking boot cast. Then she turned and went back to work, dismissing him just as quickly.

He patted his chest, but he had no pockets and no pen. His shoulders slumped. Now he had to ask her a dumb question. "Excuse me, do you have an extra pen?"

She turned back around with a semi-annoyed expression. Rhee wanted to turn and go somewhere far away.

She grabbed a pen from a nearby holder and slid it towards him. "Take a seat and wait with the other applicants." She pointed over Rhee's shoulder.

Five other potentials waited for an interview. Four of the young men appeared to be post college, eager and fit, and all were wearing ties; the other was a young woman dressed in a dark blue track suit with UC Berkeley stenciled just below her left shoulder.

Self-consciously, he felt for the tie that he wasn't wearing. His eyes fell and revealed his T-shirt and shorts. He suddenly felt the bulky weight of his walking cast, realizing it made him the worst choice in the room.

He turned back to the young woman. "Thanks," Rhee said, sheepishly. He crossed the room and sat on the remaining empty chair, placed his cane under it, and settled in. He looked around for a hard surface to fill out the application. All of the other potentials had got to them first. Rhee finally flipped his backpack to his lap and scribbled.

An older man kicked the front door open, startling Rhee and the other candidates. None of the office bees paid any attention. Rhee stopped filling out his application. The older man's hands and arms were loaded with soccer balls and basketballs. He wore the typical coach's regalia and school colors: maroon shorts with matching maroon polo shirt top, a whistle dangling on faded leather around his neck.

His mangy head of blond hair was faded gray, and the lines on his face indicated many possible visits to late-night bars, poker games, and a general aggressiveness towards indulgence, regardless of the effects on his health. His belly pushed his shirt over his belt line. One side of his mouth sagged a little, probably where he held whatever he was inclined to smoke. His breathing was short and rapid.

"Hit the switch, little Lynn," the older man said. It annoyed her. She looked at Rhee, who looked down. Rhee registered her name, Lynn.

"Hello, Coach Holt," Lynn said.

She reached under the counter and pushed a button that made a loud buzzing sound. This man was a coach? Coach of what, exactly? He was caught between pushing the little door and juggling the balls. He dropped the balls and they bounced all over the room.

"Shit! Dammit!" Coach Holt yelled.

"Coach," Lynn said, and pointed at Rhee and the other applicants, who all dipped their heads and pretended not to notice the commotion.

Coach Holt never looked their way. Rhee put down his application and jumped up to help the coach round up the balls that repeatedly knocked each other and banged into the wall. Rhee gathered as many as possible and then handed them over the little door to Lynn. "Here," Rhee said. He gave her a smile. She rolled her eyes. She juggled the balls and dropped them on the other side of the counter.

Coach Holt dropped the rest of the balls behind the counter and went to take the balls Rhee held. He tried to hand the coach only one ball at a time. Coach Holt looked at Rhee. "Let me have all of them, son. I'm not dead."

Rhee felt embarrassed. "Sorry, Coach."

Coach Holt turned away from him and then turned back, narrowing his gaze on Rhee. "Well, I'll be damned. Rhee Joyce," Coach Holt said, and then motioned to Lynn with a wave. "Let us in," he demanded. Lynn retaliated by slowing down her movements.

She took her time reaching under the counter. She pushed the button and ushered Rhee with a wave. "Come on inside."

Coach Holt went through the little door. He turned back to Rhee and made a wild gesture. "Get over here. Come on in my office." He beckoned Rhee, who had yet to move.

Lynn tapped on the coach's shoulder. Rhee waited for the coach to notice she wanted his attention.

"Coach," Lynn said.

Coach Holt looked at Rhee, who felt awkward at best. "Move your feet, son. We have plenty to talk about."

She changed her tone, gave it more authority. She sounded like she might send Coach Holt to his room. "Coach Holt," she snapped.

"What? What the hell is it?" Coach Holt asked. Lynn pointed. Coach Holt looked at Lynn and followed her finger toward the other applicants. "Ah, jeez, I got nothing for them." He took a deep breath and looked at Rhee, who quickly looked away. "Do you know who this kid is, young lady?"

Lynn looked at Rhee as if he were a stinky cheese. She stole a glance at all the other applicants. Rhee slowly looked at them too.

Defeat was on every face. None of them wanted to leave because it would be unprofessional, but they had all stopped filling out the applications. Some of them actually folded the applications or put them away. "Coach Holt, all these other applicants were here before him."

Embarrassment and anger shot through Rhee's blood. He needed the job as badly as any of the other candidates. Now his reputation was going to work against him. He pointed his thumb over his shoulder. "I'll get in line."

"Nonsense. Don't be ridiculous," Coach Holt said, and ushered Rhee in. "How would you like a job coaching basketball?" Rhee stood still, unsure which way to go or how to act. Everyone looked at him, and he felt judged and maybe despised.

Rhee's tongue felt like it weighed a hundred pounds. He held up the application. "I came to fill out an application for the job." He was barely audible, and his voice cracked.

"You're hired. There is a practice game in less than two weeks, so we better get started," Coach Holt said, in the direction of all the other applicants.

Lynn stepped in front of him, her arms crossed. "Coach, you need to look at all the applications and then confer with Principal De Loach."

Coach Holt pointed and shook his finger at Lynn. "Young lady, I assure you none of those people over there know a fraction of what this kid knows about basketball. Tell Principal De Loach whatever he was going to pay for the position isn't enough. Time to increase the budget. This damn school is finally flying first class."

Lynn's eyebrows furrowed. Using her palms, she smoothed the front of her dress. She was not used to being overridden. "How can we give him a raise when we don't even know his Social Security number?" Lynn asked, and folded her arms tightly.

"Tell you what. Before he leaves my office, I promise to have him write down his Social Security number, his phone number, and every number he has on the back of my hand and you can do with those numbers what you will." Coach Holt gave her a wink.

Lynn turned on her heels like she was trying to dig a hole in the floor. "Sometimes you are so difficult," Lynn said and stormed away.

Coach Holt looked at Rhee and pointed at Lynn. "Pretty gal there, Joyce." Rhee froze, hoping that his mooning had gone unnoticed. "Get in here. We're burning daylight."

Rhee carefully walked behind the coach. "I'm right behind you." He stole a quick glance at Lynn. She sat down with volcanic stiffness.

Making the small cubbyhole an office was obviously an afterthought, but it was far enough from the front office to offer sanctuary to a cranky, old coach. It dawned on Rhee that the small room was meant to be more of an equipment room: stuffed with baseball mitts, basketballs, bats, soccer balls, orange pylons, and old sneakers.

The cleaning crew, who meticulously took care of the outer office, had hit this one with a drive by. Lopsided shelves strained to hold up framed team pictures. Various plaques on the walls revealed some of Coach Holt's past under a film of dust.

"Come on in young man," Coach Holt said. He beckoned Rhee with his hands. Rhee balanced on his cane, held onto the application and his backpack, and walked in, awkwardly. "Close the door."

Rhee shifted everything in his hands, turned, and closed the door. Coach Holt extended his hand. Rhee switched the cane from his right hand to left and offered his hand to Coach Holt, who snatched it and shook it hard. The coach's other hand was firmly on Rhee's shoulder.

Coach Holt's handshake rattled Rhee's entire body, and Rhee's voice vibrated. "Pleased to meet you, sir."

"Pleasure is mine, young man. Pleasure is mine." The coach finally let go, but Rhee still felt his arm vibrate. The old man seemed a little off, but he was the only person to treat Rhee like a star in months. "Have a seat."

Coach Holt shoved a pile from a corner of what looked to Rhee like a desk and rested his behind on it while Rhee looked around for a place to sit. There were two chairs, but they both had piles of files, balls, and shoes.

"I read last year you had signed with St. Aquinas," Coach Holt said, a look of astonishment on his face.

"Yes." Rhee kept his answers short and sweet. He still wasn't sure he had the job. This Coach Holt probably had supervisors who had the final say in the matter. He didn't want to get his hopes up to have them dashed again.

"I guess you plan to return the school to its glory days."

Rhee was caught in an awkward moment between telling a lie to get through the moment and telling the truth and risking judgment or, worse, losing the job. "That was the plan," Rhee said, with a sigh. He was sure he was under the microscope. He wanted to move through the subject of playing past high school as quickly as he could.

"Damn, I was surprised. Glad as hell, but still surprised. I thought you'd go take the 'one and done' deal at a major school like Kentucky or North Carolina with lots of television and national exposure."

Rhee was unsure how to respond. "My mom liked St. Aquinas." Rhee leaned back against the wall, feigning relaxation, even though he was far from it. Telling the truth and speaking of his mother gave him unexplainable confidence.

"Your mom must wear the big pants in your family." The coach wiped at his nose. "If you were my son, you'd play for Krzyzewski or Coach Knight."

Rhee wanted to remind the old man that Coach Knight retired several years ago but decided against it. He tried to think of a more polite response. Rhee thought of the job. There was a principal that had been mentioned by the attractive girl named Lynn. As far as Rhee knew, the principal still outranked the coach. The coach told him he had the job. But what if that meant nothing until someone higher up approved, someone other than this ball collector?

"Coach Knight is my father's favorite coach of all time."

The coach's face became stern. "Coach Knight is many smart people's favorite coach of all time, son. Your father is obviously one of them."

Rhee remembered how disappointed his father became and remained after Coach Knight retired. It was the same level of disappointment that had kept the Joyce household in a constant state of tension since Rhee's injury.

"Shitty luck about the injury." He looked down at Rhee's cast. "What kind of concoction you wearing there?"

"It's a walking boot cast. I get it off in a few days."

"Damn, sorry it happened. I'm praying you have a full recovery," Coach Holt said. "You're going to make a comeback, though, right?" His concerned gaze burrowed into Rhee.

"Hope so, sir," Rhee answered. He noticed the coach stiffen.

"No one has called me sir, not since the Gulf War. I don't have particularly fond memories of that, so I suggest you call me either Coach or Coach Holt."

Rhee felt the job slipping through his fingers. He meant no disrespect. Calling an elder "sir" was a sign of respect to him. Rhee's father made sure Rhee made a habit of it. "My parents are strict on how I speak to grown-ups."

"That's your first mistake, Rhee Joyce. I'm not a grown-up yet."

Rhee averted his eyes from the coach's gaze, unsure of a response. He noticed a plaque on his desk that read, "Coach of the Year." He wondered which year that was.

"Which brings me to one question," Coach Holt said. "What the hell brings you to this hellhole? Do you really need this thankless job?"

"Sir?"

Coach Holt gave Rhee a hard look and showed gritted teeth. "Bad choice of a noun. Call me 'Coach' or 'Jug Head,' or we're going to have a serious problem."

Rhee looked at the coach and decided he was crazy. All Rhee wanted was a job so he could go to college. "Sorry, Coach. I thought coaching basketball might be something I could try because I played."

"You more than played, dear boy. You made it to legendary status in my book. You're a McDonald's first-team All-American."

"Yes, I'm hoping my experience will help me with the job."

Coach Holt reached into the desk drawer and removed a silver flask. Rhee's eyes widened as Coach Holt twisted the top and threw back a generous gulp. The hard liquor smell reminded him of several former legends in Live Oaks Park, now pickling themselves with secret stashes in paper bags. Rhee's heart sank. The job and its importance diminished. Now all he wanted to do was make a graceful exit.

Chapter 11

Run And Don't Look Back

The coach wiped his mouth with the back of his hand. He held up the flask and offered Rhee a swig. "Mother's milk. Care to take a sample for yourself?"

Rhee held up his hand, politely. He fought back a disapproving grimace, knowing the job hinged on it. "No thanks, Coach."

He looked up at the clock. It was just after three p.m.

"Suit yourself, Coach Holt said. He tossed back another swig.

Rhee had seen men drink alcohol between games at many outdoor summer leagues, but he'd never seen anyone drink alcohol at work, especially in a school. "Do they allow you to...?" Rhee stopped in mid-sentence. This was a slippery slope. He had no idea what to do or say.

"Of course not," Coach Holt said. He turned the flask over again and sucked some more down. Rhee had no idea what the coach was drinking, but the pungent smell was a dead giveaway that it wasn't soda pop. The coach exalted and threw back another heaping swallow. He coughed as it went down. Again, Coach Holt wiped his mouth with the back of his hand.

"You want me to come back another time?" Rhee asked.

"What? Why? Of course not! And let me tell you something, young man. I don't have a drinking problem, if that's what you're thinking."

Rhee's eyes bounced from the flask to anything else in the room and then back again. From his vantage point, this man was a stone-cold alcoholic. Only an alcoholic could look at the pristine gym Rhee had seen on his way in and call it a hellhole. "Of course you don't," Rhee said. He meant none of it.

Coach Holt pulled the desk drawer open, dropped the flask inside, and smashed it shut. He stood up, which made Rhee freeze. The coach wandered around the cluttered desk and stood right next to him. He placed his hand on Rhee's shoulder, which made Rhee jump. "As long as I can find a drink, there's no problem."

Rhee had no conceivable reply. The job wasn't his yet. Now he wasn't sure he wanted it. He played it safe and remained silent. He smelt the sweet scent of cologne mixed with alcohol. It was the same sickly smell Rhee had encountered with several street players he had guarded during outdoor games at The Jungle. Seeing how Coach Holt had benched himself with booze, Rhee wondered, as great a player as Rooster was, how much better he could have played without drug-induced comfort?

Coach Holt crossed his feet. "So how bad is that damn injury?"

Rhee's nerves calcified as tight as petrified wood. "I'm going to have to pray for a miracle," he said.

Coach Holt pushed his left knee in Rhee's direction. "It was 1970. I was in high school on my way to Notre Dame. The best damn cornerback in Maryland."

Heat rushed through Rhee's body when he glanced at the long scar on Coach Holt's knee.

"Instead of the Green Bay Packers, I shoveled manure at a feed factory with my dad for two straight summers before I ran away from that steaming hell." He gave Rhee an eerie stare. "So you're really going to try to be a civilian for the time being, like the rest of us?"

Coach Holt's question sank into Rhee's stomach like lead. His mind swirled. Before Coach Holt, no one had spelled it out so bluntly. Everyone danced around it, but no one hit the bull's-eye dead center. It had been a long time since he had hit a winning bucket at the buzzer or sank a free throw to win a game or thrown a no-look pass or dunked on a defender. Rhee looked down at his hands. "For the time being, yeah, I guess."

"You all right there, son?"

Rhee looked at the scar on Coach Holt's knee again. He wanted to change the subject, especially in his own head. "I saw some good players today in the gym on my way here."

Coach Holt looked at Rhee like he was crazy.

"One of the kids can flat ball. He has real talent," Rhee said.

"What? What talent? Where?" Coach Holt asked.

"At the gym about a half hour ago. I saw a kid who had some mad skills. He had all kinds of handles and shot the ball like a Division One college player."

Coach Holt shook his head and waved at Rhee. "Don't go getting your hopes up, son. Those were just probably some of the kids from a rival school in Oakland. They come up here to use the gym since it's the best damn facility in the county and nobody around here uses it."

"What about a kid, goes by the name L.A.? He and his friends said he goes to school here."

"Never heard of him," Coach Holt answered.

"His friends called him 'L.A.' or 'White Chocolate.' I'm sure he goes to school here."

Coach Holt went back around his desk, sat down, and then picked up a magazine and browsed. "Well, he's probably too smart to embarrass himself and too rich to care. These knot heads aren't like you or me, Joyce. These brats' parents have Donald Trump-type money. You know what I'm saying?"

Rhee had no idea how to answer, what to do or say at this point. He was in a sink-or-swim situation. The job he originally wanted had started to appear crazier than the man in the room. Coach Holt obviously wasn't able to coach anymore, especially while he drank. Rhee decided to walk right into the question instead of dancing around it.

"Why aren't you coaching the team?" Rhee asked.

Coach Holt looked up. Rhee had got his attention but worried it was going to stir the hornet's nest. "You ever heard of something we in academia call tenure?"

Rhee had no idea what it meant. He thought of lying but he didn't want the coach to catch him in a lie. "No, si-- I mean, Coach."

One of the coach's eyebrows rose up as he measured Rhee. "It's kind of like being a cockroach. After being on the job for so long, they can't throw you out; they can't burn you out, and they can't spray enough poison to make your nose itch."

Rhee nodded and stole a glance at the wall clock to see how long he'd been in the coach's office. Only a few minutes had passed, but it felt like an eternity. He looked back at the Coach, who stared him dead in the eyes, catching his blunder. "So they won't let you go, but they won't let you coach anymore?"

"You're a smart kid, Joyce," Coach Holt said, nodding his head. "Anyway, a string of bad luck, two mean ex-wives, and a couple bouts with bad judgment. Now here I am, captain of nothing anyone cares about."

Rhee tossed the words around in his head. He wondered how the coach had had bad judgment, but he knew it might cripple his chances of securing the job. "Bad judgment?" Rhee asked. Drinking had to be at the top of the list, but he acted like he had no idea.

"Suffice to say, you hit the bull's-eye. They won't let me coach anymore, but they can't get rid of me. Those sons of bitches." Sunlight filtered through frosted cage windows, making the perspiration on the Coach's sallow face gleam.

Rhee diverted his attention, pointing at the plaque that read, "Coach of the Year." "Is this your 'Coach of the Year' award?" Rhee asked.

"No, son. It belongs to Eddie Murphy. I just like to hang it there to make me remember the movie *Trading Places*. It was one of my favorite films."

Rhee looked at the puckered expression on Coach Holt's face long enough to realize the old man was pulling his leg. "You must have been a pretty good coach to get that award."

"I won a dozen of those. That's the only one I didn't seem to misplace."

Rhee tried to cover his genuine surprise. "Wow! That's incredible!"

"I slapped a couple of the varmints upside the head for insubordination, and then the bastards demoted me to girls' intramurals and lunch time and afterwards school yard duty."

Rhee knew now was the time to stay quiet. At the same time, he wanted to say, "Hey, this doesn't concern me. I've got problems of my own." Though, he felt sorry for Coach Holt; the man was clearly in pain.

"Trust me, Joyce. After a few days with some of these kids, you're going to want to put a foot up their back sides yourself." Coach Holt coughed into his fist. "You may even start sipping the old brandy yourself."

Rhee waited for this opportunity so he jumped on it. "So I got the job?"

Rhee waited. Coach Holt gave him a glare.

"Of course you got the job, Joyce. Wash the wax out of your ears. I told you that at the beginning."

Rhee used his thumb to point over his shoulder. "That girl in the office, Lynn, she said the principal had to approve."

It was obvious Coach Holt was irritated. He opened the drawer and twisted the top off the flask. He threw back a heaping swallow, wiped his mouth with the back of his hand, and belched. "Like I said, first practice game is less than two weeks, and official tryouts are still a week out. The principal knows we don't have a lot of time to get someone in here. Besides, Rhee Joyce is not going to walk in here more than once. Am I right?"

Rhee nodded. He tried to reason with his own heart that this crazy old coach with the drinking problem had the authority to hire him. "Coach, I need to work at least twenty hours a week."

"Done."

"Done?"

"Tap the water from your ears, Joyce. I'll put you down for

twenty hours a week, even if you only come five."

Rhee looked at the coach, unsure what to say. "Thanks."

Coach Holt gave Rhee a dismissive wave and set to pretending he had something important to do, like find a bottle to refill his flask. Rhee silently prayed in his head: *Please, God. Never let this happen to me.*

Chapter 12

Eagles Without Wings

There was an icy silence, underlined with forced politeness between him and his parents at each meal. But today Rhee blocked it out. He hadn't bothered to tell his parents about his new job. If coaching basketball ended in failure it was better not added to the Grand Canyon size wedge that already divided the family. The fact that they manage to co-exist under the same roof was something Rhee knew had an expiration date. Leaving the home he grew up in any time soon was more like walking the plank blindfolded into a deep sea of sharks and piranhas. There was no plan in place for him to wrap his brain around, just a plummet into an unknown darkness. The tools to survive on his own had more of a chance to come from outer space than his back pockets.

Rhee cut himself off from all possible life supports other than his parents. All friendships and relationships were framed by his stardom and notoriety. Any contact with anyone in his past only shined a light on his tragic demise. And it was not just Rhee. People began to treat him like a cancer patient. The energy it took to act happy or to hold up hope drained the batteries his relationships. There simply was no sunny side of the street for anyone to stand on when they were around a fallen legend. Even neighbors who once lingered in front of their houses to catch a wave from Rhee, now quick stepped up the driveway or waited for their garage doors to close before they got out of their cars.

Building new friendships or relationships was from a mind and body Rhee only began to use. Everyday that went by he was more and more a stranger to himself. Rhee's transformation into a civilian was like teeth that dropped out on their own. It took away his smile.

Rhee wore a brand new, maroon, Nike sweatshirt and a hoodie, compliments of a recruiting trip he'd long forgotten. The maroon color almost matched the Eagles' school colors. He was relieved he was out of his walking cast boot. He had a slight limp, but the pain was less and less severe, bearable. He still needed the cane, but he went without it as often as he could.

Rhee bolted from his house carrying a clipboard and a whistle suspended by a new leather rope around his neck.

When he arrived at the middle school, he ducked his head inside Coach Holt's cubbyhole. Coach Holt clearly wasn't expecting anyone anytime soon. Leaning back in his chair, he held a vintage Playboy magazine stretched to its full length. His head was tilted, and he examined it sideways.

Rhee cleared his throat as quietly as he could. Coach Holt glanced up and saw Rhee but made no attempt to conceal his pleasure with the magazine. A flabbergasted Rhee pointed his right thumb over his shoulder and leaned his head away. "Sorry, I can come back if you're busy."

Coach Holt waved Rhee inside with one hand, while he gripped the magazine with the other. "Coach Joyce, come on in. Come on in, big guy." The coach carefully lowered the magazine, folded it gently and placed it in his drawer. He'd return to it later. "What can I do for you?"

"Today's the first day of practice, right?"

Coach Holt gave an encouraging fist punch through the air. "Give 'em hell, and don't be light on the pansies."

"Is there a roster or a sign-up sheet?" Rhee asked.

Coach Holt patted his keg-like form as if he was looking for a pen or a cigarette or a mug. Rhee had no idea which. He waited for the coach to lose interest in his pockets. The old man looked away like he'd forgotten something important.

"Coach?"

Coach Holt stood and rifled through a stack of papers and magazines. He found a torn piece of paper with some names scribbled on it. He handed it to Rhee. "Here you go. The new team."

Rhee cocked his head getting a better angle to read. He used his index finger to count, hoping it would help Coach Holt understand his next question. "All I see here are six names."

Coach Holt analyzed an old football as if there were answers written on the pigskin. "That's your team, Joyce. You've got six pinheaded imbeciles."

"Only six?"

"Yep, best turnout in three years." Coach Holt snorted loudly and coughed into a handkerchief that he retrieved from a back pocket.

"This is a joke, right?" Rhee asked. His patience with the Coach's incompetence was wearing thin.

Coach Holt shook his head and folded his handkerchief. "Two years ago we had to let girls play on the boys' team in order not to forfeit any games."

"You're kidding." For a moment, Rhee honestly felt he was getting punked. He looked into Coach Holt's eyes and saw the old man was dead serious.

"The girls weren't bad either."

Rhee tried to hold back his surprise, but his mouth opened and words blurted out anyway. "You had a Junior High co-ed team?" Rhee asked.

Coach Holt shook his head and distracted himself with an old, grass-stained softball. "Damn straight! A few years back, we had a couple girls at this school that whooped the tar out of all the boys on the court. They weren't Cheryl Miller or Nancy Lieberman, but they managed to toss the basketball into the hoop."

Rhee was too young to ever see two of the greatest female basketball stars play, but he was happy his father and high school coach told him about legendary female basketball players like Miller and Lieberman. He also knew about Denise Curry and Ann Meyers, as well as more recent stars like Swoops, Parker, Leslie, Taurasi, Lobo, Moore, and Brittney Griner, a player Rhee shot hoops with at a boys and girls all-star camp. He knew without a doubt that Pat Summit was one of the all-time greatest basketball coaches, male or female, college or professional. He looked back down at the piece of paper. "I can't believe only six guys wanted to try out." In Rhee's hand was another reason to walk away from this job.

"A lot of boys may want to play, but unfortunately they want to play at a different school."

"That's not any kind of school pride."

"Welcome to coaching at Joaquin Moraga Junior High, Joyce. There isn't any school pride."

Coach Holt slowly opened a drawer and peeked inside. Rhee knew the old man was looking to steal a little sip.

"Coach," Rhee said.

Coach Holt quickly shut the drawer. He found a stack of papers and held them up. "You probably want to hand out the emergency forms with the parents' phone numbers."

Coach Holt offered the papers to Rhee, who put them on his clipboard. Maybe there was a way to salvage this mess. He thought about the white kid with all the mad skills.

"What about the kid called L.A. or White Chocolate?" Rhee asked. "Did he come by or sign up?"

"You keep mentioning those names, and I keep telling you I have no idea who you're talking about. Don't know any 'White Chocolate,' or 'Lemon Meringue' either."

He picked up a baseball glove that looked like it should have been thrown away. He tossed a softball in the air and caught it. He stayed with the solitary game until Rhee lost all patience.

"So you never heard of him? You never saw him play?" Rhee asked.

"Like I said, never heard of him. What about him anyway?"

"If we could get him to come out for the team, it would make a huge difference."

Coach Holt tossed the softball high enough to hit the ceiling. Debris fluttered down, and it seemed to pique the coach's interest. He tossed the softball hard and chips of paint fell. "You said he was good, right?" Coach Holt asked.

Rhee covered his clipboard, looked up, and took a step back from the mess that began to litter down from the ceiling. "All kinds of talent."

"None of those six knuckleheads fits that description."

Rhee nodded and slowly turned away. The cold rush of trepidation filled him. It was the first time he could ever remember not being eager to get into the gymnasium.

When Rhee pushed open the gymnasium door, the light flickered over the giant eagle in flight. The next thing he saw was a cluster of the most unimpressive fourteen-year-old boys he'd ever seen.

Air went from Rhee's lungs as he started his trek across the gymnasium floor. He masked his disappointment as he stopped in front of six boys who sat on the bleachers. They each distracted themselves with their cell phones or portable video games. Rhee's high school coach, Dr. Robert Silva, had told his players, "Any texting or twittering during practice is an automatic dismissal from the team." Should he enforce the same policy? Or better yet, should he turn and hightail it out of here while he still had the chance?

Rhee looked down and assessed all the boys' sneakers. They each had the latest and greatest top-of-the-line footwear. The list of positives was from the absolute bottom up: great gymnasium floor, good footwear. Rhee hoped he would find more for the positive list. He read from the short list on the torn piece of paper. "Terrance Darling?"

No one said anything or looked up from texting, checking emails, tweeting, or playing video games. Rhee raised his hands and got down to business. "OK, hold up. Everyone put all y'all little electronic gizmos away, like right now."

"Here."

Rhee looked up and saw a slender, sandy-brown-haired boy wearing a T-shirt emblazoned with, "Surfers do it on the board."

"I'm Terrance, but who are you?"

Rhee gave all six uninterested players a wide-eyed stare. A few of the boys looked up. "I'm the new coach." All the boys looked up at him like he was kidding.

"Put it away now, y'all, right this second." Rhee waited while all six eighth grade boys made a show of powering down and putting away their gadgets. All told, it was two full minutes of waiting. "OK, let's get this over with."

He swallowed back the knot that rose up from his stomach to his throat. He looked back down at the torn piece of paper on his clipboard. "Doug Martin?"

"So, like, are you really the coach? For real?"

Rhee heard the voice of a man, not a kid. A thick-necked, crew-cut, Aryan-looking kid had his hand in the air. He was big and had a five o'clock shadow. The kid seemed like he'd been in a few fights but never been on a basketball court.

Rhee leered at the man-sized kid. "Yes, I'm the coach. Are you Doug Martin?"

"How old are you?" Doug asked.

"Old enough to know six egghead kids are not a basketball team." Rhee looked back down at the piece of paper. A head-on collision between him and six fourteen-year-olds mounted. He could sense it in the air, but he continued. "Asa Lieberman?"

A mousey kid with curly dark hair raised his hand. He was the only kid who paid careful attention and didn't have an electronic device on his person. He held up his hand long enough for Rhee to acknowledge him. "Right here, Coach."

"What a kiss ass," Doug said, under his breath.

Rhee gave him a cold stare. "Haters keep it to yourself until I'm finished." He turned his attention back to the kid with curly black hair. He wore eyeglasses covered by thick goggles for protection. Rhee pointed to his own eyes. "You can get sports goggles with a prescription," Rhee said. "That's only if you don't want to look ridiculous."

The five other boys laughed. Asa bowed his head, as if embarrassed. "Gotta make the team first," Asa said to the floor.

Rhee wondered if the kid was really being serious. How could this kid with goggles over his eyeglasses not know there were probably not enough players to even have a team? Rhee looked back down at his clipboard. "Blaze Hammond?"

"Yes, sir," Blaze said. The boy called Blaze was the portly one, with a doughboy face.

"You're Blaze?" Rhee asked. His disbelief was a neon sign.

Blaze nodded feverishly. Rhee lowered the clipboard. "A name like Blaze must mean you're pretty quick."

The other boys, except Asa, laughed out loud.

"I'm quick enough," Blaze said. He stared down at his own hands and feet and absorbed being the brunt of Rhee's comment.

"We'll see about that," Rhee said. His eyes slowly fell back down to the clipboard. There were so few names Rhee could have memorized them. The clipboard was just a tool to avert his gaze and hide his disgust, which took some doing. "Weston Morgan?"

"Right here, dude," a boy responded. The Abercrombie poster boy looked bored. He barely raised his head. Rhee looked toward the voice and saw the Abercrombie poster boy was the rude kid who had climbed out of the turbo Bentley and disrespected his mother the other day. Rhee leered at the kid. The kid frowned back, not sure where Rhee's obvious scorn came from. Rhee held the leer, until Rude Bentley Boy looked away.

"And Gerry Agosta?"

"Yo," Gerry said. He was a tall, six foot, three or four inches, slender kid with legs and arms like branches.

Rhee lowered the clipboard and examined the motley-looking crew: These kids were not ball players. They looked like the Keystone Kops. "I'm your coach, so you guys can call me Coach or Coach Joyce." Rhee waited a moment to see if any of these misfits recognized him. Maybe these losers would shape up and at least give him his props when they realized he was Rhee Joyce. "That's if we can even have a team. Six guys are probably not going to cut it."

One pair of eyes widened in true amazement. They belonged to Asa, the kid with goggles over glasses. "Rhee Joyce, from Davis?" Asa asked.

Rhee looked at him. What a nightmare. Only the little Johnny Neutron kid guessed his name and looked impressed. He cleared his throat and opened his mouth when something distracted him. Weston, the Rude Bentley Boy, raised his hand. "What is it?" Rhee asked.

"Can we take a five-minute break?"

Weston got off the bleachers and started toward the drinking fountain. Rhee glanced at the clock on the wall protected by an iron cage. "Are you serious?"

His throat strained and hit an unfamiliar pitch. It was the same pitch when the adrenalin took over and amplified the voice to match the feelings underneath it.

"I'm thirsty," Weston said.

Rhee eyed Weston with disdain. "Sit your butt down, soldier boy."

Weston looked at his teammates. He whispered something into Terrance's ear. They shared a laugh.

"You have something to say?" Rhee asked.

Weston curled his lips and showed his teeth. "Not to everyone, no," he said. Weston spoke like Rhee was an inferior. It made Rhee's blood boil.

"Sit down now or get out." He waited for Weston to sit and then glanced at the rest of the boys. "All right. Let's do some drills so I can get an idea of your skills," Rhee said. "Maybe see if all those $200 shoes can make you play like NBA players all y'all representing from your ankles down."

Asa leaped to his feet. The other boys begrudgingly unglued their butts from the bleachers, stood, and hopped onto the floor.

Rhee blew his whistle. "OK. Line up, two deep and three across." He couldn't believe his eyes when the boys attempted to follow the instructions but instead wandered around in confusion like lost sheep. Rhee physically pulled each of them into a place, three across with one person behind. He picked up a basketball and shoved it into the stomach of the first middle person, Weston, or 'Rude Bentley Boy,' who wheezed and groaned.

"Whoa, dude. Take it easy," Weston said.

Rhee may have hurt the smart-mouthed kid, but right then, he didn't care. "OK, three-man weave, pass and go behind," Rhee said, with an ounce of gratification.

"What the hell is a three-man weave?" Blaze asked.

Rhee turned to figure out which one of the idiots in front of him had the guts to admit he was an idiot. "Does anyone in the gymnasium know what a three-man weave is?"

The six bobbleheads shifted from foot to foot in assigned positions, shrugging at each other, no one, and Rhee. None of them spoke.

The door at the other end of the gymnasium popped open and Rama, Lam, and Cub strutted through dressed in basketball gear, unlaced well-used sneakers, long shorts, and baseball caps on sideways or backwards. Rhee put his whistle in his mouth to blow when he saw L.A. behind the three others. L.A. pimp walked behind his crew.

Rhee blew the whistle. "Take five," he said, to the six players. "Remember your positions." A pain shot up from the pins and plates of his ankle, but he tried to ignore it as he marched toward the intruders. He winced a little and just knew he was going to hit someone before the day was done.

Chapter 13

White Chocolate And The Oaktown Crew

A searing jolt of agony shot from the bottom of his foot to the top of his hip. He felt the size of his leg muscle strain. Before his recent adventure into pain, he would not have known exactly what hurt. Now Rhee knew it was his superior and inferior extensor retinaculum. The eyes of his six subpar players followed him as Rhee bit his lip and made it to the intruders. He held up his whistle. "See this?" Rhee's eyes met each of the four in turn, and his jaw muscles quivered. "For the next two hours, I own this gym, so get to stepping."

"Man, cuz, lighten up. We ain't criminals, you know?" Cub said.

"Yeah, hey, we ain't goin' mess anything up for your boys. They don't need no help with that," Lam said. The others in the group smirked and grimaced, straining not to laugh.

"All you need is Dopey or Sleepy and you'll have your seven dwarfs," L.A. said. His words released the floodgates of laughter among them. They all gave each other more high fives and held their stomachs they laughed so hard.

Rhee blew his whistle, the shrill noise cut through their chortles. These were the players he wanted. They were pretty good, and he felt bad turning them out when his team could barely tie their overpriced shoes. He spit the whistle out.

"Sorry, fellas. The gym is closed for practice."

Lam let out a very competent imitation, a sound bite of Allen Iverson: "Practice? Are we talking about practice?" More giggles from the group.

Rhee smiled despite himself. "Yeah, we're talking about practice." All the boys howled in amusement.

He knew they were laughing at a truly pathetic situation. Rhee looked back at the sorry group of boys. They stood around with no traces of confidence, staring at the floor, gazing at the ceiling, examining their hands. Rhee turned back to the intruders, and it dawned on him that the two kids he liked wasn't rolling with the rest of them. "Where is Felix Providence?" Rhee asked.

They looked at each other. L.A. patted his chest and then his pants. "Oh, damn! Guess they dropped out when we gave the bus driver our bus passes," L.A. said. His crew laughed, but Rhee didn't think the jibe was funny. He sneered at all of them.

"OK playas, out. All of you roll on out like you rolled on in, uninvited," Rhee said. He looked at L.A., who stared back with a mad-dog glaze in his eyes. "L.A., you're welcome to stay or suit up and join the team."

L.A. waved him off. "I'm good, my man. I never worked at a circus or nothing like that, right?"

"This is your school. We'd have serious grip with you on the team," Rhee said.

"My school, but not my clowns, Coach. You the one running this sideshow, boss," L.A. said. He and his crew backed up toward the door. Merciless laughter, the bounce of a ball, and squeaks from their sneakers trailed along as they made their way out of the gymnasium. Nothing but silence was left behind. Rhee wished he had a giant hook to put around L.A.'s neck and reel him back to join the team.

He dropped his head and slowly turned back to the six self-entitled, talentless, suburban, affluent boys left on the court. He walked over to the ball rack. He picked up balls and tossed them toward the six boys. "OK, shoot, rebound your own shot, and just keep shooting."

The gym came alive again with the sounds of sneakers and basketballs hitting the wood floor as they did what they were told. Their shots veered over the rim or clanked off the backboard. All except one. Terrance shot the ball with an unorthodox style, elbows out, an almost two-handed shot, but everything he threw kept falling through the rim. It reminded Rhee of an old film his dad showed him of a player named Jamaal Wilkes. Terrance had the same awkward shooting style, but he was smooth, like he was gliding. Rhee counted six, and then seven straight baskets. "Keep your elbows in, one hand, like you're shooting out of a phone booth," Rhee said.

Terrance tried to adjust his shot, but he missed three times in a row. "What's a phone booth?"

Rhee gave Terrance a look like he was the dumbest kid Rhee had ever known. Then it dawned on him that he didn't exactly know what a phone booth was either. It was just a shooting drill he'd done for years but never questioned.

"Just keep your elbows in." Rhee said.

The ball whooshed through the net, four times. Terrance went back to his natural, unnatural shooting form. Rhee forced himself to not care or be impressed, a stoic expression frozen on his face. "Ok, grab your balls," Rhee said. The minute the last syllable came from his mouth, he rolled his eyes, knowing he was easy pickings.

Doug and Weston grabbed their own crotches. "These nuts?" both of them yelled. Gerry and Blaze erupted in laughter and held onto their crotches.

Rhee stared at the two boys and just shook his head. "Okay, you got me. I just blind-walked into that one." He placed the whistle in his mouth and blew as hard as he could. The entire gymnasium echoed a piercing shrill. "Dribble to the other baseline using only your right hand and then return dribbling with only your left hand."

The boys jostled over to retrieve the basketballs and formed a horizontal line beneath the gigantic eagle on the wall. "Ready?" Rhee asked. They held onto the balls, watched Rhee with anticipation, some crouched to position themselves for the drill, but he knew they weren't ready. He wanted to tell the coach he at least tried after all the players quit, which Rhee was sure they would do. There was no twenty-hour-a-week job in this gymnasium. The best thing for these kids was ten hours a week of detention.

The boys jumped forward and attempted to dribble the basketballs the length of the court. Nearly all of them reached the first free-throw line before Doug's basketball sliced into Gerry's, and a colliding pop sent the two basketballs careening into the other players' forward motion. The domino effect sent all six players scrambling after the escaping basketballs, like toddlers at a rolling Easter egg hunt.

These kids were worse than they looked. They were worse than he had ever imagined. He blew the whistle, hard and loud. The boys stopped and raised their chins toward Rhee. Silence once again overtook the gym.

"OK, OK. Let's forget about balls for now. Everybody run a couple laps."

All six players stared momentarily at Rhee, apparently confused, but they turned towards the double doors of the gym in unison, and headed outside. Rhee grabbed his head with both hands.

"No, no, no. Run laps around the black line of the court, or the perimeter of the court." The six boys looked at Rhee, and then around at each other, perplexed expressions on their faces. "Inside the gym." Rhee said, as if speaking to children. He dropped his head in shame. He had walked into a minefield of impossibility. The utter incompetence blew his mind. After the boys completed a couple of laps around the black line, he said, "Keep going."

Rhee sat down on the bleachers and contemplated taking a nap, letting the Backstreet Boys run for a few hours. He closed his eyes and let go with a meditative exhale. A daydream came into his head. Rhee sat at the First Take desk, dressed immaculately. A perfectly tailored Stephen A. Smith and Skip Bayless trained their eyes on him, incredulous. "Let me get this straight. After your illustrious career, you walked into a middle-school gymnasium and set the bleachers on fire, while six motley, good-for-nothing, fourteen-year-olds were all duck-taped together at half court?" Stephen A. Smith asked.

"Yes," Rhee answered.

Stephen A. Smith and Skip Bayless look at one another, stupefied. "That's the most brilliant thing I've heard in the history of our show," Skip Bayless said.

Then the gymnasium door clanged open. Rhee snapped out of his daydream. A bald, squat man with eyeglasses wearing a blue, frumpy, wrinkled suit and poorly knotted gray tie ambled across the wooden floor towards him. The man had silver hair that began atop a high forehead and thinned into a comb-back, attempting to cover his mostly baldhead. His brown leather belt matched his brown leather shoes with solid black soles.

"Rhee Joyce?" the man asked. He jutted his right hand to Rhee.

"Yes." Rhee hesitated before he offered his hand. They shook. "Welcome, I'm Principal De Loach, Norman De Loach." The man's sweaty palm felt like a warm fish. "I've heard all about you coming to our fine establishment, and I'd just like to say what a pleasure it is to have someone of your caliber representing our school and coaching our young men."

He proudly surveyed the six boys hoofing around the gym, although they slowed their pace. Weston's arms hung from his sides. "Dying out here, dude."

Principal De Loach smiled wide. "Good turnout this year."

Rhee stared at him, trying hard not to gape like a fish. "Depends on your expectations, right?"

The principal caught none of Rhee's sarcasm. "Yeah, looks like a good group. The Morgan boy is related to the famous banking family," Principal De Loach said. Rhee nodded. It meant nothing to him other than Weston was rich and spoiled. "And Blaze Hammond, now there's a real fire, right?"

Principal De Loach chortled at his joke, and Rhee forced a smile. "Right," Rhee said. He feared all the training his parents pounded into him to be polite and respectful was going to end any second.

Principal De Loach gave Rhee a playful wink. "Maybe we'll break that two-year losing streak."

Rhee wanted to gently put a hand on the principal's baldhead and say, "I heard that the Titanic might come up for air and throw some hellacious prom parties." Instead, he shrugged his shoulders and mumbled, "Anything's possible."

The six boys dragged themselves around the gym and barely jogged now. They grabbed their sides and moaned. Rhee frowned, brought his whistle to his mouth to blow.

"Uh, just between you and me, if they don't win some games this year, I doubt we'll have a basketball team next year," Principal De Loach whispered.

Rhee leaned away from the principal's coffee breath. "Bummer," Rhee replied. He kept the whistle on the corner of his mouth because the principal kept talking.

"I'm sure you're old enough to understand budget cuts. There are a lot of programs to pay for, and we can't keep everything. The school board is planning athletic cutbacks, and well, Eagles basketball will probably be the first to go. It's been years since The Eagles were anything to talk about"

"Yeah, I saw some plaques on Coach Holt's walls."

Principal De Loach patted Rhee firmly on the back. "Well, I'll bet you're eager to get back at it." Rhee looked down at the black mark Principal De Loach's shoes made on the hardwood. The principal cupped his hands as a megaphone. "Go Eagles."

Rhee watched the principal leave through the double doors, and three of the six Eagles raised their middle fingers in salute. All the boys chuckled, slapped hands, and high-fived.

Rhee tightened his jaw to keep from laughing. He ushered the players off the court by blowing his whistle. "OK, that's it for today."

The boys immediately turned and sprinted towards to the locker room. Rhee witnessed the first sign of any synchronized teamwork they had shown all day. The six players obviously hustled away in fear that he just might change his mind and call them back onto the court.

When the last one disappeared into the locker room, Rhee gathered the last ball and wedged it next to another on the ball rack. The dead silence gave him the opportunity to clear his head. Taking this job was a mistake. He knew it. He was the wrong fit. There was no way he could make these know-nothing boys into actual basketball players. The moving second hand on the wall clock in its cage made Rhee feel like his time was wasting away here. This team needed a genie in a bottle to grant them all wishes to be the Los Angeles Lakers.

He stared at the locker room, took a deep breath, and drummed up the courage to go face the misfits. He decided to go tell them he was not going to be their coach.

Chapter 14

Who Is That Guy?

Rhee stepped inside the locker room. The floors were tiled, not the linoleum or cement he'd seen his entire sports career. The lockers were not crammed and stacked. Each locker expanded from the knees to the top of the head of a person easily six feet tall. The showers were private stalls with curtains. Rhee had never seen private shower stalls in a middle, junior, or high school. The lighting was not the usual florescent afterthought either. The ceiling had sconces, and the lights shined in different areas like a theater. There was no cracked paint on the walls; they were smooth with a fresh coat. Why did this school spend so much money on a gymnasium and a boys' locker room? Was there a private salon in the girls' locker?

Rhee heard the metal lockers open and slam close and then the boys' voices. He stayed perfectly still. A full-length mirror on the opposite wall reflected their images. They gathered around in a small circle.

Blaze slammed his locker. His naked body sat hunched on a wooden bench. He reached to the floor, grabbed a white towel, stood, and wrapped it around his fleshy waist. "I don't think he likes us."

Rhee rolled his eyes and almost laughed. That was the understatement of the century.

Terrance passed with a towel around his snow-white, skinny frame, his arms and lower legs tanned. "Of course he doesn't like us, doofus. We're only six players, and we stink."

Asa stood in front of his locker. He was clad in underwear and pulled a sweatshirt over his head. "You're both wrong. He hates us because of who he is."

Doug laced up his black motorcycle boots, closed his locker, and straightened his army fatigues. "What are you talking about, pencil neck?"

Asa pulled off his protective goggles and gently placed his thick eyeglasses on the bridge of his nose. "Didn't you notice how Principal De Loach almost kissed the guy? You didn't recognize him, no neck?"

Doug stepped forward and shoved his army-fatigue-attired chest in Asa's face and bumped his thick eyeglasses. "Who you calling no neck, butt face?" Doug asked. "Our principal is an idiot. He tries to tongue everyone. That doesn't make this guy special." Doug's arms puffed away from his sides. He pushed Asa's bony chest, but Asa recovered and stepped forward.

"You're a no neck," Asa said.

"Oh shit, Martin is going to pound him," Gerry said.

Doug raised his arms and balled his fists, but Asa shoved him, defiantly and bravely, although it appeared to be the bravado of the last gasp of a cornered bird.

"Get out of my face. Your deodorant is failing miserably," Asa said.

Doug stepped closer to Asa, dwarfing him, and tightened his fists. Asa calmly and casually laced his shoes, being careful to not look at Doug.

Gerry stood next to both of them, amazed. "Asa, dude, are you crazy? Didn't you hear how he pounded Casey Freeman last week? And that was just for accidentally spilling milk on him."

Again Doug displayed his muscular forearms by unclasping and tightening his fists, but Asa still ignored him. "Casey Freeman is a bully like him, so if he pounds Casey, he looks tougher. But if he pounds me, a dweeb in glasses, it won't promote his reputation as a badass."

His boldness paralyzed the big kid standing over him with his fist clenched. Asa tied a bow in his shoelace, threaded it and tightened it.

"OK, butthead, just hope you don't get a sudden growth spurt, 'cause I'll definitely smash your face," Doug said.

Weston gently stepped between Doug and Asa. He was fully dressed and looked like a budding prince of Wall Street in a Dockers commercial with his pressed khakis, polo shirt, and unscarred leather loafers. "So who is our coach?" Weston asked.

Weston and the other boys gathered around Asa to listen.

"Yeah, who is he?" Gerry asked.

Asa pushed up his glasses, looked, and saw he had everyone's attention. "Our new coach is Rhee Joyce," Asa said.

"Who the hell is Rhee Joyce?" Terrance asked. He dressed back in his "Surfers do it with a board" shirt and a Quiksilver hat, sweatshirt, and long, baggy shorts.

"I heard of him," Blaze said.

Doug punched him in the arm. Blaze fell against the lockers with a clang. "Shut up, Blaze. You haven't heard crap or you would've told us instead of Johnny Test." Doug slapped Asa on the shoulder. "Speak up."

"Our new coach is a high school legend, man, like LeBron, Rose, Davis, and Durant," Asa said.

"Dude, I have no clue what you're talking about. I've never heard of any of those guys," Blaze said.

His teammates all looked at him. "What planet did you drop from, jerk off?" Doug asked. "Everyone's heard of LeBron."

Blaze raised his shoulders and hands. "Blaze, you need some serious psychological help, man," Asa said. "Hating LeBron James has practically become a board game."

"Not everyone hates LeBron," Gerry said.

"I like LeBron," Doug said.

Everyone's mouth opened as they looked at Doug. "What's everyone looking at?"

"Dude, you hate everyone," Weston said. His teammates all nodded in agreement.

"Well, I like LeBron, and I hate just about everyone else."

"So, who is our coach?" Terrance asked.

"Yeah, Lieberman. Spit it out," Weston said.

"Rhee Joyce. He was touted as one of the greatest high school players ever," Asa said. "My dad loves the guy like a son, and he's never even met him."

"That's creepy," Terrance scowled at Asa.

"My dad is a sports junkie," Asa explained.

"So why is this guy stuck in here coaching us if he's like another LeBron?" Doug asked.

"Yeah, if he is so great, why'd he come here? Why is he coaching us?" Blaze asked. He chucked his dirty towel onto a pile of others.

"My dad said he broke his leg or something playing summer league. He said the sports writers wrote he'll never play again," Asa said.

"He's not going to play ever again?" Blaze asked.

"He's not even supposed to be walking," Asa replied.

Shocked, wide-eyed looks plastered on everyone's face.

"Oh, damn," Terrance, said.

"What?" Gerry asked.

"We're dead," Terrance said.

"Why do you say that?" Weston asked.

"Dude is probably going to snap. His life is over, right? I'd be crazy. He's probably going to take it out on us. Maybe show up one day with a machine gun and mow us all down just to make himself feel better."

There was an eerie silence in the locker room.

"He can't touch us, right?" Weston asked as he looked around at everyone, fear in his eyes.

"You don't listen, do you moron? Terrence just told you the guy may go psycho on the whole team," Doug said.

"He's only, like, three or four years older than us," Asa said. "He's not going to do anything crazy."

"I'm thinking maybe I'll run track," Gerry said.

"Maybe I should take my talents back to surfing," Terrance said.

"Yeah, we should all take our talents outta here," Blaze said.

"Talent, my ass," Rhee muttered. The words came out of his mouth in frustration. He spoke too loud and he knew it.

"Who was that?" Gerry asked.

Rhee put his hand over his mouth. He stayed perfectly still, standing on his eavesdropping bench. He held his breath.

"I gotta go," said Blaze.

The boys picked up their backpacks, slammed their lockers, and raced for the exit.

Rhee quickly hopped off the bench, landing softly on his good foot. Some of the boys stepped on his shadow as they scurried out but didn't notice him.

Rhee tiptoed across the gymnasium, grabbed his things, and left as fast as his bad ankle allowed. He got to the double doors of the gymnasium and stopped. He turned around and looked at the court. It was a really nice gymnasium. He planned on never seeing it again.

Chapter 15

The Keystone Kops

Rhee tried to figure out why he was stuck here. He came to quit and now he was back where he started.

From the corner of his eyes, he saw Coach Holt brooding atop the bleachers. Even from this far away, he felt the old man's contempt. He kept wondering if the coach actually found a gun and planned on taking them all out -- Rhee included. If he heard a gunshot, he hoped his instincts triggered him to cover behind one of the players. *Better one of them than me*, Rhee thought.

An errant basketball rocketed toward Rhee. He knocked it down inches from his face. The ball rolled toward the bleachers. Rhee tracked the gymnasium looking for the culprit. He saw Asa running toward the basketball.

"Sorry, Coach," Asa said.

Rhee gave him the one eye as Asa wheeled back around to rejoin the drill. Rhee snatched a basketball from the rack, turned toward the players, and blew his whistle. The boys froze, and the sound of the whistle echoed throughout the gymnasium. Rhee stole a glance at Coach Holt, who was now lying down on the top bleacher, probably sleeping off the morning's booze consumption. The sound of the whistle caused no stir in the old curmudgeon.

"Form a circle," Rhee shouted. The six players moved as slow as snails. He got irritated. "Take the bricks out of your back pockets, and get in a circle." Rhee took a deep breath and then rolled five balls to the six players. "There are five balls between six players. One player gets in the middle. Pass the ball to the guy in the middle. Soon as you catch the ball, snap a chest pass to the man immediately across from you. The ball is a hot potato; now let's go."

Rhee blew the whistle. Asa was the first player to brave standing in the middle. The boys took turns passing the ball toward Asa, who caught it and had plenty of time to pass it out. None of the boys really knew how to snap a chest pass. They pushed the basketball like it was more of a medicine ball they were barely able to lift.

"Faster," Rhee shouted. The passing barely increased in speed. Asa handled it with ease. "Faster," Rhee shouted again.

A couple of the players increased their speed of getting the ball out of their hands, but Rhee knew it was only because they were irritated, just like he was.

"Faster, faster!" Rhee yelled. Two other players sped up, and now Asa barely got the basketball out of his hands when another ball bounced off his chest. Rhee blew his whistle again. "OK, switch. Someone else in the middle."

Asa joined the circle as Blaze meandered to the middle. Rhee shook his head. Seconds after he blew his whistle, Blaze was smashed in the face with two balls leaving behind red imprints on his cheek. The chubby kid turned his back to protect himself as three other balls smashed into his back. Rhee felt a little satisfaction as several balls scattered. The players had to break the circle to pick them up. Rhee stopped one with his foot. Asa ran over to fetch it. He kicked the ball into Asa's hands. The kid barely caught the ball before it smashed his nose, turning it a beet red. Rhee said nothing as he started to turn away.

"Coach?" Asa asked.

Rhee took his time acknowledging him. The boy had new goggles. He had taken Rhee's advice and purchased a prescription pair. Why not? The boy's parents had deep pockets. He gave Asa a cold look. "You have something to say, or are you waiting for Christmas?"

Asa pushed at his goggles and cleared his throat. "I read you were the first high school player to have a quadruple double in the state tournament."

Rhee raised an eyebrow. "That's wrong. Get your facts straight and your mind right."

Asa's face flushed with embarrassment. "Sorry." He dipped his head in shame and slowly turned away.

"You ever heard of Raymond Lewis?"

Asa turned back but timidly kept his eyes on the floor. "No, why?"

"You should study the history of the players who made the game what it is today."

Asa slowly raised his eyes. "My dad tells me the same thing."

Rhee was taken aback. "You should listen to your dad then. He's a smart man."

"I listen to him. I just never heard of Raymond Lewis."

"Raymond Lewis is the greatest player to ever play the game when he was in high school, and he had a quadruple double. So I wasn't the first."

Asa dropped his eyes, ashamed he didn't know this, and then raised them. "Where is he now?" Asa asked.

"Dead. He died in his early thirties. You wanna ask me something else?" Rhee stared at the kid, wondering if he was being brave or a smartass.

Asa shook his head. "No." The other players avoided eye contact, hoping this made them invisible.

"Let me ask you something. Who was Spencer Haywood?" Rhee asked. He waited for the kid to look dumbfounded, but instead his eyes widened with excitement.

"Leading scorer of the 1986 gold medal Olympic team," Asa said with a small smile.

Rhee was shocked, if not downright floored. "Kid Goggles" had one-upped him. He made a quick comeback. "Why was he so important to basketball?"

"His anti-trust lawsuit went all the way to the Supreme Court and was settled in his favor. It's why high school players used to be able to go straight into the NBA if they were good enough."

Rhee felt dizzy, like Kid Goggles had just pumped blood into his head. "Whoa, how in the world?" He looked at the kid as if he held a smoking gun in his hand. "How did you know that?"

"Like I said, my dad tells me all the time to study the game. He asks me questions too."

"Well, you didn't know who Raymond Lewis was, and my quadruple double was the semi-finals," Rhee said, daring him to make a smart remark. Asa just smiled. "What?" Rhee asked. He was mad as hell. The kid had won.

"Are you coaching us because you got in some sort of trouble and you're having to do community service?"

Rhee picked up the last ball and gave a quick glance toward the other players who stood around. They braced themselves, expecting him to lob the ball at one of them. He held onto it instead. "Look, Kid Goggles, I'm here because I need this job, OK?"

Asa lowered his eyes to the floor and bounced one of the basketballs. "Yeah, sure, no problem."

He ran back to the circle, which was now misshapen. All six players struggled to get back into it. No one walked into the middle. Rhee gave up on the drill. He took the whistle off his neck and blew it.

"Five suicide sprints, well, at least we will call them sprints, beginning right now."

"Oh, Coach. Do we have to run?" Weston asked.

Rhee ignored the question and glanced at the wall clock. He waited a few moments before blowing the whistle, a shrill, piercing blow. To his surprise, the boys broke away from Weston and obediently lurched forward and began striding into a sprint.

He shot Weston a look. "We're waiting on you. Waiting for Christmas?" He looked at the Rude Bentley Boy until he grew tired of it. "Get going, kid. You're burning daylight."

Weston shot a resentful look at Rhee, who ignored it. Rhee just sucked on his teeth. The kids were right. If he had to stay out here, he was going to torture them to the bone.

The double doors of the gymnasium swung open and exposed the bright California sun. Principal De Loach stepped into the gymnasium, pulling a hand trolley stacked with two large boxes behind him.

"What now?" Rhee asked himself.

Principal De Loach looked up into the bleachers and waved at Coach Holt. "Hey, Coach."

Coach Holt lay on his back with his fingers intertwined like a corpse in a coffin.

Rhee placed the whistle in his mouth and blew, extra-long and loud. "Take some laps around the gym. Inside the gym."

The six teammates clutched their sides in agony as they hemmed and moaned. Little by little and one by one, they began to jog. Their line staggered, and none of them kept close to one another. When the boys jogged behind Principal De Loach, Doug and Gerry gave him their middle fingers.

"Doug and Gerry, what does that mean, exactly?" Rhee asked, loudly.

Principal De Loach turned and looked at the boys, missing their middle fingers in the air by an eyelash. The two boys looked at Rhee.

"Thanks a lot, Coach," Doug said.

"Yeah, Coach. Thanks for looking out," Gerry added.

"No problem. Just keep running."

Principal De Loach wheeled the two boxes up to Rhee. "I apologize for disrupting practice, but I thought you and the boys would like to see the new uniforms."

The boys slowed the lackluster saunter that they believed was a jog and came toward the boxes. Asa was the only one who continued to dutifully run. Left to his own, Asa picked up his pace. "Hey, what are you all doing?" Rhee asked. He pointed at Asa. "Y'all better not let Kid Goggles lap you."

Rhee's warning worked. No one wanted to be passed by their teammate with the new title of Kid Goggles. To his surprise, Kid

Goggles ran down every single player. Kid Goggles was not only smart, but he was also fast, exceptionally fast.

Principal De Loach pulled the boxes off the hand trolley and sliced open the tops with a small box cutter. "Wait till you feast your eyes on these," Principal De Loach said. "Especially this one."

Rhee's eyes widened. Principal De Loach handed him a brand new uniform top. It had the number thirty-two in the middle. It was Rhee's number in high school. "Unbelievable," Rhee muttered.

Principal De Loach kept handing parts of the uniform to Rhee. The deep maroon warm-up tops and pants with breakaway Velcro. Emblazoned across the tops in bold, golden letters was "The Eagles." Rhee examined the uniforms. They were hands down as nice as any uniforms he'd seen, especially for middle school or high school for that matter. Damn, they were as nice as some NBA uniforms. A twinge of jealousy poked at him. He was a first team All-American, touted to be one of the best high school player in the last decade, and he'd never worn a uniform this nice.

Principal De Loach unpacked more of the plastic to expose the crisp new uniforms inside. Rhee noticed a maroon, zip-up jacket with an eagle embroidered on the left breast. The principal pulled it on. "I ordered these special, for a few members of our staff."

Rhee blew his whistle and ushered his players to join in Principal De Loach's fashion frenzy. "Bring it in." He was surprised how fast the boys ran over to see the bounty. It might have been their top speed. The new uniforms rejuvenated the boys, who already began to quarrel over the numbers sewn on each jersey. Two of the boys reached for the number thirty-two, but Rhee turned the uniform away from them. Not one of these boys deserved to wear his old high school number.

He swept up every clothing item with the number thirty-two before any of the players laid a hand on them. He planned to steal them or hide them. One thing was certain, though: no one would see number thirty-two again. He jogged the uniform over to the bleachers and sort of tucked it under. Everyone was so excited no one noticed. Coach Holt sat up like a vulture and stared down at him. Rhee waved at him. Coach Holt continued to stare at the commotion.

Rhee turned back to Principal De Loach, who caressed the sleeves of his new jacket. "Got to admit, these are pretty smart." He gave Rhee a Christmas morning smile.

The principal proudly touched a uniform. Rhee took a quick appraisal of the principal's body without an ounce of muscle and knew he'd never been touted or coveted for his athletic achievement. He'd never made any team and had never seen his name in the newspaper, scoring a touchdown, making a basket, or hitting a home run. Yet he looked the part. Rhee noticed the uniforms sparked a fantasy in De Loach's eyes.

Rhee pointed toward the locker room. "There're a couple of full-length mirrors in the locker room. Go cape up in your new digs." The boys raced toward the locker room. They pushed and shoved one another as they each disappeared inside.

Rhee stood alone with Principal De Loach, who had a strange exuberance in his demeanor. "Why don't you go check it out? Those are cool jackets," Rhee said. He tilted his head toward the locker room, and the principal bounced on his toes and darted in the direction of the boys' locker room.

"I'll just take a quick peek."

"That'll be it for today," Rhee said to no one.

The uniforms made everyone forget about practice. Rhee expected little else. When everyone was gone, he turned and stared at the basketballs scattered all over the gymnasium. He grabbed the ball rack and set out to collect them. Once he picked up the last one, he navigated the ball rack toward the closet. He made it as far as the three-point line and stopped. He looked at the rim and then looked at his ankle.

He spun the ball rack around in the same position, like the NBA three-point contest. With his eyes locked on the rim, he caressed the grooves of the black lines and the little bumps on the first ball. He then pulled it from the rack and shot. Right when the ball went through the rim and the net jumped, he shot the next ball, then the next, then the next, and then the next. Six straight balls went through the rim. He shot the seventh ball, and it rattled around the rim and came out.

The error seemed to run through his veins as cold as ice water.

His body shivered. His eyes stayed on the rim as he pulled the ball rack close and got ready to shoot the remaining five basketballs. But he stopped. His face flushed. His hand trembled. He tried to remember the last shot he ever took in a game. The memory was fading. It was the last game he'd ever played and that too was a bit of a blur. The last shot, the last game, they were behind him, and he could see nothing coming up on his horizon. Those last five seconds stood as a statue of his last five seconds of fame.

He couldn't believe this was his life now. He started to gather the errant balls again. When he finished, he headed toward the uniform he'd stuffed away.

Once he crammed the brand new uniform in his backpack, he closed the gymnasium doors and walked toward his mother's car, backpack slung over his shoulder. He glanced up as a Bentley rolled up to the curb, the attractive woman behind the steering wheel. She smiled at him, and he returned the gesture with a slight wave. The silent exchange evaporated when Weston jogged up to the car, hair wet, and his backpack on his shoulder.

He snapped open the door. "Where the hell were you today? I fucking called you twice."

Rhee saw the attractive woman slump and lose the luster she had displayed seconds before. Her face flushed in embarrassment.

"Hey," Rhee yelled, but it was too late. Weston was in the car, and the car was sealed, sound tight. Rhee watched the boy as the car rolled away.

He tried to picture his own mother's expression if he were to speak to her in that way, but he drew a blank. A clear image of Mr. Joyce charging at him with a knife came to him. He shuddered when the knife plunged into his chest.

Weston continued to verbally assault the woman -- his mother, Rhee assumed, as they drove away. Rhee narrowed his eyes. The ill-mannered Weston chewed words like a deer chewing grass in a hunter's crosshairs. Only the hunter was Rhee Joyce, and Rhee couldn't wait for a clean kill.

Chapter 16

Runway To The Promised Land

The six Eagles players sat on the bench in front of the lockers, donned in their nice, new uniforms. Rhee paced back and forth in front of them. His ankle had healed faster than expected; he didn't need the cane. He wore a maroon pullover polo shirt that sported an eagle in flight and a pair of wrinkled slacks. His pathetic team waited to hear something inspirational, but he had nothing.

He never listened to any of the pregame speeches. His skills were so unique he'd never needed to listen to the encouragement. Now he wished he had so he could just regurgitate it. The only inspirational thing that played over and over in his head was how awesome the uniforms looked. Other than that, the boys he paced in front of had no outside chance of beating a team of elderly nuns.

Rhee stopped. His players looked up. He rubbed his hands together. "I know we haven't had much time to learn any offenses or defenses, and I know the Cougars are defending champions. Just remember, it's only a practice game." He looked down at his players. They stared up at him, some with mouths open like baby birds waiting for more nourishment. "Right. Well, whatever you have inside you, leave it all on the court," Rhee added. There was no truth the way his words came out.

He turned and walked away. The six Eagles players slowly stood and moseyed behind their coach. Doug leaned toward Gerry. "That was supposed to be a pep talk?" Gerry rolled his eyes in agreement. The six Eagles trotted out of the locker room like a bin of beef rolling toward the lion cage.

Rhee entered the gymnasium and was amazed. The entire visitors' bleachers were filled. The Marshall Cougars from Oakland had cheerleaders rattling their pompoms, doing splits and somersaults while song girls clapped out a beat to sing to. A coaching staff of five paced along the sidelines, and every fan carried a gold and red pennant. They had enormous painted signs with a large cougar carrying an eagle in its mouth.

The Eagles' home bleachers were scarcely filled. There were a couple of faculty members Rhee had seen but not met. There was a dark-haired man with silver temples, who had on creased slacks, a button-down white shirt, and a jacket with patched elbows. The man had a remarkable resemblance to Asa "Kid Goggles" Lieberman. When Kid Goggles gave his father a small wave, Rhee knew it was more than a resemblance.

Coach Holt sat by himself in the far corner. Rhee waved. Coach Holt gave a small salute that felt a bit like a farewell. Rhee's eyes fell on Weston's mother. She looked like a woman right off the cover of Vogue. She smiled at him; he smiled back.

He made his way over to his home coaching seat. He looked across the gymnasium. L.A. sat on the Cougars' side with a couple of African-American kids. Ninety percent of the Cougars fans were African-American, including the cheerleaders, song girls, and coaching staff.

Rhee stared in amazement. When he played basketball, his skill set and talent transcended race. He was better than most of the people he played against -- black, white, or green. The outcome of the game was all that mattered. Now he looked across the court at all the different African-American faces. His own skin color strangely loitered in the back of his mind.

His mouth dropped open when he saw Prov, Cub, Lam, Rama, and Felix, all of whom were part of the Cougars' fifteen-man team. The team was impressive. They were leapers, smooth and skilled. Several players dunked.

Rhee sat, shriveling into himself by the second. None of his players came close to touching the rim. He heard the Cougars fans laughing. They howled with amusement.

The six Eagles players had collectively stopped their pregame warm-up drills. All of them stood and watched the Cougars go about their pregame warm-ups. They stood in awe like they were watching fireworks.

Rhee stood up and waved at his team. "Let's go guys. Our basket is over here."

The laughter continued. A ripple of anger coursed through Rhee's veins. No one ever laughed at him when he played. They stomped, whistled, and cheered but never laughed. No matter how many points his team slaughtered their opponents by, he never laughed at any players, no matter how bad they were. He looked at the Cougars fans angrily. His anger-filled gaze landed on L.A., who was not laughing. His friends roared with laughter and high-fived, but L.A. watched Rhee watching him. He stared at L.A. for a moment until the Cougars' head coach approached.

The Cougars' head coach was a balding, African-American man with a serious expression, who wore a brown suit that bulged at the seams from his muscular frame. He fixed his yellow tie and then extended his hand toward Rhee. "Hey, Coach. I'm Coach Leonard." He gripped Rhee's hand with the strength of a steel vice. Rhee felt his knuckles crack.

"Rhee Joyce," Rhee said. He quickly took back his hand. Coach Leonard nodded, and a look of recognition leaped into his eyes.

"You're Rhee Joyce from Davis?"

"Yes, sir," Rhee replied.

"I'll be damned," Coach Leonard said. Rhee's unease increased during Coach Leonard's slow and careful examination of him. He looked at Rhee with a mixture of reverie and pity. "I read about your injury. I didn't know you had gotten into coaching."

Rhee turned and looked at the six Eagles players. A person had to have a real team to be a real coach. Technically, he had not gotten into coaching. He had only gotten into a hot mess.

The Cougars' coach shook his head. "You guys are still having trouble getting ballplayers, huh?"

"Yeah, seems like," Rhee said.

The already deafening sound levels of the Cougars' band belting out the school fight song, shrieks and yells from cheerleaders, and fans increased so loudly, Rhee and the coach had to raise their voices.

"It's a crying shame, man. This is the nicest gymnasium in the whole county." Coach Leonard looked around with profound appreciation of the facility and then turned his attention back to Rhee. "I saw you play in TOC year before last. You were a helluva player. One of the best I've ever seen."

As time went by, Rhee was less and less moved by praise about his past. He attempted a polite nod. It came across more like a twitch.

"You guys always have such a big turnout for practice games?" Rhee asked.

Coach Leonard flinched as if Rhee had said something bad about the man's mother. "Practice game?"

Rhee looked down at the program in his hand and saw in bold letters: "THE EAGLES VS. THE COUGARS: A PRACTICE GAME." Rhee tapped the program. "It says 'Practice Game' right here in the program."

Coach Leonard folded his arms, a noticeable display of agitation. He stepped up to Rhee and pointed toward the six Eagles players. "Coach, you see your players over there?"

Rhee refused to look at his players. "Yes."

Coach Leonard looked at the Eagles players and then looked back at Rhee. "All your players come from large homes, filled with the best computers, video games, bicycles, motor bikes, tutors, and all the rest of the things money can buy." He looked straight into Rhee's eyes. "You know why there're only six players on your team?"

Rhee shrugged his shoulders. "No one around here is that interested in playing basketball?" Rhee asked, not expecting an answer.

Coach Leonard shook his head vehemently. "No. No, Rhee. It's because they've got all of the choices open to them. This is just a building to them, a place to kill some time, get some exercise," Coach Leonard said. He turned and pointed toward his Cougars players. "See my players?"

Rhee nodded.

"This isn't a gym to my players. It's barely even a building," Coach Leonard said.

Rhee struggled to hear. The noise increased even louder as the Cougars cheerleaders rattled off some cheers.

Coach Leonard pointed around the gymnasium. "You know what this is -- those rims, that score board, this sound system, the bleachers...?" He raised his voice to stay above the noise in the background. "This is an airport runway."

Rhee moved closer to him. He wasn't sure he'd heard Coach Leonard correctly. "A what?" Rhee asked.

"A runway. Departures only. There's an airplane that flies in here every few years. That airplane is going to take only one or two of my players out of their underprivileged, meager existence to the Promised Land."

"Promised Land? What Promised Land?" Rhee asked.

"The Promised Land where there is a slim-to-none chance to get a scholarship to go to college, to get an education and -- God willing -- carve out a better life," Coach Leonard said, "and maybe have two or three choices, compared to the pile your guys are sitting on."

Rhee was struck by the coach's words. He was, of course, right. Most of the great players Rhee had competed against were also from disadvantaged backgrounds. The best players always talked about basketball being their one-way ticket out of their impoverished life.

Coach Leonard gave Rhee a pat on the shoulder. "None of our games are practice games. OK?" He flashed a fractured smile Rhee believed was not friendly or warm. "Good luck."

"Yeah, you too," Rhee said, knowing full well the Cougars needed no luck.

He felt ill as he turned and trudged back to his seat. The Cougars' coach implied his players were hungrier and more motivated because they were poor. Rhee thought about how hard he'd practiced and played even though his parents had a decent home. He thought about players like Austin Rivers, Klay Thompson, Chris Webber, Stephen Curry, and Grant Hill, who all had mad skills like Rhee's but also didn't come from a meager existence. But for some reason, the universe tended to glorify black athletes from the ghetto. Rhee knew many white basketball players whose parents were poor as dirt, yet that was more the exception than the rule, so it was never newsworthy. The issue of color and money no longer loitered in the back of his mind. It moved to the forefront of his mind and beat his brain like a sledgehammer. He thought about his own parents.

They had packed his bags and put him on that same airplane. He had made it on board. Only his plane had to make an emergency landing. He had to get off the plane because his broken bones were like sticks that set it on fire. He stood and watched his plane burn to the ground. He wasn't allowed to catch the next one, nor the one after that, nor the one after that. He was going to spend the rest of his life watching those airplanes take off and land with no hope of ever earning a ticket or catching a ride again.

Tears welled in his eyes. He burned with anger. He wanted to take on the Cougars' team by himself. He wanted the Cougars' coach to take back his words. Hunger and desire had little to do with privilege. Rhee wanted to win today. He wanted to win badly. He looked at his players and felt the cold, sobering realization that a win was not going to happen today or any other day.

Chapter 17

Not So Funny

All five African-American players that Rhee had seen his first day in the Eagles' gymnasium were Cougars starters. Felix and Prov turned and gave Rhee polite waves. He tilted his head up and gave Felix and Prov a small grin. He liked Felix Duncan and Kenny Providence. He even liked their names. Rama turned to Rhee and gave him a thumbs down with an evil smirk. Rhee pretended he did not see it. He stood and clapped his hands, hard. "Let's go Eagles."

None of the Eagles players looked over. He understood they were probably too petrified to look at him. He had no idea why he was cheering his players on. There was no cheering a hopeless situation. They were lambs to be slaughtered. There was no time to teach them how to play against insurmountable odds.

The referee blew the whistle at half court. "Everybody ready?"

The Cougars players lined up with precision, and Rama stepped into the circle.

Rhee knew they had a set play for the jump center tip-off. Rhee cupped his hands and shouted, "Gerry, you jump."

Gerry stepped into the half-court circle. The referee tossed up the ball. Rama out-jumped Gerry with ease, his fingers deftly tipped the ball to Cub, who drove straight down the center of the court and scored.

Rhee looked down at Blaze, who buried his face in his hands. "Oh, dear Lord," Blaze said.

The Cougars fans stood and filled the gym with loud cheers and applause. They jumped up and down and waved their pennants.

The Cougars cheerleaders rifled off some backhand springs and cartwheels. Rhee clapped his hands harder. "It's all right. Let's go, Eagles."

"Yeah, let's go," Blaze added.

Rhee gave Blaze an unquestionable expression of hopelessness. "Get ready to go in," Rhee said. Blaze looked like he'd just been told his arm had to be cut off.

Asa grabbed the ball and stepped behind the line. He tried to throw the ball to Terrance, but Rama stole it and passed to Prov, who leapt in the air for an uncontested layup. Prov turned and shot Rhee a look. "Sorry, Coach. This is too easy," Prov said. He looked apologetic.

The route to a blowout was on. The Cougars scored at will. They even scored when they didn't try. Their fans slapped their knees and howled with laughter. Rhee lowered his head to hide the shame for his team. The Eagles were terrible, and they were a joke, but he still believed no one should be laughed at like they were fools. It felt like the Cougars were playing a pickup game and the Eagles were just watching. He kept his eyes on the floor as the seconds seemed like hours. The gymnasium emanated with riotous laughter, and then it started to slowly fade. He thought something bad had happened.

Rhee looked up and witnessed the oddest event he'd ever seen. The Cougars fans, coaches, cheerleaders, and players stopped laughing. What they were witnessing stopped being funny. The Eagles were so outmatched and outplayed it became unsettling, even to the opposition. Even the Cougars players backed off and let their feet off the gas pedal. They slowed down the pace. The Eagles were still not able to stop their opponents.

Rhee clapped his hands. He was unnerved. "That's OK." His claps were now loud enough for all of his players to hear. The gymnasium was so quiet, when Blaze coughed, it echoed through the building. It was the echo of the mausoleum where the Eagles would be laid to rest.

Rhee's face went ashen. He felt sick. His players went from being the biggest joke to the biggest tragedy. The experience ripped away Rhee's will to continue. He wanted out. He wanted to get out of the building and run, never to return. Yet, even at the young age of eighteen, he believed it would be inhumane to leave his team on their own. Rhee watched what seemed like an arduous autopsy on his team, and the cause of death was humiliation.

It took an eternity for the horn to sound and put an end to the horror. An exasperated Rhee looked up at the scoreboard: Visitors 45, Eagles 9.

He threw up his hands. "Thank you, God, it's over!" Rhee shouted.

Blaze tugged on his shirtsleeve. "Coach, it's only half time."

Rhee looked down at Blaze and then back up at the scoreboard. It had to be the longest first half in history.

"That was bad, really bad," Rhee said and then headed toward the locker room, not to encourage his team but to hide.

The somber atmosphere in the locker room rivaled a funeral. None of the Eagles said anything or made eye contact. With long faces, they avoided each other while they drank water and went to the bathroom. The only chance the second half would be different than the first half was if five NBA players miraculously replaced them.

Rhee looked up at the wall clock. It sickened him that it was almost time to go back out there. He swore time slowed down in the gymnasium but sped up in the locker room. The most merciful thing to do would be to walk out there and wave a white flag: We surrender. We surrender.

When it was time, he followed his downtrodden team back into the gymnasium. The Cougars' head coach cut off his path.

Coach Leonard spoke under the noise of the Cougars band. "Don't worry about this half," Coach Leonard said, barely audible.

Rhee wasn't able to hear. He leaned forward. "What'd you say?"

"How do you want to work this?" Coach Leonard asked, with a raised tone.

Rhee pulled back and measured the Cougars' coach. He asked

Rhee a question he didn't know how to answer, but he tried.

"Keep it real. It's good my team has a reality check of how much work they need." He saw the surprised look on Coach Leonard's face. They both understood Rhee's team needed more than work.

"I'll play the third team this half," Coach Leonard said. "That will be real enough." He marched off, a pinched look of annoyance on his hard face.

The gymnasium quieted considerably. Empty seats were peppered throughout, and more fans were still filing out. The Cougars band played, but the fans who remained, the cheerleaders, and the coaches sat quietly while the Cougars players finished their polished warm-up drills.

Rhee had no idea how to handle this situation. He'd never lost a game by more than five points. In his entire four years of high school basketball, he'd lost only five games, total. Three losses came in his freshman year. His junior and senior years, he lost only two league games.

The horn sounded, and the six Eagles meandered to the bench. They barely took any warm-up shots. Rhee ushered his team into a huddle. They stood around Rhee, once again, the hungry baby birds waiting to be fed encouraging words. Rhee's ability to deliver a pep talk was just leaving the solar system.

"Same starters. Let's get through this with as much pride as we can. No matter what happens, keep your heads up." Rhee ignored all the bewildered expressions from his players and led a haphazard cheer. "Go Eagles." His players all turned and ambled back into the butchery.

When the final horn blew, Rhee blinked back tears as he looked up at the scoreboard to make sure his eyes had not deceived him. It read: Visitors 83, Eagles 22. The Eagles players stood like orphans on the court. The Cougars players lined up and walked toward the Eagles, who all straggled off the court.

Weston breezed past Rhee. "Thank God, it's over."

Rhee grabbed Weston by the shoulders and turned him toward the Cougars players. "God doesn't like ugly. If you can't learn to play, at least learn to be a good sport. Go shake hands."

They all turned back and reluctantly complied. Rhee was mesmerized by how erect, alert, humble, and well mannered the Cougars acted. The Eagles were slouched. They carried themselves like old men coming off a double shift in the coalmines. Rhee trailed behind them, equally as beaten but working at a poker face.

He shook hands with Felix. "Good game, Coach," Felix said. He gave Rhee a sheepish look.

"You played good, man. You are a leader." Rhee gave him a nod and then shook hands with Prov, Cub, Lam, and Rama, who was the only Cougar player that carried an evil smirk. Rhee shook with the rest of the team and coaches. When all the pleasantries were exchanged, he turned to head into the locker room. He jogged pass his players. He needed a moment alone to gather himself before his team arrived.

Rhee paced back and forth in front of them. His hands buried in his pockets. He wore down the tiles beneath his shoes. His mind raced trying to organize his thoughts.

"That was... that... was... amazing," Rhee said.

The six Eagles players sat in the locker room with quiet disgrace. They all hunched over with their eyes pointed at the floor. Their once pristine uniforms now dripping with sweat. "Tell us about it," Doug said, to the floor.

As Rhee's pacing sped up, the more perplexed he became. "It was 83-22. Isn't that some kind of record?"

None of the Eagles players remotely acted like Rhee's words affected them. He stopped pacing and looked at the reddened, flushed, faces of his team. They were rich, spoiled kids, but they'd been humiliated. He saw six kids who probably had been beaten down for the first time in their lives. Maybe they didn't need any more.

"OK, you guys. Get showered. I'm going to go find a church," Rhee said. He turned to leave.

The Eagles looked at one another, until Terrence spoke. "Why are you going to find a church?"

Rhee stopped and turned back to them. He took a couple steps in their direction. "During the game, I said some things to God that I didn't exactly mean. I'll see you guys at practice." He turned to walk away but stopped. "No, actually, bad idea. No practice tomorrow. Take tomorrow off."

The six Eagles glanced at one another. Gerry looked at Doug, who looked at Asa, who looked at Terrance, who looked at Blaze. Each player passed the responsibility to respond down the line. Weston stood at the end of the line.

He inched forward, reticent. "Can we at least come in and shoot around?"

Rhee looked at him and then looked at the rest of the players. Why the team wanted to show their faces again was lost on him.

"Yeah, sure. Practice is totally voluntary tomorrow. Have a good weekend." He nearly made it out of the locker room, when he came back. "Hey, Kid Goggles, I just want to get something straight."

The players stopped changing. "Yeah, Coach?" Asa said.

Rhee looked at all of them. "After this practice game, we play everybody twice during the regular season, right?"

"Yeah, that's right. Except the Cougars we only play one more time 'cause we just played them in a practice game," Asa said. "We play them again the last game of the season."

Great. The Eagles were going to begin with a slaughter by the Cougars and end it the same way. Rhee looked straight up and pressed his hands together. "Thank you, Lord, dear God, for the small salvations. But please beam me to another planet." Rhee looked back at Asa. "That's sixteen games, counting this one, right?"

"Yeah," Asa answered.

The entire team looked at Rhee with a mixture of confusion and unmistakable disapproval. He didn't care.

"OK, I was just checking," Rhee said. He spun around and quickly headed off.

Chapter 18

A New Sheriff In Town

Rhee sat by himself on the bleachers. He still suffered from the hangover of the worst defeat he'd ever had. It surprised him that being the coach of a bad team would be as miserable as actually being on a bad team.

The school bell rang, and Rhee sat up. He knew none of the players had the nerve to show their faces after the beatdown by the Cougars. He was wrong.

One by one, the six players strolled out of the locker room and wandered onto the court, soldiers trampling across the field of their demise. They wore their new practice uniforms, resplendent in maroon and gold: the only bright thing about them.

Rhee's stomach went tight and burned when he fixed his gaze on Weston. He stood and blew his whistle. "OK, form a circle over at half court for stretching," Rhee trumpeted.

The players looked at one another, confused. They awkwardly trotted to half court. Weston protested first. "I thought you said this was a voluntary practice."

Rhee gave Weston an icy stare and watched him look at his teammates to see who else had the gonads to speak up. None of them did. "All practices are voluntary when the coach doesn't show. But I'm right here. Bad luck, right?"

Rhee kept his eyes on all the players to see who would challenge his authority. He put his whistle in his mouth and gave it a quick blow. "Form a circle and start stretching." The players slowly formed a circle and began to stretch. They straightened their arms. They touched their toes and bent their legs. While they halfheartedly went through the motions, Rhee strolled up behind Weston and tapped him on the shoulder. "You've got some work to do before you can practice."

The Rude Bentley Boy gave a confused look. "Excuse me?"

"Have you heard of a mop-up?" Rhee asked. Weston stepped outside the circle of boys.

"What?" Weston asked. His tone was confrontational, which Rhee had anticipated.

"That's right. You and that smart mouth of yours have some work to do." Rhee repeated the question to everyone. "Have any of you heard of the mop-up?" Rhee asked. This time his voice found its bass. All the boys shook their heads. Weston looked away. "Well, Weston here will introduce us to it."

"What?" Weston asked. "Why me?"

Rhee marched towards Weston. He glared at the eighth-grade boy. "Take off your shirt, hold it with both hands, and push it like a wide broom across the floor," Rhee said, nonplussed.

"Are you kidding?"

"Do I look like I'm kidding?"

Rhee pointed his index finger like it was shooting bullets. "Start at one baseline and mop to the free-throw line and back, then to half court and back, then to the far free-throw line and back, and finally all the way to the other baseline and back."

Weston's eyes darted around like a bird on a wire. Rhee smelled fear and uncertainty. He was looking for any kind of a rescue. None was coming, which was exactly how Rhee had planned it.

"You will complete five mop-ups before you touch a basketball again." The other five players swallowed any temptation to laugh or chuckle.

"This is a joke, right?" Weston asked.

The other players hid their faces and pretended to stretch. Rhee raised his chin at Asa.

"Kid Goggles, do I look like I'm joking?"

"No, Coach," Asa answered with just a little less fear than Rhee wanted.

Rhee pointed toward Doug, who bent over and stretched toward the floor. "Muscle Head, do I look like I'm trying to be funny in any way?"

Doug kept his head down. He hid the smirk on his lips. He acted like he was warming up for a gold medal game.

"You look as serious as a heart attack to me."

Rhee nodded and then turned back to Weston. "You just heard it from two eye witnesses who said I'm not joking. So get going." Rhee looked at the other teammates. "You want to be on my team; you do things my way," Rhee said. "That goes for all of you pinheads."

Weston gave Rhee a defiant expression and then turned towards the baseline. He flung his reversible practice shirt toward the baseline.

"How long will this take?" Weston asked.

Rhee looked Weston up and down. He saw the fear behind the young kid's bravado. "It depends on you and how fast you mop."

He turned back to the other players. He had their attention. The chastising of Weston served as a double-edged sword. He wanted to bring the ill-mannered kid down several notches and get more respect from the other players. It worked.

He blew his whistle, loudly. "Bring it in, now." His tone was all business and no smile. "OK, let's talk offense. You guys are going to learn basketball -- even if you can't play basketball -- or you all will be mopping and making this floor clean. And I mean shiny clean." Rhee pointed at the big clock near the scoreboard. "Two more hours, and you're going to work every single minute." The players, in unison, stole quick glances at the clock.

A half an hour later, Weston was flat on his back. His chest heaved in and out while he looked straight up. His rib cage expanded in and out like he was nearly hyperventilating. His muscles quivered. His soiled practice shirt was on his chest, and he sucked in as much air as possible. "I'm gonna die," Weston said. "We were right. Dude is crazy. He is trying to kill us."

Rhee stuffed the whistle in his mouth. The shrill noise it trumpeted brought the other players to a stop. He stood at one end of the court and pointed at the free-throw line.

"Everyone grab a ball and come stand single file on the free-throw line."

Sneakers squeaked as five of the boys raced over to the ball rack, grabbed balls, and dribbled over to Rhee.

"Each of you will shoot, and however many you all miss is how many suicide sprints you have to run." The five players looked at each other with panic. "Don't look so scared, guys. All of you can fill it up. You're good shooters, right?"

Rhee watched them all point toward Terrance, insisting he go first. Weston was still on the floor, panting. He looked up as Rhee loomed over him. "Yo, Mr. Mouth, if you need to die, drag yourself to the side so we don't step on your body. If you're not going to die, get over here and shoot."

Weston rolled over and somehow made it to his feet. He stumbled toward the basketball rack, snatched one, and made a crooked line toward the other boys. "Jeez," Weston sighed.

"OK, let's get started," Rhee said.

Doug raised his hand. "Coach, can Terrance shoot for us?"

Rhee gave Doug a quizzical look and shook his head. "Heck no. Get your mind right, Thickness."

Doug threw his head back and raised his hands. "Oh, man."

"Hey, come on guys. If we make them all, we don't run," Asa said. Rhee smiled at Asa's optimism.

"Yeah, and if we miss them all, we run six," Terrance said.

Rhee walked over to the bleachers and sat down. He stretched his arms, knowing this was going to take awhile. He chewed on his whistle for entertainment. Then he straightened up. "Let's go, fellas."

Terrance, Asa, and Doug made their shots. "Yes," Doug yelled and pumped his fist. They jumped up and down and gave each other high fives. Gerry sank his free throw and then Blaze stepped to the line. His teammates encouraged him by being completely silent. Weston paid no attention. He held onto the ball and slumped over. The guys held their breath as Blaze's shot rolled around the rim. It finally dropped in.

"Yes!" Blaze jumped higher than Rhee had ever seen.

All five players started cheering on Weston, who finally stood straight up. His breathing had slowed, but his face was beet red. "Don't miss, Bentley Boy," Rhee said under his breath.

"Come on, Wes... you can do it," Asa said.

"Yeah, Wes... make it," Gerry said.

"Dude, you make this shot, I will be your personal bodyguard the rest of the year. I'll jump on a grenade for you. Just make the shot, please," Doug said. Weston stopped. He and all his teammates looked at Doug, who looked back at them. Doug raised his hands. "Yeah, I said it. I'll pound anyone he wants, even you guys."

Rhee stood up and headed toward the boys. As he approached, he wanted to clap his hands, blow his whistle, stomp his foot, anything to guarantee Weston missed the shot. Rhee decided he didn't need to do anything. Weston was going to miss. Rhee almost laughed when he saw Blaze close his eyes and cross his fingers.

Weston threw up the shot as if the ball slipped out of his hands. Time seemed to slow down as the basketball banked against the backboard and went in. "Oh, my God," Weston said. He even surprised himself.

Everyone jumped up and down and rushed to pat Weston on the back. "Can we go now, Coach?" Doug asked.

At first Rhee was too stunned to answer. "Yeah," Rhee said. All the boys celebrated. "All except Weston, he's got some more running to do." All the boys stopped.

There was a deafening silence inside the gymnasium. Rhee was in charge, and now he was going to hand Weston huge doses of humility. The other five players kept still.

Chapter 19

Payback

"What? I made my shot. Why do I have to run and no one else does?" Weston asked. He opened his mouth and looked at his teammates. They all lowered their eyes and turned away from him. He put one hand on a hip and wedged the basketball he was holding into his side. "I don't have to run. I made my shot, and I already did the mop-ups."

Weston's teammates meandered around. Rhee wanted to tell them to leave, but he also wanted them to witness the next few minutes. Rhee clenched his jaw and barely opened his mouth. "You run, or you're off the team."

Weston slammed the ball to the ground. It bounced high off the floor and headed toward the locker room. "Fine, I'm outta here. We all quit." Weston marched past his teammates. None of the boys moved a muscle. Weston stopped and turned around. "Come on, guys. Let's blow this joint. This dude has lost his mind." He looked at each one of his teammates. None of them offered any solace.

Rhee stood stalwart, as Weston looked to them to support his mutiny. "Go on, fellas. Make my life a lot easier," Rhee said. The five players looked at each other. No one took a step to join Weston.

"Terrance, you were right. He only came here to make us pay for his stupid injury," Weston said as he gave Terrance a friendly push. Terrence stood stone still.

Rhee used his eyes to give Terrance permission to stay out of it. Terrance looked down and then back up to Weston. "Dude, Coach kicked you off, not us."

Weston tried to usher Doug into his battle. "Doug, everyone heard you say you'd pound anyone I wanted you to pound."

Doug looked at Rhee, who showed no fear as he stared at Doug. Their eyes stayed on each other. The tension in the gymnasium was thick as soup. "Make your move, Thickness. You want a shot at the title, just holler."

Doug turned his attention back to Weston. "Weston, dude, you're high. I'm a tough eighth-grader. Coach is a tough college guy."

"You said you'd jump on a grenade for me," Weston said, desperation palpable in his voice.

Doug dropped his eyes. He wanted no part of challenging this coach. "I said I'd jump on any grenade for you but not a nuclear bomb."

"You guys aren't going to put up with this shit for long," Weston shouted and then turned and stalked off, mumbling as he went into the locker room.

The other players collectively sighed. "That was awkward," Blaze said.

"Shut up, Blaze," Gerry said.

Rhee took a deep breath. "Anyone who gives me fifty free throws before they leave I'll assume wants to stay on the team." Rhee stared into each player's eyes. They all appeared uncertain. "I don't care if you all walk out, but if you stay, I'm in charge. So it's my way or no way." He waited for someone to say something or move.

"Coach, how are we going to play with only five players?" Blaze asked.

"Not my problem," Rhee said. He walked over to the bleachers and sat down, picked up his backpack, and rifled through it until he found a water bottle. He twisted the top off and drank.

"What are we going to do?" Blaze asked his teammates. No one answered. Asa made the first move toward the ball rack. Doug followed, and then the rest retrieved basketballs. Three boys went to one basket, and two went to the other. They started to shoot free throws and then stopped and stared.

Rhee followed their gaze. Weston marched into the gymnasium. "What the...?" Rhee stood and braced for a physical confrontation. The other players froze.

Weston stopped a safe distance from Rhee, and then, pointing his finger at the floor, he yelled. "I demand to know what the fuck is going on."

Rhee looked at the other players, who seemed as stunned as him, now covering their mouths. Rhee stepped towards Weston, who took a step back. All five players scurried to position themselves in a semicircle behind Rhee. "What's up, man? I thought you were out," Rhee said. His tone was measured and controlled.

Weston looked like he was about to blow a fuse. Rhee shifted his weight in case Weston snapped and charged.

"Tell me why the fuck I'm being singled out," Weston shouted. Rhee let the kid's demand linger between them until it lost some of its power. He slowly turned to the other players who now looked shocked.

"Listen up. This gymnasium is my church, and I am the minister. My word is gospel; my directions are commandments. If you're not a believer, don't come to my church. Anyone swears in my church, from now on, is off the team, until I'm no longer the minister." Rhee's voice filled the entire gymnasium. The other five players nodded quickly, and Rhee returned his glare back to Weston. "You're interrupting our service. You're going to have to go, or I'm going to drag you out of here by your thumbs."

Weston's eyes narrowed in defiance. "You're not a saint. I heard you swear."

Rhee locked eyes with Weston, who now trembled from the confrontation. "You're right, I'm not a saint, but from now on, I'm a Disney character. From now on, PG only in my church. And you don't have to quit 'cause I am booting your butt off of the team."

Weston looked shocked. Tears of confusion filled his eyes. The smart mouth had probably never been reprimanded. No one came to Weston's rescue or defended him. "Why are you doing this?

What did I do?" Weston asked. His voice cracked liked thin glass.

Rhee stepped forward, careful not to physically threaten the kid. "Because you're rude and you don't have manners. You can't get through life without manners. Like me, no one wants to be around your rudeness. So turn around, and step off. You're done here."

"What are you even talking about?" Weston asked. "I was never rude to you."

"I saw the way you talk to your mother. That's not cool," Rhee said. He turned to the other players. "If you're on this team, you all gotta mind and respect your parents."

Weston's expression changed. Something threw the kid off balance. His bravado and sense of entitlement appeared to melt away. His lips shivered. "You're not my dad."

"True. True that. But, unfortunately for you, I'm the coach of this team. Now turn around, and do your talking with your walking." Rhee took two small steps toward him and Weston backed up. "I don't care for your attitude, Mr. Mouth, and I especially don't care for the way you speak to your mother."

"Mother? What the hell are you talking about?"

"I'm talking about the way you talked to your mother yesterday, and every day I've seen you with her." He noticed another change in Weston, who now appeared confused.

"My mother?" Weston asked.

"Yeah, your mother. I saw the way you talked to her the first day I came here and yesterday after practice, and you gave her no respect. So I don't want to coach you or be around you. Now make a beeline for the door before I put my foot up your behind."

Weston spoke clearly and quietly in an effort to keep himself from exploding. "That woman you saw is my stepmother. You don't know nothing about me."

"I don't care if she's your distant cousin's friend. You don't talk to people that way. Does your father know the way you speak to his wife?"

Weston looked over Rhee's shoulder at the other players. It was the first time in minutes that Rhee remembered the other players had not left.

He turned to them. "Practice is over, guys. Rude Boy made me lose my desire to be here." None of the players moved. He held up his right hand and spread his fingers. "OK, then five minutes of fresh air."

"But Coach..." Gerry protested. They were all glued to their places see this out. They all wanted to know how it ended.

"Get gone, fellas," Rhee said. The five players slowly turned away and began to file out of the double doors marked "Exit." Rhee watched them until the flash of sunlight went away, and they were all outside. The gymnasium doors slammed shut. Rhee turned around. Weston came apart at the seams. His hands and knees shook. "And you're still here? What part of get out of my gym don't you understand?"

"You're kicking me off the team because of the way I talked to my stepmother?"

"I'm kicking you off the team 'cause I don't like you or your attitude, and if I was your father, I'd kick your butt."

"My father doesn't care what I do," Weston mumbled.

Rhee reached into his sweat pants and pulled out his cell phone. "OK, go get your cell phone so we can call him and ask."

"No!" Weston pleaded, panic spread all over his face.

"Why not?" Rhee asked.

"Because he gets pissed if I call him at work."

Rhee blew a long exhale from his mouth. "Look kid, truth is I heard y'all talking about me, and a lot of it is dead right, on the hundred. I really don't want to be here," Rhee said. "If I'm going to drag my butt down here every day, I'll need y'all to have some integrity. Translation: a good attitude toward you and me and your teammates. No head cases. I need effort. That means hustling your butts off. And I need to see some manners. All you dudes come from crazy-rich families, but that doesn't mean y'all can't be good people. I'm not looking for anyone to kiss anyone else's butt. Just be cool, and check your attitudes at the door. None of you are Division One scholarship players. But at least you might get stronger and faster and learn how to acquire skills and not to quit." Rhee stopped to check if Weston was listening. The kid barely looked up. "Did you hear any of that?" Rhee asked. Weston nodded. "Then read it back to me."

Weston slowly raised his head. "You want me to have a good attitude. You want me to try, and you want me to be polite."

"Not just when you're here. Try to be cool at home and with other people too."

Weston stared into Rhee's eyes. Rhee measured the eighth-grader's expression. His lips quivered as he struggled to blink back tears. Rhee waited it out. Maybe if the kid pulled it together long enough he might speak and shed some light on things. "Why are you out here, kid? Why don't you just pack it up?" Rhee asked. He felt his hatred of Rude Bentley Boy begin to fade. He had no idea why.

Weston looked away. He hid the few tears that rolled down his cheeks. "I got in trouble."

"What trouble?"

"I got in a lot of trouble after..." Weston stopped and lowered his eyes. The gymnasium was silent. Only the wall clock ticked audibly.

"After what?" Rhee asked.

Weston remained silent, but then his sniffles grew louder, and tears streamed down his cheeks and over his hand. His body trembled. "After my mom died," Weston murmured, "I got in a lot of trouble."

Rhee felt a pang. He wondered if he had made a mistake. He thought he was going to lose his balance. "Say again."

"After my mom died, I started 'acting up.' I was expelled from like three schools. My dad got sick of moving me in and out of different ones. He threatened to put me in a military school."

Rhee listened intently, but the thought of his own mother dying clouded his ability to hang on every word Weston said.

"Please, don't make me call my dad. This is the longest I've been able to stay at any school in three years. He'd lose his mind if you told him I was getting kicked off the team."

For the first time, Rhee felt bad for the rich, spoiled white kid. He wasn't ready to be Weston's number one fan, but little by little, Rhee started to feel differently about him. Rhee looked into the kid's bloodshot eyes.

Weston dropped his head and began to cry. Rhee watched him sob like he'd been storing those tears for years. Rhee looked away, not knowing how to handle this boy's pain. He locked his own tears into a vault so no one would think he was a punk. But he didn't feel Weston was being a punk. The kid was self-entitled and a bit out of control, but he had a lot of pain too. Rhee slowly wrapped his arm around Weston's shoulder. He crumpled against Rhee. The spoiled, rich white kid cried like he'd been stabbed.

The gymnasium door opened, and the five other players filed inside. They all stopped when they saw their coach holding up Weston. Doug spread his arms and plowed his teammates back toward the doors.

Weston dipped his head and pulled away. Rhee put his body in front of him so Weston had a chance to pull it together.

Rhee motioned for the other players to walk on. "You guys put the balls up and hit the showers. We're out. This voluntary, come-to-Jesus practice is over."

Weston walked and sat down on the bleachers, his knees spread wide as he clasped his hands and kept his head down. Most of the players finished putting the basketballs in the ball rack and headed toward the locker room. Rhee checked his keys, opened the storage room, and then went back to put away the ball rack. When Rhee came from the storage room, he saw Asa had sat beside Weston. Neither of them said anything.

Rhee gave Asa an appreciative nod. He was glad someone showed Weston some love. Asa stood and walked toward Rhee. Asa kept his head down and his voice so low Rhee barely heard him.

"Coach?"

"What?"

"About the come-to-Jesus thing, I'm Jewish."

Rhee fought with all his might not to smile. He touched Asa on the shoulder. "That's cool. So was Jesus, and I grew up hearing he was a pretty great guy."

Asa let go with a broad smile. Rhee gave him a nod. Asa picked up his energy and sprinted toward the locker room. Weston stood up and trotted after Asa.

Before Weston disappeared into the locker room, Rhee shouted, "Hey, Bentley Boy." Rhee's voice resonated throughout the gymnasium. Weston stopped. He made a half turn. "See you at practice tomorrow. Don't be late."

Weston's eyes widened with surprise. Rhee hadn't planned on reinstating the spoiled, smart-mouthed kid on the team. It just happened. Not waiting for a reaction, he turned to pick up his backpack, clipboard, and sweatshirt. As he headed out of the gymnasium, he had no idea how it was going to play out.

Chapter 20

Phoenix Rises From The Ashes

Rhee pounded through one of the big double doors. His team watched him as he tossed his backpack onto the scorer's table and removed his whistle. He pulled the leather rope over his head and looked up at his players. They all stood at attention in a huddle.

Rhee marched up to Weston, who froze. "We cool?" Rhee asked.

Weston nodded. "We're cool."

"Good." He stuffed the whistle in his mouth, blew loud, and then clapped his hands. "OK, grab a ball, three-man weave." None of the players moved. They all looked at him, incredulous. Rhee clapped his hands again. "Let's go. I'm not paid to babysit. I'm paid to coach. Just because you got your butts kicked, doesn't mean you can't learn the game properly."

The players sprang into action. They formed two lines of three under the basket. Asa threw the ball to Terrance and then ran behind him. Terrance snapped a pass to Doug and ran behind him. Rhee watched them move down the court without a misfire. Asa finished with a layup. Rhee held back his smile as the three-man weave started back toward him. Rhee had the six players' undivided attention.

Rhee held onto a basketball under the rim as the team listened with intent. "This is a rebounding drill. Gerry, you Blaze, and Doug will box out Asa, Weston, and Terrance," Rhee said.

"Hey, that's not fair, Coach," Asa said.

Rhee turned to him with patience. "Why not?"

Asa pointed at the three bigger players. "Those guys are twice as big as us."

Rhee smiled. He pointed at Asa, Weston, and Terrance. "OK, you three come over here," Rhee said with a devilish smile. He knelt down and waited for Asa, Terrance, and Weston to surround him. "Look, you guys are smaller, but you have the advantage."

"How's that, exactly?" Weston asked.

Rhee looked up at Weston. "How does Chris Paul or Derrick Rose ever get rebounds?"

"'Cause they can leap out of the building?" Terrance asked.

Rhee waved him off. "Quickness and using their heads. Now, listen. When I shoot the ball, you guys fill a gap and beat them to it. Don't think about how big they are. Use your speed." He waited until the three players around him looked like they understood. "All right, now let's do this." Rhee stood and walked back to Doug, Blaze, and Gerry. "Here we go. Everybody get ready."

Rhee bounced the ball to Terrance and caught him by surprise. Rhee stuffed the whistle in his mouth and blew. Terrance held the ball. Rhee's whistle dropped out of his mouth. He held up his hands in disbelief. "What?"

Terrance continued to hold the basketball. "What do I do?"

Rhee rolled his eyes. "You're the shooter."

Terrance flashed a wide smile. He looked at the rim, happy. "Coolness. Thanks."

"Don't mention it." Rhee scratched his head. He placed the whistle back in his mouth and blew.

Terrance squared his shoulders and shot. The ball went straight through the net, swish. Doug, Blaze, and Gerry stood around clueless since they had no rebound.

"Sorry about that," Terrance said, raising his shoulders apologetically. He turned and shot the ball again.

Rhee watched the basketball go right through the net again.

"Dang, sorry. My bad." He shot the ball again, and again it went through the rim, nothing but net.

Doug stood under the net, ready. He caught the ball. "Coach, can somebody else shoot the ball? He never misses," Doug protested.

Rhee stepped toward his players. "What?"

"The guy hardly ever misses. He made sixty free throws in a row before you came here today," Doug said.

Amazed, Rhee turned to Terrance. "You made sixty free throws in a row?"

"Sixty-one. My personal best is seventy-two," Terrance said. He tried to hide his smirk but failed.

Rhee marched over to Doug and snagged the basketball from him. He turned and walked toward Terrance. "You made seventy-two free throws in a row?"

"Yeah," Terrance said calmly. He looked at his teammates.

"When?" Rhee asked.

"A couple of weeks ago."

Rhee stared at Terrance with as much disbelief as he could muster. "Where did you grow up?"

"Hawaii," Terrance said.

"Your parents from Hawaii?"

"Why?" Terrance asked.

"Can you just answer the question?"

"My dad is in the Navy. My mom is from China," Terrance said. "Why?"

"I'm trying to figure out where you learned to shoot like Larry Bird," Rhee said. He turned to the rest of the team. "Anyone doesn't know who Larry Bird is can start running." The players looked at each other. No one ran. He knew one of them had to be lying.

Rhee looked at Blaze. His teammates all let out disappointed sighs. "Who is Larry Bird, Mr. Man?" Rhee asked.

A look of blind panic came to Blaze's face. His eyes darted

around.

"Oh, dude. Come on. Everyone knows Larry Bird," Terrance said.

Blazed closed his eyes. "Boston Celtics. Played on the first 'Dream Team' and played against Magic in college."

All the players let out collective sighs of relief. Sounds of handclaps as they took turns giving Blaze appreciative high fives.

Rhee turned to Terrance. "OK, so your mom is Chinese."

"My mother played for the Chinese women's national basketball team," Terrance said, embarrassed.

"Oh, so your mother taught you to shoot the rock."

"Is that a problem?"

Rhee stared at Terrance. He was beside himself with surprise. The kid was a pure shooter, and it had slipped right by him.

"Wait a second, here," Rhee said. He bounced the ball to Terrance. "Shoot it again, from behind the three-point line."

Terrance backed up behind the three-point line. He squared his feet with his shoulders. He made a perfect U with his thumb and his index finger. His elbow was still too wide. His left hand guided his aim. His forearm flew forward like a perfect human trebuchet. His fingers rolled along the black lines on the ball, giving it a nice spin that added to the swish sound at the basket. He held his stance until the ball cleared the rim. His heels hit the floor a second before the ball bounced off the wood floor under the wagging net.

Rhee grabbed the basketball and rifled a chest pass back to Terrance, who shot it again. Again, the hand, the elbow off, heels set, and nothing but net.

Rhee grabbed the basketball. "Son of a bitch."

"Hey Coach, no swearing in the church," Weston said.

Rhee torched the kid with a mean glare and then smiled. "OK, OK. You got me. My bad. I'll watch myself." Rhee held the basketball on his hip and turned his attention back to Terrance. "How many threes have you made in a row?"

Terrance looked down and shuffled his feet, nervously. "I don't know, maybe twenty," Terrance uttered under his breath.

"Twenty?" Rhee boomed at the top of his lungs.

Terrance was startled. He shuffled his feet again. His sneakers squeaked on the shined floor. "Yeah, nineteen or twenty."

Rhee was astounded. "Boy, why didn't you shoot like that in the practice game when we were getting our butts beat to oblivion?"

"I never got to touch the ball," Terrance said.

Rhee slapped his own forehead. He stood and stared at Terrance and then addressed the team. "Why didn't any of you guys tell me we had someone on the team who could fill it up?" All the boys shrugged their shoulders. "OK, just 'cause I'm a little older than you all doesn't mean I won't bust y'all upside the head." Everyone stood frozen until Rhee started to laugh. Clearly, they still thought he was crazy.

"Hold up," Rhee said. He turned and flew out of the gymnasium. He crossed campus to the administration building and nearly took the hinges off the door going inside. Rhee flew into the office.

"Yes?" said Lynn. She looked as pretty as always, but Rhee was on a mission.

"Coach Holt back there?" Rhee asked.

"Fermenting," Lynn said as she buzzed Rhee in.

Rhee burst into the Coach's cubbyhole. Coach Holt had his feet up, his head back, snoring.

"Coach? Coach!"

Coach Holt snapped to attention and nearly fell out of his chair. He put both his hands on his desk and braced himself. "What? What is it? Fire? What?"

"Do we have a rebounding grill?" Rhee asked.

"Jesus, Mary, and Joseph, Joyce, you scared the snot out of me," Coach Holt said.

"Sorry, Coach."

"You damn better be," Coach Holt said. He reached into his drawer and found his flask. He twisted the top off and chugged a quick one back and then pointed to the top of the shelf behind Rhee. Rhee turned and saw the orange rebounding grill. It looked completely new and unused. His body thrummed with excitement as he quickly scaled the wall and plucked it down.

"Thanks, Coach," Rhee said, and flew out of the little office.

The six Eagles players waited for Rhee to come back down off the ladder. He had snapped the rebounding grill into position around the hoop, fully blocking the basket. Rhee wiped his hands.

"Not even a tennis ball is able to go through this rebounding grill. OK, here we go." Rhee looked at Terrance. "I'll shoot it. If you make a shot through the grill, I'll have to put a hurtin' on you." Everyone laughed. Rhee gave Terrance a wink.

Rhee shot the ball. Asa raced around Blaze before he could put his body on the little speedster. The ball bounced off the rebounding grill. Asa grabbed the basketball and held it like a prize. "You guys are slower than my grandmother," Asa said tauntingly.

Blaze shot him a hateful glare. Asa tossed the ball back to Rhee.

"Come on guys, box the little guys out," Rhee yelled.

He shot the basketball back at the grill. Weston beat Doug to the ball. He handed it to Doug, who went red with anger. "There you go, tough guy," Weston said.

Doug squeezed the basketball as if he wanted to pop it.

"You're slow as molasses, thick neck," Weston said.

"You're dead meat," Doug said.

Doug flung the ball to Rhee. He stuck the whistle in his mouth and blew. "OK, time out. Doug, Gerry, Blaze, come over here for a second."

The three beaten players slowly huddled around Rhee as he knelt. Rhee looked up at their flustered sweaty faces and made sure he made eye contact with each of them. "You guys are supposed to box out, but those three little twerps are making fools out of you."

Doug looked back toward the smaller players who were laughing. "Punks," Doug said with a scowl.

Rhee grabbed Doug's practice jersey, twisting the material in his hand. "Listen up. Focus. I want you to put a body on them," Rhee said. He turned to Blaze. "Blaze."

"Yeah, Coach," Blaze replied.

"Every time someone beats you, I want you to make them pay," Rhee whispered. He tried to get under Blaze's skin. Blaze looked confused.

"What do you mean?" Blaze said.

"I mean I want you to legally assault someone."

"How do I do that?"

Rhee looked back at the smaller players. "If there are no broken bones or no blood, then it's legal," Rhee said, and smiled.

"What about a little blood?" Blaze asked.

Rhee gave him a wider smile and slapped Blaze's shoulder. "Now you and I are understanding one another." Rhee glanced at Doug and liked the rabid look in his eyes. "Blaze, look at Doug," Rhee demanded. "Look at him." Blaze looked at Doug. "Do you see the mean in this boy's eyes?"

"Oh, yeah," Blaze said, with little doubt.

"Get some of that meanness," Rhee said.

Blaze looked back at Doug, who smiled slow and wide. He gave Blaze a nod. Blaze nodded back. The three beaten players broke from the huddle with renewed fire in their bellies.

Rhee held the ball. "You ready?" He looked at Doug and saw the mad dog in him. Rhee shot the ball and watched.

Asa and Weston crossed and tried to go around for the ball. Doug turned with his elbows out. He nearly took Weston and Asa's heads off. They went crashing to the floor. Rhee saw Blaze had pinned Terrance all the way off the court into the bleachers. Gerry easily snagged the ball.

"Now that's what is called boxing out," Rhee shouted. "It's a little too on the mixed martial arts side, but it's a start." Rhee raised his whistle. "OK, guys, let's see some Lambier and Rodman."

"Who are Lambier and Rodman?" Gerry asked. Rhee gave him an incredulous look and shook his head.

"Everyone listen up," Rhee hollered. "Make a circle."

The boys made a circle around Rhee. "Who wants to get out of running?" They all raised their hands. "No problem." Rhee gave each of them a hard stare. "Anyone who can name ten of the NBA's fiftieth anniversary top fifty players gets to not run." Rhee looked at all his players. None of them moved. Asa slowly raised his hand. "Kid Goggles, what up?"

"You want them alphabetically or in chronological order?"

Rhee shook his head. "OK, anyone but Kid Goggles who can name ten players voted the top fifty players doesn't have to run for three practices." Rhee waited. Nothing. "Come on now, guys, in order to know this game properly, y'all got to know the players that made the game what it is today. You need to know the coaches too." Rhee gave each of his players a long gaze. "Anyone who cannot name ten of the fifty best players in the history of the NBA by tomorrow will have to do ten mop-ups before and after practice."

Rhee took off his whistle and dropped it on the floor. He turned and marched away from his team.

Chapter 21

Glimmer Of Sunshine

Practice was almost finished, but an animated Rhee coached with an enthusiasm the players had not seen. They all stood around and listened to him generously share his basketball knowledge. He deftly moved the ball to demonstrate some of the finer points of passing.

Weston tried to perform the way Rhee demonstrated, but he was not quite getting it. "Hold up. Hold up. Stop. Stop, please," Rhee pleaded as he made the time out sign with his hands. "Weston, my man."

Weston held the ball on his hip. "Yeah, Coach?"

"Weston, you telegraph all your passes so badly that I can tell you were gonna throw the ball last week."

Weston pushed the hair out of his eyes. "You could?" Weston asked.

Doug and Blaze laughed.

"Thickness, who is John Havlicek?" Rhee asked. Doug panicked. He looked at Asa. "Don't look at him. I didn't ask Goggles. I asked you."

"Ah, he was a good player," Doug said, struggling. He snapped his fingers.

"You're staring at ten mop-ups," Rhee said.

"He played for the Boston Celtics," Doug screamed.

"OK, that's good."

Doug let out a huge sigh. Rhee turned to Weston. "Bentley Boy, what famous coach played on Havlicek's college team?"

"Coach Bobby Knight," Weston said, and pretended to look at his nails. His teammates nodded, impressed.

"Nice," Rhee said. He took the basketball from Weston and tried to encourage him. "Ever heard of a no-look pass?" Rhee asked.

"Yeah, well kinda." Weston looked at all the eyes on him, decided to come clean, "No, not really," he answered.

Rhee demonstrated by looking away, then he quickly sent a bullet chest pass toward Gerry, who had his hands on his hips. The basketball hit Gerry squarely in the head and knocked him over.

Rhee raced over to Gerry and kneeled next to him. Gerry was out cold. Rhee gently smacked his cheek. The other players gathered around. Rhee tapped both sides of his face. Gerry's eyes fluttered.

"Mom?" Gerry asked.

The other five players howled with laughter. Rhee helped Gerry to his feet.

Practice extended way past the usual end time, and none of the players complained. Rhee had his six players line up on the baseline. They were coiled and ready to run. Rhee blew his whistle, and the players took off the length of the court and sprinted back. Rhee saw Asa finish ahead of the players by fifteen feet. Rhee looked at his watch and then blew the whistle. Asa finished ahead of the other five players by an even wider margin than before. Rhee blew the whistle again, and again Asa finished way ahead of the pack.

"OK, this time, whoever finishes ahead of Kid Goggles will not have to run anymore," Rhee shouted.

"No way," Terrance protested, and gasped for air. He put both hands on his head and sucked wind.

Doug raised his hand. "Yeah, Coach, time out. Give us something in the realm of possibility." He wheezed for oxygen.

"Are you guys telling me that no one can beat Kid Goggles?"

"Coach, no one in this school could beat him with a 100-meter head start," Gerry said. He leaned on Blaze, who was bright pink from exhaustion.

"The dude is Speedy Gonzales and the Flash rolled into one," Blaze said.

Rhee looked at Asa. He was the only one not panting. Rhee turned and went to his backpack on the bleachers. He picked it up and pulled out a stopwatch. "Kid Goggles, over here. The rest of you off the court." The other teammates happily accepted the break and moseyed off the court.

Asa trotted over. "Yeah, Coach?"

Rhee pointed. "I want you to start at the baseline run the length of the court, touch the other baseline and run back. Got it?"

Asa nodded and dutifully jogged over to the baseline. Rhee held up the stopwatch. "On three, start running. One, two, three..." Rhee clicked the stopwatch on. Asa raced down the court, touched the other baseline, and sprinted back. Rhee clicked the stopwatch off. He looked down at the time. The kid had beat Rhee's high school record from baseline to baseline line by a sixteenth of a second. He was floored. "All right, five-minute water break," Rhee ordered. The players meandered toward the water fountain. "Kid Goggles, get over here."

Asa turned and sprinted over to him. "Yeah, Coach?" Asa asked.

Rhee noticed the young boy was not even breathing hard. "Listen up. I need you to come clean with it, on the one hundred. Are you on steroids?" Rhee asked.

Asa looked up at him, confused. "Steroids?"

"I've never met anyone as small as you who could run that fast, unless it was from the police or he was on steroids. So what are you on?" Rhee asked.

Asa raised his hands and shoulders. "Hebrew school, I guess."

Rhee stared at him with amazement. "You're on Hebrew school? What kind of drug is that?"

"I'm not on Hebrew school, Coach. I got fast because of

Hebrew school."

"They make you run at Hebrew school?" Rhee asked.

"No, Coach. When I was little, every day after Hebrew school, these big guys would always chase me and try to take my yarmulke. I guess I kinda got fast from running away from them," Asa said, shyly.

"Fast? Kid, you make Usain Bolt look like a pigeon-toed snail."

"Coach, snails don't have toes," Asa said.

"You obviously haven't been to my neighborhood. Now get to steppin', Flash." Rhee ruffled Asa's hair. Asa beamed. He turned and headed for the drinking fountain. "Do they take black guys my age in Hebrew school?" Asa belted a laugh so hard it made Rhee laugh too. "I'm dead serious. If I need a recommendation, are you gonna help a brotha' out or what?"

"You're funny, Coach," Asa said. Rhee watched him shake his head and run off.

"I'm not that funny, and if you don't run track in high school, I'm coming after you." Rhee shouted.

A while later all six players stood around and watched Rhee put on a dazzling display of basketball wizardry. He was dribbling the ball around his feet, through his legs and behind his back. The players were overwhelmed. Rhee dribbled the basketball like it was on a string.

One of the double doors opened. Rhee and his players looked at each other while Coach Holt huffed and puffed as he climbed the bleachers. He found a seat a safe distance away. Rhee stopped his dribbling. His eyes fixed on Coach Holt while he spoke to the six Eagles players.

"See, none of y'all knew I'd get my handle back, but I'm cane free now, so don't even think about picking my pocket on the court."

Rhee was surprised how well his ankle held up. Then he felt a twinge, so he immediately stopped. He was just a little short of breath.

"The reason we couldn't bring the ball past half court was

because none of you are confident with the rock," Rhee said.

"Were you using mirrors for that little ball handling demonstration?" Weston asked.

Rhee smiled and broke his gaze from Coach Holt. He looked at Weston and spun the basketball on his finger. "I started carrying the basketball everywhere I went when I was five years old."

Chapter 22

Progress Report

Rhee leaned over the desk and handed over his pay stubs. "How is the job going?" the Assistant Dean asked. He examined the pay stubs and then pulled out a ledger.

Rhee thought about the question and had a lot of responses, but he knew the Assistant Dean wouldn't understand. "I'm coaching a bunch of misfit, spoiled rich kids."

The Assistant Dean wrote in the ledger. "You're getting paid to coach basketball, though. At least you're not doing telemarketing or stacking ice like some of the other students. Plus, we've got all the paperwork filled out so there's a good chance you can start classes next semester."

Rhee stared him into silence and then turned his attention back toward the window. As every student passed by, it made him wonder what their story was or if they had to go through anything as hard as what he was going through. Everyone he saw looked so happy they seemed to walk on air. He'd been there once, when he was somebody; now no one even remembered his name.

"It feels like I woke up one day and realized my whole life was just a dream. One day I'm a hero, and the next, I'm a nobody," Rhee said.

The Assistant Dean leaned back in his chair. He acted like he cared but probably didn't all that much. But he listened, so Rhee continued.

"When I was in ninth grade, I got a letter from Coach Bobby Knight," Rhee said. He turned his attention back to the Assistant Dean. "How many ninth-graders can say that?"

"Not more than a handful, I'm sure," the Assistant Dean said. He stared at Rhee with a look of compassion.

Rhee looked out the window again, his thoughts reeling. "By the time I was in tenth grade, people were offering my father money for my autograph." Rhee turned back to the Assistant Dean and saw genuine amazement on his face. "Do you know what it was like to be fifteen and be asked for your autograph?"

"I've never been asked for my autograph, unless I was applying for a credit card." It sounded flip, but it was honest.

Rhee looked out the window again. The light and people walking by helped him organize his thoughts, which were now free-flowing. "As long as I was scoring thirty points a game, I had an identity. Now, everything is different. I walk around, and I'm invisible. People pass by me and are afraid to look me in the eye or say anything. It's like I'm handicapped or something."

The Assistant Dean narrowed his eyes and shuffled in his seat.

"I got a job, just like you told me the other day, coaching kids that can't even play."

"You got a job, and that's what matters."

"We lost our first practice game by sixty-one points," Rhee said.

"Ouch! Sorry to hear that. I'm sure, with your guidance, you will win some games."

Rhee thought about the players. "Normally, losing a game is not such a big deal, right?"

"Losing isn't the end of the world," the Assistant Dean said.

Rhee felt a wave of sadness rise up inside him. He was petrified he might start crying like a punk in front of the Assistant Dean. Rhee took a deep breath until the wave of sadness passed. "What if the losing never stops?"

Rhee's eyes filled with tears. He leaned forward and snatched a tissue out of the Assistant Dean's leather Kleenex box. Rhee blew his nose and then composed himself as best he could. "Do you know what it's like to be a nobody?"

"Just because your basketball career ended, doesn't make you a nobody," the Assistant Dean said. "School teachers, garbage men, postal workers don't think of themselves as nobodies. The world doesn't operate that way. You're going to have to reorient your way of thinking."

Rhee sat back and tried to drink in the Assistant Dean's words. No one had ever said these things to Rhee. He had no way of processing the logic.

"Ever since I was ten years old, people told me I was special. They told me I had what it took to go all the way." Rhee folded the Kleenex. Rhee heard laughing outside, so he looked out the window again. "I keep having this dream that I'm on the court, and the gymnasium is packed. I'm holding the ball, I look up in the stands, and no one is cheering. They just stare. I hold the ball and wait for them to start cheering again, but they don't," Rhee said, his mouth quivering.

His voice left him at that point. He drew on all the dignity he had and reached for another Kleenex. He blew his nose and waited for his voice to return. The Assistant Dean sat perfectly still with his eyes trained on Rhee.

"The most messed-up part is no one even attempted to prepare me for this -- this failure. I mean someone, anyone, should have told me that the fame and the recognition could be taken away in an instant. It's like some big-ass lie. It's a full-court lie. Everyone told me it was all going to work out: smooth sailing to a bright future. How was I supposed to know? I'm just a teenager. I just wanted to have a cool car, buy my parents a big house, and tell my dad he never had to work two jobs again." Rhee took a deep breath. He fought back his urge to fall to the floor and sob. "Now everything is different. I'm supposed to just fall into the world without missing a step, right?" Rhee looked out the window. "The only people I'm kicking it with are a bunch of rich kids I can't stand and can't stand me."

The Assistant Dean said nothing. He slowly stood, walked around his desk, and put his hand on Rhee's shoulder. "I can't tell you how many times I've sat with students who I knew didn't have a chance in hell of surviving this school or any school." He eased his hand off Rhee's shoulder. "I know you'll make it because you're a winner. That doesn't need to stop because the basketball stopped."

Rhee looked up. He felt the salt from his tears sting his eyes. "I had no idea when I won the league championship game with five seconds to go..." His lips quivered. His throat felt like he swallowed a rock. "It was going to be the last five seconds I was ever going to get to play."

The Assistant Dean looked at Rhee like he really cared. More tears fell unhindered from Rhee's eyes. Maybe the man really did care. Maybe he was really trying to look out for him.

Rhee stood, feeling like he'd completely punked out. He had to get out of the Assistant Dean's office before he became any more foolish. He started toward the door. Rhee was surprised that the Assistant Dean walked him there

Rhee put his hand on the doorknob. "You sound just like my mom," Rhee said to the door. He looked back at the Assistant Dean. There was nothing more to say. There was much more to do.

Chapter 23

The Turnaround

The gymnasium was filled with screaming fans all waving their cardinal-red pennants. The Lafayette Cardinals had several hundred spectators in their home bleachers. Three championship banners adorned the wall over the scoreboard. Next to it loomed an oversized cardinal bird to intimidate visiting players. In the visitors' bleachers, rows of empty seats were dotted with no more than twelve spectators for the Eagles.

Rhee sat next to Blaze on the bench. When the horn sounded, Rhee looked up at the scoreboard and saw the miserable truth. The scoreboard read: Visitors 14, Cardinals 35.

Rhee raised his hands, stood up, and voiced his familiar mantra, "Finally! I thought it'd never end." His players meandered, heads downcast, toward the sideline. Blaze pulled on Rhee's shirt. "What? What is it Blaze?"

"Coach, it's only halftime," Blaze said.

Rhee looked at him as if he'd slapped him silly across the head. "Again? It's like a recurring nightmare that won't stop. How do we make it stop?" He looked up to the heavens. "Please, God, make it stop."

Rhee leaned against the locker in front of his dejected players. Their heads were all down. He wanted to say something, but all he could do was stare at the floor with them in silence. There was a minute between each second that passed.

Rhee thought about Coach Holt's warning. The old man was right. Rhee knew it. This was the Titanic, and Rhee's job was shuffling deck chairs before the ship went down. He had to let this go. He had to let it all go. Rhee thought about what the Assistant Dean had said about Rhee being a winner. How could he possibly win in this bad situation with these bad players?

Rhee looked at each of them as they continued to avoid his glare. He saw Doug, the muscly head bruiser, and Terrance, the freethinking surfer kid. Rhee looked at Asa with his goggles and Weston with his billion dollars. Rhee looked at Blaze and then Gerry. Individually, they were not bad kids. As a team, they reeked.

Rhee scanned them all again and considered. They each had something to offer but not as a team. He pushed himself off the locker. "Listen up everyone." Only Weston and Asa looked up. Rhee met their eyes. "I don't know about you guys, but I'm tired of getting my ass handed to me." The other four players joined Weston and Asa and listened. Rhee paced in front of them. "So, we're going to revert to what I call drastic measures."

"We're gonna leave?" Asa asked.

Rhee stopped pacing. He knelt down in front of the six players. "No, better than that." He looked up at the ceiling. "Forgive me, Coach Knight, for what I'm about to say," Rhee said with his eyes closed.

He opened his eyes and saw the six Eagles looking at one another. Rhee taught them all about Coach Knight and a lot of other great coaches. Now he was going to teach them about another coach. Rhee rubbed his hands together. He was excited. The players obviously had no idea why.

"I'm going to teach you guys something called street ball," Rhee said, excitedly. "'Run and gun' was made a science by the legendary coach Jerry Tarkanian."

The six Eagles players were not able to join in their young coach's excitement. They eyed him like he was crazy.

"What's street ball?" Weston asked.

"What's run and gun?" Blaze asked. They verbalized the perplexed looks on all the players.

"Street ball, or run and gun, means there's no better defense than a strong offense," Rhee explained.

"You don't want us to play defense?" Doug asked.

"The good news, Doug, is you're not playing defense now, so it's not something you're going to have to worry about. In fact, if they score it's a good thing," Rhee answered. He saw his players deflate from his statement. Rhee kept his energy high. He was not going to let them deflate any further. "What I'm saying is save your energy for offense," Rhee said. The six Eagles players glanced at one another, confused. "Street ball means don't worry about defense, just outscore your man." He looked at each player and saw the lost looks of confusion in their eyes. "Terrance," Rhee snapped.

Terrance sat up straight.

"Yeah," Terrance answered.

Rhee duck walked over to him. "You ever heard of Reggie Miller?"

Terrance half smiled, confused. "He played eighteen seasons with the Indiana Pacers. He was the all-time three-point shooter until Ray Allen broke his record."

"How do you know that?" Rhee asked.

"Coach, you told us to study the history of the game."

"That's right. I did." He looked at the other teammates and then back to Terrance. "You know what a pure shooter is?"

"No," Terrance answered.

"That's you. You're our pure shooter." He put his hand on Terrance's shoulder, trying to encourage him. Terrance feigned a smile.

"I am?" Terrance asked.

"Damn right. You're one of the best young shooters I've seen in years. I've played against some great ones, and you're right up there." He knew he was stretching the truth, but when he saw his young player smile and perk up, Rhee realized it was working. "All I want you to do next half is shoot the ball. You got me?"

Terrance nodded. Rhee knew he was not one hundred percent comprehending. "Don't worry about your man. Every time you get your hands on the ball, I want you to shoot. In fact, start shooting now, and don't stop until we get back on the bus, OK?"

Terrance smiled nervously. He nodded. Rhee stood up and walked over to Asa. "Goggles?"

Asa straightened his back. "Yeah, Coach?"

"From now on, you're not Kid Goggles. You are the cheetah from Hebrew school," Rhee said. "Your new nickname is 'Flash,' OK?"

Asa smiled wide. "OK, Coach."

Rhee looked at the rest of the team. "This is Flash. Everyone got that?" Rhee asked. They all nodded. "OK, Flash, every time they shoot the ball, I want you to take off toward our basket. I don't care if they miss or make it, I want you to be a cheetah or a gazelle," Rhee said. Asa nodded in belief. "There isn't a player in this league who can run with you. You got that?"

Rhee wanted to be sure Asa believed it. When Asa smiled, a glint in his eyes, Rhee knew he was beginning to believe. Rhee smiled back and then turned to Doug and Gerry. They straightened their backs. Whatever Rhee was selling, they wanted to buy.

"Doug and Gerry." He walked over to them. Their eyes were wide with eagerness. "Who is Dennis Rodman?"

Doug and Gerry looked at each other. They spoke at the same time. "Championship player for the Bulls and the Lakers."

"That's right." Rhee smiled wide. "Rodman was a rebounding machine. Every time the ball came off the glass, Rodman got the ball. Tonight I want you both to be Dennis Rodman. When the other team shoots, I want you to crash the boards. It's time that you guys take advantage of your natural born gifts."

"What's that, Coach?" Doug asked.

Rhee gave them a winner's glare. "Rebounding," Rhee said with an infectious smile. Doug and Gerry smiled. "I want to see bodies on the ground, all right?" Doug nearly jumped up and ran back out to the court. He was so enthused. "Whenever you guys get the ball in your hands, find Weston to pass the rock to, OK?" Rhee stared at them long enough for them to swell with excitement. Rhee winked and patted Doug on the head. He turned to Blaze. "That goes for you too, Blaze. I want you to think of yourself as the Hulk."

"I'm going to play?" Blaze asked, his eyes wide with disbelief.

"Of, course! And when you do play, I wanna see bodies on the ground."

"Yeah, come on Hulk, take some heads off," Doug yelled at Blaze.

It was the first time in a long time that Doug had not made fun of Blaze. And that made Blaze swell with confidence.

His players all listened intently for the first time. A charge of excitement began to dissipate the stifling gloom. Rhee walked over to Weston. "Weston, I want you to be the outlet. Every time Doug or Gerry gets a rebound. I want you to yell, scream, and flap your arms. They are going to get you the ball, or they'll have to answer to me," Rhee said.

He saw that Weston was not as sure as his teammates. Rhee knew he had to win him into the plan. He kneeled in front of him. "You're my main guy. You're the quarterback. Without you, none of this will work. So I need you to cape up."

He waited for Weston to believe. Weston smiled. "I got my cape on, Coach." He was won over.

"I see it." Rhee patted Weston on the shoulder and turned to Doug, Gerry, Terrance, and Blaze. "On every made or missed shot, I want you guys to look for our quarterback, Weston. He's going to get the ball to Asa down court. In fact, just chuck the damn ball down court. Flash will catch up to it."

Rhee took a step back and measured his players. He saw hope in their faces as they bounced with excitement. "You guys now know who Jerry Tarkanian was as a coach. We're going to give them our best impersonation of one of Coach Tarkanian's old teams, called 'The Running Rebels', or better known as 'Runners and Gunners.' Our new creed is: 'Forget about defense. Just outscore your man.'" He studied his players. "You guys with me?" Rhee shouted.

The six Eagles snapped back. "Yes."

"What's our new creed?" Rhee asked.

"Forget about defense. Outscore your man!" they all yelled.

Rhee smiled. He held his hand out. All six players leaped up and reached over to Rhee. A mound of hands formed on top of his.

"OK, let's have some fun."

Rhee followed his six Eagles players back onto the court. Rhee looked up at the scoreboard, but it didn't faze him this time. He glanced over toward the Cardinals players. They were well organized. All the players were white and had crew cuts. They ran their warm-ups with skilled and restrained discipline.

The Cardinals' coach approached Rhee. He also had a matching crew cut. He was well built, with hairy, Popeye-like forearms. Rhee waited at half court. The Cardinals' coach extended his hand, and Rhee received the gyrating handshake.

"Hey, Coach," the Cardinals' coach said. His expression was one of mercy. "Don't worry about this getting out of hand. I'll play the second string the entire second half. There's no need for your kids to be ridiculed the entire season."

"Thanks, but you might not want to do that," Rhee said.

The Cardinals' coach looked at Rhee like he was crazy and then turned away and trotted back to his team. Rhee watched him kneel in front of his players. The Cardinals' coach said something that made his team laugh. At least the sounds of their amusement were drowned out by the cheering Cardinals fans.

Rhee turned away. He had a small smile no one in the entire gymnasium noticed. Rhee looked up at the visiting bleachers and saw that every seat was empty except for two Eagles fans, probably the last in the world. One of them was Mr. Lieberman, who faithfully sat in the stands. Rhee gave Asa's father the thumbs up. The other was Mrs. Morgan. Rhee acknowledged her with a nod as she clapped her encouragement. She looked exquisite, as usual.

Rhee took a seat and studied his six motley Eagles running and passing the ball to each other, doing a shoot around. The scoreboard sounded. The head referee blew his whistle. The Cardinals fans screamed. They had not cared about the score.

They wanted to see blood. Rhee stood up and encouraged his team by clapping. This time he meant it. He believed.

"OK, Eagles, over here." His team sprinted over to the sideline and huddled around their coach. "It's just like we talked about, street ball, run and gun."

"OK, Coach," they all said in unison before breaking out of the huddle.

Rhee saw a new enthusiasm in his team as they sprinted back to the court. He didn't care if no part of his plan worked. He was glad he was able to give them hope. Sometimes that was all a person needed to perform miracles.

One of the referees handed Asa the basketball under the Cardinals' basket. The Cardinals' coach had kept his word. His entire second string was in the game. Asa tossed the basketball to Weston, who struggled but managed to bring the ball up court. He passed the ball to Terrance, who was several feet behind the three-point line. Terrance held the basketball.

"Shoot the ball. Let it fly," Rhee screamed.

The Cardinals cheerleaders yelled and rattled pompoms so loud that Terrance wasn't able to hear him. Terrance nervously held the basketball and saw Rhee motioning to shoot the ball. Terrance turned and shot the basketball.

Rhee balled his fist, watching the basketball in flight. The basketball bounced off the back of the rim and flew out of bounds. Rhee saw Terrance's confidence deflate. Terrance clapped his hands hard, with noticeable disappointment. "Dag," Terrance yelled at himself.

Rhee clapped loud and gave Terrance the thumbs up. "That's only one, Terrance. Keep shooting. Don't worry about it. Take a thousand shots."

A Cardinals player inbounded the basketball to his teammate, who dribbled up the court. The Cardinals set a play and executed it perfectly. One of the Cardinals players was so open he had to shoot. The basketball hit the front of the rim and bounced high in the air. Rhee watched on the sideline, mouth agape, speechless, as Doug boxed out a Cardinal, leaped in the air, and grabbed the basketball.

Weston jumped up and down, waving his hands. "Over here. Right here."

Doug spotted him. He snapped a chest pass. Weston fumbled the basketball. He gained control of the basketball, and he let go with a lame duck pass to Asa, who was streaking down the sideline.

Asa raced ahead of his defender by several feet and surprised himself with an uncontested layup. A look of shock on his face as the ball dropped through the basket. Rhee and Blaze jumped up and down in celebration. The five Eagles players in the game looked at one another in surprise. Ruckus cheers from the Cardinals fans were hushed.

All of the Eagles glanced over to the sideline to observe their coach's reaction. "See, just like I told you. Now pour it on."

The Cardinals set their offense easily. There was no pressure from the Eagles defensively. A Cardinals player shot the basketball and made it. No sooner than Rhee was able to yell, Gerry quickly took the basketball out of bounds. He flung the basketball to Weston, who turned and launched a ridiculous pass way over Asa's head. Asa then broke from his defender and raced past him to catch up to the basketball. Asa made another uncontested layup. Mr. Lieberman jumped to his feet. His cheers sliced through the collective groans from the Cardinals loyal crowd.

Blaze leaped up and pumped both his fists. "Yes!"

The Cardinals players stood around in shock. The Cardinals' coach screamed and kicked his bench. The Eagles jumped up and down with excitement.

The momentum quickly changed. The Cardinals players became flustered. They hurried their next few shots without setting up their offense. They shot and missed and shot and missed. Doug and Gerry rebounded with a vengeance. They took turns throwing the outlet pass to Weston, who flung the basketball to Asa, who executed layup after layup.

Rhee looked at the Cardinals' coach, who began to pace and turn beet red with panic. He yelled a time-out. Rhee looked up at the scoreboard. It read: Visitors 24, Cardinals 41. Rhee heard the referee blow his whistle. He glanced over to the scorer's table and noticed the Cardinals starters had been sent back into the game. Rhee felt a surge of energy rush through his body. The other team was starting to realize the Eagles were no joke.

Terrance made a three-pointer, and his confidence began to soar. He made his next eight shots in a row. The Cardinals players managed to slow down Asa only by fouling him. Terrance was another matter. No matter how many defenders they put on him, Terrance drained shot after shot.

Rhee was not able to believe his eyes. Terrance took over the game. He was on fire. After every shot he made, he grew more and more confident. Terrance backpedaled down court holding up three fingers.

Rhee leaped to his feet and yelled at him. "Go on with your bad self. You the man. This is your house."

Terrance looked over at his coach, and Rhee saw fire in his eyes. Terrance pointed both index fingers to the floor. "This is my house, Coach. We play by my rules." Cheers from the crowd to encourage the Cardinals fell on deaf ears.

The horn blew loudly, ending the game. Rhee looked at the scoreboard, and it read: Visitors 59, Cardinals 53. The Cardinals fans and players were stunned as all eyes gawked at the score.

The six Eagles players were also in shock. They barely celebrated their victory. The Cardinals' coach was red-faced and flustered as he ushered his dejected players to the sideline. The entire gymnasium was silent. Rhee saw Weston hand the head referee the basketball. The Eagles walked toward Rhee. He frantically ushered his players to reverse and form a line to shake hands with the Cardinals players. The Eagles seemed more bedazzled than their opponents. With stunned expressions, they exchanged handshakes with the twelve Cardinals players. Rhee headed toward the Cardinals' coach, but he wheeled around and jogged into the locker room.

In the Cardinals' locker room, Rhee stood in front of his players. They waited for him to speak. Rhee looked around without a smile. The Eagles looked worried.

Rhee cleared his throat. "Do you feel that? Do you feel what I'm feeling?"

They looked at one another, not understanding. Rhee moved close to his players and spoke softly. "Winning feels different. It's contagious. The more you win, the more you want to win -- the more you will win," he said.

He looked them all in their eyes before he walked away. Rhee didn't have to turn around because he knew something had changed today, not only in his players, but in himself too.

Chapter 24

Recruiting

Rhee navigated his mother's car through the Orinda Hills. He passed a school where a few kids were playing basketball in the schoolyard. He was forty yards past the school when he veered into a turn lane and wheeled the car back toward the schoolyard. Rhee got out of the car and walked toward the kids on the playground. A warm breeze carried the shouts of youthful voices in his direction.

There were six white teenagers playing three-on-three. They were older than the fourteen-year-olds Rhee coached. Their skills were marginal, but they trashed talked, hacked, and shoved one another like they'd been playing forever.

Rhee noticed one of the teenagers was not too bad. He wasn't a great player by any means, but he had a little game. What struck Rhee was that this particular kid kept trying incredible circus moves. He twisted, double clutched, and shot blindly over his head. Once in a while, the kid's acrobatic attempts would actually go into the basket. He celebrated a miracle basket with his hands in the air, followed by a few rigid dance moves, no better than his athletic skills.

Rhee smiled. The kid was not good enough to play on a high school competitive level, but he really enjoyed imitating the professional players he obviously watched and admired. Either that or the teen was a Harlem Globetrotter fanatic. He trash talked even when he got beat or missed a shot by yards.

It amused Rhee, and then it triggered something inside. Rhee spun around and hastily hobbled to his mother's car. The yells from the kids and sounds of the ball hitting the pavement faded behind him. He started the engine with a roar, and it hit him that his ankle felt pretty solid. There was no pain. For a brief moment, Rhee thought the win against the Cardinals might change his luck. The wheels smoked as they spun. His mother's car fishtailed down the street.

Rhee burst into the reception area of the middle school. He raced up to the counter. His backpack was on his shoulder.

He was a bit thrown when Lynn turned around. She looked down at her watch. "You're early. Don't you have a couple hours before practice?"

Rhee was a bit distracted. Lynn's hair was up in a tight bun with a couple chopsticks through it. She had small ears and a slender neck. Her shoulders were straight as a coat hanger, but they were small and delicate. Her dress was thin and floral, with spaghetti straps. She reached for the buzzer to let Rhee behind the counter, and he caught a quick peek of ample cleavage for such a slender girl.

"Do you want the coach?" Lynn asked.

Rhee pulled his eyes off Lynn's breasts as fast as he could. He wondered if it was too late. Her relaxed eyes and manner let him know he was still, at least temporarily, in decent standing. Rhee needed to act on his inspiration before he lost any enthusiasm or a shade of doubt crept into his mind.

He waved her off. "Nah, that's OK." Their eyes were on each other. Rhee thought he sensed something. He went with quitting while he was ahead. "Can I ask you something?" Rhee asked.

"Yeah, sure," Lynn said. She gave him a curious, small look of suspicion.

Rhee looked into her hazel green eyes. He felt a tug; something was preventing him from remembering exactly what he had originally wanted. He knew his thoughts were much better served without gazing at her, so he looked away. Then he snapped his fingers.

"White Chocolate," Rhee said.

"What?" Lynn asked. The small spot between her eyebrows wrinkled. Rhee thought it was cute.

"I need the class schedule of one of the students," Rhee said.

"What student? Do you have a name?" Lynn asked.

"He calls himself L.A." Rhee said. "I'm not positive, but he might have a photographic memory." He noticed that a small grin appeared on Lynn's mouth. He wasn't sure if he was being funny or if she knew something he didn't. "What's so funny?" Rhee asked.

"Nothing. I just never heard anyone call him White Chocolate before," Lynn said. "And he does have a photographic memory."

"You know him?" Rhee asked.

"Very well. Why do you need his class schedule?" Lynn asked.

"We need his help."

"Who are we?" Lynn asked.

"The Eagles, the basketball team," Rhee said.

Lynn shook her head and laughed. "He's not going to be able to play for your team."

"Why not? Does he have bad grades?

Lynn laughed a little louder and gave Rhee a stare he wasn't able to decipher. "He was the class valedictorian in sixth and seventh grade. He'll probably make it again this year."

Rhee's thoughts skipped a bit. The kid he asked about never remotely acted like he had any intelligence. He was sure they were talking about two different people.

"I don't think we're talking about the same kid," Rhee said confidently. He tried not to act cocky. It was the longest she'd given him a dose of actual smiles and laughter.

"He's a straight-A student in the accelerated program, all college preparatory classes. Most of the teachers say his IQ is off the charts."

Rhee stared at her while her words rattled around in his brain. Her perfume wafted into his nose and lured him into a trance. He shook his head to snap out of it. "Nah, that ain't him," Rhee said, emphatically. "I'm talking about a kid who acts all hard like he's straight out of East Oakland."

Lynn laughed and covered her mouth. "White Chocolate's name is Leslie Adams."

"Leslie? Adams?" Rhee asked.

"White on the outside, black on the inside, kind of a gangster-talking, good-looking boy, with sandy-blond hair, right?" Lynn asked.

Rhee nearly bit down on his tongue. She described the right kid, though. "Are you telling me the kid I'm asking about is some sort of nerdy bookworm?"

"No, Leslie Adams is no 'bookworm.' I don't think I've ever seen him with books." Lynn raised her two hands and displayed two fingers like quotation marks. "I think he hides them 'cause they ain't cool. Besides, he's a speed-reader, and his comprehension is stratospheric. He's scary smart."

"So why can't he play?" Rhee asked.

Lynn turned around. She went to the filing cabinet and took out a thick folder. She opened the file and read. "Leslie Adams, thirteen, born May 7, 2000. He has a 4.8 grade-point average. He takes two courses after school at St. Aquinas College."

Rhee raised his hands in disbelief. "Are you saying he's thirteen and taking colleges classes?"

"Exactly. You're a quick study, Coach Rhee."

Rhee gave her a sidelong glance. He looked around. "Am I getting punked here?"

Lynn raised her right hand like she was giving a sworn testimony. "White Chocolate is an academic standout," Lynn said. "He can skip high school entirely if he continues at this rate. Probably one of the brightest kids -- if not the brightest -- to ever attend this school."

Rhee took a step back. "That's crazy talk." He reached out and put two hands on the counter; he was feeling a bit woozy. "Damn, I'm busting my hump to get into college, and this little eighth-grader breezes up there on skates four years before he can even go?" Rhee slowly pushed himself off the counter. A cool dread started at the top of his head and slowly sank through his body to his feet. "My bad. I just thought he might change his mind if he heard we actually beat a pretty good team."

Lynn folded her arms and tapped her foot. "Yeah, a lot of the teachers are mad at you for ruining the office pool."

"There's an office pool?"

Lynn looked over both her shoulders and then stepped up to the counter. She used one hand to hide her statement. "Yeah, there is a pool on the number of points you guys are supposed to lose by," Lynn whispered.

"That's cold," Rhee blurted. "It's downright nasty."

Lynn used both hands to try to get Rhee to lower his voice. "You didn't hear that from me." She put her right index finger on her lips to emphasize she needed him to keep it on the down low.

Rhee took two steps back from the counter. "So, in the mean time, you're going to help keep White Chocolate off the team so you can keep the pool in check, right?"

Rhee measured her to see if he was kidding himself or he actually had her on the spot. "I would help you and those poor kids if I could." There was a defensive tone in her voice.

"You could come play for the team," Rhee said.

"Now, that's crazy talk," Lynn said.

"Tell you what, you just hold up that file, and I'll pretend to be passing by, and I'll look at it like I thought you were giving me a note from the principal," Rhee said. Lynn smiled wide and laughed. Her smile lit up the room. And she smiled. A big smile too.

Lynn wiped the smile off her face. She turned and looked behind her. She placed the file on the counter in front of him. She folded her arms and shot him a playful yet threatening glance. He looked down and read the file. It looked like something he couldn't decipher. He scratched his head.

"I have no idea what this says." He watched her arch one eyebrow.

"We have modular scheduling," Lynn said.

"What does that mean?" Rhee asked.

"His last class was Advanced Calculus. He gets out early. You'll have to catch him on his way to the college."

Rhee straightened his back and grabbed the shoulder harness of his backpack with both hands. "So I'll have to go to his house."

Lynn closed the folder over the file. She gave Rhee her first coquettish smile. "At the risk of being shot for trespassing."

"Oh, my goodness, she has a sense of humor."

Lynn put her hands on her hips. "Who said I was trying to be funny?"

"You were being funny," Rhee said. He looked down and noticed her waist was as small as one of his thighs. He wanted to talk to her about something else, maybe ask her out. "Where is he now?"

"Probably on his way home," Lynn said.

"Can you give me his address?"

Lynn stared at Rhee suspiciously. She reopened the folder and turned it around. "If someone burns his house down or even steals his newspaper, I'm going to report you," Lynn said.

Rhee held up his hands. "If someone burns his house down, it'll be because they thought he was black, not because of me." Lynn let go with a hearty laugh. Rhee gazed at her, taken aback. "I made you laugh." He gave her his sweet smile. At least he thought it was sweet. He was out of practice.

"You're just walking by, right?" Lynn asked.

"Yep. I'm just walking by. Pimp walking too."

"OK, Mr. Pimp." Lynn put the index finger on the upper corner of the file. "I hope you read fast."

Rhee quickly slid his backpack off his shoulders and dug into it for a pen before she changed her mind. He tore a piece of paper from his folder, scribbled, then folded the paper, and shoved it into his pocket. Lynn picked up the index card, turned, and went back to the file cabinet.

"Thanks, I owe you one," Rhee said. He waited to see if she gave him any signal. Anything that revealed he had an opening. She only folded her arms. Nothing. He took in the silence of the office, that they were the only two in the room, and used it to fuel his courage, "So this means you're going out with me?" He knew full well he was now over the line.

"Don't push your luck," Lynn replied.

"I haven't had much luck to push in a long time." Lynn folded her arms and gave Rhee a sidelong suspicious glance. "What?" Rhee asked.

"I'm sure a guy like you has his pick of the litter."

"A guy like me?" Rhee put a hand on his chest to highlight his innocence. Lynn's eyes narrowed. "What'd I do?"

"I know how to Google."

"Oh, so now you know all about me?"

"I know you're famous."

A kaleidoscope of emotions surged through Rhee's body. He was exhilarated she took the time to look up his name on the Internet. He was disappointed his fame was now a fraud. It was a moment in history no longer useful enough or valid enough to still gleam admirers. He backed away from the counter. "The guy you looked up on Google isn't that guy, anymore."

With that, Rhee turned quickly and left the office. He was happy for two reasons: he now had L.A.'s address, and Lynn's eyes were on him when he left.

Chapter 25

The Drive-By

Weston leaned his arm against a wall while smooth-talking a young girl. She smirked and smiled at his banter as a breeze blew through her tousled hair. Rhee cleared his throat and brought up the bass in his voice.

"Mr. Morgan," Rhee said. Weston pushed off the wall and straightened up, the moment between him and the young girl broken. "At ease, soldier. You're cool. This ain't a jack." Rhee was amazed at how many different shades Weston was able to blush.

"Hey, Coach," Weston said.

Rhee took a minute to appreciate the new respect he was receiving from this once self-serving pain-in-the-ass kid. He waited for an introduction but realized Weston had lost his cool, smooth attitude.

"I'm Coach Joyce," Rhee said to the nervous young girl. A quick inventory told Rhee she was undeveloped but pretty. She had the standard barely visible silver nose ring and wore the latest fashion, which showed too much belly and a navel piercing. Her ears had more than the standard amount of piercings. She was too young to appreciate the manners of saying her name, so Rhee turned his attention to Weston.

"What's up? Hope you're not up to no good," Rhee said. He watched Weston look around like a kid who had been caught doing something he wasn't supposed to be doing.

"Not at all, Coach. We're just hanging," Weston said. The girl turned on her heels and skirted off. Rhee waited for her to get out of earshot.

"Why aren't you in class?" Rhee asked.

Weston stumbled and fumbled over his words. "I've got study hall last period. It's kind of like a free period."

Rhee glared down at him. "Then why aren't you in the gym practicing your jump shot?"

"I think there's a P.E class in there..." Weston stammered.

Rhee pulled the paper out of his pocket and showed it to Weston. "You know where this place is?"

Weston turned his head as far as he could read the scribble on the paper. "Yep. It's close to my house."

Rhee folded the paper and stuffed it back into his pocket. "Want to take a ride?"

Weston looked around to make sure no one was close enough to hear the conversation. "I'm not supposed to go off campus until after school."

"I thought this was an open campus," Rhee said.

Rhee saw Weston dip his eyes in shame. "It's part of my probation. If I get busted, I could be expelled."

Rhee studied him. Weston shifted uncomfortably under his suspicious stare, until Rhee slowly started to smile, a devilish smile. "Then we have to make sure you don't get busted."

Weston looked up at him with a grimace, skeptically. "You sure about this?"

Rhee gave him a glare. "Are you being nicer to your stepmother?" He studied the small line of perspiration that moistened the young boy's adolescent mustache.

"Yes," Weston said. He followed it with a furrowed brow and a nervous swallow.

"Good. Then if you decide to buy drugs or rob any liquor stores, I'll vouch for you." Rhee turned in the direction of his mother's car and started to walk off. Weston hesitated. He looked over both shoulders and then hustled to catch up with Rhee.

Weston got into the passenger seat and closed the door. Rhee saw his eyes dart around. "Where are we going?" Rhee rolled down the window to release some of the stifling air.

"To talk to Leslie Adams. You know him?" He waited for Weston to buckle his seatbelt.

"Yeah, we used to hang out when we were little, but it's not like we're good friends anymore."

Rhee pulled out of the parking lot and drove to the campus stop sign. "Left or right?"

"Right and then turn left at the next stop light."

"Why aren't you friends with him anymore?"

"He's kind of a brainiac," Weston said and then hesitated. The words almost came out before he calculated what he was going to say.

"And what?" Rhee asked. He used his gaze to put Weston under the spotlight.

"He doesn't hang out with anyone around here," Weston said.

"I've noticed. Why not?" He fired off the questions in hopes of getting to the bottom of it. Rhee could have guessed, but he wanted to hear it. Weston continued to pause before speaking.

"Don't know. I guess he's into other things. Turn right at the next light." He was more comfortable giving directions than answering Rhee's questions.

"Like what?" Rhee asked.

Weston shifted in his seat. He looked out the window at trees and other cars going by. "Like hip-hop and black people, I guess."

"Black people? I'm black, and he doesn't seem to be into me," Rhee said. Weston placed his hands under his thighs. Rhee smiled, knowing the kid was not going to go down any racial road with his coach. They drove down the street in silence while Rhee stole glances at Weston. "Can I ask you something?"

Weston shrugged his shoulders. "Sure."

"How did your mom die?" He saw Weston's laid-back attitude fly out the window. "You don't have to talk about it if you don't want," Rhee said, too quickly to be natural.

Weston looked out the window, and Rhee understood it was to hide the eighth-grader's face. Rhee waited. His head fought for a way to make things easier but failed.

"Car accident," Weston said, punctuated by sniffles.

Rhee acted as casual as he could. "Dude, I'm really sorry."

Weston trained his eyes on something out his window and then pushed the button to roll it down. "So was the fifteen-year-old kid who was joyriding with his homies," Weston said, so softly Rhee barely heard. It kicked him in the gut nonetheless.

Next to his career-ending injury, this moment was one of the most difficult. Rhee had no idea what to say or how to ease the moment. He reached over and patted Weston's leg. Rhee felt his player's knee jerk.

"I don't know what to say, dude," Rhee said from the pit of his stomach. He felt selfish because explosive, violent thoughts bounced around in his mind. Rhee visualized hunting down the joyrider and killing him, if it were his own mother. All of a sudden, Rhee felt he understood Weston a lot better. Rhee understood the kid's anger and bad behavior. It all fit. It all felt right.

"Coach?" Weston said.

"What's up?" Rhee asked. Now he'd jump on a grenade for the smart-mouthed kid.

"You're a pretty cool dude," Weston said.

Rhee had no idea what to say, so he let the silence say thank you for him.

Minutes later, Rhee drove through one of the most exclusive neighborhoods he'd ever seen. The expansive homes had acres of manicured gardens with long security-gated driveways. Each house was modern but custom-built to resemble an earlier and more stylized period of architecture: large antebellum columns of Greek revival, sweeping curved steps of Federal colonial, and ornate Spanish-style homes with balconies and tiled roofs.

"Damn, look at that one. I can't believe only one family lives there," Rhee marveled. He pointed at a grand Georgian-style home. It sat back off the road on two or three acres of land.

"Only one family does live there," Weston said.

"How you know that?" Rhee asked.

Weston turned his gaze away from the house, disinterested. "'Cause it's mine," Weston said.

Rhee nearly drove off the road. He looked at Weston to see if he was joking. He wasn't. Rhee hoped the weight between them had lessened. "Hey, how much ransom money do you think I could get for you?"

Weston looked up. Rhee waited for him to laugh, but he didn't. "Not much. Why? What are you planning?" He looked at Rhee suspiciously.

"I'm not planning; this is strictly a spontaneous train of thought. I'm improvising." He stole glances at Weston, who looked away and avoided Rhee's eyes. "I'll let you go home in exchange for the Hummer."

"My dad will probably just tell you to shoot me and dump the body," Weston said. Not a hint of sarcasm in his voice.

Rhee shot a couple glances at Weston. The kid forced a smile, but Rhee felt he was not joking in the least bit. "Things aren't perfect with pops, huh?"

"Not exactly," Weston said.

Rhee drove a little ways in silence. He thought about the cold shoulder he was getting at home from his own dad. More importantly, he thought of the conversation about Weston's mother. "We can start our own club. My pops and me aren't hitting it off too good either."

Weston's eyes widened. He stared at Rhee. They gave each other a few sympathetic glances at one another, until Weston pointed. "That's it," Weston said.

Rhee looked to his left. His mouth opened. He slowed in front of an immense home. It looked like a compound. "That's it?" Weston nodded. "You're telling me Leslie Adams lives in that little city?"

"Yep."

Rhee stared in disbelief. "Dude, that's a big-ass crib. Does it have its own zip code?"

Weston shrugged his shoulders again.

"His daddy must have more money than your daddy," Rhee said. "From the looks of your house, your daddy has some serious ends too."

Rhee's comment brought a wide grin to Weston's face. Rhee was happy some of the weight had lifted.

"My daddy has more money than a lot of people. His daddy has more money than God," Weston said.

Rhee tried to figure out where the property began and ended. That was going to take some driving time. "What the hell does he do for a living, rob banks?"

"Why would he rob banks when he owns them?" Weston shrugged his shoulders again like it was no big deal.

"Any of you guys ever get used to having all this money?"

"I don't know what you mean."

"Why do you guys go to school at all? I mean, why don't you just hop a plane and travel the world until you're around thirty and then come home and collect all the interest from your inheritance?"

"I don't know. Maybe if we hopped on a plane and didn't come back till we were thirty, there would be no inheritance."

"You may have a point, but you people are something else, my man," Rhee said.

"What do you mean, you people?" Weston asked.

Rhee turned the car into the long tree-lined driveway and slowly glided up to the massive, ornate, wrought-iron security gate. "You people. Like you people who are born into all this bling." Rhee rolled the car down a long driveway and found a gate that was built to make people keep driving on by. There were even security cameras in trees. Rhee pulled up to a keypad with an intercom. It gave him a double take before he reached out and pushed a small square button on a keypad.

"Is there some catchy phrase that keeps a brotha' from getting shot?"

Weston smiled slow and wide. "You could try, 'please don't shoot.'"

"Oh, so you're a comedian and a terrible basketball player."

"You're too easy, Coach."

"OK, wise guy. The minute I hear gunfire, you're a human shield."

A man's voice came over the intercom. "May we help you?"

He sounded formal and all business. Rhee looked at Weston. They both covered their mouths to suppress their simultaneous laughter. Rhee found his composure. He found the bass in his voice and spoke.

"Ah, yes, I'm from the faculty of Joaquin Moraga. I'm here to discuss an after-school program with Leslie Adams," Rhee said.

There was a silence, until the gate slowly pushed toward the Adams's home. Rhee rolled the car into a property that appeared to have several houses. When they came to an opening in the tree-lined estate, a house came into view that was the largest Rhee had ever seen. The massive brick structure had more windows and fireplace chimneys than he could count. There was a huge fountain at the top of the circular driveway. He turned off the engine and leaned back in his seat. Rhee stared straight ahead, processing his game plan.

"You know you're wasting your time, right?" Weston asked.

"What do you mean?" Rhee asked.

"He'll never come out for the team."

They both sat in silence, until Rhee quickly wrapped his hands around the door handle and pulled. "This is a black thing, between two black guys, so stay out of it," Rhee said.

Weston cracked an uncomfortable grin. The door swung open, and Rhee placed one foot on the ground.

"Want me to come with you?" Weston asked.

Rhee turned around and looked at Weston then at the large

mansion. Rhee gasped as the enormity of the home overwhelmed him. He shot out of the car, closed the door, and then turned around. He stuck his head in the window. "If things don't go well, I'm going to steal something and run like hell back here. So have the motor running."

Weston laughed. "Is that also a black thing?"

Rhee pointed at him. "You're not as dumb as you look."

"Thanks, Coach, you're like a serious confidence booster."

"No worries. If you hear any gunshots, make a run for it and save yourself."

Rhee spun around and headed toward the front door. He took brave steps up a flight of marble stairs to the massive double mahogany doors. He stood on the front steps and looked up to notice the home was a towering three stories. He raised the heavy brass lion's claw that was a doorknocker. It was mounted on a large brass plate. Rhee raised the lion's claw and let it fall on the brass plate, four times. The sound was deep and echoed like someone was trying to beat the door down with a battering ram. He stepped back to appreciate the enormous size of the door.

The door creaked open, and a distinguished older man stepped out into the sunlight. He was the man Rhee had seen chauffeuring L.A. back and forth from school.

He was almost the same height as Rhee. He had a long face with gray temples and sideburns. He was dressed in dark pants and a white starched shirt. A speechless Rhee was fascinated that he was standing in front of a real manservant. All of a sudden, he felt underdressed in his tracksuit and sneakers.

"Can I help you, young man?" the man asked. He didn't sound British, like in the movies Rhee had seen. His accent was homegrown, like Rhee's.

Rhee extended his hand and immediately wanted to retract it, but it was too late. "Please to meet you." He waited for the man's response. The man did not offer his hand to shake but nodded politely.

"Clayton Weatherspoon."

"Please to meet you, sir. I'm looking for Leslie Adams." Being polite and well mannered served him well. Clayton looked Rhee up and down.

"Senior or junior?" he asked. His tone was not impolite, but it was definitely not warm. He was a professional through and through.

"Junior, I think. Unless senior is an eighth-grader at Joaquin Moraga," Rhee said.

Clayton never changed his expression or demeanor. "Who may I say is requesting his audience?"

Rhee started to answer, when a small devil appeared on his shoulder. "Michael Jordan," Rhee said.

He waited for Clayton to laugh, but Clayton looked Rhee up and down again, never giving away if he knew Rhee was Michael Jordon or not.

"One moment, Mr. Jordan." He turned and walked into the home. Rhee peeked inside, his breath taken away at the sight of the gymnasium-sized entry hall, a big gymnasium.

A few moments passed before L.A. came to the door. He wore an over-sized Philadelphia 76ers NBA T-shirt, with a large number three in the middle. His jeans bunched at his ankles from being pulled down low. He had on a pair of yellow Timberland hiking boots. When he saw Rhee, he sucked on his teeth and frowned.

"What are you doing here?"

Rhee straightened his back to emphasize his steep of height over the younger boy. "Leslie? Is that you?" Rhee noticed the involuntary cringe the eighth-grader gave at the sound of his real name.

"Nobody around here is buying what you're selling, so bounce on outta here, Mr. Hoorider," L.A. said. He turned to head back inside when Rhee tried to lasso him verbally.

"Hold up. I didn't come out here to throw down with you. I came out here to ask you something."

L.A. squared on Rhee and threw up his fingers like an MTV rapper. "So why don't you say what you gots to say and bone-out,

Saddidy?"

"Come, little man. Lighten up. You're not all hard like you act. I know there is a whole different side to you so let's just get down to business. Is that cool?"

"Nah, it's not cool. It's not cool at all," L.A. replied. He started back inside. Rhee shoved one foot in the massive doorway.

"Come on, 'Shorty.' You know why I'm here. I heard you were the smartest kid in the universe, so stop fronting."

"How long you been on the crack pipe, Coach?" L.A. asked.

"Only thing I smoked was the guys I played against and the scoreboards. And that's 'cause I had heart to back up my skills," Rhee said. "I thought maybe you had the same."

Rhee searched for something in the kid's expression that indicated Rhee was getting inside his head, but L.A. only sucked on his teeth and grabbed his crotch.

"Come on, little man. Do you want me to beg? You got skills and mad talent, and we could use you."

"No, Mr. Jordan, I don't want anybody to beg. I'm just not interested in playing with a bunch of rutti poo chumps," L.A. said.

Rhee started to feel uncomfortable. He knew his anger might take this whole situation in the wrong direction. He thought about discipline. He took a deep breath.

"Ah-ite then. That's your choice, Slim Shady, but let me tell you something about those chumps. They may not have an ounce of your talent, but they got something that you seem to be lacking in spades, spade. It's called courage. I'm sure you have the brain mass to figure out what that means."

L.A. gave his back to Rhee but turned around again. He stepped out into the sunlight and pulled the large door to a crack. Birds chirped throughout the surrounding beautiful grounds, creating a warped soundtrack for L.A.'s hard-core façade.

"Why are you doing it anyway?" L.A. asked.

"Doing what?" Rhee asked. He raised his shoulders and showed L.A. his hands, feigning ignorance.

"Why are you wastin' time with those poo butts? So you won a game. That doesn't mean anything. Those guys are a bunch of losers." His eyes burned into Rhee's with defiance.

"Who said I was wasting my time? You?"

L.A. dropped his hands to his sides. He tilted his head, and Rhee almost came out of his shoes when the kid they called White Chocolate mad dogged him. "I know who you are," L.A. said.

"Oh, is that right? Tell me who I am, then," Rhee replied.

"I went to some of your games. So you're a real baller, the next great pimp with all the bling bling. The papers said you could have skipped college and gone straight to the dance, but now look at you, coming around here like a Girl Scout selling cookies."

Rhee shifted his weight. The young boy's words cut into him, deep. The urge to grab the kid by his neck and squeeze the life from him welled up inside. Their eyes stayed on one another. Rhee itched to drag the young boy out of his mansion and slap him into humiliation. It was going to take every ounce of will Rhee had to back away. Somehow he managed it. Rhee stepped back. He shook his head and donned an uncomfortable grin.

"OK, little man, I can see you are used to having things go your way," Rhee said.

"You know everything, right Mr. Jordan?"

Rhee retreated further back to make sure his fist couldn't reach the kid. He looked around the property of a massive manicured lawn dotted with sculptured bushes and fruit trees. "Yeah, you livin' real chilly. It must be great to be born into all this money." Rhee continued to back away. "Yeah, dog. It must be great to act black when you never have to fight for anything. But what do I know? I'm just a coach trying to recruit a good player." He stared at L.A., who he could see was now getting uncomfortable.

"Ah-ite, then stick to coaching. I don't ask you why you act so white," L.A. said.

Rhee froze. He felt a volcanic eruption of anger while L.A. tossed in a gangsta sidelong glance for effect. Rhee stepped back toward the kid.

"What'd you say?" Rhee was so insulted it took time for him to feel how much he'd been dissed.

"You heard playa. You put me on blast by saying what you've observed about me. And I'm just saying what I've observed about you. What's good for the goose should be good for the gander, right homie?"

"What are you talking about?" Rhee asked. He was dazed like he had been judo flipped.

"Look in a mirror, playa. You act like you white as snow," L.A. said. "I act like I act, and you act like you act. What's the problem?"

Rhee was completely thrown. No one had ever said anything like that to him. He'd heard every kind of trash talking on the court, but no one ever called him white before. Rhee's lips curled back, his facial reaction giving more information than he ever normally would have volunteered. He struggled for a moment.

"I don't have to look in a mirror. I know I'm black," Rhee said.

"Yeah, right," L.A. said. He waved Rhee off with a teenage roll of the eyes.

Rhee wasn't having it. "What? You think I need to talk jive, walk like a gangsta, and hold my dick? Then you'd think I was black?"

"Whatever, playa. It's yo world," L.A. said.

The hairs of Rhee's neck rose. He was interested in L.A. He wanted to know what made him tick, but he was not going to take a busload of attitude from a thirteen-year-old wannabe gangsta.

"No, not whatever. I wouldn't say you're in the position to know what it means to be black. You're not exactly Malcolm X, little man," Rhee said. Contempt and defiance colored L.A.'s expression. "Talk to me. Use sign language if you have to."

L.A. sucked on his teeth and practiced improving his mad dog glaze. "Whatever." Rhee's kettle whistled from the boiling steam of ire.

"Boy, you better be glad you're standing in front of your house and not in the street. I'd beat you down like a cut snake. All you white kids who listen to rap music and watch music videos think you have any idea of what being black means? Oppression and bigotry is a bitch, not a privilege. Have you ever had someone lock his or her door in the supermarket parking lot just because of the color of your skin? Have you ever seen a lady clutch her purse and cross the street just because you were walking in her direction? You ever been called nigger, spear chucker, or baboon by someone who didn't even know your name?"

L.A. yawned and looked around like he was bored. Rhee stepped as close to the kid as he could without being charged for assault. "I may not act hard and talk like I'm from the hood, but I am black. I'll always be black, and don't you forget it, white boy."

"I don't need this. Go lecture someone else," L.A. grumbled.

"Of course you don't need this. You were born with a silver spoon in your mouth. What you need is an old-fashioned can of whoop ass," Rhee said.

"You finished, crackerjack?"

Rhee wanted to kill the little punk with his bare hands but slowly regained a modicum of self-control. He backed away to keep from choking him.

"Nah, playa, I'm just getting started. You supposed to be all that in the classroom, but you must not have read your history books. All that cool and hip-hop confidence you've adopted comes from black people who have actually had to fight their way out of oppression and degradation for hundreds of years. That took more heart and courage than you'll ever know or ever have. So you can go on with all that drink drank, gangsta armor you wear, but you and I actually know who is really frontin', don't we?"

"Nah, you are finished. I'm out." L.A. wheeled around and walked back into his house, his swagger in full regalia.

Before he closed the door, Rhee let his venom spew. "Boy, you'd be a real good reason to go to jail, but you ain't worth it. 'Cause you ain't nothing, and you'll never be nothing 'cept money." Rhee backed all the way off. He was spent.

L.A. turned and saluted with his right middle finger. When he slammed the large door, Rhee stood and stared at the brass doorknocker. It took all the nerve and control he had to not pick up a rock and throw it through one of the plate glass windows.

Rhee got back in his mother's car and slammed the door. His eyes were scorched with anger. He was so mad his hands shook as he started the car, and he temporarily forgot Weston sat beside him until the eighth-grader spoke.

"What'd you say to him?" Weston asked.

Rhee took a deep breath, pressed the gas, and heard the engine roar. He slowly turned to look at Weston. "I told him he had a nice crib," Rhee said as steam came from his ears.

Chapter 26

Role Model

It was Sunday, and Rhee slowed his mother's car to a procession of African-Americans leaving a Baptist church. All the women, men, and children were decked out in their Sunday best. Several women wore large ornate hats. The men sauntered in their sharp suits. Little girls skipped around in flowered dresses with frilly ankle socks. Little boys cast off their suit jackets to run free around the cars unencumbered by wardrobes. There were no millionaire sports stars or celebrities, but Rhee had never seen a finer looking bunch of people.

The minister stood on the steps shaking hands with the departing worshippers. Rhee had no reason in particular to smile, but he did. He navigated the car back into the lane of the road and drove on.

There was a lingering residue of anger that stuck in Rhee's side like a thorn. Less than a few days had gone by, and the unpleasant confrontation with the sassy rich kid stuck to him like glue. He had been accused of acting white. And it wasn't an accusation from another African-American. It was by a smart-mouthed little rich boy. What was wrong with the kid? Rhee drove by modest homes of people watering their lawns, taking groceries from their cars, etc. His mind went back to L.A.

He had it all, even mad skills on the court that rivaled Rhee's mad skills. And more than Rhee, the damn kid had two good legs. Rhee thought of the Fab Five documentary, where a large community of African-Americans were segregated from one another; one side was accused of being Uncle Toms because they came from good families and chose to send their kids to schools like Duke. The other side was maligned for being too street and thuggish by several of the college basketball fans.

He never thought of himself as a straight-laced, white- acting African-American. To him, he was just a kid who had fallen from grace. It didn't matter what he had been accused of; none of it brought back his star basketball career with a charted dial set straight for the NBA.

He kept driving and lost track of where he was going. He saw a street sign that read: Martin Luther King Jr. Boulevard. He finally had a small sense of where he had navigated the car. He drove under the Mason Dixon Line, which was called the Macarthur Freeway. He was now deep in the hood of Oak Town -- Oakland, California, to most.

He understood bad things could happen to people who didn't know exactly where they were going in this part of town. It was a place that you didn't venture into without a plan because a wrong move made you part of someone else's plan. Rhee just wanted to keep driving until some of his mental anguish subsided. The rundown buildings of the poverty-stricken residents encroached on the few well-kept homes of its working-class occupants. Rhee took in the sad realities of poverty and inequities and came upon a schoolyard where a young boy was alone, shooting baskets in a hoop without a net.

Rhee pulled up to the curb and noticed that the young boy shooting by himself was Kenny Providence. He had a Cleveland Cavalier's jersey on with the number twenty-three. *Since LeBron James returned home, he's been everywhere,* Rhee thought.

He drove his mother's car up toward the playground and got out. Weeds burst through cracks on the asphalt; broken glass and food wrappers were littered throughout. Rhee watched Prov practice his crossover moves; he was a spinning Earl the Pearl Monroe on the blacktop. Prov executed each move as if the NBA's best defender guarded him. Rhee walked toward Prov when the young boy finally looked up. Rhee flashed the kid a smile as he deposited jangling keys into his pocket.

"How long are you back in Cleveland, Mr. James?" Rhee asked.

Prov looked at him and the flash of recognition came to his

face. "Hey, Coach. What brings you to the hood?"

"My bad, I thought you were LeBron." Rhee said. "I was just cruising, trying to stay black."

"Once you're black, you can't go back, Coach." Prov set up for a jumper. He shot the basketball, which went right through the rim.

"You sure you're not Lebron? You shoot just like him."

Prov held the basketball. "Shoot, I wish. He's my favorite player, Coach. Just don't know why he's on blast all the time."

Rhee wanted to tie his shoelaces and get out there with the youngster. Prov shot the basketball, and it sailed straight through the rim without a net. Rhee trotted and retrieved the ball. His ankle felt tender, but he moved fine. "Lebron James is on blast because he broke the code."

"What code?" Prov asked.

"Back in the days of Jordan and Bird, Johnson and Thomas, all the best players liked to go against the other best players." Prov looked perplexed. "Ever heard of Jordan, Bird, Johnson, and Thomas?" He waited while Prov worked it out.

"Yeah, I heard of some of them."

Time stood still as a breeze blew through the air. Rhee was only four years older than Prov, but he knew all the old greats. His father had drilled him every day and made him watch classic NBA TV. Even when Rhee went to basketball camps with other All-Americans, none of them knew Charles Barkley, David Robinson, Jerry West, Elgin Baylor, or Gale Goodrich. He even knew Ernie DiGregorio. He knew playground legends like Herman the Helicopter and Raymond Lewis. He even knew some great players from the Jewish summer leagues.

"You ever heard of Earl Monroe?" Rhee asked. He bounce-passed the basketball to Prov, who caught the ball and placed it on his hip.

He shook his head. "Nah, I haven't." He spun the ball in his hands and sized up his next shot.

"He was one of the greatest players in NBA history. They called him Earl the Pearl." Prov soaked it in. "That reverse spin move I saw you practice was invented by him."

"That's cool," Prov said.

"Oh, he was more than cool. He was so cool they called him 'Black Jesus.'"

Prov held the ball, thinking. "I've never heard anyone called that."

"I promise, you never will again," Rhee said.

Prov shot the basketball, and it went through the hoop with no sound. Rhee caught the ball. He made a small pivot. His ankle continued to feel fine, but he knew not to push it.

"Why aren't you in church?" He sent a crisp chest pass to Prov, who caught it and let the worn basketball fall on the blacktop. He bounced it through his legs a few times.

"Mama makes me go to early service so she can go to work," Prov said.

Rhee thought about God and his own faith. He realized he'd not prayed since his injury. Before that, Rhee had prayed every morning and night and before every game. It made him feel ill that he hadn't had a powwow with the highest power upstairs. He was mad at God, and his instincts told him he'd have to deal with it sooner or later. Maybe God had dealt with him already.

He approached Prov and asked for a pass with an open hand gesture. Prov snapped a crisp chest pass to Rhee, who received the worn basketball like his hands were made of cotton. There was no sound. He still had soft hands.

"Where does your mama work?" Rhee asked. He bounced the worn basketball on the blacktop and noticed it sprung back up in the air at an awkward angle. The worn basketball was a little lopsided.

"She works for BART," Prov said.

Rhee smiled. He once got lost trying to take the Bay Area Rapid Transit train from Walnut Creek to Berkeley. He ended up in San Francisco, where there were no playground games.

Rhee bounce-passed the worn basketball to Prov. The young

boy caught it. His sneakers squeaked as he practiced a couple stutter step moves. Prov went around Rhee and did a reverse spin. The ball bounced off the backboard with a thud and glided through the rim.

"What about your daddy?" Rhee asked.

Prov stopped. He held the basketball. Rhee prayed the kid's father was not dead or in prison. "He's a security guard up at Berkeley. He works graveyard shift, so mama doesn't make him go to church with us."

Rhee was relieved he dodged a bullet on that one. He smiled. Providence had a father that was home, unlike seventy percent of all inner-city African-American kids. It now made sense why Kenny Providence had manners and a level of respect for others. He came from a solid household with two parents.

"Where's your posse?" Rhee asked.

Prov held the ball and looked around. He shrugged his shoulders high. "Doing they own thing, I guess."

Rhee looked around. The playground was dilapidated as much as any inner-city school. The tetherball poles had only rusty chains and no balls. The baskets had all been bent out of shape with no nets. "What's doing they own thing around here?"

Prov dribbled the ball. He stopped and tucked the ball on his hip with his forearm. "I don't know, Coach. Some people be going to church, some people be chilling or banging."

"Where are Cub and Rama?" Rhee asked.

Prov was about to turn and shoot, but he stopped, obviously uncomfortable with the question. It was as if he wanted to say something, but the words were forbidden.

Prov spun the worn basketball in the air. It bounced in front of him and jettisoned back to him. He caught it and bounced it around his back. Rhee took in the sounds of rubber hitting asphalt and appreciated how well the young boy could handle the rock.

"Cub is up in Richmond at his auntie's; Rama goes up north to see his daddy on Sundays," Prov said.

"Where up north?" Rhee asked.

Prov's face grimaced. He shifted and tossed the ball up in the air. Something made him unable to look at Rhee. He bounced the ball once, twice, a third time, until he held the ball in his hands.

"San Quentin."

Rhee stared at Prov. There was an awkward silence, and Rhee heard sirens in the background. The only thing Rhee knew about San Quentin was that it was a very bad prison for very bad people. That's why Rama had so much anger and mistrust in his eyes. Rhee sensed it from that first day he met the boys.

He decided to change the subject. "So, how did y'all meet Leslie Adams?"

Prov held the worn basketball with a frown of confusion. Rhee realized that Prov and his posse did not know L.A.'s real name. "L.A.," Rhee added.

Prov's forehead jumped back with understanding. "Oh, white boy with crazy game."

"Right," Rhee said.

"What did you call him?" Prov asked.

"Leslie Adams," Rhee said.

"Oh, yeah, Rama said he had some jacked-up girl's name." He held the ball and gave Rhee an awkward look. "I'm sorry, Coach. What was your question again?"

"How'd you guys meet the white boy with crazy game?"

"Oh, yeah. My bad. We all met him at a concert up at the Greek."

The Greek Theater was an outdoor concert pavilion up in Berkeley. The last time Rhee had been there was to see Lil Wayne. "How did you fellas end up hanging with Richie Rich?"

"We didn't know he was rich. We didn't find out until Rama told us."

"How did Rama find out?" Rhee asked.

"I'm not sure. L.A. and Rama became tight. They always do the hubby and marinate. Rama said white boy's parents have more money than LeBron and Tiger put together."

"So how did he make the grade with an Oak Town boy with a daddy in prison?"

"Don't know. All I know is he's real cool. Not like a lot of rich people who be acting all saddidy."

"Are you serious? You think that wannabe gangsta is real cool?" Rhee asked.

"I know he's cool. He always has us over to his crib. He lets us sleep over and eat all the food in the house. He helps all of us with our homework. Yeah, he's a real cool white boy."

Prov turned around and went to the free-throw line. Rhee stood dumbfounded. L.A. had the stamp of approval from a bunch of underclass kids from the ghetto. Yet the kid seemed to despise Rhee.

"I've got to shoot some throws. If I don't get home on time, my daddy is going to skin me alive."

Rhee watched Prov take measured steps to a makeshift free-throw line because the blacktop didn't have the standard painted ones. Hoopsters had to estimate where the line would be in this neck of the woods.

Rhee walked to the basket and rebounded Prov's shots. Most of them went straight through the rim. Rhee caught the shot attempts and bounce-passed them back to Prov.

"When it gets dark, without a net, how do you know if you made it or if you were a foot short?"

"Welcome to the neighborhood, Coach," Prov said, with a crooked grin.

Rhee watched him square up on the imaginary free-throw line. This boy wore the look of someone determined to get out of the hood. Rhee believed he would. Despite all the odds stacked up against him, Kenny Providence had a leg up on everyone. He had two parents who loved him.

Rhee spent the next half hour retrieving free throws for the young boy from Oakland. The orange glow of the setting sun made Rhee squint as he walked toward his mother's car with Prov.

"That your hubs?" Prov asked.

Rhee searched his pocket, pulled out jingling keys, "My mom's car."

Prov bounced the worn basketball around the car, excited. "This is fly. Are your parents rich?"

"Nah, not even. They just work hard," Rhee said.

"Dag, this hoopty is smooth."

"You want a ride home?"

Prov smiled wide. They both got into the car.

Rhee eased his mother's car to the side of the curb next to a modest but well-kept house: freshly painted, with a manicured lawn and blossomed flowers in the heart of the Oakland ghetto. Prov reached for the door handle.

"Thanks, Coach," he said.

"Anytime," Rhee replied.

Prov opened the door and stepped onto the sidewalk. He turned back and tapped on the window. Rhee pushed a switch to roll the window down.

"What up?"

"My daddy came to our practice game," Prov said.

Rhee felt his face flush with embarrassment. "Don't remind me."

Prov leaned into the window. "He talked about you after the game."

Rhee sat up in his seat and clutched the steering wheel. "Let me guess. I'm the worst coach he's ever seen."

"Nah, he didn't care about the game too much," Prov said. "He said you were special 'cause, even though you couldn't play anymore, you still trying to make something of yourself." Prov bounced the worn basketball close to the car.

"He said you're a better role model than most black folks 'cause of that. He told me and my little brother that you weren't going to end up in the streets 'cause you're going make something out of your life."

Rhee stared at Prov speechless. "You OK, Coach? I say something wrong?"

"No, not at all. I'm good," Rhee said.

Rhee was lost for words. Prov held onto the worn basketball and leaned further into the window.

"Coach, do you think I could play in college?" Prov asked.

Rhee smiled wide. "Prov, I promise you if you keep your head on straight and stay out of trouble, you can play at any college."

Rhee watched Prov celebrate by throwing the basketball high in the air. "Thanks for the ride, Coach."

"No problem. See you soon."

Rhee waved and rolled up the window. Kenny Providence waved back. Then both of them jerked when they heard two gunshots. Pop. Pop. It was the unmistakable sound of gunfire. Rhee rolled the window back down and looked at Prov with concern.

"You OK?" Rhee asked.

Rhee scanned the area from left to right. He looked in all his rear view mirrors.

"I better get inside, Coach. Thanks again for the ride."

With that, Kenny Providence ran into his house. An uncomfortable heaviness settled over Rhee as he pulled out of the driveway. Prov's neighbors watched him with curiosity. He wished the kid was going to be lucky enough to make it out of the neighborhood. Rhee drove off, worse for the wear.

Chapter 27

New Addition

Rhee clapped his hands. "Come on, Flash. Wake up." Asa's eyes were glued on the other end of the gymnasium. "Come on, Flash. Pull it out of your behind."

"Sorry, Coach," Asa said. His eyes kept darting across the gymnasium. Then the eyes of the other five players followed Asa's across the gymnasium. Rhee turned to see what distracted his players. His mouth opened when he saw L.A. standing just inside the double doors.

He leaned against the wall with his hands pressed firmly in his pockets. He wore basketball attire: long shorts, a jersey on the outside of a white T-shirt, and expensive high tops. What surprised Rhee was that L.A. wore the color maroon that matched the team color of the Eagles.

Rhee raised the whistle to his mouth and blew. "OK, five-minute water break." Rhee walked toward L.A. The six Eagles slowly dispersed, but they all kept their eyes on the situation.

"Salaam Alaikum, my soul brother," Rhee said and extended his hand.

L.A. pushed off the wall and turned to leave. "I'm outtie."

"Hold on a minute. Wait a second." L.A. had both hands on the door handle under the exit sign. "Just hold on a second, L.A."

L.A. turned around with an acid expression across his face. "I didn't come here to get clowned."

"I'm not clowning you, dog." Rhee forced a friendly smile "So, what's up?"

L.A. glanced over Rhee's shoulder. All six Eagles players stood together and stared at him. "I heard you had a long rap with one of my boys," L.A. said.

"You mean, Prov?"

L.A. kept his eyes trained on the six Eagles players, who all kept their eyes on him. "He said you was hella' cool," L.A. said. "He said you told him about the old great players, who used to want to play each other instead of being on the same team."

"Dang, you and Prov must have had a seriously long conversation. Anyway, I don't know if I'm hella cool, but I must be hella crazy to still be out here," Rhee said.

L.A. let his watchful gaze go from the Eagles players to Rhee's eyes. "Why are you out here?"

Rhee was a little thrown by the question. "Dude, honestly, I have no idea. I mean, I'm trying to get into college, but only a crazy person would want to coach this team."

"Are you going to stick it out?" L.A. asked. "Like stay the whole season."

"I'm open for suggestions."

Rhee looked back at the six players, who all stole glances toward them. He looked back at L.A.

"I'd be a liar if I told you I didn't think about walking out on these guys every day." Rhee laughed. "Now I just want to see how many games we can win."

"How'd you do it? How'd this team beat the Cardinals?" L.A. asked. "It's like, they're the second-best team in the league."

"A little luck and a little heart, I guess," Rhee said. L.A. looked over Rhee's shoulder at the other players.

"You want me to bounce?" L.A. asked.

Rhee played it cool. He wanted to come out of his skin. Was this kid really considering coming out for the team?

"Nah, it's cool. You can stay. You can even play with us if you like. It's your school. I'm down with it."

L.A. was like a nervous little bird. "I'm sorry for calling you white. I was just being a dick."

Rhee took two steps back and placed his hand over his heart. "Oh, my God. Did you just apologize? I'm gonna have a heart attack." L.A. dipped his head down to hide his wide smile. "Next thing I know you'll be telling me you want to play on the team."

Rhee feigned a laugh but measured the kid. He turned and looked back at his six players. They all pretended to not be eavesdropping.

"Believe it or not, there are actually some decent players just waiting to break out of the bodies of those bumbling geeks."

L.A. stayed true to himself by displaying his carefree attitude.

"So what up, Mad Skills? What other shocking news you gonna bring to the table?"

L.A. looked down and traced an invisible line on the court with the top of his sneakers. "I was thinking about something you said about them." He indicated the six Eagles players by raising his chin.

"What's that?" Rhee asked.

"They must have some heart. The Cardinals are a fly team."

Rhee glanced back at his team and noticed they were getting impatient. "Yeah, they might look like geeks, but they got heart."

"Some places it's cool to be a geek," L.A. said.

"Yeah, like where?" Rhee asked.

"Math and Science Club."

Rhee shot him a look. "You're in Math and Science Club?"

L.A. gave Rhee a defensive expression. "What if I am?"

Rhee looked at the kid and decided there was no way he was going to blow this opportunity. He gazed back at his team. All six of them sat down in a circle at half court. They looked bored.

"It's your move, kid." He held his breath while the kid gave Rhee a dead-serious look.

"Cool," L.A. said. "Is there an extra uniform?"

Rhee looked at L.A. with wide-eyed shock and then looked around. "What is going on, kid? Where are the cameras? I'm being punked, right?" L.A. fought off a grin. Rhee knew he had to act fast before the kid changed his mind. He held up his hand. "Wait here."

Rhee trotted over to his backpack and pulled out the uniform with the number thirty-two on each item: shirt, pants, warm-ups, and practice jersey. He offered L.A. the uniform. "I saved this 'cause I didn't think anyone should wear it."

L.A. reluctantly took the uniform. He looked it over, curiously. "Why? What's so special about it?"

"It's been my number since the eighth grade."

"Cool," L.A. said, and shrugged his shoulder like it was no big deal.

"Cool?" Rhee asked. "That's all you have to say after I poured out all this love?"

L.A. said nothing, but his expression was enough to satisfy Rhee for the moment.

"We're cool, right?" Rhee asked.

L.A. looked over Rhee's shoulder at the other players. "Yeah, Coach. We're good."

Rhee moved toward his other players. "Yo, Birdmen. Come check out our newest Eagle."

The six Eagles all stood up and looked at one another in disbelief. Asa started to move out of the pack when Doug grabbed him by the arm.

Rhee and L.A. approached the skeptical and distrustful group of players.

"What's this about?" Doug asked. He appointed himself as the spokesperson for the entire team. None of the other players dared to challenge him.

Rhee stopped in front of his players. L.A. stood just behind him. He appeared vulnerable, using Rhee as a shield.

"This is L.A. He wants to play with our team."

"So," Doug said. He folded his arms and flexed his teenage rebellion.

"What do you mean, so? This kid's a good player."

All the players shifted uncomfortably, but Doug held his ground. "We know he's a good player. He's a great player, but he's too good for us, isn't he? He sure acts like it."

"Yo, if we don't let him play, the NAACP will be breathing down our necks." Rhee laughed, trying to temper the mild mutiny with a little humor. No one laughed. L.A. dropped the uniform on the floor and turned to walk away.

"I knew this was a mistake," L.A. said as he waved his arms in the air. Rhee turned on his heels and shouted to L.A.

"No, hold up. There's no mistake, L.A," Rhee said. "Get back here, Cool Breeze." He picked up the uniform off the floor. Rhee wheeled back toward his six players. "I invited him to play."

"Then where has he been?" Doug asked.

Rhee looked at Doug and the rest of the team and then back toward L.A. He was across the gymnasium just feet from the door. "Yo, L.A. Come on now. Get back here," Rhee shouted.

L.A. stopped and turned around. Rhee motioned him with a hand gesture and then turned back to his team. "I'm the coach, and I say he's on the damn team."

The Eagles looked at one another while Weston inched forward. "Coach, there's no swearing in the church."

Rhee looked at Weston. "You right. You're right. My bad," Rhee said, apologetically. Weston stepped back into the circle of his teammates. Asa raised his hand.

"Why don't we take a vote?" Asa asked.

L.A. slowly returned to the group. "Yo, fellas. This is not a democracy. I'm the HNC, and what I say is gospel," Rhee demanded.

The six Eagles banded together in solidarity. Rhee stared at them in disbelief. He wondered if he had made a big mistake asking L.A. to join the team.

Asa separated from his teammates. "Coach."

Rhee turned toward him. "What's up?"

Asa inched as close to Rhee as he could. "What's an HNC?"

Rhee looked at Asa and wanted to laugh out loud. Only this wasn't the right moment to laugh out loud. Rhee was still recruiting. He raised his hands to his players. "Hold on a second." Rhee turned to L.A. "You know what HNC means?"

L.A. put on his stone face and nodded. "Yep."

"You wanna tell them what it means?" Rhee asked.

L.A. looked at the other six Eagles. He shook his head emphatically. "Nah, that's ah-ite."

Rhee turned back to his players. He cleared his throat and sucked in enough air to make his voice have more authority. "I'll tell everyone what HNC means if we win our next game." He checked the faces of all his players. None of them looked at their coach. Their eyes stayed glued on L.A.

Asa took a step toward L.A. and then looked back at Doug, who narrowed his eyes with displeasure. Asa extended his hand to the new recruit. "Welcome to the team."

L.A. glanced down at Asa's hand and then looked at Rhee. Weston stepped forward, so did Blaze, then Terrance and Gerry. Doug stayed back. L.A. stepped forward. He reached out and accepted Asa's hand. The other four players joined and welcomed him with more handshakes and pats on the back. Rhee narrowed his eyes and looked at Doug, who didn't flinch.

"Whatever," Doug said. He shot Rhee a disapproving gaze and then turned and headed for the drinking fountain.

Rhee followed Doug and caught up to him. "Yo, what gives?"

Doug looked over his coach's shoulder after he took a mouthful of water. He swallowed. His eyes trained on L.A. "That jerk shouldn't be allowed to play with us."

"Is there some sort of thing between you guys I should know about?"

Doug pulled his mistrustful eyes off L.A. He leaned over and filled his cheeks with water then spit back into the fountain. He wiped his mouth with his practice jersey.

"A few times I tried to get in a game with him and his friends. They laughed and shined me on. They told me I should stick to football and bull riding. I guess I wasn't black enough for them." His face reddened like he was going to blow a fuse.

Rhee held up both his hands and smiled. "Then there isn't any problem."

Doug turned his angry eyes on Rhee. "What are you talking about?"

Rhee patted Doug on the back and started to walk away. "You're black enough for me."

Doug tried to hold onto his contempt, but Rhee's comment got under his funny bone. Doug smiled.

Rhee ushered him to follow. "Come on, let's practice."

Doug slowly followed. "I still don't like the guy."

"Once you've knocked him down in rebounding drills a few times, it'll make you feel better." Rhee saw Doug try to contain his smile, but the offer sounded good.

"Sounds good to me," Doug said, with a sinister expression.

Chapter 28

Throw Down

Rhee was pleased the Eagles players had raised their level of competition. L.A. wore his new maroon practice uniform and was embroiled in a three-on-three game; his teammates were Asa and Gerry. They scrimmaged against Blaze, Doug, and Terrance.

Terrance tried to defend L.A. by using size, but L.A. easily broke him down and scored at will. The humiliation seemed to set a fire under Terrance. If he could not cover L.A., he was going to outscore him.

He responded by trying to outplay L.A. on offense. He made nearly all his shots. Asa, Gerry, Blaze, and Doug faded into the background. The three-on-three became one-on-one. L.A. and Terrance scored on each other at will. Rhee was mesmerized, though not surprised. A pure scorer against a pure shooter was always entertaining.

L.A. was spectacular. He drove to the basket, made no-look passes, beat his defenders off the dribble, and drained shot after shot.

"That guy is unbelievable!" Weston said.

"Yeah, he's good, but look how much harder everyone else is playing," Rhee replied. "When was the last time you saw Terrance play that well?" Weston turned back to watch. Rhee looked over at Weston, "Go in for Terrance."

"You want me to try to stop that guy?" Weston asked, his eyes wide.

"Do your best," Rhee said. "Worked for Terrance, right?"

"But I can't shoot like Terrance," Weston protested.

"Find a way to score even if you have to pass the ball." Weston stood petrified with uncertainty. Rhee blew the whistle. "Terrance, take a break."

Terrance held up his hands in protest. "Coach, don't take me out. I'm on fire."

Rhee blew the whistle, again. "Sub coming in."

Terrance threw his hands in the air. "Coach, I'm just finding my stroke."

Rhee picked up a basketball and snap passed to Terrance. "Find another basket and keep shooting."

"Should never mess with a guy when he's hot, Coach," Terrance muttered.

Rhee waved him off the court. "Well, find a way to stay hot all the way through our next game. That's when it counts." He bit down on the whistle between his teeth.

Terrance pulled on his jersey and ambled toward the sideline.

Rhee walked over to him. "How do you feel?"

"Like playing some more," Terrance said.

"Good. Keep that enthusiasm for the whole season." He patted Terrance on the shoulder. "You're a good shooter, Terrance. Keep that up, and you might take that to the next level."

"Like high school?"

Rhee bit on the whistle, hard. "In the right system, kid, you might tear it up in high school. Maybe even go a little farther."

"Are you saying I could play in college?" Terrance asked.

Rhee heard the question, but he was distracted. A bad feeling jumped into his gut and burned.

Doug had a crazed look in his eyes. He fixed on L.A. like a heat-seeking tracking device. He started to slack off his man defensively. Rhee's bad feeling got worse when L.A. tied Weston in knots with a killer crossover dribble. He drove the baseline and had a clear layup.

Doug streaked toward L.A., undercutting him after the basketball went through the rim. The boys collided and twisted. L.A. landed on his back.

Rhee ran toward them. "Back up, and give him some room." Doug ignored his coach and balled both his hands into tight fist as he stood over L.A., who writhed in pain. "Get away from him." Rhee blew his whistle.

Recovering, L.A. jumped up and squared off with Doug. "Are you crazy or just stupid?" L.A. asked. "Coach said back the hell up."

Doug stepped nose to nose with L.A. "What'd you say punk?"

Rhee got between them, but L.A. threw a haymaker and caught Doug on the side of his head. The punch didn't hurt Doug, but it awakened a beast in him. Rhee made a big mistake and turned around, leaving his back wide open and lost momentary track of Doug, who was now nitroglycerin.

"Knock it off," Rhee yelled, but it had no effect.

"I'll kill you, bitch," Doug grunted as he pushed Rhee aside, tackled L.A., and pinned him to the ground. He pulled back his fist and was set to fire a crushing blow.

Rhee grabbed him, but Doug was thick and heavy for his age. It was like trying to pull a small car out of a trench. As Rhee pulled with all his strength, he saw L.A. seize the opportunity. L.A. got off a couple wild punches that grazed Doug's forehead and cheek.

Doug snorted like a rabid animal. "I'll kill you."

The kid was a bull. His rage had increased his size and power by at least twenty pounds. He carried Rhee on his back. Rhee had no idea how strong the kid was as he managed to punch L.A. in the nose with his right fist and follow with a left to L.A.'s left eye. L.A. stumbled backwards and almost went down.

Rhee rode Doug like he was a bull in the rodeo. "Knock it off, both of you."

L.A.'s left eye swelled immediately and blood gushed from his nose. "Fuck you, punk motherfucker," L.A. screamed. Red spit jettisoned out of his mouth. Gerry and Weston jumped in front of L.A.

"OK, little girl. I'm happy to mess you up good," Doug spewed.

"No swearing in our church, dudes," Weston said with his finger close to L.A.'s face.

L.A. slapped Weston's finger away. Blood sprayed from his mouth. "Get the fuck outta my face."

Rhee managed to maneuver off Doug and get in front of him. Finding strength he forgot he had, he shoved Doug and the force sent him off his path. He went sideways. He beat his chest. "You want some more, tough girl. Come get it," Doug yelled.

Rhee shoved Doug again and now the kid felt the force of his coach. It distracted him long enough for Rhee to see in Doug's eyes the realization he was being outmanned.

"That's enough," Rhee yelled as he pointed a threatening finger at Doug. "You're on blast, and this is your last warning."

"He started it," Doug yelled back.

"No, he didn't," Rhee hissed through his teeth. "Settle down. Chill out."

Doug's gaze tracked over Rhee's shoulder to L.A. He pointed at him. "Come get it, punk. I got more than enough for your little punk ass."

"I said that's enough." He kept his glare on Doug to make sure the kid did not rush and try to continue the altercation. "It's over." He got right in Doug's face and put his finger on the kid's chest. "You wanna throw down with your bad ass self, then you have to go through me. I'm the 'Head Nigga' in Charge' You ready for that?"

Doug took a step back; tears of rage filled his eyes. Rhee's use of the 'N' word sucked the air out of the entire gymnasium. Doug's fists were large, tight balls. His chest heaved in and out. Rhee looked down at Doug's fist. They were clutched so tight the kid's knuckles were white. They were also scraped and scratched.

"Relax your hands right now, or you're gonna need them against me. You want to throw down, I'll be happy to go with any of you."

Doug backed away another step. He realized the situation might go to a place no one wanted. "That idiot means that much to you, Coach? You want a guy like that on our team?" Doug's voice cracked with each question. Rhee wanted to stay neutral, but he was willing to defend L.A.

"Yeah, matter of fact, he does mean that much to me. I asked him to come here and promised I'd have his back. Just like I got Gerry's back, Asa's back, Blaze's back, Terrance's back, Weston's back, and I got your back." Rhee looked at Doug square in his eyes. He was mad, but Rhee felt his anger came from a deeper place. Rhee noticed the lips tremble on this bull of a kid.

"You said I could knock him down," Doug said.

"I said you could box him out hard as you want. That's part of the game." Rhee pointed toward the visitors' bleachers. "Get over there, now." Rhee's voice was hard. "If I hear another curse word in this gymnasium, I'm gonna kick someone's butt myself."

Doug turned around and stomped off toward the visitors' bleachers. Weston and Gerry released L.A. His mouth and nose poured with blood. He looked like he was on the verge of exploding again.

Rhee pointed at the floor in front of his feet. "Get over here," Rhee ordered.

L.A. stayed where he was. Blood oozed from his mouth and nose. There was an accusation of betrayal in L.A.'s expression.

"I said come over here, right now," Rhee yelled.

"You best deal with that dumb-ass buster. Boy is crazy." L.A. touched his mouth and looked at the blood on his hand. "I don't need this bullshit."

"Swear one more time, rich boy. One more time." Rhee held up his finger threateningly.

L.A. pulled off his practice jersey and tossed it on the floor. "I'm out." He started for the exit.

Rhee turned to the rest of the team, who stood around, uncertain of what to do next. He pointed toward the home bleachers. "Everyone on the bleachers -- right now!" The players, taken aback by the fire in Rhee's eyes and voice, obeyed him, tripping over each other as they hustled for the bleachers. "At least we know what 'HNC' means," Terrance murmured to Weston.

"I can't believe Coach said that word in our church," Weston murmured.

Rhee grabbed a towel off the bench and raced after L.A. He caught him just outside the doors. He paced back and forth like a wild animal, shirtless. Steam came off his body. Rhee saw a few other kids gather around, pointing. He tried to put his hand on L.A.'s shoulder. "Hold up."

L.A. slapped Rhee's hand off. "You told him to knock me down?" He continued to pace and dab at his bleeding mouth.

Rhee glanced around and saw a few students start to make their way toward them from curiosity. They definitely didn't need an audience. He opened the door. "Back inside, now."

"Are you crazy? Get your mind right, Coach. I'm not going back in there unless it's to bust a cap in that punk's ass."

Rhee held the door. He looked over L.A.'s shoulder and saw a small crowd gathered around, all trying to see what was going on. Rhee tossed the towel and it hit L.A. in the chest. He had to catch it.

"Clean yourself up. Let's take our business back inside. Too many curious monkeys out here."

L.A. threw up both his hands. "Oh, hell nah." He walked in circles with his head down. One hand was a fist clenched; the other held the towel on his nose and mouth. "All of y'all are out to get me. I'm no fool."

Rhee's eyes darted between L.A. and the curious onlookers. The last thing he needed was one of the looky-loos telling the principal about what they'd seen. "I told him to box you out. I didn't tell him to take a cheap shot at you." He stepped inside the gymnasium and held the door wide open. "Come inside. Cool your jets."

L.A. finished one last circle and marched into the gymnasium. The second he got inside, L.A. stopped and wheeled on Rhee. He held up the blood-soaked towel, inches from Rhee's face. "He boxed me all right. You satisfied?"

Rhee let the door close. "I'm sorry. You're right. It's my fault."

L.A. pointed his finger at Rhee and spit furry at him. "Yeah, it's your fault. You set me up." L.A. touched his mouth and nose with the towel to see if it was still bleeding. It was. "I knew it was a mistake to come here. I knew you'd never watch my back."

Seeing the boy's pain, suffering in his eyes and on his face, filled Rhee with guilt and dread. He took a deep breath and struggled to be calm and deliberate. His words came out of his mouth with no conviction. "It wasn't a mistake, and I got your back."

"What? Are you high?" L.A. asked incredulously.

They looked at one another for several seconds. Neither of them moved. Rhee turned and looked to see what the rest of his team was doing. Five of the players sat together on the bleachers. Doug sat far off by himself.

Rhee turned back to L.A. "Look, you can leave but not until practice is over."

"Oh, it's definitely over. You best believe that." He kept the towel pressed on his face and glared at the other kids like they were his enemies.

Rhee picked up L.A.'s practice jersey off the floor and marched straight over to Doug. "Come over here," Rhee said. "Right now."

Doug slowly stood up and walked across the court behind Rhee, who handed L.A.'s jersey to him. L.A. clutched it in his hand but did not put it on. Doug stood a careful distance away and made no eye contact.

Rhee stepped back and pulled Doug by his bicep. "Shake hands."

"Hell no," L.A. said.

"Why should I?" Doug asked.

"I'm not asking you to be girlfriend-boyfriend. I just want you to be teammates." After a few moments of hesitation, the two boys reached and barely touched fingertips with no eye contact. "Go over there and sit down." Neither of the boys moved an inch. "Seriously. Go sit down before I beat both of you."

Doug eyed L.A. -- not in a friendly manner -- but to make sure L.A. didn't jump on him when he turned around. They separated and walked over to the bleachers, where the rest of the team sat in shocked silence. Doug and L.A. sat down on opposite sides of the other players. Doug stared at the floor; L.A. kept his eyes on the exit sign like a bird that wanted to escape its cage.

Rhee paced back and forth in front of his players, thinking. He stopped and stood in front of the team, staring at Terrance, who squirmed in his seat.

"Did I do something?" Terrance asked.

Rhee said nothing and then took two steps, stopped, and turned back toward all the players.

"When I first came here, I thought you guys were a joke." Five of his players looked up and gave their undivided attention. "My life was a shit storm." Weston started to say something and Rhee pointed his finger at him. "I get one, just one. OK?"

"Yeah, but you also used the 'N' word in our church."

Rhee looked at Weston and the rest of his players. "I'm sorry. But this is a black church so it happens more than you think."

"We don't like that word, Coach," Asa said. He kept his head down.

Rhee took inventory of his entire team. The boys were fractured. He knew it. He looked each one of them in the eyes, one at a time. "I'm sorry. My bad. It was uncalled for. I won't do it again. Rhee trained his eyes on Weston.

Weston nodded. "OK, Coach.

"Thank you," Rhee said and then gathered his thoughts. "Today I watched you practice, and I saw something I hadn't seen since I've been here. You guys played hard, really hard." Rhee noticed Doug look up for a brief second. L.A. still acted disinterested. "People fight and argue every day." Rhee looked at Doug and L.A., who both avoided his gaze. "Especially teammates."

It still had no effect on the two fighters. Rhee touched his own chest.

"I've had fights. You can't compete without fighting." Rhee's eyes volleyed between Doug and L.A. Rhee was afraid to lose them, so he spoke from his heart. "Look, y'all. I'm only a few years older, and I don't know what the hell is going on. I came here feeling sorry for myself; I still do. I was supposed to be somebody, you know. I was somebody." Rhee felt himself choke up. He knew he couldn't punk out now and cry, so he sucked all the air in that he could. "But now when I wake up, part of me can't wait to get here."

Expressions of surprise lighted on all their faces.

"We only have fifteen more games. You guys don't ever have to talk to one another after that."

L.A. looked away and murmured, "Bet that."

Rhee gave him a look and then continued. "No one even thinks we can win. They think our last game was a fluke. After watching you today, I think we can win. When I first came here, I didn't believe that." The boys shifted in their seats. A couple of them looked down after Rhee's confession. He continued, "Now I do." Rhee took his time and studied the faces of all seven boys, every one of their eyes on him now. Satisfied they all had taken an ounce of his conviction, he turned away.

He headed toward the ball rack. The wheels on it squeaked as he pulled it to the center of half court. He grabbed some basketballs and turned. "Anyone who wants to leave now, it's cool by me. I'm down." Rhee looked at Doug, and then he looked at L.A. "Anyone who wants to stay and see how many games we can win, I got your back. You still have a coach. I'll go to war with any of you 'cause I believe in all you knuckleheads." Rhee threw a ball to all the players except Doug and L.A. "Pair up, and shoot free throws. One day you might get fouled."

Rhee looked at Doug and L.A., who continued to sit away from one another. Finally, Doug stood up. Rhee rolled him a ball. Doug stopped the ball with his foot, looked down at it, and finally picked it up. Rhee watched him dribble over to a foul line with Weston.

Rhee held the last ball and walked over to L.A. He sat down

next to him. L.A. had his head down. He stared at the Eagles practice jersey. Rhee offered him the ball and waited. L.A. stared at it. Their eyes stayed on the ball until L.A. stood up, and Rhee handed it to him.

"Who am I going to shoot with?" L.A. asked.

"Me." He watched L.A. pull his practice jersey over his head. "Does this mean you're staying?"

L.A. dribbled over to a foul line. Rhee watched the kid with dried blood on his face and under his nose as he lined up a free-throw shot.

"It means I'm going to shoot these free throws and get the hell out of here." He shot and Rhee watched the basketball go through the rim without touching, iron. Swish.

Chapter 29

The Dougie, Jerk & Nae Nae

Rhee kept a roll of adhesive tape in his mouth while he kneeled in front of Weston and wrapped tape around his ankle. The rest of the players ran laps. "You know this leg is going to have to completely come off before I let you get out of doing your laps."

Weston kept his hands under his thigh so he could continue to hold up his ankle. He grimaced. "I swear I broke it, Coach."

Rhee shook his head in disbelief. He finished taping Weston's ankle and waited as Weston struggled to put his sneaker back on. "It's not broken, and it's not even swollen, so stop stalling."

Weston laced his sneaker, stood, and watched the other players. "Are you as surprised he hasn't quit?" Weston asked.

Rhee turned to see L.A. trying to stay up with Asa, but Asa pulled away from all the players behind him. Rhee raised his index finger to his lips. "Don't jinx it," Rhee whispered. Weston smiled.

"Forget I asked," Weston whispered back.

"I already changed the subject in my head," Rhee said, with a small smile. "Stop stalling, and go run."

He pushed Weston's back to help him fall in line behind the other players. Weston forgot to sell the fact that he was hurt. The kid never hobbled or even limped.

"Hey kid, that ankle looks mighty good for being broken," Rhee yelled at Weston, who looked down at his ankle as he ran.

"Oh, check it out, Coach. You are a miracle worker. I'm cured," Weston said. "You should quit coaching and become a doctor."

Rhee held up his fist. "You're cured all right, but you're about to get busted up for real," Rhee said, threatening. Weston quickly fell in line with the other players.

The tension between L.A. and Doug took the level of competition to a whole new height every practice. The two boys always seemed on the threshold of another altercation. Only, they turned their intense dislike for one another to the basketball court.

Rhee figured L.A. had never quit because he had something to prove. He watched L.A. one-up Doug with his skills. Doug accepted the challenge every day. He almost sprinted into the locker room to get dressed every time. The other five players sucked up L.A. and Doug's competitive oxygen.

Rhee routinely observed L.A. in his own world, off by himself shooting baskets away from the team, until Rhee blew the whistle to officially start practice. L.A. saved his entire personality and attitude for then. He hardly looked anyone in the eye and said no more than was necessary to let everyone know he still had the power of speech. He nodded to Rhee before practice, and he nodded on his way out of the gymnasium. He was the first one on the court and the last one to leave. He enjoyed his dominance on the court. He savored the moments when the other players gawked at his moves. He knew they admired his skills. It was obvious they longed to be just like him but knew they never could.

L.A. had a profound influence on the team; yet, as good a player as he was, the other players seemed to lack his atavistic feel for the game. The other six players never adopted L.A.'s natural rhythm. They played harder, but his street moves and smooth, dance-like quality had not rubbed off on any of them. He had soul.

Rhee wondered what to do about that. Their next game was only three days away. He had to get the six original players on the same page as L.A.

Rhee inhaled, stuck the whistle in his mouth, and blew long and hard. The seven Eagles turned and looked at him. "L.A., come here a sec."

L.A. stared at Rhee, doubtful, while he crossed the court. The kid was always careful how close he stood to Rhee. He treated him with the same caution he used for the other players.

"Come here. I'm not gonna bite you. I need to ask you something." L.A. inched closer, remaining at arm's length. Rhee stepped toward him. "Remember, the first day I came here, you and your friends were playing some tunes on the sound system?" L.A. nodded. The kid was unsure where this was going. "You have some of those CDs?" L.A. nodded again. Rhee could tell the kid was still unsure where the inquisition was leading. "Can you flip one of them into the sound system?"

"No doubt," L.A. said and cracked a smile. Obviously, he liked the request but still didn't get where Rhee was going with it. L.A. turned. The wooden floor squeaked under his heels, and he raced into the locker room.

"Yo, Coach. What's going on?" Asa asked.

"What's going on is I'm coaching the team, and you're on the team, Curious George with Goggles," Rhee answered.

Asa fought against laughing. He backed away and joined the other five Eagles players, who all stood on the baseline. They each held a basketball in their hands. The gymnasium was cloaked in silence.

Rhee waited patiently, until L.A. came out of the locker room and raced up to the scorer's table. He picked up his own basketball and joined his teammates on the baseline. Fifty Cent blared over the sound system. The beat was tribal and hard. The rap lyrics were laced with profanity.

Weston covered his mouth and yelled, "Yo, Coach. That isn't exactly church music."

Rhee blew the whistle. The seven Eagles players dribbled down the court. Rhee started to rock and sway to the beat.

"Everybody feel the beat. Try to dance with the ball," Rhee said.

He saw L.A. pick up what Rhee was trying to say. L.A. dribbled down court. He was Fred Astaire; he was Michael Jackson with the ball. His game, his weightlessness, his speed, his tightness, and his moves were synchronized to the music.

Rhee looked at the other players. They had improved their ball handling, but they were out of sync with the beat. "Come on y'all, try to feel it. Move to it. Basketball has a rhythm." Gerry raised his hand. "What up, Gerry?"

"Coach is you tripping? Have you been smoking tree?" All the players howled with laughter. Rhee pointed at Gerry.

"OK, just 'cause I'm only eighteen doesn't mean I'm not allowed to come over there and whoop on your behind like you were a baby."

Everyone laughed. Gerry held up both his hands in a mock surrender. "No worries, Coach."

Dr. Dre and Eminem now shook the walls. Rhee was in front of his players listening to the beat. He shocked them all when he broke out with a couple of old school dance moves as the Eagles watched. Their mouths opened in shock. Their eyes bulged from their heads in utter disbelief.

"You got to feel the beat. Let it move through your body," Rhee bellowed.

He assembled a few combinations of outdated dance steps. All seven of his players roared with laughter as he busted a move. Weston and Gerry fell to the floor and convulsed in hysteria. Doug and Asa pointed. L.A. turned away. Rhee stopped dancing. He raised his hands.

"What? Y'all don't know the Dougie or the Jerk or the Nae Nae?"

Rhee's players struggled to contain their laughter. Some of them had to hold their sides; others discreetly covered their mouths. Rhee folded his arms, defensively. L.A. covered his mouth to hide his bellowing laughter as well.

"What?" Rhee asked.

"Coach, that ain't the Dougie or the Jerk," L.A. said.

Rhee set him on fire with a laser stare. "What was it then?"

"We don't know what that was. Looks like it came from the eighties or something," L.A. said.

Rhee watched L.A. high-five with Doug and Terrance. The

entire team fell to the floor.

"I'd like to know what was so funny. I'm trying to teach you guys about the beat and rhythm of the game," Rhee said.

Asa let go with a loud cackle but covered his mouth. "Sorry, Coach." He attempted to apologize, but the laughter had seized his body. Asa tried to reel it in, but it erupted uncontrollably through his tight expression, his eyes sparkling as his mouth clenched. "It's just that -- " Asa had to hold his side with one hand and cover his mouth with the other.

"Just what?" Rhee asked.

"I've seen dinosaurs with newer moves." He had barely got out the last syllable when the raucous laughter returned and echoed throughout the gym.

The players laughed so hard, they all fell back down to the floor. Doug kicked his legs in the air. Rhee stepped back defensively.

"OK, so all of you who have the nerve to clown the coach. Would like to run some laps, liners, and mop-ups instead of getting hip to what I'm teaching?"

Doug stood up with his hands in the air so he was able to breathe. "Please, Coach. Let us run so we don't have to see you do that anymore."

Rhee stepped back and folded his arms defensively. "All right. Let me see one of you have the gonads to kick down more modern moves."

The players rolled over and looked at one another, daring each other on. DMX vibrated the speakers in all four corners. They all slowly stood up. Rhee was mystified when all seven players breakdanced, pop and locked, spun wildly on the floor, and contorted into the latest and greatest hip-hop steps.

"That's what I was trying to show you," Rhee shouted. The players stopped. They looked at Rhee and started howling again. Rhee waved them off and walked away in shame. "All y'all can go on So You Think You Can Dance, but you kill yourselves trying to play basketball." Rhee decided he'd had enough of being clowned. "Weston." His tone said he meant business.

Weston stiffened and dusted off his wide smile. A couple chuckles slipped out. "Yeah, Coach."

"Who was George Mikan?"

Weston looked at Asa, who stared back.

"Take your time 'cause if you don't know, all y'all gonna do mop-ups until Christmas." He acted like he had a watch on his wrist. "Santa Claus will be here in fourteen days, and I can't have all y'all coming back with fifteen extra pounds." He put the whistle in his mouth to show he meant business. "So let's lose the weight before you leave for winter break."

The entire team looked at Weston with panicked expressions. Weston's eyes rolled around, thinking. "George Mikan, ah, the first big player, ah, played for, ah, the Minneapolis Lakers."

All the players celebrated and high-fived until Rhee barked. "Gerry."

"Yes, Coach."

"Who was Wilt Chamberlain?" Rhee asked and immediately knew it was too easy of a question. His players knew what followed and formed a shoulder-to-shoulder line. Some of them continued to smile. Rhee was going to change that.

"Wilt Chamberlain was the only NBA player to average fifty points in one season," Gerry answered.

"Blaze."

Blaze raised his hand. "Right here."

"Jerry West," Rhee snapped.

Blaze stood straight as a soldier in boot camp. "Jerry West went to the University of West Virginia and played his entire NBA career for the Lakers and is the silhouetted logo for the NBA."

"Weston."

"Coach."

Rhee studied Weston, who looked like he was ready for any question. A slow smile spread across Rhee's lips. "What did Bill Bradley do after his NBA career?"

Weston deflated and pointed to Gerry and Blaze. "And they got Wilt Chamberlain and Jerry West?"

"Answer the question, Bentley Boy. We're all waiting for those pre-Christmas mop-ups," Rhee said, like a drill sergeant. Weston folded his arms and looked at Asa. "Why are you looking at him? Don't look at him."

"Bradley went into politics," Weston said, nonplussed. "He was a senator, and I don't like the look on Goggle's face."

"The name is Flash to you," Asa said.

"Whatever," Weston said, with an impressive roll of the eyes.

Rhee looked at Asa, who indeed sported a devilish smirk. "Mr. Flash."

"Captain, my captain," Asa said and went stiff as a board.

Rhee walked up to him, looked him up and down, circling. "You look like the perfect guy for the twenty mop-ups."

"Twenty?" Terrance blurted.

Rhee whipped around and used his eyes like a blowtorch. Terrance inched behind Doug, just out of Rhee's eye line. Rhee took his time turning back to Asa and eyeballed him. "Tell me Bob Cousy's first cousin's, sister's name." Asa looked at Rhee with the appropriate glaze of uncertainty to satisfy the eighteen-year-old coach. "Can't do it, can you?" Rhee asked.

"I mean, Coach, come on. Who could answer that?"

Rhee put the whistle in his mouth and took a stance like he was ready to frog march up and down the court. "OK everyone, line up for fifty mop-ups," Rhee shouted. He blew his whistle, turned, and marched toward the locker room, hiding the silliest grin as his team stood, bewildered.

Rhee heard moans and groans like troubled children. He turned back to his team, pointed in their direction, and winked. "Gotcha," Rhee said and howled with laughter. "See you chumps after the holidays."

Chapter 30

Second Opinion

The sound of dribbling basketballs and squeaky sneakers tore at his inner core. Rhee entered his high school gymnasium with a myriad of emotions rushing through his body. Mingled in was a feeling of guilt that he'd interrupted practice. It dawned on him that he hadn't taken the time to think that it was nearly three months into the school year and he was not attending any school for the first time in thirteen years. He needed to run something by his old mentor. Now it felt like a huge mistake.

Too late. Dr. Silva turned and saw him. A couple of old teammates saw him too.

"Hey, Coach," Rhee said.

Rhee's ex-teammates and some new players all shook his hand and dapped. Dr. Silva blew his whistle.

"Five-minute water break," Dr. Silva yelled. The players ran toward the water fountain like a stampede. "Rhee, how are you doing?" Dr. Silva asked. Rhee's old coach approached with his hand out but gave Rhee a big hug instead. "I see you're getting around like you're ready to get back out here and play."

Rhee smiled. "From your mouth to God's ears, Coach." He wished it were true. His leg and ankle felt better, but there was an occasional jolt of pain at random moments that reminded him of his tragic accident. "How's it going?" Rhee asked.

"It'd be better if I had a Rhee Joyce in the lineup, but we're competing." There was an awkward moment of silence before Dr. Silva cut through the pleasantries. "What can I do for you, Rhee?"

Rhee stared at his old mentor and tried to think of the right words. "Coach, do you remember telling me about that Maravich guy that you said was magical? You said he would have averaged nearly sixty points a game in college if the three-point line had been brought into the game."

"Yeah, of course I remember. Pistol Pete Maravich. He was one of the greatest offensive players of all time. Some might give a strong argument he was the greatest college scorer of all time. Why do you ask?"

Rhee looked at his old mentor and tried to find the right words. "When did he die?"

"January 1988. Why?" Dr. Silva asked.

Rhee's mentor answered the question so fast Rhee hadn't organized his next few sentences. He was at a loss for words, so he decided to let it out from the heart.

"I think he's come back. I think I'm coaching him right now." Rhee thought what he said sounded wrong but felt no other words were able to convey his message. Dr. Silva never batted an eye.

"Where is he? When can I see him play?"

Rhee pointed over his shoulder. "I got a job coaching down in the bay area, near Oakland," Rhee said. "We'll be starting up again after the holiday break."

"Congratulations, Rhee. I'm really proud of you." Dr. Silva looked down at his watch with a look of concern as sounds of sneakers returned to the court. "I've got to finish running practice. But stick around so we can talk more about your special player." Dr. Silva turned back to his practice, and then he quickly turned around and pointed at Rhee. "In fact, I have a great idea. I'll tell you what it is right after practice."

Rhee watched his mentor trot back to his players. Dr. Silva blew his whistle and shouted instructions to them. Rhee ambled over to the bleachers and found a seat. He sat down as the players positioned themselves around the court per instructions Dr. Silva bellowed. Rhee realized he was watching his old team and some of his old teammates. Rhee's face flushed hot. His hands started to sweat. A sudden nausea came over him. He quickly stood up and headed out of the gymnasium.

Outside, Rhee leaned against the wall and breathed deeply. Although he was light-headed, he eventually found his balance. He heard the faint sound of basketballs bouncing, sneakers squeaking, and then he heard the shriek of Dr. Silva's whistle.

Rhee was wakened to the reality that coming back to his old high school drummed up something he'd kept down as long as humanly possible. But now it came to the surface. Rhee leaned his head back against the wall and realized he wanted to play again.

Chapter 31

The Eagles Find Their Wings

A car rolled to a stop at the sidewalk in front of The Jungle. The passenger door opened, and out spilled all seven of his rich, white, middle-school players: Doug, Gerry, Weston, Asa, Terrance, Blaze, and L.A. They were all dressed in matching maroon sweats with a logo that read, "The Eagles." Their senses were on full alert after gazing out their passenger windows at dilapidated homes, corner drug deals, and scores of RIP murals honoring fallen loved ones from the neighborhood. The weary fourteen-year-old boys semi-filed behind Rhee and followed him to the outdoor, street ball courts.

Rhee stepped through the fence and found a seat on the metal bleachers that faced the courts. His players sat down around him. The air reeked of alcohol and cigarette smoke.

A game was in progress on each of the two full courts. The nearest full-court game had been temporarily halted by a heated argument, accompanied by a shoving match between two hard men who looked like they each had learned how to play basketball in prison. Profanity rained down like a torrential thunderstorm.

Rhee's middle school team sat next to him with their mouths wide open. He knew none of his players had ever been this close to pimps, junkies, drug dealers, and felons, who all had game or at one time had been legendary basketball players. All the players squeezed in as close as they could to their coach. He gave them all quick glances and saw their eyes darting around like squirrels that had gotten too close to alligators.

Asa leaned in close enough to whisper. "Coach, didn't someone get shot here not too long ago?"

Rhee shrugged his shoulders and nodded. "I think I heard about that, yeah," Rhee said. "Right after Christmas." Rhee watched a couple of his players turn white with fear. "Someone always gets shot around here for the dumbest reasons. I just hope and pray guns don't start blazing while we're kicking it."

Rhee didn't have to look at any of his players to know he had just put the fear of God inside them. But that's exactly what he wanted. It was exactly why he'd brought his eighth-grade basketball team to The Jungle.

He waved at a self-appointed sideline coach, who drank rotgut wine inside a twisted brown paper bag. "Happy New Year, Mister Green," Rhee said. Otis looked over at Rhee with his players. The clean-cut youngsters stuck out like seven sore thumbs.

Otis was the same disheveled, toothless man Rhee had known for nearly five years. His clothes were threadbare, but his sneakers looked brand new.

"Happy New Year is for white folks. Black folks have nothing to be happy about, 'cept a president white people hate," Otis said and strolled over, giving Rhee a fist-to-fist dap.

Otis placed the twisted brown paper bag in a safe place under a bleacher. He slid behind Rhee and tapped Rhee on the shoulder. Rhee smelled the familiar blend of alcohol and strong aftershave. "Good to see you Rhee," Otis said. His hot breath caused Rhee to pull back an inch. It made Rhee's eyes water.

"Good to see you too, Mr. Green," Rhee said, respectfully, because long ago, Otis Green once was touted as the best basketball player in America.

Otis inspected all seven of Rhee's middle school players. They all looked away as Otis sized them up. "You got five dollars I can borrow?" Otis asked Rhee.

Rhee glanced over his shoulder, smiled, dug into his pocket and pulled out three one-dollar bills. "Three is all I got." He handed the dollars to Otis, who inspected them and then counted to three silently.

"Then three is all I got now too," Otis said. He caught one of Rhee's players staring at him. "Whatchu looking at, boy?"

Asa snapped back around and pretended to watch the game.

Otis kept his eyes on all the players. He used the back of his hand to hit Rhee on the shoulder. "Whatchu up to, Rhee? You got yourself involved with some white boy walking association?"

Rhee looked at his team, who all looked away and tried hard to be invisible. He smiled. "Nah, Mister Green. I'm coaching them."

Otis reared back in disbelief. "Coaching them? You coaching these boys in what?"

"Basketball, Mr. Green. I got a job coaching basketball. I figured it was time for them to see how the game is really played," Rhee said.

"Hell, boy. These kids look kinda soft, like pink cotton candy."

Rhee's eyes swept the nervous faces of the Eagles. He smiled. "I was soft when I first came here too. Took a while, but you can't be soft and survive The Jungle. Right, Mister Green?"

"Sho' enough, Rhee. It worked for you so I guess it'll work for these sorry-looking whatchamacallits," Otis said. All seven fear-stricken boys diverted their gaze from the toothless professor of street ball.

Rhee smirked at their discomfort and turned his attention back to the game. There was little to watch at the moment because there was another altercation, and two men had to be separated. They yelled obscenities at one another until they were equally satisfied. The action finally picked back up.

Rooster yelled at the top of his lungs after he dunked the basketball. Rhee looked over. Rooster was the same ole dark, shirtless player who helped toughen up Rhee back in the day. He was still muscular and broad as a linebacker, like he was when Rhee first faced him. He wore his usual jeans and had run-down, untied sneakers. Rooster had to be over forty, but he moved as quickly and was as lithe as any of the younger players.

Rhee kept his eyes on Rooster while he beat his defender off the dribble, drove down the center of the key, and slammed over a player who was at least six foot nine inches. All the men on the sidelines howled in appreciation. They high-fived and were careful not to spill a drop of alcohol or drop even a roach of marijuana.

Rooster tilted his head back, screamed, and beat his chest again until he ran off the court, grabbed a brown bag off a spectator, and drained a large swallow of bubbly beer, which ran down both sides of his mouth. He handed it back and ran back down court -- just in time to swat an attempted shot clear out of bounds. "Get that weak-ass, Betty Crocker, Dr. Phil bullshit outta my house," Rooster yelled.

Rhee's team watched with their mouths still open. Otis nudged Rhee. "Rooster's been out of jail just under a week, and he's already back in form."

Rhee cupped his hands and shouted through them. "Way to bring it, Rooster." Rhee and Otis high-fived.

"That man may be the devil's best friend, but he's still got a little game left in him," Otis said.

Rhee looked around at all the faces. He noticed an ominous-looking man with a dark blue hoodie pulled over his head. The ominous man's face was silhouetted in a shadow. Rhee slowly pulled his gaze from him. "Where is Red, Mister Green?" His eyes lingered a little longer on the hooded man.

Otis looked at each of Rhee's players and then leaned forward. "Red got shot," Otis said.

Rhee sat frozen. "Is he dead?" He paid little attention to his wide-eyed players, who eavesdropped.

Otis picked up his brown paper bag and pulled a hard swallow of his beverage. "Nah, that nigga' ain't close to being dead." He shoved Rhee's shoulder. "He's not dancing too good, though."

"Was he robbing some place?" Rhee asked.

"Shit, no," Otis said. He held the brown bag in front of his mouth and then took a swallow. "His old lady came home from work early and caught that nigga' on the down stroke. She shot the girl he was with too." Otis laughed out loud so hard he nearly fell sideways.

Asa leaned into Rhee. "Somebody you know got shot?"

Rhee glanced at each one of his players. MTV made street life glamorous and cool to all his privileged white players. *Now they are hearing how cool it really is*, Rhee thought. He pointed at the court.

"Don't worry about it. Y'all watch the game and learn," Rhee said.

Blaze looked directly at Rhee. "Yeah, but who is going to watch us?"

"Just watch the game, Blaze. I promise you'll learn something."

"Like what, Coach? How to drink and point a gun?" Blaze asked. Rhee ignored the comment.

"They cool with us watching?" Weston asked. "I mean, it's not gonna make anyone want to shoot us for watching, right Coach?" He kept his voice low, and his eyes roamed in case he had to run for his life.

Rhee turned around and faced his players. The moment of truth had arrived. He looked at each and every one of them. "Watch? Heck nah," Rhee said. "We didn't come here to watch. We came here to play." Before anyone could protest, he turned toward the game, cupped his hands and hollered. "We got next!"

Rhee looked over all of his players, who shared the exact same expression, like they were rabbits being prepared for rabbit stew. Even L.A. looked petrified. "School is about to be in session, boys," Rhee said and gave them all a thumbs up.

"Oh God, Coach, you brought us here to die," Weston said. The entire group of fourteen-year-old rich white kids shared a look of utter panic.

Chapter 32

We Got Next

The losers of the previous game struggled to catch their breaths as they shuffled behind the winners to the drinking fountains. Rhee seized the moment to grab the court. He turned and signaled his players with his hands like a conductor.

"Come on, everybody up." The seven Eagles froze. Rhee knew their butts stayed glued to the benches on the sidelines because of fear. "Let's go, fellas. We got next. Get out here and warm up."

Rhee grabbed a couple of loose balls sitting near court one. He picked them up and waited until, one by one, each of the boys got up and straggled onto the court. Rhee tossed L.A. and Asa a ball each.

"Get some shots in and stretch out. Next game starts in a couple minutes."

Someone crashed into Rhee's back and sent him flying. He twisted, bounced a few times, and then checked his ankle. There was no pain, so Rhee turned to see the perpetrator was Rooster.

"Sorry 'bout that, little fella'. You got to keep your head on a swivel around here 'cause there is no telling when a nigga' might run into you," Rooster said with a grin.

Weston and Asa trotted over to Rhee. "You OK, Coach?" Weston asked.

Rhee wanted to laugh, but he held it back. He grabbed his back like there was a jolt of pain. "I'm good. It was an accident. Don't worry about it. Get back on the court and warm up."

"He looked like he did it on purpose," Weston said.

"It only looked like he did it on purpose 'cause he did do it on purpose," Rhee said, grimacing for effect.

Rhee stood and kept his back bent. His players were more concerned with him than playing. Rhee got what he wanted. He clapped his hands encouragingly.

"Let's go, Eagles. The game is about to start."

Weston and Asa turned back and reluctantly took to the court. Rhee looked up to the sky and said a silent prayer: *Please, God, no injuries or dead bodies today*.

He headed for the sideline. He spotted an open seat on the lowest metal bleacher and sat down. Rhee looked toward Rooster and his fellow tattooed, street-battle-scarred, criminal-looking teammates as they took the other court. They all looked back at the Eagles players and laughed. Rhee put his hands under his thighs and waited for the game to begin. Rooster rolled a basketball that hit L.A. in the back of his heel.

"Take the ball out, little girls. School's in session," Rooster hollered.

L.A. picked up the basketball and looked at Rhee, who clapped. "Take it to them," Rhee shouted.

L.A. tossed the basketball to Doug, whose foot stepped out of bounds and tossed it back to L.A. The game started.

Five of Rhee's players -- Doug, Gerry, Terrance, Asa, and L.A. -- were mired in a full-court game against five street players, all menacing and intimidating-looking men, especially Rooster.

Gerry crouched low in a defensive position. His feet shuffled with nervous, scared energy. He held his hand up and tried to stay with the Rooster, who dribbled the ball on the left baseline. Rooster scanned the court, looking for one of his teammates to set a pick. When no pick came, Rooster took matters into his own hand, as he lowered his shoulder, ran right over Gerry, and flattened him like a pancake.

Rhee winced while Rooster slammed the basketball through the rim, crashed landed on top of Doug, and shoved him. Doug did a soft somersault and got to his feet. Gerry stayed on his back. All the onlookers screamed with excitement. Rhee saw both his players manhandled in less than three-tenths of a second.

Rhee stood up. "Charging," Rhee yelled. He pointed at Rooster. "Play the game right, Rooster."

Otis stood up too. "That's right, Rooster. Learn how to play the game the way it was meant to be played," Otis said. "This ain't no damn football game. Lawrence Taylor had no place in this game. He was a hall of fame football player. You a hall of fame knucklehead."

Rooster grabbed his crotch and then gave Rhee and Otis the middle finger. Rooster ran down court and swatted at his arms as though he was irritated. "Damn gnats are all over me," Rooster yelled.

Rooster's admirers laughed hard, slapped their knees, and drank their hidden alcohol.

Rhee clapped his hands, encouraging Gerry. "Get up buddy. You're OK."

Gerry rolled over and peeled himself off the concrete. He looked at Rhee like he was crazy for putting the fourteen-year-olds in a game against tough, mean, street ball players. Rhee sat back down on the metal bleachers. His right knee bounced nervously.

Blaze cupped his hand and whispered in Rhee's ear. "Coach."

"What?" Rhee asked.

"Do we have a first aid kit?" Blaze asked.

Rhee looked down at Blaze like he was going to strangle him. Blaze shrank back as Rhee let his eyes turn back to the game.

L.A. dribbled around and actually dazzled the defenders with his ball-handling skills. Nerves zipped through him as Rhee watched L.A. bounce the basketball behind his back and through his legs. He crossover dribbled and took the basketball behind his back. L.A.'s defender lagged behind by a step. Gerry crossed the lane and set a screen. L.A.'s defender plunged into Gerry and sent him flying. Gerry tumbled and rolled over backwards.

Blaze put his hands over his eyes. "That's gotta hurt."

Rhee nudged Blaze. "Just watch and learn," Rhee said. "You'll be going in any second." Blaze looked at Rhee like he should be institutionalized in a psych ward.

L.A. beat his man with a killer crossover dribble, drove the lane, and went up for a layup. Out of nowhere, Rooster went airborne and swatted the basketball over the backboard, over the fence, and across the street.

The onlookers leaped to their feet and yowled.

Rooster placed his sweaty chest in L.A.'s face. "Welcome to my house, little man."

Otis stood up, gestured wildly at Rooster. "'Lot of good that does, Rooster. The kids still get the ball."

Several young kids scurried after the ball. It was as close to stardom an eight- or nine-year-old received at The Jungle.

When two boys returned grappling with the basketball, trying to rip it from each other's hands, the game started back up.

The Eagles passed the basketball around like a hot potato. Rhee rose up. "Shoot the ball," he hollered.

Terrance received a behind-the-back pass from L.A., turned, and fired. Just when he released the shot, a muscular, tattooed Mexican man shoved him in the chest. Terrance went down. The basketball rattled around the rim and went in. The tattooed Mexican man held his hand in front of Terrance and hoisted him off the ground.

"Good shot," the tattooed defender said with an evil smirk.

Rhee clapped and held up one hand. "That's one," he yelled, clapped hard, and rolled his fist in a circle.

Rooster threw a lazy pass to one of his teammates, when L.A. jumped in front of the pass and stole the ball. He threw it back out to Asa, who was so surprised he almost lost the ball.

Rhee stood up. "That's it, guys. Take it to them."

Asa dribbled the basketball in front of a bearded man, who looked like an Aryan Nation prison inmate. His head was bald. He was covered with satanic tattoos. The bearded man plucked the basketball from Asa's grasp and raced down the court. He had a clear layup but bounced the basketball high. Rooster flew through the air and then dunked it backwards with two hands.

Rooster turned to the crowd, all yelling his name in praise. Rooster beat his chest with his fist and spread his hands on his chest like Superman. "It's 15-2. Next!" Rooster yelled at the top of his lungs.

The five defeated Eagles players ambled off the court, dejected. L.A. marched straight up to Rhee, who stood on the sideline. "Yo, Coach. Can we bounce from this hell, now?"

Asa followed right behind him. "Yeah, Coach. Let's hit the road before sundown. These guys might turn into wolves and vampires, like I know they are for real." Asa waved his hand in front of his own nose. "And they all smell like alcohol."

Rhee stared right into Asa's eyes. This was all part of Rhee's mad plan. "They only smell like alcohol because they've been drinking all day."

"Yeah, that might make you smell like alcohol all right," Doug said. He waved his hand in front of his own nose.

Rhee gave his players a look of determination. He knew they wanted to leave, but he wasn't going to let them go. Not yet. It wasn't time.

Chapter 33

Fearless

"Come on, Coach. Let's just quit while we're still alive," Terrance said. All his teammates agreed with emphatic nods.

"Now, listen to me. There is no way we're going to bail like a bunch of little punks. We're not tucking our tails between our legs and hiding. We're just getting started, fellas."

All seven of his players looked at Rhee like their eighteen-year-old coach had also been drinking. They reluctantly gathered around him, leaned over, and clutched their shorts. Rhee knew from their expressions they wanted to run, but he needed to prove his point to all seven of them.

"Not yet. That's not the plan," Rhee said.

"Coach, maybe sitting around here gave you a contact high." Gerry said. "All the tree getting smoked on the sideline is messing with your mind."

Doug straightened and wrapped his fingers behind his head. He sucked air, desperately. "High or not. We need to get gone, Coach. I promise I'll run a thousand laps -- whatever you want."

Weston hunched over with his hands planted firmly on his knees. "If it's money you want, we're all rich. We can rob our parents," Weston said. "We're too young to die."

Rhee waved all of them off. He was ready to share his crazy plan. "Everyone shut up a second, and listen to me." He knelt in front of them and showed them great enthusiasm. "Listen up. Next time we go out there..."

"Next time?" Blaze asked, incredulous.

Rhee shot him a cold gaze. "Next time we get on the court, forget about their size, their color, their age. Forget about the prison tattoos. I want you to forget about everything except playing the game."

"Those are prison tattoos?" Blaze asked.

"So there's going to be a next time?" Terrance asked. His eyes widened. "That's plain crazy talk, right Coach?" Terrance asked.

Rhee studied all of his players individually. None of them were able to meet his piercing gaze. Rhee turned to Terrance and pointed at him. "Terrance, shoot the damn ball; stop trembling with fear."

Rhee then looked at Asa. "Flash, I want you to run like the wind. Listen to me. I have played against all these guys, and none of them are faster than you. Not one of them can outrun you. I promise." Asa was mystified by Rhee's words.

Rhee's eyes searched and found Gerry. "Gerry, I want you to try to block every shot that's put up. I don't care if it's taken from half court." Gerry appeared puzzled. Rhee wasn't going to wait for him to figure it out.

Rhee found Doug. "Doug, I am giving you permission to knock someone down. If you get shot, I'll tell your parents you died gallantly."

"Thanks, Coach. That's really gonna make me feel better in heaven," Doug said.

"Shut up for a second, and pay attention. I played out here since I was your age, and I'm still alive."

"Coach, didn't you also have a career-ending injury out here?" Asa asked.

Rhee was temporarily thrown. He looked at the court. A game was in progress, but he saw the spot he went down, where his ankle betrayed him and nearly severed itself from his leg. A chill went through his body. He took a deep, cleansing breath and let it out slowly, and then he looked down at Asa.

"You're right. I got hurt here." He looked at all of his players one at a time. "But I left everything out on that court every time I came to play. I pray to God that he will show me enough mercy to allow me to get out there again. And you know why?" Rhee looked at each of his player's blank expressions. He touched their jerseys one by one. "Because I learned to play without fear. No matter who I played against. No fear fellas. No fear. That's the only reason I brought you here today." Rhee gave each of them a long gaze. "I want you to go back out there and pay them back for what happened to me. I want you all to just play, but play without fear. I want you to leave every ounce of energy you have on that court." Rhee waited for one of them to break through their cloud of fear and believe, but all he saw was sagging shoulders from their collective self-doubt.

Only Doug nodded. Rhee glanced at L.A. and saw he wasn't afraid, only bewildered. Rhee saw there was a glint in his eyes. L.A. turned and watched the game going on behind them. There was something in his expression Rhee liked. He had to catch it.

"Yo, White Chocolate with mad skills." L.A. looked back at Rhee. "You ready to show these old guys how it's done?"

He waited until L.A. nodded. Rhee smiled at L.A. and then shared the same smile with the rest of his players. "This is street ball. You already know how to play street ball. Remember what you did to the Cardinals. Out here is playground rules, so you've got a license to run and gun, and you know how to do it 'cause I taught every one of you." His players all stared at him.

"Forget about defense, and outscore your man?" Terrance asked.

"Hell, yeah. That's what I want to hear," Rhee said.

His ambition surprised his players since it showed how much he believed in them, and it seemed to pump them up. They all glanced at each other wide-eyed as the sounds of yelling and bouncing balls clamored in the background. Rhee turned away from them before his players had a chance to protest.

"We got next," Rhee shouted and then turned back to his team. "If you all are willing to stand up to these felons and thugs, then playing other eighth-graders is going to be a walk in the park, not this park. I'm talking Disneyland during the day." A couple of the players laughed. Rhee knew he had got under their skin. Finally.

He put his hand out.

"Who is with me? Who is willing to go to battle as a team?"

L.A. was the first one to put his hand on Rhee's hand. "Let's do this." He looked at his teammates. "No punks on the Eagles."

Doug put his hand in, hard. "Hell nah. No punks."

Asa jumped in with both his hands. "No punks."

"We die, we die together," Weston said and put his hand in.

Terrance and Gerry put their hands in. Solidarity.

Rhee smiled. For the first time since he went down, he felt like going to battle on the court. He needed this moment. He wanted this moment. His veins felt hot with anticipation, just like when he played.

"Go Eagles!" they all yelled.

Chapter 34

Eagles Fly

Rooster sailed through the air for a slam dunk and finished the game with a two-handed jam. He hung on the rim and finally let himself fall back to earth. The defeated team walked off the court, panting from being out of breath, heads bowed, and sour faces glistened with sweat.

Rhee studied his players. He looked each one of them in their eyes. He felt their excitement. He felt their anxiousness. He felt their fear temporarily subside. "Go warm up."

The players walked onto the court and warmed up. As they did, Rhee watched Rooster walk over toward the sideline. He stared at Rhee, and Rhee stared back. A man on the sideline handed a beverage wrapped in a brown paper bag to the big man. He took a few swigs and burped. Rhee shook his head. Rooster walked over to Rhee. They each made fists and dapped.

"Haven't seen you around here for a good while," Rooster said with a small grin.

"I heard you've been on vacation," Rhee said. He watched his players practicing blocks and passes. They looked back to see him talking to Rooster.

"Three squares and a cot," Rooster said.

A loose basketball rolled in Rhee's direction. He picked it up and bounced it to Terrance, who wheeled around and shot. The basketball went straight through the net, swish.

Rhee looked at Rooster and smiled. "How old are you now, sir? You were approaching a hundred when I was fourteen," Rhee said. "I'm almost nineteen, so you must be 103 or 104, right?"

Rooster folded his arms and watched Rhee's team practice free throws. "My mama lost my birth certificate after I was born, so I have no idea, but you might be right. I can't run as fast or jump as high, so I must be around a buck fifty by now."

They shared a laugh. They both turned back and looked at the ominous-looking man, still silhouetted by his hoodie.

"I see he's up there again."

"He's the biggest pimp out of all us out here. You should know that," Rooster said. They looked at each other for a long while. "Niggas told me you may not play no more."

Rhee turned his eyes on back to his team. "Early retirement, maybe," Rhee said.

"You'll be back."

"What makes you think that?"

"The look in your eyes, young buck. You wanna be the king again."

"From your mouth to God's ears?"

"Just tell him what you want. Do the work and he'll meet you half way. That's why I'm the king now," Rooster said.

Rhee pulled his gaze off his players and stared Rooster in the eyes. "You preaching, now?"

"Just telling it like it is, young buck."

"You were always king, Rooster. I was just your stand-in while you were on vacation once in a while."

Rooster studied Rhee. "There was a time you were king. And you will be king again. Maybe not out here, but some place bigger. Believe that."

"Thank you, sir," Rhee said. Rooster offered no response to Rhee's thanks. After a moment, they shook hands, hugged, and patted each other on the back. "Don't ease up on them. They need this," Rhee said.

Rooster saluted with three fingers and gave Rhee a nod. "The king eases up on no one. You should know that." He turned and walked away.

Rhee watched him go look for some more alcohol. He found someone's brown bag, guzzled from it, and corralled his teammates.

Asa dribbled over to Rhee. "You played against that guy?"

Rhee turned just in time to see Rooster, high over the rim, slamming the basketball with thunderous authority. "Yep, and proud of it, just like you will be one day."

"How can he play like that and drink alcohol at the same time?"

Rhee looked down at Asa for a while. "I can't tell you, Flash. What I can tell you is that with the exception of my dad and my coach, that scary looking man taught me more about the game than anyone else."

Asa kept his eyes on Rooster, who was now on the sideline drinking from yet another brown bag. "He really shot someone?"

"Not this week, anyway, but the day is still young. Are you ready?" He gave Asa a smile and saw his player swallow back the fear that started to rise.

"I heard him say you were the king," Asa said.

Rhee gave Asa a stern look. "You weren't supposed to be eavesdropping. You were supposed to be warming up. Besides, Rooster puts a lot of salt and pepper on everything."

"Salt and pepper?"

"Exaggerates," Rhee said.

Asa raised his hands to his side in defense of himself. "I don't think so, Coach. My dad told me the same thing."

Rhee shrugged his shoulders. "It's time for you and your teammates to be kings for the day."

Asa smiled wide. He turned and dribbled back to take a couple more shots.

Rhee looked over toward Rooster and saw him play boxing with a young gangsta-looking man. Rhee looked around, taking in the faces he remembered had been legendary at one time or another.

Rhee wondered if they looked at him and thought the same thing. Maybe one day.

"Coach, are you OK?" Blaze asked.

Rhee's players huddled around him. He snapped out of it and clapped his hands. "OK, let's get at it." He held out his hand and looked at his team. "Any last prayers?" The Eagles froze, unsure, until Rhee laughed. "You guys are too easy." He led them in a chant.

"Go Eagles," they all shouted.

Rhee looked up in time to see Rooster and his teammates looking at them and laughing. Rhee turned his attention back to his team. L.A. was the last player onto the court. "Yo, L.A.," Rhee called. L.A. turned around. Rhee motioned to him. "Come here a second. I need to holler at you."

L.A. slowly wandered over. "What's up, Coach?"

Rhee measured his words and stared at him for a good while. "You and I know how good you are. This is a good place to find out if it's real or all in your head." L.A. showed a nervous smile and looked up at his coach. "You know the best thing about street ball?" Rhee asked. "It teaches you to want the ball."

L.A. looked confused. "What do mean?"

Rhee got in close to him. "All the bickering and fights and the ball hogs start to get on your last nerve. Then you just get this hunger to touch the rock. You know if you give it up, chances are you'll never get it back."

Rhee looked at his star player and saw he slowly began to understand.

"Word," L.A. said.

"Go out there, and light it up," Rhee said. "This is your team. It's time to put them on your back."

"I think I can do this."

"I know you can," Rhee said.

Rooster stepped right in front of L.A. and glared down at him. "After today, white boy, you're going to have nightmares for weeks.

Don't let it bother you none, son," Rooster said. "After a few years, you'll be able to sleep with the lights off."

L.A. stared up at him and then turned to join his teammates. "Whatever, dude. You need to brush your teeth," L.A. said.

Rooster jogged over to Rhee. "These kids are so cute. They make me want to have kids of my own." He trotted backwards onto the court. Rhee turned and found a seat next to Weston and Blaze.

Asa chucked the basketball inbound to L.A., but Rooster was all over him. He hand-checked L.A., pushing him back. "Come on, baby boy. Yo mamma never told you I was your daddy, did she?"

Rhee shook his head and buried his face in his hands. Otis tapped him on the shoulder. "Did you loan me that five dollars already?"

Rhee laughed and looked back up to the game to see L.A. slapping away Rooster's hand check and dribbling the ball up court sideways. Doug ran up to the top of the key and braced his body to set a screen for L.A.

Rooster stayed in L.A.'s face, shoving him aggressively. L.A. dribbled behind his back and ran Rooster into Doug's screen. Doug flew back but did not fall. He was a wall. L.A. squared up to the basket and started to shoot. Rooster went airborne, but L.A. had not left the ground yet. Rooster was in the air when he realized L.A. had juked him with a pump fake. L.A. waited for him to fly by.

L.A. left his feet and shot a perfect jump shot that found the bottom of the net, swish. Rhee leaped off the bleachers and pumped his fist. "That's what I'm talking about. All day long." Rhee turned to high-five with Otis.

Asa looked for L.A. on the wing. He passed the basketball, but Rooster intercepted and raced down court for a two-handed jam. Rooster celebrated his uncontested dunk by high-fiving his teammates. He was so busy congratulating himself, he didn't notice how fast Doug inbounded the ball to Gerry, who zipped a pass to Asa, streaking down court and making the layup before any of the street players made it to half court.

Rhee jumped up. "That's it Eagles, here we go. Pour it on." Weston and Blaze leaped in the air next to Rhee. They double high-fived and bumped their chests against each other.

Rooster dribbled the ball and waited for his opportunity. Doug guarded him, but Rooster paid him little attention. The tattooed Mexican man broke across the foul line and set a screen. Rooster faked left and went right, but Doug stayed with him. When Rooster dribbled toward the screen, Doug lowered his shoulder and plowed into the tattooed Mexican man. The tattooed Mexican man went flying.

"Oops, my bad," Doug said.

Rooster reversed his dribble and went toward the rim. He left his feet, and Gerry closed his eyes and sacrificed his body. Rooster plowed into Gerry and lost the basketball out of bounds. Gerry soared backwards but stayed on his feet.

"There you go, Gerry, my man. You the man," Rhee yelled. Blazed jumped up and down and pumped his fist. Rhee pushed him. "Go in for Doug." Blaze froze in panic. "Hurry up."

"Coach, Doug just leveled a guy. They're gonna want revenge," Blaze said.

"Good, that means they're on his heels," Rhee said.

He pushed Blaze on the court. Blaze trotted onto the court and tapped Doug on the shoulder. They slapped hands.

"Give 'em hell," Doug screamed. He grabbed Blaze by the shoulders and shook him hard. Doug sprinted off the court. Rhee gave him a firm slap on the rump.

"You the man," Rhee said. Doug smiled and took a seat.

L.A. dribbled the ball up court, a defender hunkered down to block him. L.A. crossed over left and then back right. The man tried to turn with him but twisted his ankle and fell.

Otis leaned down. "That's what is known as an ankle breaker. I haven't seen a boy that fast with that kind of handling since you was out here."

Rhee smiled and watched two men help the man with the twisted ankle off the court. Rooster shoved a man guarding L.A. "I got him. Get out of the way."

He matched L.A. step for step as L.A. brought the ball up court. It was not necessary for Rooster to shove L.A. with aggressive, challenging, hand checks, but he did anyway. He tried to rattle the young boy's nerves. L.A. had to swat at Rooster's large hands with each dribble.

"Hey. Watch the hand checks," Rhee shouted.

Rooster continued to shove L.A. He glanced over to Rhee. "Sit your ass down. I'm the king now. This is my court," Rooster shouted.

Rhee started to sit down but caught himself. He stayed standing.

The Eagles were up by one. If they managed to score, they would have pulled off the upset of the century.

L.A. sized up the entire court. His teammates scurried around trying to set screens, but they were manhandled. The street players pulled them down or bulldozed through them.

"Let's do this," Rhee said. He clapped his hands. "Let's finish it."

L.A. dribbled the basketball at the top of the court.

Rooster taunted him. "What's the matter, little man? You heard your coach. One more basket, and you're home free. Don't choke little man. Little girls don't like no little boys who choke."

L.A. kept his eyes on Blaze, who stood alone under the basket. "Pay attention, king. School's in session, and your teacher's about to teach," L.A. said, just when he faked left and went right.

He beat Rooster off the dribble. Rooster let him go, intentionally. L.A. played right into his plan. L.A. drove toward the basket. The defense collapsed on him.

"Let him go," Rooster yelled to his teammates.

Rooster's teammates sagged off. L.A. dribbled down the right side of the key. L.A. left his feet and went up for a layup. Rooster followed him by two steps and timed it perfectly. Rooster soared into the air with both arms fully extended. His hands slapped the backboard, hard. L.A. was in mid-air when he switched the basketball to his left hand and acted like he was going to throw the ball to the right. All the defenders went right. L.A. wrapped his entire left hand around his own neck and passed the ball left. The basketball floated into Blaze's hands. Weston jumped up and covered his mouth. Blaze froze in terror. No one was on him. All the defenders and Rooster tried to recover. They lunged at Blaze.

"Shoot," Rhee yelled.

Blaze launched the basketball toward the rim in desperation. The backboard was still shaking from Rooster's powerful two-handed slap. The basketball rolled around the rim as everyone watched. It rolled and rolled until it fell through.

Gerry grabbed the basketball and flung it into the air. Doug and Weston rushed Blaze and picked him up. Rhee leaped off his feet and realized he was going to land on his bad ankle. When he came down there was no pain. Rhee pumped both his fists. He looked up. "Thank you, God," Rhee yelled.

L.A. tapped Rooster on the shoulder. Rooster turned around, angrily. "Off the court, your majesty. This is our castle now," L.A. said.

Rooster glared down at him and then slowly, almost without notice, he broke into a grin. He turned and saw Rhee looking at him. Rooster gave Rhee a wink. Rhee winked back. When the next team trotted onto the court, Rhee was elated.

The Eagles held the court three more games before they were overtaken. Rhee knew his team was spent, but they had learned -- a lot.

Rhee exchanged hands with several men and finally Otis. "Good Lord Almighty, that white boy can deal," Otis said.

"All that and a bag of chips," Rhee said.

A strange look came over Otis. "Let me ask you something."

"What?" Rhee asked.

"Can I borrow five dollars?"

Rhee laughed and gently pushed away from Otis. When all his players headed to the drinking fountains, Rhee turned and walked toward the ominous-looking man in the hoodie. He pulled his hoodie back just when Rhee arrived. Rhee smiled at Dr. Silva, and they hugged.

"What do you think?" Rhee asked. He watched Dr. Silva stare at the courts.

"He's got a ways to be like Pete Maravich, but he's on his way, isn't he?"

"You'll talk to him?" Rhee asked.

Dr. Silva had already started toward the drinking fountain. Rhee watched his mentor tap L.A. on the shoulder and begin speaking. L.A immediately fell into the coaching spell. He listened as Dr. Silva talked basketball with his hands, just like he'd done all those years with young Rhee Joyce.

Rhee's eyes filled with tears. An involuntary tear went down his cheek, and he wiped it away before anyone could see it.

Chapter 35

New Jungle Legends

Rhee and his father whittled their dialogue down to just about a head nod. No conversations in his house lasted for more than a sentence. Rhee was getting used to the quiet yet mannerly distance between himself and his parents. Ever since Rhee could remember, he and his father had routinely sat down and watched the lineup of ESPN shows, like His and Hers, Pardon the Interruption, and First Take. Now all Rhee and his father watched were the back of one another's heels as they headed in opposite directions.

Thanksgiving was a symphony of utensils against plates and an uncomfortable silence after prayer. Mr. Joyce went to the football game before dessert, which Mrs. Joyce served him on the tray of the La-Z-Boy.

Rhee skipped the pie and sat in his bedroom fantasizing about making a comeback and living on his own. He would send money and presents as a reminder of his success in the NBA and his decision to discontinue communication with his mother and father. Both of them would pine for his company and regret they had treated him so poorly. It was a wishful fantasy.

Christmas was worse. Rhee spent as much time as he could out of his house to avoid the cold distance from his parents and unexpected visits from friends he'd not heard from because they were off to college. He wanted no part of the humiliation of stories about the excitement of higher learning on top of questions about his grim future.

Rhee had money from his coaching job, but his stomach knotted with the idea of shopping for Christmas presents for parents he grew farther from each day. He planned on putting it off until seconds before Christmas Day. The only change in his daily routine of avoidance came when he asked his mother for his cell phone.

It was not cancelled, but the voicemail was full, and no one could contact him. He only put the names and numbers of his players into his contacts in case he wanted to organize a couple of shoot-arounds. Rhee started to miss his team, which was a big surprise to him. There was a moment while Rhee showered that his middle school team were the only friends he valued. He tried to towel off the revelation but it stuck to him like glue. Rhee actually missed the Eagles, each one of them.

The New Year came and went without any jubilation in the Joyce household. Rhee's parents went out for dinner and came home early. He watched the crack under his door as their light went out. They went to bed without a whisper of "Happy New Year" to Rhee. He sat back against the headboard on his bed and was glad they never bothered.

The trip to Live Oak Park gave Rhee a little light of joy. His players managed to man-up and do what he asked them to do. School was about to begin, and the Eagles were going to start practice. Rhee wanted to be in the gymnasium with his new friends. A couple more days, and Rhee was going to be coaching again. It started to grow on him.

He looked down at his trilling cell phone to see Flash was calling; Rhee answered immediately. He closed his cell phone and floated down the hallway to find his mother in the kitchen.

"Mom, can I use your car?"

"Of course, Rhee. Will you be home for dinner?"

"No. I'm eating with one of my players tonight."

"OK. How is that going?"

"Fine." He couldn't find any other words for her.

"How is your ankle?"

"Fine."

"You have a checkup appointment second week of this month."

"Cool."

Rhee checked the kitchen wall clock. He breathed a sigh of relief. There was just enough time to race off and miss his disgruntled father. He grabbed his mother's car keys and turned to head out the front door. He nearly collided into his dad, who carried a small stack of books when he opened the front door.

Rhee tried to sidestep him, but his dad caught him off guard with a complete sentence. "Someone left these for you on the front porch." Mr. Joyce shoved the books into Rhee's chest.

"From whom?" He took the books and saw yellow Stickies on the top of each book.

"I have no idea," Mr. Joyce said, a perplexed look on his face. "The note is addressed to you. Looks like a bunch of books on coaching."

Rhee read the note and recognized the handwriting. It was from Dr. Silva, and it was a small stack of books on coaching by some pretty reputable coaches, including John Wooden, Dean Smith, and Mike Kryzewski. Rhee only glanced at the books while he continued out the door. He didn't want to get into any further awkward dialogue with his father, which was exactly what happened.

"How is that job going?" Mr. Joyce asked.

Rhee stood sideways with one foot on the front porch. He pushed the screen door back and the front door forward. The stack of books almost eclipsed his vision of his dad. Rhee saw the top of his father's head.

"OK, it's going OK." Rhee flew out the door without anything further to say.

The utensils quietly chimed as Rhee sat at the dinner table with Asa and his parents. The silence would have put anyone else on edge. For Rhee, it had the familiar ambiance of home. The food smelled different from his mother's, but it was good enough to tease an appetite.

Mr. Lieberman had thick wavy hair and thin spectacles he frequently took off to pinch his nose. He was taller and thinner up close. He looked like a college professor, which was exactly what he was. And he knew more about sports than Rhee, including basketball.

Rhee fought the urge to ignore Mrs. Lieberman and ask Asa's dad questions about the old ABA and several players he only knew a little about. Players like George "The Iceman" Gerven and George "The Baby Bull" McGuinnis. Mr. Lieberman did educate Rhee on the old Jewish summer leagues, which was technically one of the first professional leagues because players were paid to play for certain teams, and there were championships that came with a little extra cash.

Mrs. Lieberman picked up a bowl of potato salad and offered it to Rhee. "Have some more, Rhee."

Rhee had already eaten as much as he could. Though he presently felt no overwhelming loyalty to his mother, it was a fact that no one's potato salad rivaled Mrs. Joyce's.

"Everything was so good, I can't possibly eat anymore," Rhee said.

Mrs. Lieberman put down the bowl and kept her eyes on Rhee. There was something about her that made Rhee feel unnerved. She had grace but a stern expression that made him lose his train of thought. Idle chatter wasn't her thing. She only spoke when necessary. And she looked through Rhee like she was examining everything he did for hidden meanings. She treated Rhee like an adult. But something was on her mind.

"Practice went rather late last week. Are you overworking our son during the holiday vacation, Coach Joyce?" Mrs. Lieberman asked.

"It wasn't an official practice, mom," Asa said.

Rhee stole a quick glance at Asa long enough to understand he had not told his mother that Rhee took them to The Jungle. He reached for the glass of water to buy some time. To Rhee's surprise, and relief, Mr. Lieberman jumped into the conversation.

"I gotta tell you, Rhee. I've never seen anyone get the boys to play at the level you've managed to get them to play," Mr. Lieberman said.

Rhee breathed a sigh of relief. Mr. Lieberman had saved him

without Rhee having to avoid Mrs. Lieberman's line of inquiry or possibly lie to her. This had to mean Asa had told his father -- but not his mother -- that Rhee had taken his team to Live Oak Park.

"So if it wasn't an official practice, what was it?" Mrs. Lieberman asked.

Rhee looked at Asa, who smirked between bites. "Coach gave us a couple weeks off to celebrate our own family traditions," Asa said.

Rhee opened his eyes wide and sat up straight. He never considered any family traditions. He just wanted to let everyone chill until the New Year.

"Oh, that's nice," Mrs. Lieberman said. "What did your family celebrate?"

Rhee looked at Asa and Mr. Lieberman for help.

"Christmas and New Years, Mom," Asa said. "Not everyone is Jewish."

Rhee felt Mrs. Lieberman's lie detector turn to full volume. Her eyes followed his every move.

"I know that honey. I'm just trying to learn something about Rhee and his family," Mrs. Lieberman said.

She looked at Rhee, and he finally figured out what made him nervous. This woman reminded him of his own mother. She was after something, and it was a matter of time before she got it.

"We celebrate Christmas," Rhee said. "This year we were quiet. We all did our own thing."

"I see. Had you planned an outing for the team, or was it impromptu?"

"Mom," Asa pleaded.

"Ava, Rhee doesn't want us to prod into the way he coaches his team," Mr. Lieberman said.

"I'm not prodding. I just want Rhee to tell me why he took our son to a park where there has been three murders in the last six months."

Rhee felt hot as burning coal. The shoe finally dropped. This was just like his mother, who skated around the real thing she wanted to talk about until she'd discovered if Rhee was going to volunteer the information.

Mrs. Lieberman looked down at her fingernails as though she was calculating which finger of Rhee's to cut off first. "My son and husband didn't volunteer the information. I had to find out from one of the other mothers, Mrs. Agosta."

A bead of sweat pooled under Rhee's nose. He sat up straight. He was in front of the firing squad, Mrs. Lieberman's firing squad. She folded her hands and looked right into her son's eyes. Asa looked at his dad, who looked at Rhee. The dining room had turned into dead man's corner. In this case, it was one dead man and two young men.

Mr. Lieberman looked at Rhee. It was a clear signal for Rhee to skate the question if he wanted. Rhee's eyes volleyed between Mr. Lieberman and Asa.

"I took them to play at Live Oak Park," Rhee said. "It was where I learned how to play."

Mr. Lieberman sat up with a smile. "Live Oak Park? My son played ball at Live Oak Park?" Mr. Lieberman asked, his voice tinged with pride. He reached over and tussled his son's curly hair. "That's great son. You're almost a man now. Only the best players to come out of the Bay Area were able to hold their own at Live Oak Park." He smiled at his wife. "Did you know that, dear?"

Rhee was grateful for Mr. Lieberman's effort to diffuse the bomb placed in Rhee's lap, but he was not yet off the witness stand. Mrs. Lieberman had more interrogation. Rhee felt heat, the same heat his mother gave off when she needed to melt down the truth. His mother had the same eerie style: ruthless patience.

"We lost our first game, but then we held the court for three straight games," Asa said proudly.

Mrs. Lieberman raised an eyebrow of concern. "Wasn't someone shot at Live Oak Park this past summer during one of those games?" Mrs. Lieberman asked.

Rhee, Asa, and Mr. Lieberman panicked. Their eyes circled one another. Rhee looked for an open door or window. Mr. Lieberman pushed back from the table and loaded as many plates off the table as he was able to carry. "I'll clear the dishes."

Asa leaped out of his chair. "I'll help you, dad."

"Why don't all of you just relax? I'll get dessert," Mrs. Lieberman said. Asa and his father slowly sat back down. Rhee's chair settled in quicksand. "I just want to know why I didn't get a permission slip or document request to take our son off campus -- especially since you didn't exactly go to a museum."

Rhee looked at one of the windows, just left of the dining room. It wasn't a huge window, but Rhee thought he could make it through with a dive. The glass might shred him to pieces, but it was better than sinking in quicksand.

"Honey, Rhee has taken our boy and the entire team further than any other coach in the school's history. Sometimes, in order to turn around a fledgling sports program like Joaquin Moraga, you have to think outside the box."

Rhee loved Mr. Lieberman. The man took a bullet for Rhee, who gave him a small, barely noticeable nod of gratitude. Mr. Lieberman looked at Rhee as if to say, "Don't even try to take on this woman."

Rhee avoided her gaze. He wasn't sure the tigress was going to rip his throat out first or her husband's. When Rhee looked up, he found her gaze fixed on him.

"I'm sorry, Mrs. Lieberman. I should have done the right thing. I didn't think it through," Rhee said, straight into the tigress's eyes. "I'm so new at this coaching thing. Trust me, this wasn't the first mistake I made. I haven't been able to get a lot of my job right. I should have asked for your permission," Rhee said. "I should have asked for all the parents' permission. I'm sorry."

Mrs. Lieberman's eyes softened. The hard look on her face changed. Rhee was unsure what he had said for that to happen, until she spoke.

"Rhee, one of the most important things in our home is the courage to be accountable and brave enough to tell the truth." She gave a warm smile. "I know nothing about you, but my son idolizes you. I'd bet my life that you have good parents." Mrs. Lieberman turned to her husband and son. "Maybe next time my husband and son will decide to be accountable too." Rhee tried to find something to look at other than the guilty party. "Now, who wants dessert?" Mrs. Lieberman asked.

Rhee exhaled. He wasn't sure how long ago he'd stopped breathing. Whatever dessert this woman was going to bring, even if it were paste on a brick, Rhee was going to eat it all.

Chapter 36

Richie Rich

Blaze took off from the diving board and managed a respectable cannonball, which was soundless because of the hip-hop music that blared from the hidden speakers of the backyard surround sound. The audio was loud yet crisp and clear, without a trace of harmonic distortion. Rhee counted five high-definition flat screens larger than any Rhee had seen in any Best Buy. Doug and Gerry moved life-sized chess pieces on a grass chessboard, easily forty by forty feet. Even that was dwarfed by the acres of manicured gardens, a tennis court, and a basketball court, hidden in exotic foliage.

Rhee glanced at the sun through discount store sunglasses. It was a typical eighty-degree January on Saturday in California. He took a moment to consider the layers of clothing he'd have to wear in the first week of January had he gone to Kansas University. It was a good school and, most likely, his first choice. Bill Self was his favorite coach. Allen Field House was his favorite recruiting trip. Lawrence, Kansas, was the most beautiful campus in his mind. Instead, he sat shirtless in knee-length swim shorts under an umbrella on a lounge chair so large it made him feel like an infant.

Rhee lowered his sunglasses and took in the enormity of L.A.'s backyard.

Clayton wore a Golden State Warriors T-shirt and matching long basketball shorts with white tube socks and sandals. He wore an apron with a blown-up photograph of Lil Wayne.

He used a long wooden spatula to flip the meat at a brick barbecue pit the size of a school playground.

There was a canvas overhang that shaded the barbecue area

to seat a hundred people or more. Mist came from pinhole areas, and Rhee wasn't sure if the moisture was for the sweet molasses-smelling barbecue or to keep Clayton and everyone cool from the dry heat.

L.A. sat next to Rhee and shoved him. "What up, Coach?"

Rhee put down one of the coaching books he thumbed through. "From where I'm sitting, it's your world, and I'm just a squirrel trying to get a nut," Rhee said.

"Dag, Coach. You talk so eighties."

"How would you know, Shorty? You weren't even alive during the eighties, or nineties."

"And you were? Oh, that's right. You were four."

"Believe that. I'd already had my first haircut, little man."

"Come on, Coach, you'd just been potty trained."

"Right. It was an amazing sign of my maturity. You, on the other hand, were still trying to work out the backstroke in your mamma's belly."

"True that," L.A said. He tilted his head to read one of the coaching book titles. "Who is John Wooden?"

Rhee gave L.A. an incredulous expression. "You know you just committed a sin, right?"

"What are you talking about?"

"One of the Ten Commandments is: 'Thou shall always know who John Wooden is' -- you little midget."

"I'm almost taller than you, Coach. What up with all the shorty and midget references?"

Rhee shook his head and leaned back in his lounge chair. He looked around while L.A. glanced at the other books. The other kids splashed and roughhoused in the pool. Rhee couldn't hear laughter over the blaring hip-hop music, but their wide smiles were an obvious clue.

"Is one of these books by that guy I met at Live Oak Park?"

Rhee shook his head. "No, the guy you met gave me these books to read."

"I don't doubt that. Dude knows a lot about basketball."

"He taught me almost everything I know about the sport."

"Is he some kind of coach or something?"

Rhee picked up one of the books and waved it in front of L.A.'s face. "He's kind of like a cross between Dr. House and one of these guys."

"That guy at the park talking all that basketball is a doctor too?"

"Yeah, man. There are other brainiacs in the world besides you," Rhee said.

"I ain't no brainiac," L.A. protested.

"Tell me the truth." Rhee held up five books. "How long would it take to read all these?"

L.A. looked over the books and shrugged both shoulders. "I don't know, maybe an hour."

Rhee almost flew off the lounge chair. "One hour to read all these? Dude, you're not a brainiac. You're a freak."

"Who are you calling a freak?" L.A. asked.

"Rich white kid right in front of me."

They laughed. L.A. waved him off. Rhee shook his head and looked around. "Can I ask you something?"

"If it's about your virginity, that's none of my business," L.A. said, with a laugh.

Rhee picked up one of the coaching books and threatened to crack L.A.'s skull. "So, you wake up, open your blinds, look out into a backyard the size of a national park, and think, what?"

L.A. cocked his eyebrow then shrugged his shoulders. "I don't know. Guess I think about finishing my chemistry homework or who's on the cover of this year's Sports Illustrated Swimsuit Edition," L.A. answered.

A slow smile spread across Rhee's lips. "Fair enough." He

raised his head and pointed his chin over L.A.'s shoulder. "Who is the Mafia-looking dude staring at us?" Rhee asked.

L.A. turned around. A salt-and-pepper-haired man dressed in a creaseless gunmetal-gray suit removed his sunglasses and looked around like he was inspecting the place for vermin.

L.A. shrugged his shoulders. "He calls himself my dad, but I kind of doubt it sometimes."

"That's your pops?" Rhee asked.

L.A. shrugged his shoulders. "Whatever."

"What about your mom?" Rhee asked.

"What about her?" L.A. asked.

"Is she around?"

"Why you putting me on blast about my parents, Coach?"

"I'm not. Just want to get to know you."

"I can ball on the basketball court. That's all you need to know," L.A. said, a scowl on his face.

"Come on, coolness, cut me a little slack."

"My mom is out shopping or running some charity. You happy now?"

"Right as rain," Rhee said.

Asa spun a basketball on his finger as he wandered over to Rhee and L.A. "We're thinking about a game of horse. Are you guys in or out?"

L.A. nodded and started toward the courts. Rhee looked back just in time to see L.A.'s dad walk back into the main house.

"Nah, I'm good. I think I'll go holler at the dude with the one-million-dollar suit," Rhee said.

L.A. stiffened. "You should leave that alone. Squash it, Coach, I'm asking you nicely before I have to get violent."

Rhee pointed at Asa. "I got this. Don't worry. Ask Flash if I'm down with parents." He gave Asa a glare. "Jump in any time, little man."

"He's cool with parents. He ate at my house. My mom decided she liked him -- even though she thought he tried to get us killed by taking us to Live Oak Park to play hoops."

A worried look came over L.A. All his cool and bravado slid off his body. "Coach, you're wasting your time," L.A. said.

Rhee turned on his heels and went toward the house anyway. "I'll be right back. Don't worry. I'm not going to talk about politics or religion."

"That's 'cause you don't know anything about politics or religion," L.A. said. He stared at the back of Rhee's head.

"You funny. You're just a funny kid," Rhee said.

"Coach, I'll give you some serious ging if you stay out of my house," L.A. yelled.

"Look at me. I coach at a middle school. I got all the ging I need. Gonna buy me a place like this at the end of the season."

He picked up his pace and marched up the staircase that led to the main house. A few swear words rang behind him.

Rhee slipped through a French door he found at the top of the staircase from the backyard. He stood in an entry hall that was so large it cautioned him to not call out for fear of an echo. His eyes roamed around the cathedral-beamed ceilings. There was a huge Rumford fireplace in a hallway. Rhee immediately wondered why anyone needed a fireplace in a hallway?

A man's voice emanated from a large mahogany door that was slightly ajar. "Yes, I'll take that into consideration."

Rhee hesitated but overcame his anxiety. He pushed open the large mahogany door and peaked inside to find Mr. Adams on the telephone.

"Sorry, my bad." He eased back out of the room. Mr. Adams raised his hand for him to wait.

"I'll talk to Roy. He said the subsidiary company was releasing the quarterly profits report on Friday."

Rhee backed away. Mr. Adams held up his index finger.

"George, I'll call you back." Mr. Adams never bothered to say goodbye and only hung up the telephone.

"Can I help you?" Mr. Adams asked. He never bothered to stand up. Rhee crossed the room with surprising confidence. It deflated slightly as he extended his hand too soon. He miscalculated the size of the desk Mr. Adams sat behind. The reach made it only halfway across the expansive desk. It forced Mr. Adams to stand.

"Mr. Adams, I'm sorry. I was looking for a bathroom."

Mr. Adams shook Rhee's hand as if it were contaminated but feigned a smile. "Leslie should have told you there are four bathrooms outside."

Rhee stiffened and pointed over his shoulder with his thumb. "He probably told me, and I spaced it. Anyway, I'm glad to meet you. I'm your son's coach."

Mr. Adams sat back down and made a steeple with his fingertips in front of his face. "That's nice. What do you coach?" Mr. Adams leaned back in a chair that cost a truckload of money.

"Basketball," Rhee said. An uncomfortable confrontation bubbled, but he kept his poise. "Your son is the star player for his school team."

"Oh, OK. Yes, I was a little surprised when Leslie told me he was going to move some classes at the college so he could join a team." The whole sentence was punctuated with irritation.

"Well, we're real lucky he made the sacrifice." Rhee smiled widely and uneasily. "Your son is such a good player, it has changed the makeup of the entire team."

Mr. Adams folded his hands on the desk and straightened his back like he wanted Rhee to leave. "Oh, very good. I'm glad to hear he is contributing." Rhee noticed the scowl now present on Mr. Adams's face. His previous charm evaporated.

Mr. Adams turned his chair. He stood and moved toward the window. Rhee spoke to his back. "Oh, he more than contributes. L.A.... Leslie is the kind of player that doesn't come along too often. He can handle the rock as good as any kid I've played against, I mean, seen in a long time."

Mr. Adams continued to look out the window. Rhee took inventory of the room while the man kept his eyes out the window. There were paintings, ornaments, leather-bound books, and a flat screen that projected stock exchange numbers. Everything was foreign, putting him in a daze, but he shored up his nerve again.

"I guess what I'm trying to say is your son can flat out play. If he wants to get a scholarship, it's within his reach. In fact, it's right under his nose."

Mr. Adams slowly turned around. His eyes seldom registered another person was in the room. "That's all well and good, but both he and Leslie's sisters are going to Harvard, like their father and my father. We're pretty sure we've got our son's future under control."

Rhee balled his hands into tight fists. He backed away. "It was good to meet, sir."

"Nice to meet you. If there is anything you need, I'm sure my son can point you in the right direction."

Rhee gave a failed wave and started to leave. Something made him stop and turn around. "Mr. Adams, have you ever seen your son play basketball?"

Mr. Adams sat back down and gently put his hand on the telephone to indicate the conversation should end. "No, I haven't."

"He's really good. Got serious, mad, crazy skills for his age."

Mr. Adams started punching numbers. Rhee raised his hand to half-mast, turned, and left. He got outside the door and stopped. The meeting felt sour in his stomach. He started back into the room, but just outside the door, he heard Mr. Adams clearly back into a conversation.

"No, George, you know that's not my judgment to make. The kid is barely any older than Leslie."

Rhee clumsily turned back to leave when he heard more of the conversation.

"I just think it's funny that a black kid has managed to get my son to spend some time with kids his own color."

A fire lit and burned through Rhee's body. He balled both his fists and stomped heavily back into the room so his entrance was heard.

"Hold on, George." Mr. Adams placed the phone on his shoulder and looked at Rhee, who fumed. "I'm sorry I'm on a business call. Can I help you?"

Rhee slowly uncurled his fist and forced a smile. He shook his finger at Mr. Adams. "Nah, you're not going to do me like that."

"I'm sorry. Do you like what?" Mr. Adams asked.

Rhee waited for the boil inside him to simmer. It never happened; he stayed hot inside. "Maybe your son has black friends because his white father doesn't pay any attention to him," Rhee said through clenched teeth.

Mr. Adams cocked his head like a puppy trying to learn a command. The silence between them thickened the air. It was hard for Rhee to breathe. His nostrils flared.

"Mr. Adams, kids your son's age face a lot of peer pressure. It's all about being down or cool. That's why he likes rap and has black friends. It tells people he's cool and is maybe a little different."

Mr. Adams said nothing.

"I don't know how long he's going to play, but I know for sure it would mean a lot to him if you just came to see at least one game. And it may really make him feel great if you said something like, 'Good game, son' or 'You are quite a player, kid,'" Rhee said. "That'd mean the world to him or any kid his age."

Rhee turned around and marched off before Mr. Adams had any chance to reply. Rhee got outside, and L.A. nearly pounced on him. "What'd my dad say?" L.A. asked.

"Oh, he was cool. We kicked it for a minute. We had a couple drinks. Then he told me you had a couple fine sisters you'd been hiding and I should get to know them. Maybe even marry into the family and live nappy."

L.A. gave Rhee a sidelong, worried gaze. Rhee grabbed him, put him in a headlock, and noogied his head. "I gotcha didn't I? You're too easy, Kid Skills." He let go and walked away. L.A. stared at him with a look of utter disbelief.

When Rhee reached the lounge chair, he punched the cushion so hard his knuckles tore the seams. He looked around and quickly stuffed feathers back into the hole he had made.

Clayton turned around with a king-size plate of ribs, steak, and chicken.

Chapter 37

Eagles Start To Fly

A loud shrill cut through the air as Rhee blew his whistle.

All seven of the Eagles players were shirtless and hunched over, wheezing from doing mop-ups.

"Everybody over here," Rhee shouted.

His sweat-drenched players dragged themselves over and plopped down on the bleachers in front of Rhee. They leaned on one another to keep from falling over. He looked at them and waited. He picked up one of the coaching books and paced in front of them while he read. He stopped.

"Any of you knuckleheads ever heard of the word 'manifestation'?" Five of the players nodded unconvincingly. L.A. and Doug leaned against one another, too tired to hate on each other. "Thickness and Richie Rich."

"Yo, Coach," Doug replied.

"What up?" L.A. asked.

"Why am I even talking if y'all gonna tune me out?" Rhee asked, one eyebrow raised with irritation.

"You asked us if any of us heard of the word 'manifestation,'" Doug said.

L.A. pointed at Doug. "Whatever he said, Coach. Me too."

"Why did everybody nod except you and White Chocolate?"

"I don't know," Doug said.

"Then one of you knot heads tell me what the word means."

Doug bit his fingernails. L.A. stared 100 yards off into the abyss. "Hey, muscle neck. Talk to me."

Doug spit out his fingernail. "It means when you create something or make something happen, sometimes out of nothing."

Rhee stared at Doug. "So you were listening but just acted like you weren't." Doug looked at L.A. Rhee noticed they both bit down on their lips to keep from laughing. "What's so funny?"

Doug straightened up and sat erect. "Nothing."

Rhee eyed him and L.A. "Not too long ago, you two were gonna rip each other's faces off. Now everything is funny?"

L.A. quickly raised his hand. "Actually, I'm still going to rip his face off, Coach, if that's OK?"

All the players fell to laughing. Rhee stared at L.A. The kid had just got the best of him. He liked the fact that the players had built some camaraderie. Still, he had to keep a semblance of authority.

"Oh, so all of you didn't get enough running and mop-ups?" Rhee asked. The players sat up and smothered their laughter. "OK, smart butts. That's more like it." Rhee waited. "OK, then, listen up." He paced. He stopped and looked at each of his players. "When pro athletes sit in a room, they picture themselves doing one thing over and over and over, whether it's draining a three or catching the winning touchdown."

"Or riding the perfect pipeline," Terrance said.

Rhee waved them off. "Black people don't surf, so I have no idea what that meant."

All of his players shook their heads in disagreement. "Not true, Coach." Terrance said. "Nick Gabaldon, Tony Corley..."

"Yeah, Coach there are a lot of black surfers," Gerry added.

Rhee's eyes jumped between them. "Well, there shouldn't be. Black people are from Africa. Over in Africa, lakes, rivers, and the ocean mean alligators, big ole snakes, and piranhas. Anyway, stop getting me off track. I'm black, and I'm in the middle of explaining something."

Asa raised his hand and spoke before Rhee said he could.

"Coach, you were the one who said black people don't surf."

Rhee put his hands on his hips. "I swear y'all are getting on my last nerve. You guys speak for rich white kids, and I'll speak for black folks."

Doug pointed at L.A. "Actually, he's kinda' black."

The players all laughed. "Go ahead, muscle man. Keep making jokes, and I'm gonna just knock one of you out and let them lock me up, happy?" Rhee stared at them all into silence. "From now on, the rule is if I fall over and die, one of you can talk. Until then, shut it." Most of the players pulled their jerseys up to hide their chuckles and smiles. "OK, so Thickness was right. People create something from nothing by visualizing it over and over and over. But there is something better than that. There is a higher form of manifestation." Rhee examined each of his players to make sure they were not drifting off. "It's when you say the word 'done,' and at that moment, there is no doubt that you will do whatever you set out to do. Like when you see a pretty girl and one day you just know you're going to get to talk to her. Two weeks later, bam, there she is with her mom right in front of you at the mall. So, from now on, that's our motto. Get in here, and when I say 'one, two, three,' you say what?"

"Done," all the players shouted.

Rhee put out his hand. They all stood and one by one put their hands on Rhee's hand. He had their attention now. He felt their hot breath on him. He liked that they were coming together.

"Now we're going to win a lot of games. Everyone understand?" All the players nodded. "OK, one, two, three..."

"Done," all the players yelled.

Rhee's ear rang from the player's loud intensity. He looked at all of them. He had them believing. And believing was halfway to being.

The Eagles won five straight games. They beat the Benicia Vikings, the Rheem Bears, the Orinda Bulldogs, the Berkeley Yellow Jackets, and the Danville Ironmen, all with ease.

L.A. tore through the league like it was a paper bag. He averaged twenty-seven points a game. His legend grew with each new game. But L.A. was not alone. Terrance averaged nineteen points a game, and he and L.A. were the only two players taken out when the Eagles were up by more than twenty points, which was all the games they played.

Weston averaged twelve assists a game and set a league record of twenty-three assists in a single game. The Eagles and the Cougars were both undefeated. They were set to meet the last game of the season.

Rhee stopped in his tracks outside the Eagles' gymnasium. A sound resonated that his mind never associated with this gymnasium at this middle school. He quickly stepped to the double doors, yanked them open, and walked into the gymnasium. His mouth dropped.

There was a small group of boys and girls with instruments. There was a drummer, a trumpet player, a trombone player, a bass player, and a tiny little girl holding symbols. This shocked Rhee enough, but then he saw five girls wearing shorts and sweatshirts, shaking pompoms, practicing synchronized cheerleading moves and cartwheels, and yelling out cheers. A cluster of other kids stood around and watched. Another cluster of kids sat on the bleachers. Rhee turned around and left the gymnasium.

He entered the administration office at Mach speed. "Is Coach Holt around?" Rhee asked.

"I think so. Why?" Lynn asked. She hit the buzzer as he breezed through the small door.

He pointed his right index finger over his left shoulder and opened his mouth to speak. He waved Lynn off and kept going. He turned the corner to step into Coach Holt's little cubbyhole of an office, and the final shock wave shot through Rhee's entire body.

Coach Holt's office was spotless and organized. There were shelves Rhee had not seen before. One of them was lined with trophies. There also were three chairs Rhee had never seen. All the loose balls and equipment were in plastic bins. On top of all the present marvels, the bins were labeled. Rhee failed to conceal the shock on his face.

Coach Holt turned around, a duster in his hand. "Don't give me that look, Joyce. The fact that you've won six straight games in a row is more of a miracle than my office being clean." Coach Holt pulled open a drawer in his desk. "That reminds me. You're just in time. I saved this for you." He pulled out his silver flask. He dropped the flask into the trash basket. It clunked as it hit the bottom.

"Say what?" Rhee asked. He sat down. He tried to pull his gaze from the trash basket, but he was dumbfounded. "What's going on around here?" He continued to stare at it.

"Whatever do you mean?"

Rhee pointed at the trash basket. "There's a band and cheerleaders in the gym, and now you're doing this?"

Coach Holt looked at the trash basket, so Rhee retracted his finger and put his hand under his thigh. Coach Holt looked back at Rhee, "School spirit. It's contagious."

"School spirit?" Rhee said as he stared at Coach Holt, incredulous.

A smile formed across Coach Holt's face, "What's wrong, Coach? You're so deep into the forest you can't see the trees?"

Rhee stayed in shock at Coach Holt's lively demeanor. His mind raced. "Excuse me?"

Coach Holt turned around and dusted the shelves. "The stars are aligning for you, Joyce. Try not to step on your own toes."

"My own what?"

"Your toes, Joyce. Remember the one thing I learned a long time ago about winning or losing."

"Let me guess. It doesn't matter if you win or lose; it's how you play the game, right?"

Coach Holt turned and pointed the duster at Rhee. "No, smart-ass. In the words of the late Henry Wadsworth Longfellow, 'Most people would succeed in small things if they were not so troubled with great ambition.' At least I think that was it. Since I stopped drinking, everything in my head is a fog."

Rhee looked back down at the trash basket. The silver flask shined like a blinking neon sign. "You seriously stopped drinking?"

Coach Holt reached up, wiped a shelf with his finger, and examined it for potential dust. "Three days now. That's three more days than I've rallied together in the last fifteen years."

"I don't understand."

"What's not to understand? Look at what you've accomplished. If your team wins the next nine games and the Cougars win too, you play them for the city championship. You're lucky the practice game where they stomped you didn't count. What was that movie about the deaf and blind gal?"

"No idea," Rhee said. He sat back and exhaled. He watched Coach Holt snap his fingers until a thought came and he spoke. "It was called *The Miracle Worker*. You never saw it?"

"Nah, Coach. Not unless it became a DVD. I'm only eighteen years old."

"I know how you feel, Joyce."

"How do I feel?"

"It's like you're standing on the street corner watching everyone running around acting crazy and you're thinking: 'Are they crazy or am I missing something?'"

"Who said that?"

"No idea, Keats or Wadsworth maybe. I read it when I was drunk," Coach Holt said.

"I'm surprised you remember anything."

Coach Holt gave him a cold stare.

"Get out of here, Joyce, before I kick you in your bad leg. Oh, and go see that little dweeb. He was looking for you."

Rhee stood, ready to leave. "Sorry, Coach, but there are a lot of little dweebs in this school."

A smile took its time spreading across the coach's face. "Point taken. The principal was looking for you. Don't be surprised if he's got some adoption papers in his office. He may want to change the school's name to 'Joyce Place' and have you bronzed while you're still alive."

Rhee looked down the hallway to make sure no one was near. "Thanks for the heads-up, Coach."

Coach Holt gave Rhee a respectable salute.

Rhee left the cubbyhole and headed for the front desk. The day wasn't more than halfway over, and it had him upside down.

Chapter 38

The Recruiters

In a daze, Rhee walked into the reception area and stood. He was still reeling from the transformation witnessed in Coach Holt's office. Lynn's back was turned. She wore a short denim skirt, tight on her hips. Her blouse was white and sheer. Even with all the distraction, this girl still managed to push his confusion aside and generate some excitement inside him. He cleared his throat and successfully got her turned around.

"Principal De Loach is looking for you," Lynn said.

"I heard." He kept his gaze on her eyes even though he wanted to check the rest of her out.

"There are some other guys in his office."

"What guys?"

"No idea. Fancy-looking guys in suits."

"Should I wait?"

"No. They said they all wanted to talk to you."

"About what?"

She cocked one hip. "Do I look psychic?"

Rhee took a beat to soak in her looks. It had little to do with psychic ability.

"No, but you always look hella fine."

Lynn smiled from being pleasantly surprised, "Thank you."

"You're welcome." Rhee said it with unwavering confidence.

She looked at him beneath the dark hood of her long eyelashes. "Some of my friends are getting together Friday night for pizza and soda, maybe a movie."

"Are you kidding?" Rhee asked. "You're playin' me, right?"

"Do I look like I'm kidding or playing?" Lynn asked with a stern look on her face.

He looked over both shoulders. "Did I come to the right school today?"

"Yes, I think so, why?"

Rhee pointed over his shoulder. "There are cheerleaders and a band in the gym; Coach Holt cleaned his office; and now you're inviting me out? I didn't think you even liked me."

She folded her arms protectively. "You've changed."

Rhee mimicked her stance. "No, I haven't," Rhee said. "Maybe you've changed. Maybe you're the one who judged me wrong."

Lynn kept her arms crossed and stood her ground. "Yes, you have changed. That dark cloud you used to carry around over your head isn't there anymore."

He stared at her as long as he could until words formed on his lips. "You might be right. They've been replaced with a few lightning bolts, especially when I got here today, and especially when you asked me out."

Rhee turned and took his sweet time going to the principal's office. He carried with him an ear-to-ear grin.

The door was ajar. Rhee carefully stuck his head in. An African-American man who wore a blue suit and red tie crossed his legs and checked his watch. A Caucasian man who wore a coffee-colored suit with a yellow tie stole glances out the window. Both men had creaseless white shirts; both sat in front of Principal De Loach, who sat at his desk and tapped a pen on his day planner. He stood with a too-happy look on his face. "There he is, the young man of the hour."

Rhee hesitated. He kept his eyes on Principal De Loach. "You wanted to see me?"

The principal came around his desk, pulled out a chair, and patted Rhee on the shoulders, like they'd been best friends for years. "Come on in. Have a seat. Glad you're here."

Out of the corner of his eye, Rhee noticed both men in the suits stood up and waited to shake his hand. This was like the old days when recruiters came to Rhee's house. He sat down without bothering to shake any hands and then made a show of looking at a clock on the wall. His practice started in less than twenty minutes. In ten minutes, he was going to pull the pin and leave, no matter what this was about.

Principal De Loach raced back around his desk and sat down. He pointed at the African-American man first. "Coach Joyce, this is Mr. Barns." Rhee waited for the principal to point at the other man, and he did. "And Mr. Wallace."

He recognized Mr. Wallace. When Rhee was a sixteen-year-old sophomore in high school, he opened the front door and saw a very confident, composed recruiter, who wore a Stanford University baseball cap. That Stanford recruiter was a younger Mr. Wallace.

He pulled his cell phone from his pocket and put it up to his face in an exaggerated motion. "I have a practice to coach in fifteen." An overwhelming dose of sour grapes kept him from being the same kid he was one year ago.

"I know, Coach. We won't take up too much of your time. These gentleman are from Stanford University," Principal De Loach said. He expanded his chest proudly.

Mr. Wallace gave him a wink like they were old pals. Rhee quickly looked back at Principal De Loach. "What's up?"

Principal De Loach smiled and leaned back in his seat. He enjoyed the attention. He looked at the men from Stanford. "You two gentlemen, take it from here."

The two recruiters stole a glance at one another. Mr. Wallace leaned forward. "Rhee, you know better than most people that colleges are taking a valued interest in players even before high school. You also know its protocol to talk to the player's coach."

"Let's cut to the quick. Leslie Adams is the exact profile of the student athlete we want at Stanford University," Mr. Barns said.

The silence choked the room, until Principal De Loach squirmed in his chair. He leaned forward and snatched a pen off his desk and then tapped it on the leather day calendar.

"Has Leslie said anything about playing in college?" Principal De Loach asked.

Rhee's eyes volleyed between the principal and the recruiters.

"Not yet. He's only in eighth grade, and this is the first team he's played on." He took a deep breath. "L.A. hasn't even talked about playing in high school." It dawned on Rhee that he'd never asked his star player what his future plans in basketball were.

Both recruiters frowned at the same time. "Who is L.A.?" Mr. Wallace asked.

Rhee let the question hang in the room for a moment. He gave Mr. Wallace the best disapproving expression he was able to muster. "L.A. is his nickname."

Mr. Wallace leaned back in his chair. "Oh, OK."

"The only person I've rapped with about his future was his pops, who told me he was going to Harvard."

Another awkward silence smothered the conversation. This time Mr. Barns broke it instead of the principal. "That's promising. We get a lot of kids who planned on going to Harvard. Stanford is the Harvard of the West Coast, with much better weather."

A swarm of jealousy and resentment rose from Rhee's stomach. "That's cool." He made another show of looking at the wall clock. "We have nine more games to play. I've just taught the guys an offense and how to play against a zone."

The recruiters looked at one another. They were losing their patience. They had a backup plan. Recruiters always had backup plans.

Mr. Barns crossed his legs and pulled on his tie. "That's something we also wanted to talk about." He turned to Mr. Wallace and gave him a nod to pick it up from here.

This had to be their backup plan. The two recruiters now

worked in tandem.

"Your principal has told us how you put this middle-school basketball program on the map. Have you thought about going to a school like Stanford to learn about coaching or, you know, to get your physical education degree?" Mr. Wallace asked. He looked back to Mr. Barns and handed him the baton.

"We've heard about your incredible coaching skills. Stanford University has an excellent program to help you, and we have some internships in coaching already in place for you."

Rhee looked at the two men one at a time. It was as though they had rehearsed in the car. He never noticed these routines when he was being recruited as a player. How had he been so blind to it? He touched his chest and felt his heartbeat. It pounded through his sweatshirt.

"Me, go to Stanford? How? I mean my parents can't afford the local schools." Mr. Barns started to speak, but Rhee cut him off. "Honestly, I'm in over my head. None of the 200 colleges that recruited me ever mentioned the price of tuition or books. And to be honest, most of them talked about paying me to go to college." Rhee's eyes volleyed between the two men. When they both squirmed, he was satisfied his insult landed. "I've never coached. I only took this job because I had to or give up on going to college altogether."

"That's why we wanted to talk to you about our educational scholarships," Mr. Wallace said.

Rhee ignored Mr. Wallace. "I'm just trying to get through the day. This is the first time I've ever been part of a team and not made a pass or scored a basket. Most of the players on this team can't really play."

"That sounds like coaching material to me," Principal De Loach said. He leaned back in his chair and gave Rhee a wide smile.

Rhee turned his attention back to the recruiters. "They're not winning because of me. Like I just said, I haven't taken a shot or even passed the ball. These kids are winning 'cause they have heart and they're busting their humps."

Mr. Wallace and Mr. Barns looked at each other. "Someone

made them believe in themselves. You're being too modest, Rhee," Mr. Barns said.

Rhee saw right through it. It was all a sales pitch, all a con. "If you'll excuse me, I have a practice to run," Rhee said. He stood up and didn't offer anyone a handshake. He turned to Principal De Loach. "We've got a band and a cheerleading squad we never had in the gym. Can you tell them to practice after we're done?"

Principal De Loach glanced back and forth between the recruiters and Rhee. Mr. Wallace gave the principal a nod. The principal stood up and reached his hand out to Rhee.

"You got it," Principal De Loach said.

Rhee turned away with smooth grace. It took him less than five minutes to get from the principal's office back out to his mother's car. Rhee got in and closed the door to decompress from the most awkward meeting with recruiters he'd ever had. All the years and all the daily detailed attention paid to him were based solely on his abilities as a player. Nothing ever was mentioned about his personality, especially not his skill to motivate and organize spoiled, ill-mannered rich kids. Rhee wondered if this was really his future? Could he be the next John Wooden, Bobby Knight, Mike Kryzewski, Bill Self, Jim Boeheim, Pat Summit, or Geno Auriemma? Rhee took a deep breath to collect himself. Nah, no way. He popped the door open and headed back to the gymnasium. When he entered, the entire gymnasium was empty. He heard the faint sound of a band playing over an even fainter sound of cheerleaders practicing. Somehow Principal De Loach had managed to move everyone into another room on campus in less than five minutes. Impressive.

He was glad the gymnasium was empty when his players came one at a time out of the locker room. L.A. trotted out of the locker room with his shoelaces untied. He stopped, sat down, and started tying them. Rhee crossed the gymnasium and sat down next to his star player.

"Hey, Coach," L.A. said without looking up.

"What up?" Rhee asked. He tried to keep it casual, though there was a clear agenda in his head.

L.A. laced one sneaker and started on the other. "It's your

world. I'm just a squirrel trying to get a nut," L.A. said with a devilish grin.

Rhee looked L.A. over and examined the kid's physique. He was slender but muscular and had a more mature body than Rhee had at his age. He was in great shape and had the physique of a professional basketball player.

"You live at a house the size of a small country. I think you got more than a nut," Rhee said.

"Word," L.A. mumbled. He concentrated on lacing up.

"What do the guys think of the new band and cheerleaders?" Rhee asked. He needed a lead into the conversation that had nothing to do with what he really wanted to know.

"They were here when we got here and then gone." L.A. snapped his fingers. "Just like that." He shook his head "They're whack, Coach. It was embarrassing."

"Word," Rhee said. It made L.A. chuckle.

Rhee wanted it to stay casual. He looked across the gymnasium intentionally so L.A. didn't feel like he was being seriously questioned. "Can I holler at you about something?"

"Literally or figuratively?" L.A. said, with a smirk.

Rhee showed him a tight fist. "Knucklestively."

"That's not a word, Coach."

"I know, Shorty. It's a threat."

They shared a laugh. "Coach, seriously, you need counseling."

"No worries. You ever thought about playing in college?"

L.A. looked up, surprised. "Where did that come from? I'm not even in high school, yet."

Rhee shrugged his shoulders like it was no big deal to him. "Just curious. We never rapped about it."

L.A. looked at Rhee with a hint of suspicion. "You think I'm good enough?"

Rhee shook his head vehemently. "No chance, not even good

enough for high school." Rhee said. "You suck."

L.A. smirked at him, "Thanks for the vote of confidence, Coach."

"Don't mention it." Rhee stood up and blew his whistle. He turned back to L.A. Under normal circumstances he would already be at the basketball rack to snatch a ball and practice some moves or take some shots. Rhee had got the kid thinking, and he knew it. It had got him thinking as well.

"Don't ever tell anyone I told you this," Rhee said.

"What?" L.A. asked.

"You're better than I was at your age," Rhee whispered, just loud enough for only L.A. to hear.

The kid stiffened. He waved at Rhee. "What? Come on, Coach. You're high, right?"

Rhee looked at L.A. to really make sure he paid careful attention to what he was saying. "Dead serious, kid. You might be the best player I've ever seen at your age."

Rhee casually started to walk away to make sure L.A. had no chance to respond. He ignited a forest fire of thoughts in the young eighth-grader's mind. L.A. stood up, and Rhee watched him stagger from the weight of what his coach had just told him.

Chapter 39

Change

Rhee stood in the kitchen doorway and watched his father. Mr. Joyce, nestled in his worn, cracked, leather La-Z-Boy and held a newspaper open to the sports page in one hand and the remote control in the other. His bifocals sat on the bridge of his nose. His eyes went back and forth from the Lakers game on the television to the newspaper. In between, they slowly shut until he jerked and started the routine over.

"Out of the way," Mrs. Joyce said.

Rhee stepped to the side. "Sorry about that."

His mother scampered past with a glass of lemonade in her hand. "I see you're getting your speed back," Mrs. Joyce said over her shoulder.

Rhee sprang forward, caught up to his mom, swiftly rolled in front of her, and snatched the lemonade from her hand. They looked at one another until he knew she understood.

His mother turned and went back into the kitchen. He crossed the room with light footsteps and placed the lemonade on the built-in tray of the La-Z-Boy. He took the remote from his dad's hand, pointed it at the television, and turned it off.

Mr. Joyce, startled, sat up. "What in tarnation?" He removed his bifocals and looked at Rhee. Their eyes were on one another as Rhee rallied his nerves.

"You haven't said more than ten words to me since I got out of my cast," Rhee said.

Mr. Joyce grumbled and went to his newspaper as a barrier.

Rhee thought about walking away but stayed.

"I know I'm not your favorite person, but I need you to listen to me for just a minute."

Mr. Joyce turned the pages of his newspaper and searched for an article. He looked at his watch. "What time does that game come on?" Mr. Joyce asked.

Rhee knew this routine all too well. His dad wanted no part of any intimate conversation, but Rhee continued anyway.

"Just about every game I ever played, back to Little League, I'd look up in the stands, and you were always there. Sometimes it was cold and raining, but I'd look up and you were there. A lot of other kids' parents never came even in the perfect weather. But you did."

Rhee stopped to notice his dad acted like he wasn't listening, which meant he was listening. His dad had mastered the art of waiting for a seam to break into his own opinion.

"I know you're disappointed in me, but I just want you to hear me say thank you. Until recently, I never realized what sacrifices you made so that I could play. Now I do."

Rhee waited a beat. When his dad cleared his throat, Rhee knew that meant he had heard every word. He turned around and pointed the remote as he clicked the power button. The game came back on the television. He turned and walked away.

"You're welcome," Mr. Joyce said, barely audible.

Rhee kept his back turned to hide his own smile. "Your mother told me about the kids you're coaching, and she told me how hard you're trying to get into college."

Rhee took a deep breath. These conversations could go north or south, depending on his dad's mood. He slowly turned around. His eyes dropped to look at the floor.

"Doing what I can," Rhee said, barely audible himself.

"She cut out an article and put it in my lunch box. It said something about your team might play for the city championship if you win the next couple games."

Rhee looked up and saw his dad pretending to read, but he'd already given away the fact that he wasn't.

"Imagine that," Rhee said.

Mr. Joyce flipped through the pages. "You must be quite a coach! The article said that school never won more than two or three games since that old coach retired."

"I'm no Bobby Knight."

Mr. Joyce finally looked at Rhee. No one was allowed to speak of Coach Knight with any trace of disrespect in the Joyce home.

"Only Bobby Knight is Bobby Knight. Don't forget that," Mr. Joyce said. It was so stern it cut through most people. Rhee grew to only let it graze his skin now. Sometimes the look drew blood; lately, it didn't.

"How could I forget, dad? You've been telling me that ever since I could walk."

Rhee felt his dad's measured, hot gaze on him. His dad picked up the glass of lemonade and drained almost half of it. When his thirst was quenched, he turned his attention back to the Lakers game. The Lakers were winning. The Joyce home ran a bit more smoothly when the Lakers won.

"It won't be the first championship game for you."

Rhee knew his dad's way of saying "good luck." He also knew when his dad was saying, "This conversation is over."

He turned and left the room while he was ahead and before the conversation with his dad went south. "Oh, yes, it will," Rhee murmured, for only his own ears to hear.

It was Sunday and Rhee needed to celebrate nearly making amends with his dad. It wasn't just Rhee's dreams that went down the drain when his injury occurred. His dad was still in mourning about it also. It was in his dad's eyes every day he passed him.

"What a great, friggin' nice gym," Rhee said to himself. He turned on the lights of the gymnasium. He unlocked the storage room and wheeled out the rack of basketballs. He looked down at his sneakers and his taped ankles. This was just a pipe dream. A moment revisited only by memories. This was no reality. So why was he doing it?

Rhee shrugged his shoulders as if someone had actually asked him, shrugging off the question as if it didn't matter right now. He removed a CD from his pocket, unzipped his sweat jacket, and tossed it close to the bleachers. He gripped the balls -- one by one -- and carefully placed them in key positions inside the half court.

Rhee fumbled around the scorer's table until he found the CD loader. He put it in and pushed the song queue. When Eminem's "Till I Collapse" started playing over the gymnasium speakers, nearly full tilt, Rhee picked up random basketballs and shot baskets.

It took four missed shots before the basketballs began to pour into the net: swish, swish, swish. He kept shooting. The balls missed the rim and dropped straight through. Rhee shot set shots until his nerves found building blocks.

Little by little, he jumped higher and higher. Now it was all about no fear. No fear of shattering the ankle rebuilt with pins, plates, and screws. His coach and doctor said his ankle might shatter. He wanted it to. It had betrayed his hopes, his dreams, and his life.

He abandoned all concern as he picked up the basketballs and shot in time with the music. The balls bounced and rolled to places not meant for shooting. He shot anyway. The balls kept dropping in the net as if making fun of him. This was all there was ever going to be, alone, without a crowd, without a team, without an opponent. The song ended right when Rhee squared up for his last shot. He heaved the basketball as hard as he could. It caught a light close to the top of the high ceiling and smashed it.

Rhee sat on the gymnasium floor, drenched in sweat, tears in his eyes. He had lost track of how many shots he had made. It might have been twenty-five consecutive shots in a row, twice. He had lost track of the misses. He fell back and let his head hit the hard floor. It pained him some, but it helped him forget the rest. He had even failed to notice that his ankle never hurt or shattered.

Chapter 40

The Big Secret

The smell of cooked cheese, tomato paste, and beer created a haze in the pizza parlor. The loud chatter competed with the noise of a bad speaker system and video games.

"I totally disagree with Charles Barkley that star athletes aren't role models," Rhee said.

He rambled nervously, but he'd just been introduced to Lynn's three friends and already had forgotten all their names. They all sat in the booth and stared at one another.

A jolt went through Rhee's body when his finger accidently touched Lynn's. Their hands rested on each other's. She slowly pulled her hand away but traced the top of his hand with her fingers. They amused her friends with their nervous attraction.

"You really think athletes are role models?" Lynn asked.

Her friends stared at him and waited for an answer. They sought a sign whether he was "the one."

"Of course! When I was in eighth grade, if someone told me LeBron James ate mud before games, I would have done the same thing." Lynn's friends stared at him like he was an alien. "Maybe not mud, but you know what I mean." The noise of beeps and tinny music from video games in the background filled in the awkward silence around their table.

Lynn nodded faithfully, but her friends looked at Rhee like he was demented. "I know what you mean." She held up the empty pitcher of lemonade. "Who wants more to drink?"

L.A. slid into the booth. "Yo Coach, do me a solid and cop me some more quarters."

Rhee was embarrassed; he'd brought his eighth grade basketball team with him as backup against Lynn's friends. Boys need wingmen. He had seven.

"This is unreal. Richie Rich is asking me for quarters, when his dad owns half of the United States." He dug into his pockets and ignored the fact that all of Lynn's friends rolled their eyes. He dropped all his leftover change he had into L.A.'s hand.

"Peace out," L.A. said. "Hey, did Coach tell you guys he's still a virgin?" L.A. flew out of the booth before Rhee could grab him and pummel him.

All of Lynn's friends covered their mouths. They turned their faces and giggled into their hands. Lynn tried to smile, but her lips went crooked.

Rhee was going to kill L.A. and his entire family. How could Rhee be more embarrassed? It wasn't just that the kid said it, but the fact that it was true. Rhee was a virgin.

He'd never discussed sex or his sex life with any of his players. It wasn't like he was Tim Tebow or anything. He just spent all of his time practicing basketball. His father told him that girls would always be there. Now there was one girl and her three friends, who were speechless. Rhee wanted to slide under the table.

Asa slid into the booth right when L.A. left. "Hey, Coach. Do you need a wingman?" Asa said. He sat down so close to Lynn that she slid closer to Rhee. Their thighs touched. It made Rhee dizzy. He closed his eyes. The date was a complete and utter disaster -- worse than his first Eagles game. But this moment filled him with the joy that had abandoned him since his career-ending injury.

"Who wants to spend time with a real man?" Doug asked.

Rhee looked to see Asa, Doug, and Blaze all sitting in the booth across from Lynn's friends.

"You guys are going to do mop-ups until next Christmas. I swear. Even after you graduate from middle school, I'll find you."

Rhee's players slid out of the booth as fast as they had slid into it. Rhee was so embarrassed he couldn't manage to look at Lynn.

He dropped his head in shame. When he felt Lynn's hand on top of his hand, he looked up.

"Maybe you can take me home now?" Lynn asked.

Rhee raised his hand high in the air. "Check please."

Rhee pulled his mother's car in front of Lynn's house. He kept the car running and hoped she'd make a graceful exit. Now that the overwhelming smell of pizza and beer had left his nose, he caught a whiff of her perfume. They sat in silence. All that played in his mind was: *Virgin, virgin, virgin, Rhee is a virgin.*

"Maybe we could just go out by ourselves next time if you want," Lynn said.

Rhee wanted a "do over," and part of him wanted to go home and just die. "I'm surprised you even want to talk to me after tonight. I'm going to kill those guys."

"Don't be silly. I'd like to see you again."

I'm not silly. I'm just a virgin and now everyone knows, he thought, but he said, "Done."

"Done? What do you mean, done?"

"Oh, it's just an expression. It sort of means when you can see something already, it's done."

"I like that."

"Thanks."

She leaned over and kissed him on the lips, and held it. Rhee's eyes popped open and saw her eyes close. His eyes blinked, not sure to stay open or close or pop out of his head. He inched back and she inched forward. Rhee smelled her. Her breath was minty. Her perfume was light. He thought of honey suckle and sweet cream. The world stood still, and all his thoughts floated away. His eyes closed as he fell into a trance. "Good luck against the Cougars," Lynn said. Rhee felt himself swim to the surface from some enchanted place. He opened his eyes. He never felt her pull away. She had a smile on her face and a look in her eyes. He'd seen admiration in stranger's eyes. Rhee hadn't seen these eyes. There was warmth in them, and a glow his he never experienced. Her eyes mesmerized him. An urged swelled in him and he wanted more. It was an instant addiction. He wanted to dive back before the urge faded. She reached for the door handle and got out of the car. She walked up her driveway. He waited until she was completely out of sight before driving away. He had not been this far up in the air without jumping in his life.

Chapter 41

Championship Game

The Marshall Cougars' middle school gymnasium was packed, tight as sardines. The overflow of the Cougars' parents, friends, students, and relatives had to sit on the side, along with the Eagles' parents, friends, students, and relatives. There were a lot more Eagles fans than their first game, a whole lot more.

The Eagles band competed with the Cougars band, note for note. The new Eagles cheerleaders and cheering section yelled and rattled pompoms as they tried their best to out-scream the Cougars cheerleaders.

Rhee carried a large ball bag and clipboard as he entered the gymnasium. He looked up, and his eyes zeroed in on the prettiest young woman in the building: Lynn. She wore an Eagles T-shirt over her floral dress. She held maroon pompoms and waved them at Rhee, who couldn't believe his eyes. Coach Holt sat in the stands next to her. He was shaved and groomed and wore a nice blue suit and maroon tie.

Rhee did a quick inventory of the crowd. Mr. Lieberman, Principal De Loach, and a few faculty members sat close to each other. There were a dozen scouts sitting close to one another. A few of them pointed at Rhee and whispered in one another's ears. Rhee cringed. How many more stories did they have to talk about his fall from grace and how they all pitied him?

Rhee shook it off. He was the coach now, not a player. He was also dressed in a suit and tie. He was in camouflage. Hopefully, half the scouts didn't recognize him.

He made it to half court. He made a beeline toward the locker room, where he knew his players were putting on their uniforms and lacing up their sneakers, but he was intercepted by the Cougars' coach.

"Coach Joyce," Coach Leonard yelled over the dueling bands and cheerleaders. He quickly stepped up to Rhee and gently pulled him by the arm. "How are you feeling?" Coach Leonard asked.

Rhee shrugged his shoulders. "I was just headed to check on my team."

"No problem. Just wanted to wish you good luck," Coach Leonard said. "If that practice game counted, my team would be city champions."

Rhee nodded and smiled wide. "Good thing it didn't count then, right?" He didn't need to wish Coach Leonard luck. His team had won the city title nine years straight, and two years before that, they had had another eight-year streak.

"After the game, I want to invite you out to grab a bite to eat and talk with you about a couple things," Coach Leonard said. "Let's be real, Joyce. If you can get that team to play out of their minds, what could you do with a team like mine?"

Rhee had an overwhelming sensation as if time had stopped. Had this guy just offered him a job? He started to pull away when Coach Leonard yelled something that made Rhee stop.

"Try to get the Adams kid to relax and play his game. He's the best player out here if he wants to be."

Rhee took a step back toward the Cougars' head coach. "I'm sorry?" Rhee asked.

"He may freeze up is all," Coach Leonard said, matter-of-factly. "He's never played in competition against all his buddies." He was definitely trying to get into Rhee's head. First, he offers Rhee a job, and now he told him his best player was not going to play well.

"I'll try to remember that," Rhee said, not loud enough for anyone to hear and gave Coach Leonard an unbridled expression of suspicion.

"See ya after the game," Coach Leonard yelled. "My offer still stands."

Rhee turned away from him and saw L.A.'s dad, Mr. and Mrs. Adams, walk into the gymnasium. Rhee's heart skipped a beat. They looked lost. The couple was so misplaced. They looked like Madison Avenue socialites who stepped into the gymnasium to ask for directions back to Fifth Avenue.

Oh, damn, were the first words Rhee's mind formed.

Rhee entered the visitors' locker. The cracked paint, rust, and water stains throughout did nothing to dampen the atmosphere of the room, where a new look Eagles team waited. The Keystone Kops were gone. In their place were seven kids who filled out their uniforms with pride and confidence. They stood solidly in their shoes. Their shoulders were erect. Their heads were higher. Fear was not in the room. It had evaporated weeks before.

Rhee cleared his throat to announce his presence. The Eagles players circled him. He took the position that felt familiar, center stage.

"OK fellas, bring it in," Rhee said. The Eagles players drew in tighter around their coach. He rolled his program and hit his thigh with nervous excitement. "We're probably going to see a box-in-one to try to stop White Chocolate." Rhee looked at Terrance. "So Terrance, I want you to go off. You might score a hundred points today. If they play zone, I want you to score 200 points, or you're getting a beat down from me."

Terrance shook his legs and nodded. "You got it." There was no doubt in the boy's eyes. Rhee smiled wide.

He looked at Asa. "No pressure, Flash, but I don't want anyone in the stands to know your number. In fact, I don't want anyone to know you wear goggles. You know why?"

Asa shook his head. "No, Coach."

"'Cause I want you just to be a blur. Your nickname is Flash, so I want you to streak up and down that court so fast that the Cougars think we're cheating by putting a sixth man on the court. Do we understand each other? Are we crystal clear?"

Asa smiled, wide. "Yes, Coach, we're crystal."

"Good. When I say Usain Bolt, I want you to think the dude is a slowpoke."

The team laughed. Rhee slowly took his eyes off Asa and looked at Weston. "Weston."

Weston perked up. "Yeah, Coach."

"When you go in for Asa or L.A., you're Magic Johnson, John Stockton, Steve Nash, Tony Parker, Russell Westbrook and Chris Paul tonight. I want you to set the middle school record for assists tonight."

Weston nodded. "OK."

Rhee's eyes volleyed between Gerry and Doug. "You guys own the glass tonight. Anyone gets a rebound other than you two guys, I want you to be offended. Show out, boys. You two are Dennis Rodman, Dwight Howard and Tyson Chandler." Doug and Gerry looked at each other like brothers going into battle together.

Rhee turned his attention to Blaze. "Who are you? Who let you in this locker room?" Blaze froze. He went blank until they all started laughing. Rhee messed his hair. "I'm just clowning you, Blaze. You're just as valuable as anyone tonight. I need you to be aggressive, and I want you to foul out."

"Seriously?" Blaze asked.

"Seriously. When I put you in the game I want you to knock someone down. We don't need any flagrant two shots, just a couple of flagrant ones."

"What's the difference?" Blaze asked.

Rhee gave him a slow, broad smile. "The amount of blood on the floor." All the Eagles laughed when Rhee turned his attention to L.A. "White Chocolate, I don't want you to do anything different. You got us here by being you. So you just be you. Ball out, you understand?"

L.A. showed no reaction. Rhee studied him. Something felt wrong. L.A. displayed no confidence.

"You good?" Rhee asked. L.A. nodded unconvincingly. Rhee held two fingers up to his eyes and pointed the fingers at L.A. and again back to himself. "Are we good? Tell me we're good."

"We're good," L.A. said with irritation.

Rhee put his hand out. All the players put a hand in too. "Now listen. If it comes down to the last shot, who is taking it?" All the Eagles pointed to L.A. Rhee shook his head, emphatically. "Wrong. No one is going to take the last shot."

The Eagles looked confused. A slow, wide smile spread across Rhee's lips. "It's not coming down to the last shot 'cause we're running these suckers out of the building," Rhee said. "We already played these guys, and we know what to expect. Do your best, have fun, and no matter what the outcome, leave it all out on that floor. One, two, three..."

"Done," everyone said.

Rhee kept his eyes on L.A. as the team lined up and got ready to go out for warm-ups. He opened the door to the gymnasium and recognized the sound of thunderous applause and the hum of anticipation.

The gymnasium walls nearly came down as the Cougars trotted onto the court to a standing ovation. None of the Eagles players looked back at the Cougars team like before, except L.A.

Rhee met with Coach Leonard at the scorer's table. He felt the coach's eyes on him. "Listen, Coach. I've been offered the head coaching position at the high school Oakland Tech. I wasn't trying to diss you when I asked you to come out with us. We're all proud of what you've done. We want to see what you can do with a real program and a real team."

"You're right, Coach," Rhee said. "At my kid's school, there is no real sports program 'cause they have too many choices. But tonight you're going to play a real team."

He turned and walked toward his team. He knew Coach Leonard watched him until Rhee grabbed a towel and sat down. He sat on his hands and smiled at his team's perfect three-man weave.

The deafening noise found a silent hole. A hush followed close behind. A group of black, white, and Hispanic men walked inside the gymnasium. Rhee recognized Rooster, Otis, and a few of the other Live Oak Park players.

Otis looked around until he saw Rhee, who gave him a small

wave. The shady-looking men walked toward the Eagles section, and fans slid over and made room for them to sit. Rhee shook his head. Mr. Lieberman gave him a smile and a thumbs up. Rhee gave him a thumbs up back.

L.A. warmed up with a look of shock on his face. His eyes nervously darted up in the stands. At the sight of his mother and father, the kid's body stiffened like he'd been shot.

The horn sounded for the players to go to the sideline to hear their coach's last words of encouragement. The Eagles starters pulled off their warm-ups.

Rhee studied L.A. until their gazes met. "Are you OK?"

L.A. nodded and quickly looked back into the stands. Rhee looked and saw Mr. and Mrs. Adams gave their son a tight, uncomfortable smile.

"Listen up, they're going to press you to slow down our fast break. Just don't hold the ball. We want to take a shot within four or five seconds on a rebound or missed or made shot," Rhee said over the noise.

He checked the eyes of his players, and the only one not present was L.A. He was somewhere else. The second horn sounded, and Rhee put his hand out. All his players put one hand in and waited for Rhee, who said, "One, two, three..."

"Done," the Eagles yelled. The five Eagles starters jogged over to half court to meet the Cougars.

Chapter 42

No Place To Hide

L.A.'s expression was like a deer in the headlights of an oncoming car. The five Cougars all hugged him like he was a long-lost relative. The Cougars politely shook hands with the other Eagles.

"L.A," Rhee yelled. L.A. looked back at Rhee, who pointed to his own head. "Get your mind right."

L.A. ignored Rhee completely.

The Cougars controlled the tip and ran a play to score immediately. The noise level jumped up several decibels as cheering fans leaped out of their seats. Gerry inbounded the ball to L.A., and he dribbled the basketball off his foot out of bounds. Rhee dropped his head. He shoved Weston. "Go in for Adams." Weston looked at his coach like he was crazy.

"Right now? The game just started," Weston protested.

Rhee gave him dagger eyes. "Get in there, right now."

Weston pulled off his warm-ups and kneeled in front of the scorer's table. A horn sounded, and the referee blew his whistle. He waved Weston into the game. Weston tapped L.A. on the shoulder. L.A. made no complaint. He turned and headed toward the bench like he had expected it.

Rhee tossed L.A. a towel. The kid started toward the end of the bench, but Rhee slid over and slapped the bleacher. "Sit here."

His eyes stayed on the game. L.A sat next to Rhee, who jumped up and screamed at the referee.

"Where did you learn how to referee, the Berkeley School of the Deaf and Blind?"

The referee casually turned to Rhee and made a technical foul signal and then pointed at him. "Technical foul on the Eagles' head coach."

The Eagles fans booed so Rhee poured gasoline on the fire. "Why did you give me a technical when the issue is your out-of-date prescription glasses? You know it's gonna be a good game, if you were able to actually see it."

The referee stuffed the whistle in his mouth and blew it in Rhee's direction. "Do you really want to go home this early, Coach?" the referee asked Rhee. "I can send you home plenty early." The referee meant business.

Terrance ran and stood between Rhee and the referee. Both of his hands indicated Rhee should settle. "Coach, take a chill pill."

Asa ran over and joined in the discussion. "Yeah, take it easy, Coach."

Rhee stepped back and put up his own hands. "No problem. Everything is OK. We're OK. I'm OK. Everything is OK."

Prov stood alone at the free-throw line. Both teams waited behind the top of the key. Prov bounced the ball and shot. The basketball went through the bottom of the net.

L.A. kept his head on a swivel as he looked back the entire half at his father in the stands.

The horn blew and signaled the end of the first half. The Eagles' eighth-grade boys' basketball team headed toward the visiting locker room; Rhee followed them at a distance. The Eagles' section all had disappointed expressions. A quick glance back at the scoreboard reminded Rhee his team managed only eighteen points to the Cougars' thirty-five points. It was the worst half of basketball Rhee's team had played since their first practice game.

Rhee entered the locker room. The electricity of winning, present before the first half, had dissipated. His players meandered between the bench in front of the lockers, the bathroom, and the drinking fountain. L.A. sat alone away from the rest of the team.

"Everyone put your warm-ups on and stay loose," Rhee said.

He tried to sound upbeat as he approached L.A. and sat beside him. He looked at L.A., who looked at him with sad eyes. He let the silence between them linger.

"What do you want from me?" L.A. asked.

"Did I say I wanted anything from you?"

"You don't have to say, just from your expression, I know I'm letting everyone down."

"Look kid, I'm not your father. I'm only four years older than you. I got my own problems. I have no idea what to do with my own life. From where I'm sitting, this is just another game I can't play in, so don't think you're letting me down." Rhee placed a heavy hand on L.A.'s shoulder. "The reason I took you out of the game is because you're stinking up the joint. Your mind is in outer space or something. Also, you didn't look like you were having any fun. The game is supposed to be fun, right?"

"It's the first time I've ever played against them. They're too good."

"I hope you're not stepping in the dog pile while you're lying down. Yes, they're good. You play against them all the time, and you're better than all of them put together."

L.A. looked at him with a plea in his eyes. "The reason I never joined a team was because I knew he'd think it was stupid."

"So this is about your dad?"

"Damn right, it's about my dad. Why did he come?"

"What does it matter why he came or even what he thinks? So what if he thinks it's stupid. It doesn't matter."

"It matters a lot. I wish it didn't, but it does."

"Look, Kid Skills. Parents are a drag. Just when we start to get used to hating them, they do something nice like show up at a game unexpectedly. There is nothing you can do about it."

"I still think it's stupid. All of it is whack."

"There are certain parts of all sports that are stupid," Rhee said. "Just like people and life." His words surprised L.A. "What's really stupid is we put so much importance on every game. At least I did.

When I played I always felt it meant everything in the world because my future depended on it. My father even made me feel that way. He had such high hopes for me, and he had no problem letting me know that I let him down."

"That's a drag," L.A. said, his head down.

"Tell me about it. But it doesn't have to be that way for you because your future doesn't depend on every shot you take or every pass you make or every rebound you get," Rhee said. "You can go out there and just have fun because you're still going to be rich and one of the most soulful white kids on the planet."

"I don't know about all that, Coach."

"Like I said, I'm only eighteen. What the hell am I supposed to know other than my own life is totally messed up?" Rhee kept his eyes on L.A., until the kid slowly looked back at him.

"Is your life totally messed up?" L.A. asked.

Rhee looked at the kid with widened eyes. He held up one hand and counted with the other. "Well, let me think. My basketball future is over. My dad hates me. I got only a small chance in hell of getting into college, and I'm coaching an all-white team that's getting their heads beat in, again."

"And you're a virgin," L.A. said.

Rhee's eyes went wide with shock. "Really? Seriously? You want me to kill you with my bare hands?"

L.A. let go with a small grin. "I was just clowning you, Coach."

Rhee raised his hand like he was going to hit L.A., hard. "Boy, I should send you into next week, right now."

"Sorry, Coach. You aren't lying, your life is whack." He cracked a smile. Rhee hit him on the shoulder.

"You won't say that with two broken legs." They shared a laugh, until the awkward silence sat between them. "It's just another game, White Chocolate. Don't take it so serious. I wanna see you go out there and block everything out of your head and have fun. Just ball out and show out. Show these fools that you not only have crazy game but you also have heart."

L.A. nodded. "So that's it?"

Rhee took his time. He smiled, wide. "There's one more thing."

"Kick it down," L.A. said.

"There is something called separation," Rhee said.

"Separation?" L.A. asked.

"Yeah, it's the difference between really good and really great," Rhee said. "There are two, maybe three players out there who will probably play in college on scholarship." Rhee looked into L.A.'s eyes. "There is one player out there who could go all the way to the NBA and make his mark 'cause he's that great. But now, today, he must prove it to himself. He has to separate himself from everyone else."

L.A. looked down at the floor.

"Anyone in any life has the chance to separate himself from the others; it's a gift from God that should never be refused. There are ten or eleven college scouts out there watching your every move. They are looking for separation." Rhee made a fist and offered L.A. a dap.

"Done," L.A. said. There was no doubt in his eyes. They touched their fists together.

"Done," Rhee said. He smiled and turned around to walk away but heard L.A. call after him.

"Hey, Coach."

Rhee slowly turned around.

"Do you miss it? Do you miss playing?"

Rhee wanted to think of a game plan instead of all the disappointments of his own life.

"Yeah, of course I miss it. I spend every part of my mind and body trying to stop thinking about it. Every moment of every day, I'm trying to forget my last five seconds that I had to win the game that was going to be the last time I played."

L.A. looked down and shuffled his feet. He looked up. "If you'd known it was your last five seconds, would you have done anything different?"

Their eyes stayed on each other a good long time. Rhee smiled. "I might have passed the ball and went for the assist."

L.A. stared at Rhee long and hard. "Nah."

"You're right. I always wanted to take the last shot."

L.A. nodded. "That's cool. I wish you could play again. Every time I watched you play, you separated, big time."

It took every fiber in his body not drop to his knees and sob. He looked down and blinked back the tears. He took a deep breath and looked up at L.A.

"Right now, I'm looking forward to seeing you play in the second half. So you tell me when you're ready, and I'll put you in the game."

"Thanks, Coach," L.A. said. Their eyes stayed on each other until Rhee turned around and left before he broke down.

Rhee gathered his players together. He had to find a way to light that winner's spark again. "OK guys, bring it in. The last time we played these guys, we were a different team. Now we are a team that is never out of it. We can score, and we can score a lot. This next half, I just want you go out there and have fun. Try to score as many points as possible. It doesn't matter if we win or lose. I just want you to play Eagles basketball." He held out his hand. Players put both their hands on his. Rhee made sure he looked each of his players in their eyes. "I know I haven't been the easiest guy to get along with and it hasn't all been perfect. But I know this." Rhee felt his lips quiver. "I used to wonder why God never told me it was going to be my last five seconds to play or be a star. Now I wonder when it's going to be my last five seconds to talk to a friend or my last five seconds to see my parents or my last five seconds to live. I guess it all means every five seconds is a gift." All the player's eyes filled with tears of determination. Rhee quickly rallied them. "One, two, three."

"Done!" the Eagles hollered.

When the players started their walk out into the gymnasium, Doug leaned into Gerry and whispered, "The guy saved his best speech for the last minute."

Gerry looked into Doug's eyes. "Dude, I'm going to shut my bedroom door and cry when I get home," Gerry said.

Terrance brushed shoulders with Gerry. "Me too," Terrance said.

The second half the Eagles whittled down the Cougars' big lead. Rhee looked up at the scoreboard. The Cougars had forty-five points, the Eagles now had thirty points.

Rhee looked at L.A. on the bench. His knees jumped up and down, but his eyes were focused. "Adams, come here." L.A. slid over next to Rhee, who looked him dead in the eyes. "You look like you're ready to play some basketball." He watched a confident smile spread across L.A.'s lips.

"You must be psychic, Coach. I was just thinking the exact same thing."

Rhee reflected L.A.'s smile with his own. "Ready to go out there and separate?"

L.A. looked at the game in progress. He looked back and stole a glance at his father. He looked at Rhee. "Done."

Rhee ushered him toward the scorer's table, and L.A. ripped off his warm-up sweats. "Go in for Lieberman," Rhee said.

He looked up in the stands and saw the men from Live Oak Park rise to their feet and yell things Rhee was glad he wasn't able to hear. The looks on other Eagles fans told him that things more than a little shocking had come out of the Live Oak players' mouths.

Rhee turned his attention to Mr. Adams and saw him sit up and move forward. Rhee held out his hand for Asa to slap as he came out of the game. "Good job, Flash. You're the man." He tossed a towel that hit Asa in the face. "Pay attention 'cause you're going back in soon."

Asa nodded. "Done."

Rhee messed Asa's hair. "Done."

He turned his attention back to the game to see how his star player was going to play against his friends.

L.A. went right to work. He brought the ball up the court while Cub matched him stride for stride. Rama left his man to trap L.A., but he split the defenders and went right through the middle of both of them. He drove the free-throw line, reverse spun from Prov, and let a scoop shot spin off the backboard and go through the hoop. The Eagles fans went crazy. The Live Oak Park men jumped up, and Rhee heard Otis yell, "That's my boy. I taught him that."

Mr. Adams, with eyes wide and mouth agape, looked genuinely amazed. He raised his hands to clap and then awkwardly put them down.

L.A. jumped the lane and picked off a pass from Cub to Lam, took the basketball the length of the court, and finger rolled it over the rim. It was the highest Rhee had seen L.A. jump.

"Yes!" Rhee said with a fist pump.

Rhee looked across the court and saw the Cougars' coach hit the panic button when L.A. threw a half-court behind-the-back pass to Terrance, who drained a three-point shot. The Cougars' coach crossed his hand into a T.

"Timeout," Coach Leonard screamed.

His players trotted over to the sideline just as their coach threw a towel on the floor. He stomped up to Lam, Cub, Felix, Prov, and Rama. Spittle flew as he chewed them all out only inches from their faces.

L.A. stood on the court and watched his friends get berated. "Over here, Adams," Rhee yelled. L.A. looked back several times as he headed toward the sideline. "Don't worry about it."

"He's dissin' my friends," L.A. said.

"Don't worry about it. After the game we'll dump garbage on his lawn and TP his house," Rhee said. L.A. half smiled.

Rhee checked the scoreboard. It read: Cougars 50, Eagles 49. Rhee was pleased and proud of his team. He turned to them. "They're on their heels, so now push the gas all the way to the floor." Rhee put out his hand. "One, two, three..."

"Done!" the Eagles yelled.

Rhee sat on the bench and witnessed his team finish what they had started. Even when the Cougars scored, they had no chance of getting back on defense. The Eagles turned the game into a track meet. It was beautiful to watch.

When the final horn sounded, all the Eagles jumped up and down. Rhee stared at the scoreboard, making sure what he read was correct: Cougars 61, Eagles 79. The fans and the men from Live Oak Park went ballistic. They shared hugs and high-fives.

Rhee met Coach Leonard at half court and shook his hand. Rhee stood and waited for Cub, Lam, Rama, Felix, and Prov to all shake his hand. Prov gave Rhee a hug.

"Way to go, Coach," Prov said.

Rhee gave Prov a big smile. "You're a special guy, Providence. Stay that way." Prov nodded and smiled.

The seven Eagles players lifted Rhee into the air. Doug carried Rhee on his shoulders. Then the players paraded Rhee around in front of the Eagles' section. This position was familiar to Rhee, but it made him feel uncomfortable. Not long ago, his career potential was stratospheric. Now he wondered if this was as high as he was ever going to reach. He wasn't square with that yet. One day, he might be, but right now, he didn't know.

Rhee politely found a way to slide off his players' shoulders. As well-wishers swarmed around the Eagles, Rhee found anonymity as he slipped away through the crowd.

Chapter 43

One Month Later

The Eagles logo on the front and back of Rhee's T-shirt was drenched with sweat. Rhee pump-faked under the basket and then went up for the shot. Behind Rhee, Doug swatted the ball into L.A.'s hands. Their grunts and squeaking sneakers echoed in the mostly empty gymnasium. Terrance and the others were shirtless. They were on the other team in this pickup game. Rhee quickly clapped his hands and held them out to receive the ball. "Foul," Rhee said.

L.A. held the basketball and did not toss it to Rhee. "What foul?" L.A. asked with a snarl.

Rhee clapped his hands harder. "Give me the ball, short stuff. A blind man could tell I was hacked."

L.A. remained steadfast against throwing him the ball. "Coach, that wasn't even close to a foul, unless you're calling a foul because it might rain today."

Terrance bent over and grabbed his shorts. "Wasn't a foul, Coach!"

Rhee pointed a finger at Terrance. "You stay out of this. Your back was to the basket." He walked up to L.A. and snatched it from his hands. "Play your role, small soldier. Your teammate took my head off."

Doug threw up his hands and spun in a circle. "I can't believe you called a foul."

"That's because there was no foul, college boy," Coach Holt said. He wore his same coaching regalia of maroon shorts with a matching maroon polo shirt and spun a whistle on a small leather rope. He sat on the bleacher next to Lynn, who bobbed her head in agreement. She wore Rhee's Blue Devils' lettermen jacket over an Eagles sweatshirt. Behind her, Weston was dressed in his street clothes. He paid attention to a young girl who sat next to him.

"Rhee, we all saw it was a clean block," Lynn said. "Just 'cause you're in college, doesn't mean you can change the rules."

Rhee shot her a look like she was the ultimate traitor. "What? Are you my girlfriend or a referee now?"

She waved him off and turned her head to hide her smile.

"Coach, their ball," Prov said.

Rhee looked at Prov, Cub, and Lam. They wore their Marshall Cougars' T-shirts. They were on Rhee's team but not on his side of the call. "So, now the black guys are agreeing too." Rhee pointed an accusing finger at them. "That's black-on-black crime, you know, right?" Rhee asked. Cub and Lam looked confused.

"Coach, come on. You're holding up the game," Blaze said, from the sideline. He was also dressed in street clothes.

Rhee held the ball and pointed at Blaze, who sat on the floor in front of Lynn. "You're not even in the game, and you weren't paying attention."

Rhee looked at everyone in the gymnasium. It was a mixture of Eagles and Cougars players. A few other kids shot baskets at the other end of the court. The gymnasium hummed with bouncing basketballs and shots that hit the sideline rims. Even the older kids played a couple of pickup games.

Rhee turned and surveyed his immediate audience. "Not one person in the entire gymnasium saw Thickness take my head off?" Rhee asked. Anyone paying attention kept their mouths closed or looked away to hide their smiles. Rhee tossed the ball in the air and caught it. "OK, that settles it. I didn't want to have to do this, but none of you give me a choice."

Rhee turned and darted toward the basket. It only took him two dribbles to get close enough for him to launch. He knew it was the first time he'd remotely tried to get over the rim. He took off anyway. He heard Dr. Silva's warning that his ankle could shatter. Rhee let caution go when he started his 360-degree spin. Time slowed to a crawl as his fellow teammates and foes watched with mouths agape. Rhee was way up in the air and over the rim when he slammed it with both hands.

Everyone in the gymnasium leaped up in the air. The players all shouted.

"Oh, my God!" "Did you see that?" Several high fives were exchanged.

Lynn stood on her feet with her hands over her mouth. "Rhee, be careful," Lynn said. Her voice was muted by her frightful hands.

Rhee held onto the rim of the basket. It had collapsed. He pulled his knees up to his chest and did a pull-up. "I'm the king," Rhee shouted. Now it was time for him to let go of the rim and fall down to the floor, but he lost his nerve. He held onto the rim as his body twisted.

"Rhee, don't!" Lynn shouted. She pointed. "Someone help him down."

Rhee closed his eyes, threw his head back, and let go of the rim with both hands. He plummeted back down while all eyes were on him. The last thing Rhee saw was Lynn, who covered her mouth in utter fear.

Rhee's two feet landed on the gymnasium floor. His primal scream ran up the walls and down the spines of everyone now running over to his aid. His jarring cry nearly blew off the gymnasium doors and windows.

Lynn flew across the gymnasium floor and past the players who all sprinted toward Rhee. Everyone hit their breaks when they noticed Rhee jump into the air and touch his knees to his chest. He repeatedly bounced and sprang into the air like a playful toddler on a trampoline. "Look. Look. It doesn't hurt. Everyone stood and stared at Rhee like he was a mad man. Rhee finally landed and raised both his hands up high, his fingers spread to the heavens. "Yes, Lord." Rhee hollered in jubilation. His body started to shake with unbridled excitement. He felt no pain in his ankle or soul. Rhee kept his eyes upward. He tilted his head back and spewed with all his might: "I'm back. Thank you, Lord. I'm back."

Excerpt From Book 2

One And Done

Rhee kicked open the door to the third-floor landing of his dormitory. His sour expression showed his annoyance as he did it. Another student rushed by him, accidentally bumping Rhee into the door. He dropped the duffle bag, leaned against the wall, and rubbed the scar on his leg. He stepped inside the landing as a frisbee whizzed by his head. Rhee shifted and dodged it. "Sorry, dude," cackled a young man with freckles and curly brown hair. "Errant throw, but great reflexes. You play?"

"No," Rhee replied.

"Well, maybe later, eh?"

"Yeah, maybe." Rhee continued down the hallway. As he passed open doors, he noticed guys drinking beer, pumping up their stereos, and generally preparing for the upcoming semester. Rhee stopped in front of a closed door, his.

Rhee chucked the duffle bag and backpack on the bed of his new dorm room and slouched into a wooden chair at the desk. Feeling lucky not to have a roommate, he welcomed the solitude behind a closed door.

The evening after he "purchased" his books, Rhee tossed and turned in the dark on his bed. His door remained closed, yet a festival of parties burst from all directions. Raucous laughter, screaming, wanton drunken squeals, and shouts vibrated the walls. Rhee turned over and covered his ears with a pillow and eventually drifted into the initial stages of sleep; but a rapping thump on the door jolted him back to consciousness. Rhee rose groggily and sat in a stupor, but the banging was ceaseless. He ambled to the door, flicked on a light, and soon realized that his worn boxers were too frayed for company. He stumbled to the dresser and found and pulled on a pair of sweat pants. "Brother Man! Open up! Come see the living!"

Rhee unlocked the latch and peeked into the hallway. The bright white lights momentarily blinded him. Three people stepped closer and blocked most of it. Rap music peppered with angry lyrics of, "Where you goin' bitch? Come on back," spilled out of one door. Heavy metal guitar riffs shrieked out of another. When his eyes finally focused, Rhee saw that Robert clutched a six-pack of beer as he leaned on two young freshman girls. One wore a pink halter with an invitation emblazoned across her braless breasts, "National Sex Week: Give till it Hurts." Robert and the girls grinned as Robert asked, "Can we come in?" Rhee stood speechless in the doorway as the coeds giggled with anticipation and hope that Rhee would oblige.

About The Author

Sterling Anderson is a three time NAACP Image Award Nominee for best screenwriter and winner of The Movieguide Faith & Freedom Award and the Christopher Award. His movie *The Simple Life of Noah Dearborn* received an Emmy nomination for Dianne Wiest.

He has written for some of the most popular network television shows, such as *The Unit* on CBS, as well as NBC's *Medium* and *Heist*. His teleplay *The Simple Life of Noah Dearborn*, written for CBS starring Sidney Poitier, who won the NAACP Image Award for best actor. Sterling's extensive resume also includes screenplays written for Lions Gate, Disney, HBO, TriStar Pictures and Columbia Pictures.

A graduate in English from St. Mary's College, the accomplished writer also spent five years teaching screenwriting courses as an adjunct professor at the USC School of Cinematic Arts.

Sterling has written 2 books on screenwriting; *Go To Script* and *15 Steps To Becoming A Successful (Artist) Screenwriter*. The author often guest lectures and panels on screenwriting at film schools and festivals across the country.

Born in Cincinnati, Ohio, Sterling spent his early childhood in Tuskegee, Alabama, before moving to Davis, California. His talents span far outside the world of writing. Sterling has a fifth degree black belt in Tae Kwon Do and was an award-winning winemaker in Napa Valley.

Made in the USA
Monee, IL
25 September 2023

43368384R00171